Susan Sallis is the auth[...] novels, many of which are set in the West Country. She was born in Gloucestershire and now lives in Somerset with her family.

www.rbooks.co.uk

Also by Susan Sallis

RISING SEQUENCE:
A SCATTERING OF DAISIES
THE DAFFODILS OF NEWENT
BLUEBELL WINDOWS
ROSEMARY FOR REMEMBRANCE

SUMMER VISITORS
BY SUN AND CANDLELIGHT
AN ORDINARY WOMAN
DAUGHTERS OF THE MOON
SWEETER THAN WINE
WATER UNDER THE BRIDGE
TOUCHED BY ANGELS
CHOICES
COME RAIN OR SHINE
THE KEYS TO THE GARDEN
THE APPLE BARREL
SEA OF DREAMS
TIME OF ARRIVAL
LYDIA FIELDING
FIVE FARTHINGS
THE PUMPKIN COACH
AFTER MIDNIGHT
NO MAN'S ISLAND
SEARCHING FOR TILLY

and published by Corgi

RACHEL'S SECRET

Susan Sallis

CORGI BOOKS

TRANSWORLD PUBLISHERS
61–63 Uxbridge Road, London W5 5SA
A Random House Group Company
www.rbooks.co.uk

RACHEL'S SECRET
A CORGI BOOK: 9780552157308

First published in Great Britain
in 2008 by Bantam Press
a division of Transworld Publishers
Corgi edition published 2008

A CIP catalogue record for this book is available from the British Library.

Addresses for Random House Group Ltd companies outside the UK
can be found at: www.randomhouse.co.uk
The Random House Group Ltd Reg. No. 954009

The Random House Group Limited supports The Forest Stewardship Council (FSC), the leading international forest certification organisation. All our titles that are printed on Greenpeace approved FSC certified paper carry the FSC logo. Our paper procurement policy can be found at
www.rbooks.co.uk/environment

Typeset in New Baskerville by
Kestrel Data, Exeter, Devon
Printed in the UK by
CPI Cox & Wyman, Reading, RG1 8EX

2 4 6 8 10 9 7 5 3 1

For my friends

One

We were sitting on our bikes, feet down on the rough road, the August afternoon stretching ahead promising total boredom. We had spent the morning at my house, half a mile down the rough road; I had tried to cut Meriel's hair into short curls like Ingrid Bergman's in *For Whom the Bell Tolls*, which we had seen four times already. Actually, I had done a good job, but Meriel's face was not a bit like Ingrid's and it hadn't quite worked. She was in a really bad mood.

'I'm hungry,' she announced bleakly, scuffing the toe of her sandal into the accumulated grit where the road met the grass verge.

'How can you be? You had four sandwiches—'

'Not a smear of butter. Just bread and jam. You have to have butter to call two slices of bread a sandwich.'

'I told you. Mum mixes the marg and the butter and some dried egg – it's better than plain butter and goes further.'

'I didn't notice anything except bread and jam.'

I began to feel exasperated: she was never normally like this.

'I told you that, too. The butter spread has all gone and Mum hasn't made the batch for this week, and if you think I was going to break into the rations—'

'Are you frightened of your parents?'

'Of course not! But Mum really slaves at that Ministry of Defence place and then comes home and has to make a meal from nothing—'

'Why don't you do it, then?'

'I do my own breakfast and get something at midday,' I said sullenly, knowing by now where this was going. It cropped up with other so-called friends but rarely with Meriel. In fact I couldn't remember Meriel ever telling me the obvious: that I was an only child and spoiled to death.

But suddenly, in the generous way Meriel so often did, she said, 'My mum won't let me do the evening stuff either. It seems I waste more than I cook!'

We both laughed, relieved. Then Meriel said, 'Look. If we're not going to report a German paratrooper over in the fields, what else are we going to do all afternoon?'

I had already suggested my favourite thing, which was cycling in to Gloucester and seeing if any of the ancient cathedral staff would let us play in the whispering gallery. They always did because they knew us, and they hoped that if they let us soak up the atmosphere we would become religious. The poor things were desperate. But, as Meriel had pointed out, the cathedral was for wet and windy days and today was blazing August-hot. And we'd done the paratrooper sighting before and been roundly told off for wasting the Home Guard's time.

'We could rebuild our dam down on Twyver's Brook.'

Meriel shuddered. 'I couldn't bear it if another of those little fish got caught in the twigs. If you hadn't smashed up the bloody dam and let it swim free I'd still be standing there crying!'

She hadn't actually cried, but I had known she was very close to it. She said sometimes that she preferred animals to people. Trouble was, she was also afraid of them, and she could not have gone near that dam.

I said admiringly, 'You swore then.'

'So I did. Tell you what, let's knock on Hermione's door, and if her mum answers I could try a bloody on her.'

'Don't be daft, she'd take it out on Hermione.'

Meriel thought about it. 'God. Yes. That's how it works, isn't it? Revenge. You don't always go for the culprit. You go for someone who can't hit back. That's why Dad does . . .

what he does. Because he knows he's hurting Mum.'

I frowned. We didn't often talk about Meriel's dad but when we did it was the rule that we were very matter-of-fact. So I said, 'Well . . . I see what you mean, but who is the real culprit, then?'

She shrugged. 'Maybe it is Mum . . . for having me and the boys and not being able to cope with us. But it could be . . .' She swallowed. 'It could be himself. For – for – messing everything up all the time. Can you take revenge on yourself?' She didn't look at me, so I didn't answer. At last she shook her head impatiently. 'He just likes other women. Nothing to do with revenge. Just that he's a bloody, no-good, stupid—' She broke off and laughed and looked at me. 'This is all your fault, Rachel Throstle! You've ruined my Shirley Temple curls, and Mum is going to cry when she sees me!'

I could have cried myself, thinking about Meriel and her dad. I had been with Meriel three years ago, when we were far more impressionable than we were now, and had seen her dad in the newly constructed air-raid shelters at school. He'd been with the landlady from the Huntsman then. I had not actually seen him since then, but of course everyone in the city knew about him. It was as if he didn't mind people knowing, as if he was doing something clever. And at each new story, Meriel would try to work it all out. She always ended up calling him names.

I said, as robustly as possible, 'Actually, the curls are springing back now. I think you're going to like it better as time goes on. And your mum . . . well, she won't mind. You know that.'

Meriel said nothing for ages, and neither did I. Her curls were springing back, it was true, but the close cut had made her look smaller than ever. She was older than me because she'd been kept back a class at school; it was a private school and they did things like that; not as a punishment, but to ensure we all got our matrics before we left. So Meriel was eighteen and still did not measure five feet tall. She took a size two in shoes and her enormous grey eyes took up most of her face; with her new haircut they looked bigger than ever. And you could see her ears. My dad had a saying when there was a secret to be shared – 'a word in your shell-like' – and I saw that Meriel's ears were like two delicate translucent shells. The August sun shone through them.

She said, 'I really do want to do something splendid today. Something for the war effort. Let's go and paint a sign!'

It had been all the rage. Walls everywhere were still daubed with demands to 'OPEN SECOND FRONT NOW'. Now it had happened and it seemed the end of the war was . . . well, in sight.

I said doubtfully, 'What would we say?'

'I like Ike?' Meriel offered.

Strangely enough, people didn't seem to mind General Dwight Eisenhower. Privately I thought it was a bit of a cheek, taking over our war, but Dad said they'd put so much money in it, let them have it. And anyway, General Ike had such a nice face: rather like an amiable frog.

'Well, it's quite a nice thing to paint. But . . . we'd be arrested before we got the lid off the tin!'

'That's the whole point! The danger of it!' She looked at me, all excitement, then added, 'Anyway, they don't do anything about it – you get a warning from a policeman and that's that.'

'You'd prefer to go to jail, would you?'

'I don't know . . . D'you know, sometimes I wonder what on earth life will be like after the war. No one to hate . . .'

'We'll be out at work by then. Our own money. No clothing coupons.' I crossed my fingers because there were rumours about a super-bomb that could still win the war for Hitler.

Meriel said nothing, and I was grateful because I'd spoken out of turn. I had the promise of a job at our local newspaper office so long as I matriculated, and Dad was already calling me his special cub reporter. Meriel wanted to be a hairdresser and no way would her father allow that. He had inherited Nightingale's from his father, and had watched it run downhill since the war started. It had been one of the best gents' outfitters in the city but Dennis Nightingale had failed to get the coveted 'Suppliers to His Majesty's Armed Forces' and clothes rationing had hit hard. He was no businessman and though Meriel could not spell she was excellent with numbers. He wanted her in the shop. She could think of nothing worse. If she matriculated her father had promised he would wait for another few years until she got 'some sort of degree'. We both needed that precious piece of paper.

It was then, sitting on our bikes, scuffing the grit on the rough road that led down to the fields and Twyver's Brook, that the man appeared around the bend about a quarter of a mile behind us. Meriel, who was facing that way, began to report in a low, deliberately tense voice: 'Chap in sight. On bike. Wearing civvies. Cap. Suit. Proper suit. Navy-blue. Could be a chalk stripe. Can't see yet. Coming up fast.'

I kept my eyes studiously front. I knew the drill. We'd done it before. Chosen someone – a victim, I suppose – and followed them. We'd cook up an exciting background for them en route; if they got off their bikes so did we, and we'd followed them around shops on foot. Eventually they'd arrive at their destination and we'd go home. We had always hoped for something more interesting, and this looked more like it.

Meriel suddenly got off her bike, let it fall against the grass verge, and bent down to adjust the buckle on her sandal. I followed suit, said a couple of 'rhubarbs' at her, and we both laughed. This was, of course, intended to reassure the man on the bike that we hadn't the least intention of following him.

As he drew level I started to glance up – which we had previously decided was the natural thing to do – all prepared to return his 'good afternoon' with a nod. But he kept his eyes straight ahead; I don't think he even saw us.

I tried my photographic technique, which was much more effective when I could frame my subject with tunnelled hands and spend a bit of time. This quick upward flash gave me the cap, glasses beneath, no chalk stripes: in fact a shiny serge suit, a white shirt and . . . and . . . a school tie! Not even from the boys' grammar, but from our school! The distinctive double arch of the Swallow School was unmissable.

We waited until he was almost out of sight – the rough road went on for another mile before reaching the city boundary – during which time I had passed on this vital piece of information.

'He must be one of the dads!' I gasped as we righted our bicycles and mounted them. 'How else would he get one of our ties?'

'They get thrown out, eventually,' Meriel panted. Her legs were shorter than mine by at least nine inches, and though her saddle was as low as it would go she had to stand on her pedals to get going. We concentrated on getting into a rhythm, and as we rounded the next bend there he was, still grinding along, completely oblivious to the state of the road, the heat and the two girls on bikes following him.

'Definitely not a dad,' Meriel said. 'You saw the tie. I saw the shoes. Can you spot them from here? The soles are flapping.'

He disappeared from view behind a thicket of alders, and something was hanging from his pedal. Definitely not a dad. Dads had to be earning salaries rather than wages to send their girls to Swallow. I was there on a scholarship.

We had no difficulty for the next mile or so, which took us into the centre of the city. The prongs of the cathedral tower were on our right. He turned left and so did we. We started to close the gap between us, because he had two choices now: he could go straight on over the railway level crossing or he could turn sharp right towards the city's park.

The summer afternoon was well on its way; Eastgate Street was hot and rather smelly as we passed the fruit market. We came to the level crossing – the metal lines seemed to shimmer in the heat – and the gates were closed. We couldn't see the man at first and both looked right towards the war memorial. The road was clear except for an open camouflaged truck full of chewing American GIs. No cyclists. We looked back. He was halfway across the double railway track using the pedestrian bit and wheeling his bike. He got to the other side, and as he went through there came that familiar click which meant the walk-way was also locked.

'We've lost him!' announced Meriel, looking absolutely tragic.

The time between locking the gates and a train running through was indeed long enough for 'our man' to disappear in the maze of streets and alleys leading from Barton Street to what was known as the White City and the cemetery beyond. I felt frantic.

'No, we haven't! Follow me!'

As I turned and pedalled furiously towards the park and the war memorial I felt terrific. We were both absolutely certain that we were on the trail of someone who was up to no good. We were part of the war effort. We were Doing Our Bit. This transcended painting 'I LIKE IKE' by a mile.

Once past the park, almost next to the Empire cinema, I skidded sharp left and plunged down into the pedestrian tunnel that linked the right side with the wrong side of the tracks. Up and into the heat again, I veered another sharp left, and pedalled even more furiously back alongside the railway to the other side of the level crossing. There were three cars waiting to get into Eastgate Street, four cyclists and a gaggle of pedestrians, one with a pram full of coal. I came to a stop on the other side of the street, slewed my poor old Raleigh round by the kerb, and stared along the shabby length of Barton Street. The man was just passing Silverman's Bespoke Tailoring – doing so much better than Nightingale's since specializing in alterations to officers' uniforms right back in 1939. Our man was hesitating there, his bike wobbling a bit as he glanced at the window. But then he pushed hard on the pedals of his bike and was off again. Meriel skidded to a halt alongside me, and I jabbed a finger, and we were again in hot pursuit.

I glanced at her as she did her usual thing of standing on her pedals. She was gleaming with sweat but grinning like a lunatic. And her curls were definitely coming back. I laughed, and she looked round at me and grinned, and it was like telepathy. I knew we were both thinking we were old enough to join up or make munitions or even to get married – well, she was – and here we were, acting like kids, making up games as we went along, like we always had, pretending we were rescuing the nation from a devilish German spy . . . and enjoying every minute of it.

There were more people about now, all moving towards the centre, talking to their kids in a series of hoarse commands: 'Mind that bike!' 'Get on the pavement!' 'Don't drink that pop before we damn well get there!'

Meriel looked at me and shouted, 'Holidays at Home. In the park.'

Of course. Mum, Dad, Mr and Mrs Nightingale, Meriel and the boys, Hermione Smith without her mum . . . we were all going together on Saturday evening. But it had started last weekend. I felt an extra jab of excitement: the big wheel was really big and there was something called the whip that guaranteed an upset stomach for two days after trying it. The families from the south of the town probably went most days armed with a picnic; there were plenty of free activities, the model boating pool being especially popular in this weather. No boats but plenty of muddy children.

We passed Silverman's, and I saw the notice 'closed' in the window, and wondered fleetingly whether our man had considered going in there.

'Turning right!' Meriel added and stuck out

her arm in good time. Children scattered. 'Where the hell is he going?'

'It's St James Street,' I said back. 'My gran used to live there.'

We whizzed down past Gran's old cottage with its big garden, over the ford and into Brook Street. Our man was there, wobbling again, uncertain whether to turn left or right. Right would take him back into Barton Street and would probably mean he did not know where he was going. He turned left.

He knew where he was going all right, and suddenly it was as if he knew we were behind him, too. We were in territory we did not know: the White City had been built just before the war, and was meant to house people from the city's slum area, which was due for clearance. Then the war came and the slum area was still there, and so was the White City. The new estate was like a maze, parallel roads criss-crossed by others; nobody had got around to planting trees but the names spoke of future plans for the parks and gardens department: Elm Avenue, Oak Tree Close, Poplar Road, Aspen Way. Our man knew them all and he put on speed and wove around them, doubling back so that we had to throw ourselves into gateways or behind grimy syringa bushes. We loved it, but we were apprehensive too. What if he confronted us and asked us what we thought we were playing at? What if he shouted? Or yelled for a policeman? I confided my fears to Meriel when he went into a telephone kiosk. 'He could be ringing the police right now,' I whispered. We were miles away but I dared not raise my voice.

'He isn't going to,' Meriel said confidently. 'And he must know we're here. So he's putting up with us. Why? Because he's up to no good! It should be us ringing the police!'

'I'm not ringing the police! We could end up in the cells or something.'

'I said we *should* ring them,' Meriel came back impatiently. She put on her George Formby accent. 'Eh oop! He's on the move again.'

We followed fairly decorously again, trying to look as if we were enjoying exploring this new area. He turned left into Sycamore Drive and we got off our bikes and crept up to the corner. Half-way down the road, his bike was parked neatly, pedal on kerb. No sign at all of our man.

We considered.

'Gone into that house,' Meriel said. 'Even numbers. Two, four, six . . . number eight. And they were expecting him because he telephoned from the kiosk.'

'And he's not expecting to stay because he hasn't taken his bike up to the door.' We stared at each other, amazed at our own logic.

'Ergo . . . we wait,' said Meriel.

We waited and had a depressing conversation about what would happen if we didn't matriculate. Meriel stated for the hundredth time that she was not going to work at Nightingale's and I said I only wanted to be a journalist and the *Clarion* wouldn't have me without my matric, so I would end up in an office somewhere.

'We could sell our bodies,' Meriel said gloomily.

'Oh yes,' I agreed. 'Why are we worried?'

'Or we could marry one of the Yanks at the camp and live in America.'

'Oh yes. Why *are* we worried?'

Meriel was silent for ages. I glanced at my watch: five fifteen. Mum and Dad were home any time between six thirty and seven.

Meriel said, 'He's been ages for someone who is not staying long.'

'Let's go home,' I suggested.

She was appalled. 'Don't be daft! The game must have some kind of – of – conclusion!'

'OK. We'll knock on the door and ask how much longer he's going to be.'

She tightened her lips and stood up suddenly. 'Come on. We'll play it by ear.'

I followed, twittering helplessly. She obviously did not realize how ghastly this game could become. That it was all happening in our heads, and the poor man in cap and glasses with the soles flapping off his shoes and wearing an old Swallow School tie knew nothing about it. I said something about hounding people and she turned on me suddenly. 'He could be like my dad! And this is *my* bloody revenge!'

I stopped in my tracks half-way up the path to the front door, realizing that only part of the afternoon had been a game for Meriel. She looked over her shoulder, told me to come on again, and then lifted the knocker and slammed it down hard.

I nearly ran, then. If it had been anyone but Meriel I would have run back for my bike and pedalled hard for home. We were basically nice girls, well brought up, and we might do silly, stupid things but we weren't cruel. But this was personal to Meriel. I stood next to her, trembling inside, but smiling, like Mum does when the vicar calls at the most inconvenient moments.

Nothing happened for ages. Meriel knocked again in the most imperious way she knew, and after counting a laborious but swift twenty, there were sounds inside – bolts being drawn? Then the door opened twelve inches and a woman's face appeared. She looked so much like a rabbit it was awful. Long nose, watery eyes, gingery-brown hair folded back like rabbit ears, and buck teeth that were showing even though her mouth was clamped shut.

'May we have a quick word with Mr Brown?' Meriel asked smoothly.

There was a pause while the woman organized her mouth, then all she said was, 'Mr Brown?'

'We saw him visiting you,' Meriel went on. 'We've been trying to catch up with him all afternoon. We're his nieces.'

' His . . . nieces?'

'On his wife's side. He doesn't know us but our aunt showed us his photograph and when we saw him cycling through the town we thought we would say hello.'

'I'm sorry. There is no such man here.'

I started to turn away, smiling regretfully and apologetically at Mrs Rabbit. Meriel said firmly, 'That's his bike. And we saw him come into this house.'

'Nobody has been here. Try next door.'

She shut her door softly, before Meriel could get her foot inside. We heard the bolts go home – yes, they were bolts – then silence. We had not heard her walk towards her door, nor did we hear her go away. She could have been waiting for us just the other side, and be waiting again now. It was creepy.

I practically dragged Meriel away. She kept saying, 'I know he's in there, I just know it.'

'He was in there. He's gone now. Through the back door and along one of the ash lanes.' Many houses in the city were connected by these back entrances and they were often surfaced with ashes from the house fires. They were called ash lanes.

'But his bike—' Meriel protested.

'It's too good a bike for him. He pinched it, I bet. Now he's left it.'

'How do you know he's gone? He could still be there . . . gloating . . .'

'If he'd been there he wouldn't have let her answer the door. What could we have done about that? Nothing at all.'

I was amazed at myself. I was making it up as I went along, but it was so right. I wasn't taking anything away from Meriel, in fact I was giving something back to her. Just to underline that I added, 'Some revenge, eh? You put the mockers on that. Absolutely.'

She looked at me intently for a moment, then that wonderful smile lit her face, her dimples appeared and her grey eyes leapt into life.

'Come on. Let's cycle home past the park. See what we're letting ourselves in for on Saturday.'

And that was what we did. And we both thought what a great afternoon it had been. The haircut, the butterless sandwiches, the terrific chase . . . yes, a really great afternoon. And in the end, we had hurt no one. I started to sing 'There'll be bluebirds over . . . the white cliffs of Dover . . .' And Meriel joined in. With our names – Throstle and Nightingale – we'd toyed with the idea of becoming a singing duo under the name of 'The Song

Birds'. The snag was neither of us could sing that well. We leaned over our handlebars, convulsed with giggles at our falsetto renderings. 'Don't panic, Vera!' Meriel called across the railway lines.

Two

Saturday came and Hermione's mother cycled down the rough road at eight thirty to say Hermione wasn't well enough to go to the Holidays at Home in the park. What a surprise. I heard Mum murmuring condolences at the front door. My bedroom window overhung our front door, and I peered out as Mrs Smith wheeled her bike back up to the gate and mounted it at the kerb. She was wearing one of those old-fashioned dust coats, and she had a spoke guard on the back wheel of her bike. I drowsed and wondered what kind of a job it might be to thread up those spoke guards, and whether the threader was ever tempted to crochet a pattern as she went along. In the future that sort of thing could become precious like the Bayeux Tapestry or something. I tried to imagine a crocheted spoke guard and failed. And then I thought, poor Hermione. Not even Holidays at Home. She had to be the only person in our class who hated school holidays.

When I flumped down the stairs half an hour later Dad had already left for work. He worked a six- and sometimes a seven-day week. He was a designer at Smith's Aircraft Company and had been responsible for a modification on the Spitfire's tail fin that had given it what he called 'a bit more oomph', which Mum had explained later meant more manoeuvrability. 'Could get one of those young men out of trouble,' she said in her quiet voice. Which meant that she wished Dad could be designing aircraft for international races the way he had before the war, but that if he had to make war machines she was proud of him because he could be saving lives. Anyway, what it also meant was that at times we did not see much of Dad.

'Will he be back for tonight?' I asked anxiously. It was better with Dad there, because Mum then became one of us and giggled helplessly nearly all the time. Dad was one of those people who never seemed to make their presence felt, yet . . . I don't know . . . freed everyone up to be happy and natural. There has to be a name for someone like Dad. Liberator? That was the name of an enormous plane, so it wasn't quite right. But he did liberate things. He had a way of lifting his left eyebrow and just looking at you. I don't know what it was.

Mum nodded reassuringly. 'That's why he

went off so early this morning. Long before Maude Smith came with her lame excuses. I feel so sorry for Hermione. She's ill so often it will make her properly ill one of these days.'

She looked at me and I purposely lifted my left eyebrow, and we both collapsed laughing.

We had a good Saturday. We discussed the possibility of me *not* getting my matric, and Mum said easily, 'Well, you could do a secretarial course at the commercial college. I bet Gilbert Carfax would prefer that, in a way. How would you feel? There's a good place round by the spa pump rooms.'

This whole thing at the *Clarion* office had been fixed up by Mum. She had gone out with Gilbert Carfax who owned the *Clarion* and – obviously – had dropped him like a hot cake when she met Dad at the big do at Smith's where she was waitressing. Gilbert had seen them together and known before they did. He said that was what made him such a good reporter: because he knew things before they happened. He was my godfather and I quite liked him, and called him 'Uncle Gilbert'.

She shrugged at my unspoken question. 'Well, you know. He was just ordinary. Not that good at school except that he did produce a magazine thing. He worked for his father who owned the *Weekly Post* and then his father died, and he bought the *Clarion* and Bob's your uncle.'

'And he might think I was too big for my boots if I matricked?' I asked nervously.

She shrugged again. 'I don't think so. But he wouldn't hold it against you if you didn't matrick. And he'll probably make you learn shorthand and typing anyway.'

'I don't mind that. And I don't mind making tea and things. But I would like to start learning to be a reporter.'

'So long as you don't follow in your mother's footsteps.'

She still said things like that, in spite of Dad. I reminded her that she had been the best waitress in the country, and she did the eyebrow lift and we laughed again. Then we started on the cleaning and the singing. We always sang when we cleaned the house. We harmonized, we crooned, we did instruments; we were superb doing Beethoven and Chopin. I might be on the landing using the banister as a piano and Mum might be below conducting with one of the walking sticks in the hall or my hockey stick. I already mentioned I was spoiled rotten. It was so lovely.

The Nightingales lived much nearer the city than we did, so we called for them. Dad got home in good time and we had lettuce from the garden, hard-boiled eggs from the chickens next door and plenty of bread and Mum's butter spread. One of Dad's colleagues grew his own grapes in a conservatory and had brought Dad a huge bunch. He took some of them in to Hermione's as we passed her house and asked Maude Smith whether Hermione might be well enough to come with us after all. Apparently she wasn't.

Meriel was already waiting for us outside her house. She was wearing a dress I hadn't seen before. It was dark green cotton with white bias binding along the neckline and shoulders, where the whole dress fastened with enormous white buttons. It fitted perfectly and showed off her tiny waist and burgeoning, grown-up bust. She looked marvellous but also dangerous. Her eyes were glittering. You could see them properly now that I had cut her hair. Mum couldn't get over her.

'You look like one of the covers on my magazine, Merry,' she said. 'That dress is so – so—'

'Sexy?' It was a word not much in use then and Meriel used it to provoke. I looked nervously at Mum but Meriel swept on regardless. 'Dad's sleeping with a dressmaker these days and he took her one of my old dresses and she used curtain material and made . . . this.' She looked down at it with dislike.

I nibbled my lower lip, recognizing the signs: Meriel was ripe for a rip-roaring row with her father. Or anyone else who happened to be around.

Mum said helplessly, 'Oh . . . Merry.'

Dad said, 'Is he coming to the park with us?'

'No. He's taking Mum and the boys in the car. He's got some black-market petrol and he says the car needs an occasional drive. I said I'd see them there. Shall we get going?'

Dad hesitated. 'Is your mum all right with that?' he asked.

'Of course. When he came in with the dress she said he reminded her of Errol Flynn!' The scorn in her voice made my teeth ache.

She was frenetic that night, and I went along with her because she was my friend, and because it was the best fair I'd ever been to. And because Mum and Dad looked younger than me and went on all the rides, and Dad bought loads of brandy snaps and toffee apples and funny hats and fizzy pop. I'd never been to anything like it before, where you bought fun. Our fun was everywhere but we rarely bought it. Singing. Picnics. Bike rides. Holidays in Cornwall . . . maybe we bought those. I don't know. This fun was so . . . determined. Meriel and I were old hands at the big wheel. It came to Barton Fair every autumn and we loved it. But this was a big big wheel and we did not rock the twin seat, we just screamed louder and louder. Below us, the Nightingale boys, Barry and John, tried to outdo us without success. Above us Mum and Dad just laughed helplessly. When we got out Meriel fell into the arms of one of the fairground men and pretended she couldn't stand upright, and the other one handed me out and told me that in a couple of years' time I'd have legs like Betty Grable. I was so embarrassed. But thrilled, too. We staggered across to the whip. Dad said, 'I don't advise that thing. Not after the candy floss. We don't know where that sugar came from.'

If it had been anyone else speaking Meriel would have insisted on paying out her last sixpence and climbing into one of those wicked compartments, but it was Dad, so she said, 'Tell you what, Mr Throstle. Let's do all the stalls next till we're sure the sugar was okey-dokey, then see how we feel.'

Dad seized her hand and pumped it hard. 'Done,' he agreed.

So we did the stalls. The boys stayed with us. I was glad because Meriel tailored her comments for their ears. It was they who snuffled laughter when Mum looked around for Mrs Nightingale. Barry said to her, 'They're behind the dynamo thing.'

John added, 'Spoooooning!' Meriel said nothing. She hurled the hard wooden ball at the coconuts with such force she almost dislodged one from its sandy bed. Then she just looked at the stall holder, and he grinned and fetched her a bright yellow teddy bear.

Barry won a goldfish in a jar. John scooped

up a Chinese puzzle with his long wooden spoon, and we lost about half a crown rolling pennies, and much more than that trying to spear real gold rings with crooked darts. Then Dad spotted the Nightingales, and we all walked to the fish and chip van and tucked in as if we hadn't eaten for days. We were all grinning at each other – well, not at the Nightingales, because they just grinned at each other. It had been a really splendiferous time. August 1944. Holidays at Home. The park. We were never going to forget it.

'Time for bed. Come on, girls. Back to the bikes.'

Meriel's face dropped a mile. 'You said we could go on the whip after we'd done the stalls,' she reminded him.

'But not after fish and chips.' He looked at her incredulously. She kept nodding. Her dad blinked and looked away from his wife at Dad.

'You heard what Mr Throstle said. Jump to it!'

I knew then that if she had to hang for it she'd go back to the whip.

The two of us went. The Nightingales and the boys wandered off to where Mr Nightingale had parked his car, and Dad and Mum told us to catch them up as soon as we could and they would wait for us at Meriel's house.

The whip was ghastly. It tried to dislocate the spine and very nearly succeeded on me because I had such a long one. The gorgeous fish and chip taste still lingering in my mouth changed, too. Not for the better.

We stumbled towards the park gates where we had locked our bikes. Several American soldiers were just arriving in a jeep. They took one look at Meriel and started to whistle as they spilled out of their jeep. We kept going. Then one of them shoved another, and a third one cannoned into Meriel and knocked her flying. She cried out. I wrapped her in my orang-utan arms. And from behind a laurel bush appeared her dad and . . . someone. Not Mrs Nightingale. Very dishevelled.

Mr Nightingale flew past Meriel and me, gripped the GI with his left hand – the GI was looking bewildered and concerned at the same time – and gave him a slamming punch with his right. Blood spurted like a fountain from his face as he staggered back against one of the others. Just for a moment there was a curious hiatus in the flurry of events: Mr Nightingale stood there rubbing his knuckles, the GIs were thoroughly confused – not a good sign for our second front – and Meriel and I stood apart and brushed ourselves down, although there was nothing to brush off.

Then one of the GIs called, 'No damage, sir.' And another – very odd indeed – added, 'We'll say goodnight, now.'

Mr Nightingale – who had not even glanced

at his daughter – blustered, 'I shall be phoning your commanding officer!'

And, perhaps oddest of all, the dishevelled woman, clutching her dress across her chest, said, almost shyly, 'The dress looks just lovely on you, dear.'

Meriel looked up, then lifted her head towards the top of the poplar trees that surrounded the park and . . . screamed. It was a short, sharp scream, not the sort that heralds complete hysteria; she knew what she was doing. Then she put her hands to the neck of the lovely dark green dress and pulled.

I knew that she wanted to tear the dress to shreds, but what happened was such an anti-climax. The curtain material was strong, and the bias binding which ran across from shoulder to shoulder made it even stronger, and though she pulled again and again, nothing happened. The dishevelled woman put her hands to her face and whimpered, and her dress fell open and revealed bare breasts. Mr Nightingale had turned at the scream, and stared at his daughter struggling with her clothes. I flapped around and said, 'Merry . . . please don't, please . . .'

Even then Mr Nightingale left her to whatever she was doing and strode back to the other woman saying briefly, 'Cover yourself.' Then he sort of swept the woman up and they staggered away. And then, when the soldiers had disappeared, and we were on our own by the park gates, Meriel tugged again, and one of the buttons on the shoulder of the dress came off and the neck tore.

Meriel started to laugh, and then very suddenly stopped, bent over and was horribly sick. And then she cried.

During this whole series of happenings, which probably took only five or ten minutes, I was useless. Just a bystander. I did manage to hold on to Meriel's shoulders when she was retching, but that was about it. When she started to cry, I said, 'Don't worry. It was the fish and chips and then the whip.' Then she started to calm down, and rested her head against the railings.

Eventually she nodded. 'That's what it was.' She pushed the torn neckline of that lovely dress into place and met my eyes with a funny grin. 'I suppose I wanted to show Dad how – how *awful* his – his woman looked. But he didn't so much as glance at me, did he?'

'He didn't know what to do, Merry.'

'Oh, he knew what to do all right. Hit that poor Yank and then hurry back to the bushes to finish the job on—'

'Merry, stop it. You know what he's like. If your mum can accept it—'

'Only because she adores him. More than that, she worships him. It's horrible, absolutely horrible. You've got no idea.'

I said nothing because of course she was right. I had no idea.

At last we unlocked our bikes and began to pedal slowly towards the war memorial. Because of double summertime it was still light, and I knew that if we hadn't gone on the whip we'd be going no-handed, and laughing for no reason except we'd had a marvellous evening. I tried to recapture that careless happiness by suggesting we meet after church the next day and go for a swim in the river. She said briefly, 'Can't. Helping Mum with the boys.'

'What about Monday, then?'

'Our results might be through by then.'

'Oh . . .' for a glorious few hours I had forgotten all about the results.

We cycled on in silence. Then we both saw him at the same time. The spy was coming towards us this time, from the direction of the level crossing. The bike was different – Meriel hissed, 'He's stolen a better one this time!' But he wore the same cap and the setting sun made his glasses flash. I couldn't see his tie or his shoes.

He stuck out his right hand and began to turn at the war memorial. We had intended cycling straight on and into Derby Road, but we slowed and then began to turn left. The trouble was we were too close. We should have kept going and then turned back – or not turned back, which would have been much better.

He hesitated, wondering which of us had the right of way. Then he went in front of us and his glasses flashed again as he did a double-take. It threw us for a moment. This wasn't part of the game. If he stopped and confronted us we would have lost.

He didn't stop; he accelerated frantically, not exactly standing on his pedals like Meriel did, but bending over his knees, driving them like pistons. Then, when we had dropped back considerably, he swerved across the road and disappeared in the maze of small streets that led to Russell Square. By the time we had turned right too he had gone. We pedalled as far as Eastgate and then back towards Southgate. We had always thought we knew the city well but discovered that there were alleys and dead-ends everywhere.

Meriel was the one who gave up.

'Oh, come on.' She hoisted her flapping dress up to her shoulder again. 'Let's get back to my place. Your parents will be wondering where you are.'

It was true. And surely Mr Nightingale would have gathered up his wife and sons by now and got back home. What was he going to tell Mum and Dad? I could just imagine their horror if he told the truth. Not that he would.

We emerged by the war memorial again and I turned towards Southgate Street because I wanted to show Meriel the commercial college and tell her what Mum had suggested. 'You might be able to talk your dad into letting you come with me,' I said, as much as to change the subject as anything. 'Surely it would be useful if you could type?'

She hesitated, which made me think that the idea appealed to her. I looked sideways and saw that she had not even heard me. The spy was just over the road, dismounting, propping his bike against the kerb, obviously about to go into one of the houses in the terrace next to the pump rooms. And he had seen us.

We stopped. I put one foot to the ground; Meriel had to get off the saddle and stand astride her bike. For another of those strange timeless moments we stared across the road at the spy. And he stared back. Then he walked towards us.

If I'd been alone I would have shot off, then; pedalled like mad to get away from him, the situation, everything. But Meriel held her ground, so I had to do the same. We waited. He stopped a yard away. And then he spat on to the road.

I gave a squeak and gripped my bike fiercely. Meriel . . . I will never forget this . . . Meriel spat, too. And it was as if the little spurt of desperate courage that had brought him across the road just disappeared. He drooped. He stood there and everything went out of him; even his glasses dimmed.

Meriel said almost politely, 'So you are a spy. A filthy German spy.'

His head came up. 'Is that what you think? Well, think it, then. I might as well be shot for a spy, as locked in that prison day after day.' He advanced and we both shrank back, and he laughed bitterly. 'Ah. The great English heroines, yah? You English. You think you are the best in the world. Defending little Belgium. How many countries had to go before you realized you would be next – hey? Hey?' He spat again. 'How would you be – locked up all day – how would you be, I wonder? Hey? Hey?'

Meriel said in a quavery voice, 'You're not locked up now, though, are you?'

'No, I am not. And I will not be again.' He delivered another of those bitter laughs and it was not pleasant. 'Go. Go on. Go to the police and tell them about me. Then come back here with them – yes, I will still be here—' He nodded at the house behind him.

'Come back with them so you can identify me. Hey? Perhaps the Judas kiss.' Again he laughed, and I felt like screaming, just as Meriel had screamed at her father. 'Yes, indeed. Very appropriate. Except that you would not wish to kiss me, hey?' He looked at us again. I cannot describe that look. Defiance was there, the kind of defiant courage that comes from despair. Then he turned and walked back to his bicycle, climbed the six steps to the front door of the house – number twenty-two, I noted – turned the handle, opened the door and went inside.

And we got on our bikes and pedalled towards Southgate Street where it would have been very easy to turn down towards Bearland and the prison and the police station. We did not do that. We turned right and made for the Cross and the road out of the city towards Meriel's house.

I said, ' I feel so sick.' And Meriel said, 'So do I.'

I said, 'It was almost as if he was hitting us.'

'I know. Do you think he is a spy?'

'He did not say he was.'

'But he did say he had escaped from prison.'

'The way he said he might as well be shot for a spy . . . I don't think he is.'

'I think he is. He's foreign. Sounded German.' Meriel nodded her head. 'I think he is.'

'Let's talk to my father about it. He'll know what to do.'

Meriel's head came round like a shot. 'Don't you dare! They'll take over – all of them – my father especially! It will all be their adventure then, not ours at all! Promise me – Rache, promise me – you won't say a word about this!'

'What are you going to do? Listen. Merry. I couldn't – I just couldn't point him out – identify him – I couldn't do it.'

She was silent for some time. We began to

pedal up the Pitch and she stood on her pedals and pushed her bike from side to side to get the best possible pressure. We got to the top and began to coast down the other side. We were both panting.

She said, 'OK. I'll think about it. I'll see you on Monday, right?'

I didn't bother to reply, we saw each other every day anyway; but she had gone flying ahead of me and turned into her road with a real swoop.

And there were Dad and Mum waiting outside her house, because the other Nightingales had not yet returned. Meriel fetched the house key from beneath an upturned pail and we all trooped indoors, and then the car drew up outside.

I thought it was over.

Three

On Sunday Dad was home, which meant we didn't go to church. Not that Dad was agnostic or anything; in fact he was probably a devout Christian if only he'd talk about it. But he didn't like the liturgy of a church service. He said it made it hocus-pocus for him.

It was a pity really, because I needed the hocus-pocus that Sunday. I needed to unload a lot of guilt, and it was jolly hard work doing so in my bedroom on my own. I couldn't tell Mum or Dad what had happened because I was pretty certain they would be disappointed in me. To begin with, I could have helped Meriel . . . maybe I should have confronted Mr Nightingale and forced him to talk to her. And the way I had automatically turned my handlebars left to follow him when we saw the spy. And the way I kept thinking of him as a spy! And if I really thought he was a spy, why wasn't I at the police station? And was that why I didn't want to tell Mum and Dad – because they might make me go to the police station?

It was all too much. My head ached, and I couldn't eat what Mum called our summer Sunday lunch, which was hard-boiled eggs on a bed of fresh watercress with tiny little new potatoes encircling everything. And then poached plums. They were stewed really, but Mum said poached plums sounded like the Ritz. Once, just once, Mum had worked at the Ritz. She couldn't afford to do it more often because she hadn't been paid, and had had to rely on tips.

Anyway, when I couldn't manage the Ritz-type lunch Mum knew I was ill, and she put cushions in the deckchair and an umbrella over the top, propped my legs on a kitchen chair, and brought me cold lemonade straight from the marble slab in the pantry. I felt better. And quite close to God. Maybe Dad was right. Maybe hocus-pocus sort of got in the way.

I slept and felt even better after that. I didn't move. Somewhere in the house Mum was singing softly to herself. 'We'll gather lilacs . . .' Dad emerged from the garage carrying another deckchair. He saw I was awake and set it up next to me.

'How's it going?'

'OK. What's for tea?'

'Hard-boiled egg sandwiches with watercress! Serves you right for leaving yours.' He grinned and added, 'I picked loads of raspberries.

Mum's making some of her mock cream. Will that do?'

'Oh yes.' I grinned back.

He said, 'Listen. Stop worrying about the exam. It's only a bit of paper. You're intelligent. Mum and I know that. Everyone you know knows that.'

'Oh Dad . . .' I felt my eyes begin to melt and said quickly, 'I'm not worried, anyway. I've got rich parents!'

'So you have. I'd overlooked that fact.'

We both snuffled laughs. We weren't rich, not even relatively rich. The Nightingales and the Smiths were rich. The Nightingales had their business and Mr Smith was a director of Smith's Aircraft Company where Dad worked – when he wasn't being a wing commander with a handlebar moustache. They'd had a huge house near the factory and had only moved to the rough road when war broke out so that Hermione could go to Swallow. They paid full fees. I'd got a scholarship to Swallow, and at my interview Miss Hardwicke had shaken Dad's hand and said, 'I'm a great admirer of your work, Mr Throstle. Do you think Rachel has a similar feeling for mathematics?'

Dad had grinned hugely and said, 'As you have already awarded her a place, Miss Hardwicke, I have to be honest and admit that I don't think so. But she is full of curiosity, and in my opinion that leads to learning.'

Miss Hardwicke was absolutely delighted with that, and shook his hand so hard he said he thought she might be a lady wrestler in the evenings. But he said that when we got outside.

There was a cooee from the side of the house and Hermione's mother appeared, face first. You'd never guess she was married to money. 'I knocked but . . . ah, there you are! Forgive me for intruding on your picnic.'

Dad looked up. 'My wife is in the house, Mrs Smith. Is it about Hermione?'

Mrs Smith pulled the rest of her body into view, and with it came Hermione.

'She's here. She wanted a word with Rachel, and so I walked down the road with her. I don't like her to be out on her own with the American soldiers stationed in the manor.'

Dad stood up. 'Sit here, Mrs Smith.' He smiled at Hermione. 'Are you better today?'

Hermione looked completely confused, which was her usual facial expression. Mrs Smith said quickly, 'She is much better today, thank you, Mr Throstle. We shall go to Evensong later.' She sat in Dad's chair with a thump; he'd got it on the lowest notch possible. She gave a sharp scream.

Mum must have heard her because she came out of the kitchen at a trot, saw everything was all right and forced a bright smile.

'Why, Mrs Smith! What a pleasure. Will you have some lemonade?'

Mrs Smith sat with her hand on her heart, breathing hard, saying nothing. Mum looked at Hermione who said, 'Yes, please, Mrs Throstle.' Mum disappeared.

Hermione made the most of her chance. 'I – we – wondered whether you would be going into school tomorrow, Rachel. For the results. Mother rang Miss Hardwicke, and she said they would be posted on the noticeboard on Monday, and Mother cannot take me tomorrow, so we wondered whether—'

Mrs Smith regained self-control, and leaned forward to give me a condescending smile. 'So long as you are not accompanied by Meriel Nightingale, my dear. I trust you completely. But I am sure you would be the first to agree that Meriel is not always a good influence, and she would not hesitate to cycle three abreast, which we all know is very dangerous.'

Mum arrived with the lemonade. We all had a glass except Mrs Smith. Mum said, 'Now, are you sure you won't partake—'

'Certainly not, Mrs Throstle. I refuse to indulge in the black market in any way whatsoever!'

Mum never got offended, but she was taken aback. 'We haven't the money for the black market!' she protested, very realistically. 'The lemons are from Mr Myercroft's conservatory next door, and I've sweetened them with honey from his bees.'

It was Mrs Smith's turn to be taken aback. 'It seems Mr Myercroft is a universal provider!' She was determined not to apologize.

Dad, as per usual, took the sting out of everything. He gave her his widest grin and said, 'Actually, old Mr Myercroft is in love with my wife.'

'George! Really!' Mum went pink. Hermione laughed. Mrs Smith blinked, then smirked.

'Well, in that case, Mrs Throstle . . . perhaps half a glass.'

Dad stood up. 'I'll get it, darling. Have a chat with Mrs Smith while the girls sort out times.' He looked at her with such meaning that she, too, blinked. Dad went on, 'Rachel, let Mum sit there and you take Hermione down to see the raspberries.'

Our garden was very long and the kitchen part was screened from the lawn by high trellis; in any case, the rows of kidney beans gave privacy.

Hermione said wistfully, 'Was it good at the fair?'

'Yes.' I remembered the last part and added, 'I'm not sure you would have enjoyed it, actually. Meriel was sick. We went on the whip and we'd eaten fish and chips and candy floss and she was sick.'

Hermione shuddered. 'Just talking about it . . . I had a temperature. Mother said it would be better for me to rest.'

'Yes. I think she was right.'

Hermione said, 'Actually, my father rang through. Officers are allowed to ring home from overseas but they mustn't say where they are.'

'Of course not. How marvellous. What a good thing you're on the telephone.'

'Yes. I wish you were, too. We could ring each other up and have talks.'

I couldn't think what we'd talk about, but I nodded.

She picked some under-ripe raspberries and started to eat them. 'I'm really nervous about tomorrow. What time shall we go?'

'You could telephone Miss Hardwicke tomorrow morning and check that the results are in. Then we could go whenever you like.'

'Come up as soon as your parents have gone to work and we'll telephone together.' She picked another raspberry. Dad had had all the ripe ones; she had to be desperate.

'Won't your mother mind?'

'No. She's got a taxi coming at ten for an appointment with the dentist – that's why she can't take me to school.'

'Oh. Right. I'll come to you about half past ten. We'll ring Meriel as soon as we know what is happening.'

She looked at me sharply but said nothing. We were under the plum tree by this time and I picked two gorgeous Victorias, handed her one ne other. From the lawn Mrs fluted falsely towards us.

ne! Darling! Time to get ready for g!'

mione wiped her mouth with the back her hand. She said, 'All right, then. See you tomorrow.'

'OK,' I said.

Mum, Dad and I ate our raspberries and mock cream in the garden, smiling at each other all the time. The best of Maude Smith was that when she left it was like not having toothache any more. And, at last, I'd made a stand for Meriel.

That night something awful happened. The war had not affected us personally until then. We were on a flight-line from the Bristol Channel to the industrial bits of Bristol and Birmingham, and on the night Coventry was hit we had watched the German planes go over, droning their typical uneven engine note, wave upon wave of them; sometimes they were caught in the searchlights when the ack-ack guns behind us opened fire, but they made no effort to weave. Mum had wept on Dad's shoulder and I had trembled in my pyjamas and dressing gown. It had been so . . . inexorable. For the very first time I had wondered, then, whether we might lose the war. The feeling hadn't lasted, of course. But . . . it was that inexorableness. After that, optimism had soared in again: if they hadn't brought us to our knees yet, then maybe they never would. There had been a few sporadic attempts to find the aircraft company. An occasional bomb was dropped. But the camouflage nets were everywhere and the big design and planning offices were underground.

This was different. This was what they called a civilian attack. We learned afterwards that two fighters had come over in the small hours of Monday morning and dropped their loads on the middle of the city itself. The sirens woke us at two o'clock and we all tumbled out of our beds and crouched under the stairs, where Dad had managed to fit a steel table known as a Morrison shelter. We were well wrapped in eiderdowns and blankets, supposedly to cushion the blast and protect us from flying shrapnel. Nothing happened for half an hour, and we almost went back upstairs, but Dad said we were like foxes in a den and it would be cold in our empty beds; so we cuddled down together; and I was almost asleep when the crunches came up from the foundations, gripping the floorboards just as Dad gripped us. For a moment it was hard to breathe. Then it was all right. Then it happened again, and twice more after that. Dad said quietly, 'Dorniers. I think.' We waited, still holding each other so tightly. Dad said, 'Two planes.

Two bombs apiece. All-clear at any moment.'

And it came. The long single note that told us it was over . . . for us, at any rate. We went into the front room and switched on the wireless and Dad manned it while Mum and I made cocoa. Nothing came through about the bombs. Dad stayed up, but Mum and I went back to bed. Mum had to go to work in the morning and I was suddenly terribly tired.

But everything was just the same the next day. The weather was changing and it was overcast, and the occasional breeze was suddenly non-zephyr. By the time I got downstairs, Dad had left and Mum was almost ready to go.

'Dad is going to telephone Mrs Smith,' she said to me, draping a cardigan around my shoulders. 'He'll find out about the bombs. It could be that you should not go into school today, results or no results. Anyway, Hermione will come and let you know what he says.' I shrugged off the cardigan and Mum replaced it. 'It's quite chilly outside, you'll need it.' She kissed me lovingly and wished me good luck. 'If you do go, try to ring me. There's that kiosk just outside the school and you've got my number. Here's some change. You will, won't you?'

'Of course, of course. You'll be late.'

'You could ring me anyway from Hermione's. Let me know what you're going to do.' I nodded and she said, 'Will you be all right, Rachel? You look so pale—'

'So do you!' I grinned. 'Please go. I'm really fine.'

She hugged me again and went. She tried to make me laugh by mounting her bike the man's way. She nearly fell off. Shouted back, 'Serves me right!' and wobbled away. If I didn't get that bit of paper, I was going to be more upset for Mum than for myself.

Anyway, I got cracking: washed-up, and made my bed, and peeled some potatoes for that night, and tried not to think about what would happen in-between now and eating the potatoes. Hermione did not appear, so I got on my bike and cycled up to her house. I knocked on the door unenthusiastically. Obviously Mrs Smith wouldn't leave Hermione after last night's raid, so she would answer the door, tell me that Hermione had to rest and that would be that. But that didn't happen. Hermione answered the door herself, and it was obvious she was near to tears.

'Your father telephoned.' She opened the door just wide enough for me to get into the house. 'He wanted me to walk down and give you a message but I was too scared.' She gave a dry sob. 'Mother left the house at eight o'clock this morning and I haven't seen her since! The taxi turned up at ten and she wasn't here . . . and . . . I don't know what is happening!'

I looked at her stupidly. 'The dentist doesn't open till nine,' I said.

'I know. She said the surgery might have been razed to the ground. But it can't have been, otherwise she would have been home again by now.' She closed the door, and put the bolt across, and repeated, 'I don't know what's happening.'

It was rather a turn-up for the books, Mrs Smith leaving Hermione alone after the first proper air raid we'd had.

'What did my father say?' I asked, going straight to the phone in the dark hall, as if it had all the answers.

'Four bombs were dropped near the park. What are we going to do, Rachel? What can have happened to Mother?'

'Well, the dentists' surgeries are all over that way, so perhaps there was some damage . . . I don't know.' I looked at the silent black receiver hanging on the Chinese wallpaper. 'What else did Dad say?'

'He said that everything was under control. The police had closed the area. He said that as the school was nowhere near the park, we must do what we wanted to do. There would be no danger if we wanted to go and get our results. But if we did not want to go anywhere near the city then we should stay at home.'

I could almost hear Dad's voice, very gentle,

calming Hermione down. I remembered the three of us curled up under the stairs in our eiderdowns. Like foxes in a den. Dear Dad.

'I'll ring Meriel.' I didn't ask permission, just picked up the earpiece and reached up to dial the number. Hermione was doing a little jig right by me, and suddenly said, 'I must go to the lavatory. Thank you for coming up, Rachel.' She disappeared. I was amazed. I was as jittery as she was, and she was thanking me.

Mrs Nightingale's voice was quavery, too. 'Is that you, Dennis?' she said longingly.

'It's me, Mrs Nightingale. Rachel. I wondered what Meriel was doing.'

'She's gone into the city.' Mrs Nightingale sounded on the verge of tears. 'My husband went at first light to check on the shop and he asked Meriel to go with him, and said he would take her on to school afterwards. But she said she would rather cycle a million miles than . . .' Mrs Nightingale stopped speaking and some funny sounds came across the wires. Then she went on in a stronger voice, 'She left here about an hour ago on her bike. I expect she's still at school, so you'll see her there.'

'Yes. All right. I'm leaving now. Thank you, Mrs Nightingale.'

I hadn't seen Meriel since the Holidays at Home. She obviously hadn't got over it.

Hermione reappeared. She was breathing deeply, gathering herself for something or other. Then she said in a brave voice, 'Listen, Rachel. I've got to stay here in case Mother phones or turns up. But if you don't want to stay with me, you don't have to. I mean that.' She smiled shakily. 'We've got some eggs so I could make us a proper lunch . . . if you did stay.'

I stared at her. So she wanted me to stay with her. I was almost flattered.

'I'll come back as quickly as I can. Honestly. We'll have some lunch then, if your mother isn't home.' If she was, lunch was out; no way would Mrs Smith allow me to eat one of her precious eggs. I actually took Hermione's hand. 'I have to go because Meriel has already left, and if she hasn't matriculated she's going to be pretty upset.'

'Bring her back here, if you like.' Hermione was hanging on to my hand. It was almost sweet. Especially as she didn't like Meriel.

I gave her an extra squeeze and made for the front door; it might be sweet but it was also creepy. And another creepy thing was that Hermione's school uniform was on a hanger suspended from the banisters. It was all ready for her to go back to school, and school did not start for another two weeks.

I pedalled into town as fast as I could, even standing on the pedals going up the Pitch. There was more traffic about than usual. A police car was parked at the Cross, blocking both Eastgate and Southgate. Men in Home Guard uniform were trolleying sandbags around. Nightingale's was open for business as usual; no sign of Meriel or her father. I turned down Westgate and into the cathedral precinct. Several bikes were parked outside school; but not Meriel's. The front door was open and the chattering sounded like a hen house. I manoeuvred my bike into one of the stands and joined the gaggle of girls in the hall. The noticeboard was empty. At the end of the hall the stairs rose to a half-landing and then turned; girls were sitting on every step. Twenty-six of us had taken the examination and there were at least twenty in attendance, some with mothers, some with brothers. Rosemary, Jennifer, Janet, Daphne . . . they came at me with statements about the bombing. 'Our bedroom ceiling came down and my little sister is in hospital . . .' 'I've been here for over an hour, no sign of any results . . .' 'Several casualties . . .' 'My uncle is a warden and he says . . .'

I said loudly, 'Any sign of Meriel?'

Rosemary said, 'I've been here for yonks and she hasn't turned up in that time.'

The babble went on and on. I tried to imagine what it must have been like in London and Coventry, and all the other places where the Luftwaffe had systematically blanket-bombed. Multiply this by . . . I couldn't imagine. Nobody actually knew anything, not really. And there had been only four bombs.

Janet said, 'There were so many bombs I lost count.' She grabbed my hand. 'I was so scared I couldn't speak.' She was making up for it now.

At last, when I was thinking I'd have to go, Miss Hardwicke's door opened, and she and her secretary appeared, and started to struggle through to the noticeboard. Everyone fell back respectfully. The secretary, Mrs Rolfe, was lugging the library steps with her, and she opened them up and climbed them, then Miss Hardwicke passed up a scroll of paper and, one by one, six drawing pins.

We drew back further still to get a good view, and the silence was as deafening as the babble had been. Miss Hardwicke was more important to us than the King himself. Somebody's brother asked where the lavatories were, and was violently shushed. Miss Hardwicke turned to us while Mrs Rolfe closed the steps.

'I am delighted with the results, girls,' she said. 'When you have made a note of them, please leave the school quietly and go straight home. Last night's raid has caused some disruption in the south of the city, and we would not want to obstruct any of the clearing work.' She smiled at us. 'We all want to help, and the opportunity might come our way later, but sometimes we have to be content with simply causing no trouble.' Her smile widened.

'Keeping out of the way.' She was not wearing her gown, and she stood straight and pulled down the jacket of her linen suit. 'If anyone would like to talk about their results, I will be in my office until midday. Please make an orderly queue, girls, then leave as quietly as possible.'

She was gone. I had already seen my name just above Winifred Whittingford's. I had passed. Three names above mine was Hermione's. She had passed. Six names above hers was Meriel's. She had not passed.

I stumbled outside, quite certain that Meriel would be there, waiting. The precinct was empty except for two vergers flapping towards the west door like crows, clutching books to themselves. I picked up my bike and did a slow perambulation of the cathedral. Under the archways, past the cloisters, around the bit where the grilles of the crypt offered darkness. No sign of Meriel.

I went back into Westgate and cycled towards the river, and then slowed, put my foot on the pavement and tried to think as Meriel would think. And then I turned my bike the way I had come and cycled back. I knew, quite suddenly, where she would be.

Four

The safety barriers started just by the war memorial and swept around the park railings cutting off any entry to Southgate. There was no sign anywhere of Meriel. The houses in Spa Road next to the pump rooms were . . . a mess. In the middle of the mess was a space round a crater. On either side of the space, windows and fireplaces hung in mid-air. Half a floor on the second storey still had a dressing table standing with a crocheted cover and an enamelled toilet set on it. Behind that there was a tall building surrounded by three fire engines and a crane. I knew why the fire engines were there, of course, the smell of wet ash and singed furniture was everywhere; but Dad had explained to me ages ago when I was doing things in Physics that once the centre of gravity was changed in a building, it had to be either propped up or torn down. It looked as if the crane represented the demolition squad. I remember Dad making a pile of my old wooden blocks, then just shifting one on the bottom layer. 'Tricky business, knocking it down,' he had said as I scattered the lot on to the carpet. 'Supposing there had been people around those blocks? They'd have been injured, maybe even killed by the way you knocked it down.' He built it up again and showed me how to trace the shift, and then work out where to start demolishing it so that it fell straight down or even inwards. I never remembered things like that, but I enjoyed his explanations. I've always respected mathematicians. Maybe too much.

I was staring, wondering how they would tackle that building, when a lot of shouting came from the house at the side. The next minute a man in a navy-blue siren suit, and wearing a tin hat, came out of an enormous gap in the wall, and started pulling at something. Meriel emerged, protesting loudly, grabbing on to the side of the hole with one hand, threatening to bring down the upper storey on her head. I heard the warden shout at her not to be such a little fool, but her voice was louder than his.

'There're people in there! Let me go – I think – I know—' she screamed sharply, as he gave an extra tug and the hated green-curtain dress ripped at the waist. Just for a moment she released the side of the hole and tried to shore up her dress. It was enough for the warden. He lunged forward and hoisted her over his shoulder, and the next minute he was marching her over the road to where I was waving frantically. She lifted her head and saw me, and just for a second stopped screaming to say, 'It's him, Rache. It's him.' She picked up her scream again where she'd left off; it was deafening.

I gathered her to me and yelled at the warden, 'It's my sister. We're looking for my father. She thinks – she says—'

'I know what she thinks and says, my girl.' The warden was annoyed. Meriel must have hammered on his gas mask with her sandals and it was a crumpled mass.

Meriel was hanging on to me for dear life. I realized with a shock that her tears were genuine. 'Rache, do something.' She looked up at me, her lovely grey eyes filled with tears. 'It's him, I know it is. We drove him there, Rache. We have to do something.'

I swallowed. 'Is he still alive? We could call the ambulance.'

The warden said more kindly, 'The ambulance took the injured early this morning, my dears. The others have been temporarily sheltered in the Guildhall where the WVS are feeding them.'

Meriel started to wail again. 'He's there! He's there!'

I clutched her to me to shut her up, and said,

over those short, short curls, 'There are no . . . bodies, then?'

'No, miss. The bodies have been taken to the mortuary.'

Like a Greek chorus Meriel wailed again. 'He's there! He's there!'

I said in my most sensible voice, 'Warden, please may we look – just glance – inside to check my sister's—'

'Members of the public are strictly forbidden—' he held up his hand as I started to protest. 'The buildings have not been pronounced safe as yet, miss. But I tell you what I'll do. I will go and look, and come back and report to you!' He tried to make it sound mildly funny, but it didn't sound funny even to him, and he turned immediately and marched off to the side of the crater.

Meriel didn't let me go, but she slumped a bit and steadied her breathing.

I spoke into her 'shell-like'. 'Did you really see him?' Her head nodded once against my cardigan. 'The man? Fritz? Are you sure?'

'Of course I'm not sure. But I think he's under the stairs. You know, they tell you that's the safest place in a house.'

'But you're not sure.'

'I didn't have time to dig down, you see. Just outside the stairs is this huge pile of rubble and that's where he is. But then this damned warden arrived and started to drag me away.'

'So there is just a pile of rubble there. No body or anything?'

'No body. But there is . . . something. We'll have to come back tonight when it's dark, with a spade. My God, he might be dead by then.'

'Were there sounds, then? For God's sake, Merry, you don't just see a pile of rubble and know that someone is buried in it!'

The warden was returning at a trot. He was holding something in his hand.

He said, 'You could be right, miss. I've got the rescue squad digging now. But you must realize, you cannot stay here. You must go home to your mother and the police will contact you as soon as identification is needed.'

Meriel said, 'Oh no. That's no good at all. We have to stay. Don't we, Rache?'

I said vaguely, 'The police . . . the shock . . .' I was trying to see what was in his hand, all caked with grit.

'Look, girls. I tell you what I'll do. I will come round personally to tell you whatever news there is. Probably this means nothing.' He held up his hand. 'But obviously you recognized it as the sort of thing your father would wear and therefore we are investigating. Now if you will give me your address . . .'

I moved my lips and gave my address without thinking. I could see now what was in his hand. It was a necktie. It was part of our school uniform.

Meriel had fallen strangely silent. It was she who guided me back to my bike and then on into the park, where she had locked her bike to the park gates. When we mounted and began to ride home she said quietly, 'I suppose we had to give a genuine address if we wanted to know . . . anything. And perhaps your father will understand when you explain things.' She looked at my face. 'I know it's a bit of a shock at first. But at least we don't have to start digging at midnight!'

She meant to lighten the whole thing, but it didn't work. I kept remembering the spy, and the way he had almost confessed to us; faced us defiantly and then turned and went over to the houses. Meriel was right. We had driven him there, and that was where he had died.

She said, 'Talk about something else. You've been to school for the results? Don't tell me. You passed and I didn't.'

Strangely enough, that was what finally made me cry. And that was when she got off her bike and pulled me to a stop, and said, 'Rache, don't cry. Please don't. I'm glad – I mean that, honestly. Don't you see? This is my punishment. I'll never do anything so stupid again in my whole life. I deserve not to pass.'

I still hadn't telephoned Mum about the results. I told Meriel about Hermione and Mrs Smith and asked if she would mind popping in to see what was happening there, so I could ring Mum.

'Stop sounding so apologetic, Rache. God, it's not your fault I failed the bloody exam – you can talk about it, you know!'

'I don't want you to think . . . oh I don't know. Actually, I feel just terrible.' I really did. My headache was back with a vengeance. I felt guiltier still about our poor spy, and almost as bad about matriculating when Meriel hadn't. It didn't make it better when we parked our bikes outside the Smiths' house and Meriel came at me like a little terrier and butted me on the shoulder with her curly head.

'You're an idiot. We both knew I wouldn't pass. And because of old Fritz it puts the whole exam thing into perspective, and I don't care half as much. And we're going to be friends for the rest of our lives, so you'd better get used to me failing exams and everything.'

I wished we were the sort of friends who could hug each other. I ruffled her curls instead. 'Sounds good to me,' I came back hoarsely.

We got no further because Hermione came running down to the gate. Her single plait was fraying out all over the place. She looked distraught.

'What are you doing just standing here chatting!' She actually started to wring her hands, which I'd never seen before, though in the kind of books I was reading the heroines did it all the time. 'Mother hasn't come home, and she hasn't phoned, and I rang the dentist and she didn't even have an appointment!' The hand-wringing accelerated. 'If she's left home for good, can I come and live with you, Rachel? You're an only child so there must be a spare bedroom in your house. And your mother is kind and good, and would be only too pleased to take in an orphan. It would be like war work. Wouldn't it?'

I was mute with horror. Meriel said swiftly, 'You could come to us, Hermione. Rache's mum already does war work and mine would like a chance to get in on something. Besides, you'd be a great influence on the twins.'

I said, 'Don't be so silly. Your mother wouldn't walk out on you in a hundred years, and you know it, Hermione. And we've come to give you some good news, anyway. Don't you want to hear it?'

'Oh.' She looked at me properly. 'I've tricked, have I?' It was the sort of slang Meriel used. Not Hermione.

'You sure have,' I replied with a twang.

Meriel said, 'Might as well put all the cards on the table. I haven't. But Rache has. So please be careful of my tender feelings.'

'I'm sorry, Meriel. But you always said you wouldn't. Come into the kitchen and have a drink of milk out of the fridge. It's really nice. I get extra milk because my calcium is low, and you can have some of it.'

It was the first time either of us had been offered anything by the Smiths. I think Hermione must have thought we were competing for her favours. I let them go ahead down the long dark hall and made for the telephone.

Mum said, 'Oh, thank God. I wondered what had happened.'

'Sorry, Mum. We were talking . . . you know how it is. Anyway, I got it.'

Mum made crowing noises, and there were other yelps in the background, and someone shouted 'congratulations'. She'd told everyone. I'd have to have a word with her. How would she have felt if I hadn't got it?

'What about Meriel?' she asked after a while.

'No,' I said, without explanation in case Meriel was listening.

'Oh. Oh darling. I'm so sorry. How is she?'

'Marvellous. Really good. Honestly.'

'And Hermione?'

'Yes. But rather a lot has happened there. I'll tell you later. I might have to hang on a bit. If my bike is still outside when you come home, could you pop in?'

'Of course. Nothing too awful?'

'No.'

'Mrs Smith driving you mad?'

'No. I really will tell you later. I'd better go. Hermione is getting us a drink.'

'What? I thought you said—'

'I did. And it might never happen again, so cheerio!' I could hear her laughing.

There was a grainy old table in the kitchen that didn't look too hygienic. I was glad when Hermione flapped a cloth over it. We sat there with glasses of milk – I have to say it was delicious – and discussed explanations for Mrs Smith's non-appearance. My headache got worse.

Meriel glanced at Hermione's face and said, 'Let's start at the beginning. She left for this appointment at eight o'clock.'

'Only there wasn't an appointment,' Hermione reminded us drearily. It was obvious she had been over and over this during the course of the morning.

'No. But she had planned to go out. Not until about tennish when the taxi came. It was definitely pre-arranged. She did have some kind of appointment.'

'Well . . . yes.' Hermione looked a little less fraught. 'And she was nervous, too – just like she is when she goes to the dentist.'

'Really? So she wasn't meeting an old friend?'

'She would have told me. She hardly knows a soul in this area. She would have been so happy . . .' Hermione gave a small dry sob.

I stopped thinking about my headache. I might be an only child, but I was surrounded by people who knew me because they knew Mum and Dad and they had known my grandparents. But the Smiths were not 'local'. And because they were so odd and snobby they seemed to have few friends. And then Mr Smith had been posted, and Mrs Smith and Hermione had been . . . stuck.

Meriel obviously found it impossible to imagine Mrs Smith being happy. She said, 'Perhaps she was nervous . . . for the friend? And then she left early because of the air raid. Because the friend was staying in the city and might be scared or something.'

Hermione repeated impatiently, 'If it had been a meeting with a friend she would have told me. Definitely.' She glanced at me. 'What do you think, Rachel?'

I didn't want to say, but on the other hand ignorance was not bliss for Hermione at the moment.

'She might have had a different kind of appointment. More . . . medical?'

Hermione almost wailed, 'She would have told me! She would have *told* me!'

'Perhaps she didn't want to worry you. And if it was at the infirmary it could have been cancelled. The roads are all cordoned off down Southgate.'

There was a silence. It fitted. Mrs Smith

could have set out early to find out whether her appointment was still valid, and could still be waiting in that awful out-patients' waiting room.

Meriel said, 'There are phone boxes in the entrance place, but once you've got in a queue in the waiting room you don't want to lose your place.'

Hermione said hopefully, 'Yes. I remember when I went for my tonsils . . . Yes, it could be that. And it need not be anything too awful. They do ingrowing toenails and everything.'

There was another silence. Nobody suggested telephoning the infirmary and enquiring about Mrs Smith's appointment. After a while Hermione stood up and took our glasses to the sink. 'If Mother comes in before you leave, don't say anything about the milk,' she said. And we both babbled of course not, and then mentioned that the weather was brightening. It was time to leave. She didn't want us there when Mrs Smith came home.

As we went past the stairs again I tried to get into a lighter mood. 'Still two weeks of the holiday to go, Hermione! You're a bit early with getting your uniform up together.' She laughed obediently, and I said, 'Even the pleats are tacked on your skirt. But where is the tie?'

As I spoke I wished the words back. I don't

know why. Hermione said quite easily, 'Mother thought a new tie for the sixth form would be . . . appropriate.'

Meriel spoke sadly. 'You could have had mine. It was new last year. I won't be needing it.'

That finished that. We waved cheerio and straddled our bikes. Meriel said she might as well go home. I said OK. Then, as she stood on her pedals to get going, we saw Mrs Smith. She was on her sit-up-and-beg bike with its spoke guard at the back and basket at the front, her summer boater was slightly askew, and one of her cotton gloves was missing. Strangest of all, she was coming along the rough road; not from town, not from the village, either.

We exchanged quick glances; she would not want us to see her. I turned my bike expertly and fell in with Meriel; we both stood on our pedals and whizzed around the corner towards the village. Then we got on to the grass verge as close to the hedge as we could, dismounted and crouched.

She hadn't seen us. She got off her bike and propped it against the kerb and did a quick adjustment of her hat and linen suit, and then wheeled the bike up the path.

We waited until we heard the front door open and then close. We exchanged one of our looks again, I lifted my eyebrow, Meriel shrugged, I turned my bike and started back the way I'd come. Meriel called, 'Same place. Tomorrow afternoon?'

'OK.'

I went home and took two aspirin.

Five

By the time Mum and Dad got home I was asleep in the garden. The sun really had come through, and it was a beautiful, golden evening, and I wanted it to be like the evening before when we had eaten raspberries and laughed together.

They saw me through the kitchen window, and while the potatoes were cooking they brought out the tea things and laid up the picnic table properly and placed a bowl of flowers as a centrepiece. Then they woke me.

'Am I old enough to receive flowers?' I asked primly.

'Not really.' Mum smiled lovingly. 'These are from the other girls in the office—' she held up a hand at my guffaw. 'Just you wait and see. Meriel and Hermione will always be girls to you.'

'Your girls are pleased for you. They don't know me.'

'They're pleased for all of us. And Dad and I

thought you might like—' She looked around. 'George, where are you?'

He appeared from the shed and gave Mum a package, and she gave it back to him, then they both clutched it together and held it out to me. Dad muttered, 'One, two, three,' then they both said slowly and clearly, 'Congratulations!' And I didn't have time to open it before the tears started, and then absolutely spurted, and I was gathered up between them and asked with dismay whatever was the matter. So I told them.

At the end, when I was sitting in the deck-chair again, they stood up from their squatting positions and sat down too in their chairs, and Mum said, 'How could all this have happened while we were at the fair together?'

I told her all over again, and then about our stalking expedition on Friday, and then what the spy had said to us. And then about Mrs Smith.

Mum said, 'I can't believe that in the space of three days all this has actually *happened*!'

Dad said, 'So it's thrown up three . . . difficulties. Nothing to be done about them, not really. But you will have to live with them, poppet. Number one is Meriel not getting the exam, and this problem with her father. Then it's the man on the bike, who you pretended was a German spy, and who might have been killed in last night's air raid. And thirdly, it's

Mrs Smith and the tie. Is that a fair assessment?'

Mum shook her head slowly from side to side; she didn't believe me any more than Dad did; none of it seemed real to her. I nodded just as slowly. I wasn't sure. Dad was always simplifying things, which was good a lot of the time but surely couldn't work now – this was much too complicated.

Dad said even more slowly and very solemnly, 'You and Meriel pretended a little bit too much this time, Rachel. You began to believe your own stories. There are a lot of foreigners in this region at present, some of them just waiting up at the transit camp, not knowing what is going to happen to them, and therefore unhappy and frightened. Many of them have been harassed by over-zealous patriots. It happens in time of war, I'm afraid. Silverman – the tailor in Barton Street – his windows were smashed on Saturday evening while we were enjoying ourselves on the big wheel. Perhaps your man was there at the time, and that was the cause of his angry reaction when he confronted you. And he was right, wasn't he? You were harassing him. There is a perfectly reasonable explanation for his actions, but none for yours.'

I looked at him, then down at my lap. 'Oh Dad,' I said. Then I looked up. 'But the tie?'

Dad glanced at Mum. 'Flo?' Mum's name

was Flora but he always called her Flo.

She said in a low, troubled voice, 'Old clothes go to the rag and bone man. And he sorts out anything he can sell. He might get sixpence each for old Swallow ties.'

Dad let this sink in. After a pause I said, 'So we really did harass him to death – literally.'

'Of course you didn't. You're not seeing straight on this at all, love. That man knew where he was going, and when he couldn't shake you two ferrets off, he went there quite openly. He was *going* there, sweetheart. Whether you and Meriel had followed him or not, that house was his destination.' Another pause, and then he was off again. 'As for Mrs Smith . . . her actions are always odd because she is an odd woman. Your explanation about a hospital appointment could well be the right one.' He grinned suddenly. 'Supposing she cycled home, saw your bikes propped up outside her house and thought – can't face those two perishers, I'll have a quiet cycle ride down to the fields and see if they've gone when I get back!' Mum and I had to laugh; he didn't sound a bit like Mrs Smith except for the posh-posh accent.

When we stopped laughing Mum said, 'Come on, open up your present. I'll have to go and see to the potatoes in a minute.'

As usual Dad had defused all the horrors, and Mum was picking up where he left off. I opened the little package. There was a black velvet box, and inside that was a silver bracelet, very plain, very simple. I felt the tears again.

Mum said quickly, 'We want it back. We're going to have it engraved. We couldn't before we knew that you had actually matriculated.'

'We knew you would,' Dad said. 'But Mum reckoned it was bad luck.'

I said, 'It's lovely. I'll always wear it. I just wish so much that Meriel had passed, too.'

And Mum said, 'Yes. But you know, she won't mind too much about not getting that piece of paper. It's the other-woman thing she cares about. And if Mrs Nightingale puts up with it, then I'm afraid Merry will have to do the same.'

'It was just . . . it was such a shock. And the woman must have been the one who made that dress. Meriel kept trying to rip it to shreds, and then she was sick and Mr Nightingale just . . . left.'

'Well, he'd got his wife and two sons waiting for him in the car somewhere,' Mum said reasonably. I looked at her in astonishment, amazed that she could reduce all the sordid events of Saturday evening into such neat order. Mum reached for my arm and held it so that the sun glinted on the bracelet. 'Look at how it sets off your tan,' she went on, smiling.

I got up to help her with our meal. It had never occurred to me before that jewellery was simply a way of attracting attention to the human body. And my arm did look rather nice.

Dad had asked me to pick the beans, so the next day I did that as soon as Mum left for work. Then I sorted out my school uniform, pressed everything and put it on a hanger the way Mrs Smith had done for Hermione. It was a sort of apology to her for thinking . . . whatever I had thought about her. Ever. It could be she had some terrible illness and was hiding it from Hermione . . . oh, please God, don't let that happen to Mum. I said that out loud.

It was nine thirty when I cycled into the city, turned off into the tiny lane that housed the office and print shop of the *Clarion*, and propped my bike against one of the gas lamps that still lit many of the streets then. Beyond the terraced houses opposite, the cathedral tower reared into the sky, and the smells from the vinegar factory overlaid the scent of rotting fruit that came from the market. I loved it all; I knew I belonged here.

Inside, there was a high counter, and lots of telephones all being used, as news came in from various agents over the county. A goods train from Sheffield carrying bazookas had derailed just this side of Birmingham on the Lickey embankment; cranes were being brought in. The Spitfire Fund had received a cheque for fifty pounds after a successful garden fête held by the citizens of Winchcombe. Sunday's air raid had claimed the lives of two people who had been trapped in the rubble of one of the houses when it received a direct hit. They had not yet been identified. Two people. Not just Fritz on his own. Somebody had been with him.

A voice, male but young, said, 'May I help you?' And I looked up and saw a chap, maybe a couple of years older than me, standing behind the counter fiddling nervously with a sign that said, 'Enquiries, please ring for attention.'

He was my height, which was tall, and everything about him seemed to be straw-coloured: from his aggressively straight hair and sandy-lashed blue eyes, through to his crooked nose and long mouth. Perhaps he should have started to shave, because his skin had a sort of straw-coloured sheen as the light from one of the bottle-glass windows highlighted his face. It made him seem . . . nondescript . . . but he wasn't. Not a bit. As he spoke I saw that his two front teeth were slightly prominent, and he tried to hide them by drawing down his upper lip. There was no need, it was rather attractive. He fiddled with the sign and I registered long knobbly fingers. He was certainly no Errol Flynn. But there was something . . . it was kindness. He didn't look as if he'd been one of those kids who tore wings off butterflies and stamped on snails.

His nervousness was catching, because my voice came out very shakily and all I said was, 'I wondered whether I could see Uncle . . . I mean, Mister . . . Carfax.'

'Oh. I don't know, actually. I'll go and find out. Can you wait a moment?'

'Oh yes. I've got all day.'

He smiled briefly and was gone. I used to come here often with Dad when we were going places with Uncle Gilbert and Aunty Maxine, but it was before this chap's arrival, and since the war we hadn't gone out much. I hadn't seen him before; I knew I would have remembered him. I could hear him taking the twisting old stairs two at a time; he must be fit. And younger than I had at first thought, otherwise he would have been in the forces. He was down in record time, smiling and showing those teeth unabashedly.

'I'll take you up,' he said, and indicated that I should go ahead of him.

'You go first,' I came back firmly. I was wearing last year's dirndl skirt, much too short. He hesitated, then nodded and went upstairs slowly, trying to look over his shoulder to check I was still there.

Uncle Gilbert waited at the top. 'Well done, Tom. Well done.' He never changed: words like bluff and hearty applied whether he was covering a wedding or a funeral. He wouldn't have done for Mum; Maxine could cope with him, she called him her teddy bear. He hugged me now. 'Rachel Throstle, I believe? Come to start her training? Or to tell me she's changed her mind about journalism and wants to be a famous actress instead?' He hugged me into his office, which overlooked the lane. Then, with his spare arm, he gestured the boy he had called Tom to follow us in. 'Come on, Tom. Come and be introduced to this young lady. She's my goddaughter and wants to work for the *Clarion* – can you imagine that?' Tom made sympathetic noises, which seemed to say that he too wanted to work for the *Clarion*. Uncle Gilbert sat me in a swivel chair and whizzed me round; he still thought of me as ten years old. 'This is Tom Fairbrother, Rachel. He's waiting for his call-up papers and thought he would see what it would be like to . . . guess what?'

'Work for the *Clarion*,' I said obediently. I did so much wish Tom Fairbrother wasn't there, so I could tell Gilbert that I didn't want to go back to school in September and ask if I could start working for him instead.

Anyway, Uncle Gilbert suddenly turned into the owner and editor-in-chief of a local daily newspaper and perched on a corner of his desk, rubbing his hands together as if it was mid-winter.

'Right. Quite a bond already, wouldn't you say? So I've got a job for you both. Serious stuff, but nothing like throwing you in at the deep end. The raid on Sunday night. Two bodies found in the rubble. The police are cagey. I want to know why. Ask the neighbours who they were. You'll find the survivors – most of them – still camped out in the Guildhall. Why didn't this particular couple go to the shelter like everyone else? Plenty of warning – the alert went off half an hour before the bombs fell.' He clasped his fingers and rubbed his wrists together. 'I want an angle on this story. I want people to look beyond the air raid to its victims. See if you can find something heart-warming. Maybe they were looking for a pet before they went to the shelter. Maybe they'd gone back for something.' He stood up abruptly. 'Off you go. See what you can find.'

I hadn't heard much after the first part. Definitely two bodies. One of them was – must have been – our spy. Fritz. The other . . . who was the other? I looked at Tom uncertainly. His plain, open face was suddenly animated; he was excited. What about my talk with Uncle Gilbert? I half stood up and Uncle Gilbert leaned forward and slapped my bottom.

'Jump to it, Rachel! I've got no one else who can ferret out information – all my reporters are in the army, I've got compositors who are sixty and over or . . . you two.' He aimed another slap but I skipped out of the way. To say I felt undignified conveys nothing at all.

'Uncle *Gil*bert,' I bleated.

'And if you're going to work here I'm known as the Gaffer.' He held me back and said quietly, 'Tom's a bit of an orphan. Be nice, OK?'

I nodded and followed Tom Fairbrother downstairs. Uncle Gilbert – the Gaffer – was a strange mixture. Thank God Mum had met Dad in time.

We consulted awkwardly as soon as we got outside and into the lane. He – Tom – actually offered to drop me off at the arcade where I could drink Camp coffee while he investigated on his own! I declined that, and said that we should go and see the survivors first of all. We got to the Guildhall and enquired about them. They were all at work and would be back in their temporary quarters after six that evening. It was then just gone eleven in the morning.

'What about the children?' Tom asked. 'It's still the school hols.' The way he said hols was pretty ghastly.

The woman in charge said, 'No children.'

'None at all?'

'Probably evacuated or something. Not really the sort of place for children, is it?'

Tom looked totally crestfallen. I said defensively, 'No. Not as it's right opposite the park where there are swings and a slide and a roundabout.'

Tom smiled gratefully, but the receptionist – or typist or whatever – leaned out of her cubby hole and waved us away. 'Enough of your cheek, madam! These people deserve a little privacy, if you don't mind!'

So we left and made for Spa Road.

The police cars had gone but there were big wire screens around the crater and barriers all along the terrace. And . . . people. Not many, but definitely some. I saw a glimpse of flowered material flipping through a broken doorway, and a second later an arm came out of what remained of a window and dropped a suitcase out to where the pavement had been. I looked wildly at Tom.

'Surely not scavengers?'

He pursed his mouth over those teeth. 'Don't know about that. Could be the owners collecting what they can of their belongings.' He shrugged. 'Just ordinary things like pyjamas and toothbrushes.'

I looked back at the houses and tried to imagine I had lived in one of them. They looked horribly unsafe, but if you actually lived there . . . Mum would not have let me go in but probably she and Dad and Mr Myercroft would have scrambled over the rubble and collected what they could. Books; especially books.

Tom murmured in my ear, 'There's a boy

down there, too, looking for shrapnel.' That was another thing. You couldn't stop ten- and eleven-year-old boys from collecting shrapnel.

I ducked under the barrier. 'We'd better go and have a look, then. Before they wreck everything.'

He looked at me over the red and white planking and gave that small tremulous smile. 'That was a very good example of irony.' He glanced up at the tottering buildings. 'In the circumstances.'

I laughed, and he looked at me with surprise – hadn't I laughed since I'd met him? – and laughed too. Then he joined me on the inside of the barrier and we started to clamber over the mounds of bricks and wood and glass and . . . an odd slipper and a broken chamber pot . . . it was awful. If it hadn't been that we wanted to get into the houses quickly, before anyone could start shouting at us, we would have just stood there looking; and I think perhaps I would have cried.

The boy was in the crater itself, where there were probably rich pickings to be had; maybe part of a fin from a bomb would still be identifiable. One of my London cousins was the proud possessor of a fin. The boy looked up and frowned disapprovingly.

'You shouldn't ought to be 'ere,' he said.

'We're looking for somebody,' Tom called back.

'They'm mostly billeted out now.' He jerked his head. 'Couple of sisters in there looking for their stuff.'

'We'll ask them,' Tom said equably, and began edging around the crater to the side of the house. There was a jagged hole in the wall; Meriel had been dragged out of that hole just yesterday morning. I wished now that I had asked the warden where he'd spotted that incriminating tie. Had he said it was by the staircase? Tom scrambled through the hole, turned, and leaned out to help me. He had very long legs, longer than mine, which was most unusual. I put my foot on a pile of bricks, grabbed his hand and pushed off. The bricks rolled, cascaded with me on top of them, and I ended up clutching him around the waist and doing a frantic quickstep across a dusty floor, where we ended up crashing into a sink. Tom took the brunt of all this impetus on his back.

I panted, 'Oh Lord. Are you all right?'

''Course. Another few inches and it wouldn't have been so good.'

I glanced sideways. The draining board attached to the sink had broken and a long skewer of wood pointed across the room like a spear. I shuddered.

Tom tried to laugh. 'You can see the reason behind the barriers, can't you?'

I moved away and began brushing myself down. I thought of that boy down in the crater;

supposing this house started to collapse on top of him?

Tom said, 'Let's find someone and ask questions. Isn't that what reporters are supposed to do?'

So we ploughed over to the door, which had been forced open about twelve inches – perhaps by Meriel – and squeezed through. We were in the hall; the front door, still intact, was on our left, on our right the stairs swept up in a curve. There was no wall on the other side of the hall: the ceiling was held up by scaffolding poles and planking. Dribbles of flaking plaster and dust came from above somewhere; I thought I felt the whole house move slightly as we crossed the hall to the staircase; I was terrified. There was rubble everywhere and to the left a jagged hole. 'A quick way to the basement,' Tom murmured in an obvious attempt to lessen the awfulness.

I said slowly, 'I think this is where they found it.'

'Found it?'

'The tie.'

'The *tie*?'

'Oh . . . I forgot. My friend was sure there was a man under the rubble. And the warden sent in a rescue squad because he found a tie. That was all. A tie.'

'A man . . . how did your friend know it was a man? And weren't there two bodies? Didn't the Gaffer say there were two of them?'

I looked at him helplessly; it was all so difficult.

'She just assumed . . . because of the tie. And yes, Uncle Gil . . . the Gaffer . . . did say there were two of them. But she didn't know that, of course. Because there was only one tie.'

It sounded absolutely feeble, and Tom actually drew breath to ask more of his blasted questions, when, at that exact moment, there came a cooee from somewhere, and some bricks fell, followed by a loud 'Damn!' Then there was a lot of scuffling and someone saying, 'For Christ's sake, watch it, our Doris!' Followed by steps on the stairs. The house definitely moved.

Tom stepped back to the staircase and held out a hand to someone in a flowered skirt lugging two pillow slips full of something or other. Behind her was someone else. And more pillow cases.

'Are you the owners of this house?' he asked very politely and carefully.

'Not this one, love. Two doors up. We got in through a window and it must've collapsed while we were getting our stuff together 'cos it's gone now. Thought we'd better get out while we could.' She jumped the last two steps, then screamed as the floor began to give way, grabbed at Tom, and stepped smartly away from the sagging floorboard.

Above her a voice squawked, 'I told you to be careful, our Doris!'

Doris said, 'My sister, Mavis. I'm Doris. You don't live here. The Austrian woman lived here.' Her voice sharpened. 'She's dead and gone. And someone else with her. And she had precious little in the way of worldly goods, if that's what you're after.' The sister, Mavis, came gingerly on to the hall floor, put down her pillow cases carefully and ranged herself next to the incautious Doris. They eyed us disapprovingly while my brain engaged again. This had not been home to Fritz. An Austrian woman had lived here. Fritz had been a visitor. An all-night visitor.

Tom flushed bright red. 'We were looking for them. That's all.'

'In the morgue, that's where they are.'

'Yes, well . . .'

I said, 'We're supposed to be getting stuff for the *Clarion*. Any kind of background stuff. We thought it might be . . . atmospheric or something, just to come and see where it happened.'

It sounded ridiculously feeble, but it partially satisfied Doris and Mavis. They nodded at one another. 'Newspapers!' Doris commented, rolling her eyes.

Mavis said, 'Let's get out of here. It's not safe, that's for sure.' She glanced under the stairs. 'That must have been where they sheltered.

They do say it's the safest place in most houses.' She frowned. 'What's all that rope, then?'

I'd noticed bits of rope everywhere. I pulled a couple of lengths from the rubble. We all stared uncomprehendingly.

Doris said, 'There's your story. Two of 'em were here – maybe her long-lost hubbie turned up. Maybe they felt there was no future any more.' The house lurched, and the floor dropped two or three inches. I screamed, Doris and Mavis screamed, Tom shouted. We all made for the kitchen and spent precious seconds getting the pillow cases through the narrow gap in the door. As we struggled out through the hole and into the blessed August sunshine, Doris panted, 'Suicide pact.'

Everyone looked at her. She jerked her head back. 'They din't know the bombs was coming, did they? They 'ung themselves from the stairs. Safest place, indeed!' She laughed. She was making a joke.

Neither of us commented on this; Tom was scrambling down to pull the shrapnel kid up to the street and I was struggling with four bulging pillow cases and a length of rope. But we both knew that was probably how it happened.

Six

We went to the milk bar, sat on the high stools and ordered raspberry milkshakes. The milk bar had stayed in business all through the war and there were usually queues a mile long for their drinks, but it was a dead time of the day – two thirty – and a Tuesday, so we got seats and our drinks.

By this time being with Tom was not unlike being with Meriel. Part of me was perfectly relaxed with him, I could talk nonsense and not be embarrassed; I was almost sure that later on I would be able to tell him that I might well have hounded that poor man to his death. But for now, as a reaction to that pathetic, disintegrating building and our possibly narrow escape from it, plus the somehow comic addition of Doris and Mavis and their bulging pillow cases, we needed relief, and Tom set the tone for it.

'Mr Carfax – sorry, the Gaffer – needs an angle.' He spoke nasally, like a reporter in an

American film. 'So how's about we stick with the Doris theory?'

'Which was?' I asked like an obedient side-kick.

'Suicide pact. Star-crossed lovers. Middle-aged Romeo and Juliet. He's married to someone who—'

'Doesn't understand him?' I spluttered.

'Exactly.'

'He's Austrian and he met his wife when she was on a Tyrolean holiday and . . . somehow . . . got married.' I pulled a face. 'That makes him a bit of an idiot.'

'Well, he might have been. But how about if she was dotty about him but he saw the marriage as a way of getting out of Austria and into England?'

'Brilliant. And she keeps him well under her thumb – very jealous woman.'

'I'll say. Congenitally jealous.'

I giggled and blew bubbles into my wonderful milkshake. He smiled. He liked to make me laugh, already I knew that. He went on, 'The war came. Life no fun in England. Wife ashamed of him because he is Austrian. And he meets—'

'The Other Woman,' I pronounced solemnly.

We shifted on our high stools and drank to the bottom of the tall glasses. As I placed mine on the counter I had one of those little moments when for an instant time stands still.

No, not really that. It is gathered into a droplet, like rain, like tears, and you are allowed to see it separately and to know that it is precious. So in my head I photographed everything: the milk bar, the high stools, the creamy pink residue of the milkshake in its tall glass, and Tom, sitting knee to knee with me. Such an ordinary, gangling sort of boy, waiting to go into the army or the air force, waiting to be torn out of this particular picture.

He put his glass next to mine and said in his ordinary voice, 'I heard the Gaffer tell you I'm a bit of an orphan. Please don't worry about it. My mother died when I was about three and I don't remember her at all.'

I gulped and nodded and just stopped myself from saying, 'That's all right, then.'

He smiled and stopped caring about hiding his teeth. He looked . . . lovely. 'It's great getting this assignment today. The Gaffer knows my dad – he's a cartoonist in civvie street. The Gaffer said he could use my help while I'm waiting to be called up. And to team up with you . . . he's showing us what fun it can be.' He paused and let his smile die. I thought he was going to come out with the next bit of our special report. But he said, very simply, 'Thank you, Rachel. I haven't had so much fun since my dad was reported missing.'

I heard myself make a little sound, a whistle-breath. But no words came. No mum and maybe no dad. 'A bit of an orphan—'

He said very quickly, 'Where do you think they met? Romeo. And Juliet.' It came out as a rhyme, as a Shakespearian couplet. We both laughed; it sounded slightly forced, but it was a proper laugh.

I said, 'Obvious. The overseas league place. It's in Park Avenue. She used to slip over to make the tea. Remember Mavis or Doris said she was Austrian.'

Tom nodded. 'He went there to get away from his wife.'

I clapped my hand across my mouth at a sudden, amazing thought. I knew I mustn't voice it. But I would have to tell Meriel. I would just have to.

He said, 'What's up?'

I took away my hand and swallowed deeply. 'It's OK. It's perhaps getting too real. My friend and I do this, you know. Make up stories about people. And then we begin to believe them ourselves.'

He hesitated, uncertain for a few seconds, then went on. 'We've got the rope – that will impress the Gaffer. Now, supposing we went to the morgue and asked someone whether they were dressed in their day clothes . . . just in case they were? It all happened in the early hours of Monday morning, right? If they were using the stair-well as a shelter, they would still be in their night clothes. But if they had used the stairs as a – a – gibbet? Then they would not have got ready for bed.' He looked at my face, and said quickly, 'Look, it's just another piece of information for the Gaffer. To show him we have done a proper job. That's all.'

I swallowed again; I was feeling a bit sick. The milkshake had been rich. I said, 'OK.'

We walked to the morgue near the docks, only to discover that the bodies had been taken to the infirmary. So we went there. The infirmary. Where yesterday Meriel and I had placed Mrs Smith so conveniently.

Nobody wanted to tell us anything: not where to go, nor who to speak to. Tom was like a bloodhound: leading us from ward to ward, down steps, up steps, through swing doors, accosting anyone wearing a stethoscope or uniform. Nobody could tell us a thing – good job we didn't have a body slung between us. We were directed eventually to the general enquiry office, where a woman with white hair, who was on the telephone and writing notes at the same time, stabbed her pencil in the direction of the outer door. We moved uncertainly towards it, not knowing whether we were meant to clear off or what; she nodded and jabbed her pencil up in a sort of congratulatory way, then went back to writing.

I thought that was that, but Tom was still being a bloodhound, and once out in the grounds again, he stood back and looked hard and found another door, and, sure enough, steps going up.

'That's what she meant. Out and up.' He was thrilled to bits. I trailed behind him, stone steps again, more like a prison than a hospital. At the top there were two doors, both masked by sheets that stank of disinfectant. He smiled. 'We're there.'

He lifted one of the sheets and rapped hard on the door. We waited ages. He shrugged and went to the other door, lifted that sheet, and banged with the side of his fist. The door opened. A man stood there clothed from head to foot in green material. Just his eyes showed above a mask. The eyes looked at us and became incredulous.

'What the hell are you kids doing here? For God's sake – you shouldn't be touching these sheets! Don't you know anything? Clear off before you infect us and yourselves.' He began to close the door, muttering something about the behaviour of kids these days.

Tom said, 'We're actually from the *Clarion*. Just a very quick word. The bodies brought in from the raid on Spa Road on Monday morning . . . were they clothed?'

The pathologist stopped closing the door and stared again; I thought his eyes would pop out if there was much more to shock him.

'You want to know whether the bomb blast stripped them naked?' He was absolutely incredulous. 'What the hell is Gilbert Carfax doing, sending kids like you on a job like that?'

'Excuse me, sir.' Tom was suddenly very serious and grown-up. 'It's nothing like that. We're following up a certain lead, and knowing about the clothing on the bodies would help us. We *need* to know whether they were wearing day or night clothes. That's all.'

The pathologist looked totally perplexed. He said, 'Oh.' And then his stare became less and less outraged as he thought about it. Then he said, 'They were both wearing day clothes. Is that sufficient information for your *needs*?'

We weren't entirely forgiven, and if he knew Gilbert Carfax we guessed that he would report back to him – with some annoyance.

'Thank you, sir.'

Tom added no more, no apology, nothing. He turned and indicated to me that we were going back down the steps. I half smiled and nodded at those eyes, and we left.

I felt terrible. Tom said, 'Let's just cut across the park again and go into lower Eastgate.'

'Why? We should be getting back. The Gaffer will wonder where we are.'

'It cuts off a big corner – easier to walk and talk going over the grass – and . . .' He looked at me sidelong. 'Did you know that Silverman, that tailor in the Barton, had his shop window broken on Saturday night?' I nodded. 'Well, it's another connection,' he went on eagerly. 'Silverman is also Austrian. An Austrian Jew. He came over after the Great War, back in 1918. He's been a kind of clearing house for refugees ever since. I've been looking at the old files. I reckon he's been helping Jews to escape from Germany since Hitler came to power.' He had hold of my elbow and was turning me into Spa Road once again; I hung back.

He said, 'Come on, Rachel, don't give up so easily. We know now where they did the dirty deed – we know they were fully dressed, so it was planned and nothing to do with the air raid. We've got some of the rope they used—'

'We made it all up, Tom! We made it *up*!'

'But it all fits. Rachel, we're not going to be writing this up for the paper. We're researchers and we've got some results. Let's see what Silverman has to say about it. Let's at least try, for goodness' sake!'

'I can't be long. I have to see my friend . . .' But I let myself be pulled into the park, and through the gates where Meriel had been so sick, over the railway lines set in the road and through the subway where we'd gone last Friday on our bikes . . . turn left and then right . . . we were almost running . . . and there it was across the road, identifiable because of the boarding across the broken window.

We were panting like greyhounds. Tom

gasped, 'Leave the talking to me,' and plunged us both between a couple of wagons loaded with potatoes. I actually felt the breath of one of the cart horses on my neck, and glimpsed his enormous hoof, modestly covered in a veil of horsehair, right next to my sandal. I tried to ask Tom what the hurry was all about, but it needed breath. And he wouldn't have heard, anyway.

As we did a long leap on to the opposite pavement, Tom caught his toe in the kerb; and though I managed to hold him up, we went crashing into the boarding on Silverman's window. I threw up my spare arm to protect my head, but Tom was still almost falling and hit the boarding face-on. The next thing I knew there was blood pumping out of his nose, and down his nice white shirt, and on to my dirndl, and just about everywhere. And two women detached themselves from the other shocked passers-by and came at us clucking, and telling us off, and whipping Tom's shirt tails out of his trousers and up to his face. Phrases like '. . . watch where you put your feet . . .' and '. . . no decorum, that's the word, it's all gone since the war . . . all gone . . .' buzzed around our heads like bees, and Tom was apologizing and lifting his head back, and then choking on his own blood and leaning forward again.

It stopped eventually. I always kept one of Dad's big hankies in a pocket of my dirndl, and he held that to his nose and spoke through it. 'Happens even when I don't hit it,' he explained to the women, who allowed themselves to be reassured because the crossing gates were opening. 'Honestly, I'm quite all right. You'd better cross the railway while you can.'

'Brunner's have got cakes in today,' one of the women reminded the other. 'The queue will be a mile long . . .' Thankfully they left us with adjurations about cold compresses ringing in our ears. Tom tried to smile.

'What with Mavis and Doris and now those two . . .' he said, in his new, stifled voice.

'Now can we go home?'

'We haven't seen Mr Silverman. And we're here.'

'And we can't get in. While you were bleeding to death I cast an eye around. The door to the shop is also boarded up. There's no way in.'

I wanted to get back to St John's Lane, pick up my bike and pedal like mad till I got home. Never mind telling Meriel all that had happened, never mind Hermione and Mrs Smith. I wanted the comfort of home, the waiting for Mum. I wanted to lay the table outside like we'd done yesterday and the day before, string the beans I'd picked only that morning . . .

I said, 'Come on. Let's get back to the office. You can take in your notes and the rope. Uncle – the Gaffer – will be really pleased. I have to get back home. Seriously. They will be expecting me.'

'You said you were going to your friend's first.'

'That was when I had the time to do that,' I came back bitterly.

He was leaning against the planking that covered the shop front, his head well back, wiping his nose and face with Dad's blood-soaked handkerchief. He handed it back to me and, still standing to attention, began to tuck his blood-soaked shirt tails into his trousers. I found a clean corner of cloth and dabbed at a drip on his chin. It was what Mum would have done for me. It would have given me comfort as well as a sense of cleanliness. I didn't realize that it gave her something too. A feeling of unbearable tenderness. I stopped doing it.

He said, 'Thank you, Rachel.' He tried a smile but it was a tremulous one. 'We're not going to forget today, are we?'

'No.' I crooked an arm. 'Need help?'

'Not really.' But he took my arm anyway, and we started to walk back to the level crossing. Very, very slowly.

'What was all that rush about, for Pete's sake? You could have broken your neck – we could have been trampled by that cart horse. I don't get it.'

He sighed right next to my ear; we were the

same height and I was used to Meriel being well below me. This was really easy.

'Nor me, not now, anyway. I felt as if we were catching a train. It was strange. Sorry, Rachel. God, I'm so glad it was me who took a toss. If anything had happened to you . . . don't let me do that again.'

'I don't think I could have even slowed you down.' I laughed and then stopped. Because we had come to a halt just next to the beginning of a dark tunnel of a passage leading to the backs of the houses and shops. I said, 'Oh no! Tom, come on, please. We've both had enough of this.'

Obviously he hadn't. He released my arm, which more or less set me free to stay or go. He did not say a word; he just disappeared into the darkness. And I followed him. I whined loudly about this being a complete waste of time, as it was clear that Mr Silverman could not live in the shop. But he kept going and I followed him. It was my choice. No one to blame.

The tunnel must have served other houses – it went straight on as far as you could see, but Tom turned right at the first opportunity and began to jump up and down as he walked so that he could see over the high wall and into the back yards of the buildings. We came to a door fitted into the wall and blocked with a dustbin. Tom lifted the lid of the bin and it was full of shards of glass. He moved the bin out of the gateway and tried the latch; the door was bolted. Before I could draw sufficient breath to sigh with relief, he put his shoulder to it. The door bent away from the bolt very easily. Ignoring my protests, he shoved again, then again. The bolt tore away from its screws and the door swung open.

The back yard was full of piles of rubble neatly stacked against the side wall. To the left was the outside lavatory and wash house, and straight ahead were steps going up to the shop level and another set going down to a basement. Tom made for those. I followed him, but by this time I was whimpering. I hardly knew Tom, but I thought he wasn't the sort of boy to break into someone's house, especially when the house had already been stupidly vandalized. He was going to get into trouble. I didn't want that. So I stayed with him.

The door at the bottom of the steps had been mostly glass; it was all broken and we crunched on glass shards very gingerly in our summer sandals. This door was bolted, too, but Tom just stuck his hand carefully between the pieces of jagged glass and unbolted it.

He still had difficulty in opening it over more glass. The sound of it grinding and snapping was beastly, literally beastly. And then we were through into yet another dark passage; the kitchen was on our left, it had that damp sink smell that was only a few sniffs away from being downright toxic. The next door was half-closed but it was dimly lit from another window so had to be right underneath the shop front. On our right a staircase led up to that level.

Once past the glass, Tom absolutely barged along the passage to that half-closed door. He shoved it wide, and then stopped and completely blocked my way through. He, too, started to whimper, which shut me up completely; he hadn't whimpered when he'd smashed his face against that planking. I was a yard away from him. I stooped low and looked under his spread arms.

Mr Silverman was hanging by his neck from a rope fastened into a hook on the ceiling. Below him was a chair, upside down.

Tom said sobbingly, 'I had a horrible feeling this had happened . . .'

I started to scream.

Seven

October 1945

Rache, I'm here! The boat docked an hour ago and I'm waiting in the cabin for the queue to disappear. I absolutely refuse to be one of those desperate women waving frantically from the rail whether they can see their hubbie or not. Oh Lord, just listen to that! Hubbie, indeed! It's being with this lot for a whole week. Do you know, Rache, I nearly turned back at the last minute – when I was actually on the gang plank and I looked back and realized Dad was actually crying! There were sailors helping us along, and I said to one of them was it too late to turn back? And he said, ''Course not, madam' – I'm madam now, please note – 'But your trunks can't be unloaded, not now. All your worldly goods are going to end up in New York whether you're there or not!' And as I went on walking up that plank

I realized it wasn't that I wanted to go back, especially to Dad; what was putting me right off His Majesty's good ship *Albion* were the other passengers. Most of them are ghastly, and the ones that aren't are going right up to Detroit or California or somewhere I can't get to. But I miss you already, and it's not as if we've lived in each other's pockets lately, what with me nobbling Rex and you getting your legs under the table at the Carfax *Clarion*. I know I've said this so often you must be sick of it, but I'm going to miss you, Rache, I really am. Anyway.

I hope Rex's parents, especially his 'mom', turn out to be mildly approachable, and not already cooking up a hatred of the English trollop who got herself pregnant by their son so she could shake the dust of Britain off her dinky little feet! I wonder whether Dad Robinson might have a bit of a bias too, as he teaches American Lit. Does that mean he hates Eng. Lit? But it does mean he's busy at school or in his study (Rex's words) so won't be seeing much of me. Whatever happens, Rache, at least I'll be away from this ex-troop ship with its six-berth cabins and no choice about who shares.

I'd better go. One of the bearable girls is called Rachel and she says she just loves my bubble cut. I told her you'd done it. Rache . . . I'm scared.

5 November 1945, Orion, New Hampshire

Darling, guess what? They don't have Guy Fawkes Night here, they don't even know who he is! It's such a waste because there are enough fallen leaves in our garden to make ten guys. Yes, I did say *our* garden! I naturally thought we'd have to live with Mom and Dad Robinson and it would be all awkward and they'd hate me, but shucks, that ain't the case, little lady! We're renting a gorgeous house; it's made of wood and smells of pine and resin, a bit like the bluebell woods at home. It's got a big living area – not even called a room because all the other rooms lead off it. I'm talking like them even when I don't do it purposely. Can you imagine what Miss Hardwicke would say about my grammar there? Anyway, we're renting it because Rex has put in for a job with the Space Agency. Sounds good, eh? We'd probably live in Florida. Not sure yet. Meanwhile I love it here, and Mom and Dad Robinson are great. They love me because I'm full of Rex's baby – yes, they actually speak those words! In some ways Americans are really prim and proper but in others – wow, hang on to your hat, lady! Got to go. I'm doing fried chicken and potatoes. Doesn't it sound American and grown-up and everything? Has Tom heard about his demob yet? I want to ask you what he's like in bed, but I bet you don't know yet! I discover I take after my father because I'm OK in that department. Very OK, actually. Actually, I often think I can understand poor old Dad so much better now. Wish I hadn't been so hard on him.

Honey, I know my handwriting is still pretty grim but use your imagination, won't you. And another thing, I'm going to post these two bits off just in case the airmail plane gets to crash or something – I'll never remember what I said. And one last thing, keep my scribbles, will you? When we're old ladies we'll read them together and laugh. I've got yours in a satin nightdress case Aunt Mabe gave me when I arrived. She is Mom Robinson's sister and is an absolute hoot. And another last thing, but important, stop worrying about Tom. The bloody, bloody war is over!

March 1946, Florida

Did you get my Feb letter when I was on my way to hospital with pains every five bloody minutes? Somebody posted it for me, because it was gone from my night table when I got home three hours later. False alarm, Rache. Felt such a fool. And here I am a month later, looking so much like a football I'm expecting someone to kick me at any minute. Considering the wicked deed was done on VE night, as you well know, don't you think Babe Ruth could put in an appearance like NOW! Honestly, Rache, I am so fed-up, can't tell you and won't even try, else I'll put you off glorious motherhood for ever. But I've warned Rex that if it is a girl she will definitely be called Ruth. He thinks I'm joking.

Anyway, honey, my silence since then has not been fed-upness but because we've actually moved, as you will see from the address. What a month it's been, Rache. We had so much stuff. Only been here six months but people keep giving us presents, the Yanks really are the most generous people in the world and I have to say, Rache – this sounds pretty awful, I know – they think I'm the bees-bloody-knees! Honestly. When I get spellings wrong they laugh and hug me, when I swear they absolutely curl up, then hug me – I've even tried picking my nose at a dinner party and they loved that too. Put me right off, I haven't done it again. Shame, really. But actually, Rex didn't like it. Funny, eh? I wish he didn't think I was so perfect, but he does, and I try to be because he's such a wonderful man. I know I married him for all the wrong reasons, Rache, but it's turning out OK. Honestly.

Anyway, the move. It's a long way from New England to Florida, and it was going to take a week for our stuff to get there and be unpacked, and Mom Robinson was not going to have me or her grandchild overdoing it, so we stayed with her and had breakfast in bed and a rest every afternoon. It was heaven. I get scared at times when I realize she's such a long way off, but Rex says she'd take us over if we stayed there much longer, and we're a family in our own right.

Dad Robinson came with me on the train. We had to change at New York and we decided to take a later connection, and took a taxi and drove around for two hours just looking. Fantastic. The buildings. Empire State and Chrysler and Radio City and Times Square and the Cloisters. And the little streets too, old-fashioned with small shops like in the Barton when we followed that German spy into White City. Then we went back to Grand Central and picked up the Amtrak, and before that Dad Robinson found a phone and rang home to Mom and talked to her, and then I talked to her. Grand Central is like a cathedral, bigger than ours but no whispering gallery. And I thought of Mom, folding the laundry and taking one of her fruit cakes out of the oven.

It was so strange, Rache. Underneath everything there's still this layer of homesickness for England, and now there's another layer. I'm homesick for Orion, and the wooden houses set among the trees, and the beautiful school where Dad Robinson teaches American Literature. He could have taken a job as college lecturer – almost double his present salary – at Concord which is the capital of the state of New Hampshire, but he chose to stay in Orion. I think that's pretty marvellous. To know what is important. I wish Rex was more like that.

Rache, I have to go. Maybe someone will post this for me, too! Yes, something is stirring in the woodshed. Fingers crossed. It's lovely here, but not much in the way of trees and it reminds me a bit of the Fens in a heatwave. Did you ever go there?

May 1947, Florida

Darling Rache, your last letter made me cry. Will you do me a favour, honey? Throw away – burn, destroy – all the letters you've had from me since Vicky was born. This is a serious request, Rache. I think I'm OK now. We had a little hurricane here a week ago, and believe it or not I think it took the last of my blues with it. Also I have a new friend, not a bit like you but English! She's a GI bride too, and she comes from Devon and has still got a lovely Devon accent. Her mother is one of those who always knows someone who has had the same illness as you've got. Apparently Dawn – that's her name – told her mum about me and Mum knows someone who committed suicide after the birth of her baby – cheery stuff, eh? Some women go seriously mad, too. But then they get better. And I'm getting better. I feel better just knowing that other women get this after giving birth.

Oh Rache, I'm longing to feel well again and be able to look after Vicky properly. And enjoy having sex again, too; I think Rex must be thoroughly fed-up with me and my headaches! I heard Mom say to him the other day, 'Would you be so cold with our little Meriel if you knew she had cancer?'

And Rex said, 'She hasn't got cancer, Mom.'

And Mom said, 'She's ill, Rex. She's really ill. Coming to a strange country, having such a difficult birth. Can't you see that?'

'This mollycoddling isn't doing any good.' Rex said. 'Can't *you* see that? She's taking advantage of your good nature, coming all this way to look after her—'

Mom got real mad then, and almost shouted at him. 'It's an honour to be asked to step into her shoes, Rex! She trusts me with her daughter and with you. I knew she was going downhill, and I thought she would turn her back on all of us. When she phoned and asked me if I could spare a couple of weeks . . . Oh Rex, I didn't realize you were so blind!'

I wanted to run out to them and confess to Mom how awful I'd been to Rex, always tired, always headachey. I told him one night if sex was so important to him why didn't he find a bit on the side, like my dad had done. But she has already stopped seeing me as cute and funny, and I certainly don't want her to know just how horrible I am. I've let Rex see that; I can't let Mom see it too. When I told her how much better I felt, especially since the hurricane, she called me her brave girl.

'Let me stay out this week, honey. Just to put you straight for a few days.' She's made about a million apple pies and put them in the ice box; there are cakes piled up in tins in the kitchen, and jars of jam and pickles in a long line on the shelf. Dawn tells me not to use them, just let them stay there to impress the other young mothers in our complex. She's not joking. Because all the husbands work at the agency, the complex is more of a village and is practically incestuous. Everyone is so competitive. I've been bottom of the pile since we arrived, really. Could be Mom's pickles and jams – jellies, they're called – might make a difference. See? I'm already getting into the swing of things.

I don't really care about all that. But I would like to take Vicky to the toddlers' swimming club. The pool in the complex is beautiful. I love to look out of the window and watch the maintenance man raking the leaves off the surface and cleaning up the tables and chairs. It's like being on holiday. How can you be on holiday all the time, though?

August 1947

Darling, I had to leave you then because Vicky came into the living room holding her grandma's hand and then Grandma let go and she came walking over all by herself, and laughing fit to burst. Rache, she is so beautiful, I can't tell you, otherwise I start to cry. But she is.

Anyway, I was going to go on writing to you, and then it was time for Mom to go so Dad could meet her in New York, which was great, and then I sort of had to get used to . . . everything. Babies are so full-time, Rache. I know you don't even want to get married till you're twenty-one, and then you want to wait a couple of years. But I have to tell you now, while I really know it, that babies are such hard work it's incredible. That's my excuse for leaving this letter for over two whole months! Also I wanted to be able to tell you that I am coping and everything is hunky-dory again, Rex and I are more in love than ever and I've got some marvellous news – I'm pregnant again! I know you're going to say I should have waited a bit longer, but this time it's different, honey. I'm strong and I know what I've got to face, and anyway my doctor is a poppet and is going into the whole thing – it's got a name but I can't remember what it is. He's let me have some pills that will make sure I don't get like it again. You can get pills for everything over here, Rache. It's just great. Vicky will be two by the time Junior arrives so she shouldn't need diapers any more. Rex says he's not so sure about having a big family now, and maybe if Junior turns out to be a boy we can 'get by'! Aunt Mabe has said she will come out and help, but Rex says we don't need any help and we're doing fine. Which we are.

Time for a pill, honey. Honestly, I feel on top of the world. When you decide to have a baby you must get some of these pills. They are really marvellous, Rache. If only I'd had Gus when I was expecting Vicky. Gus is this new young doctor, Rache. It's all first names here and anyway with a name like Augustus

Michaelson it's a good job, huh? Rache, here she comes. Vicky. She's had a nap and Dawn just came by and lifted her out of her cot and she's tottering across the room towards the bureau. I guess she knows her Aunt Rachel's letter is sitting here. More later.

Rache, it's midnight and Rex has at last fallen asleep. Dreadful news. Dad Robinson rang him in the office. Mom has been diagnosed with cancer. It's in two places, her pancreas and colon. They can operate on one and not the other. I don't understand it. Tomorrow I'm going to see Gus and ask him about it. I want to be with her, Rache, like she was with me after Vicky. It's amazing that I haven't been over here for two years yet, but I love her. I was always sorry for my own mum and I thought that was loving her, but it wasn't. Not properly. I should have known that, because I used to envy you your mum. And now, I've just discovered that I love my mother-in-law and it looks like she's going to die. Oh, Rache, life is so peculiar. Vicky's crying, and it's so hot I can't even cuddle her. I'll write more tomorrow after I've talked to Gus.

A quick postscript. Talked to Gus. More concerned about me not sleeping – given me some pills for nights. Says he's not really up on cancer unless it's in the uterus, in which case it's hysterectomy time. Suggests I get up there to see her as soon as poss. I'm only four months with Junior, so am over sickness and feel absolutely great – told you all that. So Vicky and I going to Orion tomorrow. I talked to Dad on the phone, and though he's far more reserved than Mom he said, 'I wanted to ask you to come, Meriel. Thank you. She will be so pleased.' I expected him to let me talk to her but he said, 'Here's your Aunt Mabe, she's been trying to grab the phone off me ever since it rang!'

Aunt Mabe said she's moved in to take care of things and it would be lovely for her to take care of Vicky. I said all chokingly, 'He called you *my* Aunt Mabe.'

And she said, 'I hope you didn't mind. You are my only hope of a niece.'

I got control of myself and told her I didn't mind. I thought I had aunts back home, but I'd never met them and it would be lovely to have a real live one. And then I lost control again because I'd said real and then live. And Mom Robinson would always be real, but it was beginning to sound as though she might not be alive much longer.

Anyway, kiddo, that's it. Gloomy. And as Rex said we have got to be optimistic, and there's no reason to be anything else. If the train is not too rackety I'll write during the journey. Vicky will sleep a lot, I hope!

August 1947, Orion

Last day of August, Rache. It's going to be an early autumn. Wish you could see the trees, honey. They are so beautiful it makes you cry. Why can't human beings look so beautiful at the end, why has all our colour got to be leached out of us like it is? It's not fair . . . I need Rex here to tell me that 'life just ain't fair, baby'. And it sure ain't.

Vicky and I have been here two weeks now, and it seems like we've never been anywhere else; Florida is an arid dream. OK, it's got the Everglades and alligators and beautiful beaches, but it doesn't suit me. It suits Vicky, though; anywhere suits Vicky. She's so happy, Rache. She adores her grandma and grandad and she is the light of their lives. Grandad nurses her for half an hour before her bed time and they go through picture books together with him teaching her a different word each evening. She never forgets them either. She turns to the right page and points and says, 'Sea!' 'Sun!' 'Stars!' Then 'Bird!' 'Boy!' 'Bucket', and Mom watches from the bed with a smile on her dear grey face and nods sagely when I pick Vicky up for bed. 'Well done, Jack. What an excellent teacher you are.' And believe it or not, Jack blushes! What's he going to do afterwards,

Rache? What's he going to do without his Ellie?

She doesn't want to talk much in the evenings. The night-time dose of morphine hasn't kicked in by then, and she is struggling with the pain. That's my time with her. Aunt Mabe and Dad try to talk to her, take her mind off it. She asked if I could stay with her because I didn't mind not talking, and I didn't get upset when she 'moaned and groaned'. She doesn't moan or groan, but when she tenses and makes little grunts, I know then that it is bad. And actually I do get upset. It's just that I don't let it show.

Only last night she suddenly sighed and said, 'It's all right now, my dear. I'll be asleep in ten minutes if you want to go and check on Vicky.'

I got up and went close to the bed and put my hand over hers; the veins on the backs of her hands are like ropes, literally. I said, 'Mom, you should have a medal.'

And she smiled with her eyes closed and said, 'Oh, I think we all get one, darling. That's the deal, as I understand it.' I put my cheek to hers and she turned her hand and held mine.

I whispered right in her ear, 'I wish I could be like you.'

And she whispered right back, 'You are. We're so alike . . . so alike . . .' and she was asleep. I stood by the window for ages, looking out. It was still light and the trees seemed to wrap around us, secure, safe. There's still hope, Rache. While there's life, there's hope.

September 1947, Orion

I meant to write a little bit each day, like a diary. I've got more time than I've ever had for sitting and thinking and writing it all down. But August has gone, and Dad has gone back to school, and there's less time, but here I am, anyway. Did I tell you that Vicky calls Dad 'Pop'? Just like a real little American, which she is, of course. I think at first it was just 'Puh' – just a noise she made when she looked at him. But he was delighted and told everyone she called him Pop, and now she does! The bed time thing in Mom's room is quite something with the two of them, and he rocks her gently as time goes on, and she likes to go to sleep right there on his lap so he can carry her to her cot. Mom says she wants to make this time really good and special and that's how it is. Not just Vicky and Pop, but Aunt Mabe and me, too. Until Pop went back to school we took Vicky for a walk after lunch, and we saw such things, Rache! A nest of mice getting ready to hibernate, and winter aconites, and a snowy owl who shouldn't have been out and about at all, but was. We told Mom about it and Vicky nodded and clapped her hands and I made proper English tea . . . I can't tell you how lovely it is, Rache. So peaceful. The baby is moving very gently, too. Rex rings most nights, and he reckons we've got a real Babe Ruth now, and he's practising right in my tummy! Rex has got time off work later this month and he's coming over. She's hanging on for that. Mom, I mean.

Rex says if you're getting married next year, maybe we can come. Depending on Babe Ruth, of course. Then I can sort out this business of Mrs Rabbit. Of course she's not following you, Rache! You've seen her twice, for God's sake. You both live in the same city so that's not surprising. Forget it, honey. Just forget the whole business.

October 1947, Orion

Darling, she has gone. Eleanora Robinson. Apparently when she met Jack he said her name was a tongue twister and he would call her Ellie. And he did. Last night Ellie went to sleep as usual and just stopped breathing about two o'clock in the morning. Rex was with her and did not even notice until that time. He knew she was still with us at midnight, but then couldn't be certain when she left. I came near to seeing a dead body before, didn't I, Rache? When we were kids . . . only three years ago. I can't believe that. Three years have made such a difference to me. Anyway, I missed it, then, thank goodness. But I wouldn't want to have missed this one. Because I know Mom isn't there. And that's important, Rache. Remember that. You need to know that the body has so little to do with the person. Ergo . . . as Miss Hardwicke would say . . . there's got to be another place for that person to be. And that must mean there's a good chance we will actually all meet up again. I bet you're choking with surprise at Meriel Robinson writing these words! But she is, and she means them. Mom, the person not the body, is still around.

Thank you for all the letters I've had from you during this time, Rache. It's been a very precious and wonderful time for me, and your letters have made it even specialer. Two arrived in one day and Mom was as pleased as I was, and told me I'd always be all right with a friend like you. I knew that, but not properly, somehow. I know how you feel towards Tom. Sort of protective. At least Tom allows you to protect him, to care for him. Rex seems to think that if he lets me in it will be a sign of weakness. Pop is the same. But Pop gets such comfort from Vicky, they've got a real bond, it's absolutely lovely. The other day she got fed-up with being told that Grandma was in heaven, and she cried – it was frustration – almost anger – because grief means nothing to her, really. And Pop held her to him, thinking she was grieving, and he wept into her hair. I was watching from the kitchen, ready to go and get her if she upset him. Then I saw that it was right for him to be upset. I do so wish Rex could get upset. He was a pall bearer at the funeral, and as the coffin went past me I swear I could hear his teeth grinding together. He's like Vicky, he's angry. That's how he is in bed. Angry. Is it with me – could it possibly be with me, Rache?

I wrote that last night. I heard him say goodnight to Pop, and I shoved everything under the bed and put out the light and turned on my side. But he didn't even ask if I was awake. He just pulled me over and made love to me, except there wasn't much love about it. There are much worse things than crying, Rache. Let Tom get it out of his system any way he can, but get it out. It was so cruel to be told that his father was in that Singapore hospital and then to find it was not his dad at all. And there must be many others who will never know what happened to their relatives in the war, too. It is dreadful, Rache.

Later

Rex is driving Aunt Mabe to her house. She is going to sell it, and is meeting a prospective buyer. She has made up her mind to come and look after Pop. He was talking of leaving the school house and taking a room in the local hotel, and Rex suggested she should move down to Orion and they could keep on the school house, which is so handy for his work, and such a lovely place with so many happy memories. Mabe was born in Orion and still has heaps of friends here. Neither of them knew what to say, but they must have talked it over quite a bit, because Aunt Mabe brought it up at the supper table last night, and there were all sorts of 'clauses', as she put it. One was that if either of them met someone else or got fed up with the situation, the arrangement would be terminated instantly.

Pop said, 'I want it known that I will not be meeting anyone else. That clause was inserted for Mabe's sake.'

Mabe is younger than Mom by quite a bit, but she is the size of a house. She tightened her lips a bit at that announcement. I burst out laughing. I couldn't help it, and Aunt Mabe knew it wasn't meant to be hurtful. Rex and Pop looked at me all askance, as you used to say, and then Aunt Mabe joined me, and it was like one of those hysterical laughs that we used to have at school: we just couldn't stop, and we both got a stitch and gasped for mercy, and then caught each other's eye and started all over again. Grief can do funny things.

So Rex and Mabe aren't here and Pop's at school and Vicky is asleep in front of the nursery guard and the baby gave me a kick like a horse. It's something you want to share, Rache. I wanted Rex to know. I mean, it just has to be a boy with a kick like that. One of the neighbors came by with a batch of drop scones and I told her, and that helped. She's had a big family, four maybe five, I'm not sure because they're all at college. She understood, and sat for ages with her hand on my abdomen, but of course nothing else happened. Except we ate almost all the scones!

Later still

It's OK, darling. Rex has felt Junior doing his stuff! We had supper, and talked properly about what Aunt Mabe wanted to bring across from her place, and how she would put the house money separately, so that if it didn't work out she could get her own place again. It was good. Everyone talking and thinking about something besides Mom. I waited till we got upstairs, and then told him what happened when Nora-Marie came by that afternoon. We stood side by side looking down at Vicky in her cot and Rex made no comment at all. And then Junior started fluttering gently, and I took Rex's hand and put it squarely on my stomach, then pressed it down. Junior went on fluttering. I whispered, 'He's taking a free kick – do they have those in American football? Now, he's coming for it. Oh my God!' It was another mighty one, Rache. Just the thing Rex needed. He looked at me, startled, wide-eyed. I grinned right up at him because it was so good to see an expression on his face again. And then he kissed me. Oh Rache, it was some kiss. Nothing like the rigid antics we've been going through night after night. Can't tell you more. It was heaven.

I'm writing this on my lap in Mom's room. She would like that. Will post it off tomorrow, honey. I send you tons, literally tons, of American love. I am happier and more fulfilled than I have ever been, Rache.

Eight

January 1948, Florida

Dearest Rache and Tom, Thank you for the lovely, wonderful pictures of your wedding. Rex never met you, Tom, but he says he would have known you because Rache described you so well. I'm glad your old school friends came down from Birmingham to 'stand by you' as you put it; I notice the Carfaxes were your guests, too, which was kind of nice. Maxine's outfit was over the top – that remark is for Rache, of course. One fox fur would have done, surely? I mean two of those mean little narrow heads peering from her bosom and then the full-length coat underneath them! A forest of fur. My Dad always fancied Maxine, but she's loyal, I'll say that for her. She and Gilbert – what a pair! I noticed Hermione and her mother in their serge coats and fur hats, but who was the chap next to them – surely not Mr

Smith? I thought she made him up. He's got a proper wingco handlebar moustache too. In fact he looks quite a lot like Jimmy Edwards.

See, Rache – I haven't changed. I'll never like the Smiths. But oh, those Throstles. George and Flora. The perfect couple. Beautiful and elegant and lovely in all their ways. I really haven't changed, I always wanted them for my parents, and you shared them very generously, Rache. Thank you.

I'd have loved to have been there, of course, but I was absolutely with you in my thoughts. May you live long and happy lives and cast your light around you like George and Flora do, so that people can come near and see properly and even warm their hands at your glow. I'm getting to be a bloody poet, Rache! More later. Ever your bestest friend, Meriel Robinson. Must tell you that some couples over here use both their names. So mine would be Meriel Nightingale Robinson. Good, eh?

Still January, Florida

Darling, thank you for the extra pic but I really can't remember what that little rabbit of a woman looked like and she is very blurred in the snap – and anyway, what does it matter? People often pass by churches when there's a wedding going on, and if the happy couple come out just as they are passing then they stop and gawp at the dress and the veil and the confetti . . . it's just a natural thing to do. I think you're all uptight after the hard work of getting married. Guess I was lucky to have a week's cruise on my own after mine! Never thought of it like that before!

Seriously, Rache, stop worrying about the woman from White City – gosh, that sounds a good title for a book! What with writing poetry and thinking up book titles maybe I should have a go at writing some of my experiences down. Perhaps you should do the same, honey. That weekend in the summer holidays was only important because nothing much else ever happened to us . . . we were always battling boredom. Surely you remember? Write it down day by day, and leave it for a bit, then read it. The four bombs and the three deaths were awful. But they would have happened anyway, Rache. Our part in the whole thing was meaningless.

What does surprise me is the way it was all hushed up. You would have thought Maxine and her teddy bear would have splashed it all over the *Clarion* but those bodies always stayed 'unidentified'. Wonder if your dad had anything to do with it? You were pretty rotten for a few weeks, weren't you? He was probably worried about you. And he always worries about your mum. Funny how she got through the war and that job at the Ministry of Defence records office and since then has become so frail. I'm real sorry about that, Rache. Give her my best love. And you two just take care. Please. I get anxious about you, because somehow from this distance you both seem so fragile. Stop grinning, Rache! I know you're nearly six foot tall and so is Tom. But you're both so thin and sort of *bendy*.

Everything is all right with me and Junior. He's not given any more of those mighty kicks like the one he gave when we were in Orion, so maybe Rex can forget the football team. Gus is keeping me supplied with pills and they suit me really well, so I've got no problems. But unless Rex is really keen, I'd prefer not to make childbirth a hobby. I do so enjoy Vicky's company and I'm rather anxious that the new baby will change that. It's bound to, isn't it? Relationships are so strange, Rache, aren't they? Ours is simple and direct, I like that.

I posted your last letter yesterday! But have to write today because I've had a letter from home, and maybe you don't know about it. It's from Dad. He and Mum are getting divorced and he is marrying the dressmaker woman. That's not the surprise. The surprise – shock – devastation – is that she, the dressmaker woman, is my real mother. Dear Mum, who loved Dad so much, was engaged to him, and he needed her family money. So when the dressmaker, I'll just call her DM, got pregnant with me – mighty careless, wouldn't you say? – he said he'd take the kid but not her. And she agreed! She actually bloody well agreed! And poor old Mum agreed, too, frightened she'd lose her Errol Flynn, I guess. And now that the twins are off to naval college, he's ditching her and going for DM. I can't believe it. I know what I said in my last letter about relationships being strange, but honestly, Rache, this is just crazy. And horrible. Poor Mum. And that cow creeping around in the background all the time . . . d'you remember that ghastly dress she made me from curtain material? Well, apparently she's a bit of a designer as well as a DM, and she's used the New Look idea and stocked Nightingale's with jersey wool dresses that are selling like hot cakes!

I just can't believe it! When I suggested opening a ladies' department, he told me I didn't know what I was talking about! More later.

February 1948, Florida

Rache, I'm here again and so is Junior, he arrived last night just gone eleven pip emma – we've got to find a name for him soon, otherwise Junior is going to stick. I had him without any trouble at all, so different from Vicky, I didn't even realize he was born. He's very small because he's 'prem', and he's the funniest-looking baby you ever saw, but none of them look that good, and I love him more for being a bit of an ugly duckling. Vicky laughed her head off when she looked into the bassinet, then she kissed him and said, 'Youse funny, baby, youse funny.' She's almost blonde now, all that black hair sloughed off. He's really dark, already his eyes are brown and his hair is black and wiry. They should look good together. Wish you could see him, Rache. Wish Mom could see him too. Maybe she can.

Haven't posted this yet. Rache, it was just marvellous talking to you on the phone, sorry I broke down and wasted precious time. I was amazed Rex phoned you and gave you the number of my phone here, that was so thoughtful and the best treat he could have given me. He's been so attentive, Rache. I haven't told you before because it didn't seem to worry me unduly, but I caught him and Dawn kissing in the kitchen. He tried to pass it off – couldn't resist English girls, all that nonsense – but Dawn was so guilty about it and hasn't been near me since and that's a pity because I miss her. We could talk about home.

The trouble with you and me on the phone, we didn't feel we'd got time to talk about the things that really matter to us. Sure, I was glad to hear that my poor mum who isn't, is still living in the house. I hope Dad hasn't frittered away all her family money. And I was sort of glad to hear that Barry came home on an overnight pass and knocked Dad down the stairs. But why was Dad in the old house and upstairs? Surely Mum wouldn't have let him into bed with her? I'm remembering her now . . . she probably would. And that might well have been the trigger that sent Barry crazy. But

I'm glad he came round to see you, Rache. He loved all three of you and it would have helped to have what he called a ranting with you. Poor kid. Well, he's not a kid any more, is he? We're all the same, we hate Dad, but we sort of love him too. What a mess. You're right, darling, I am much better out of it. And I'm not sure of my plans for a while. I feel a bit anxious actually, Rache, that's why I almost enjoyed hearing about Dad. They've taken Junior to surgery for some tests. I don't know what sort of tests but, dammit, he's only a week old. Rex looks worried, too, and Rex never shows emotions, so what's going on?

A bit of good news, though: Aunt Mabe is here. She said she would come and help out when Junior arrived but of course she'd planned it for March not February! She brought me what she calls a shape yesterday. I was mystified. It's a cross between an egg custard and a blancmange and it's supposed to nourish me much more than the ice cream they keep doling out. Even if it had been disgusting I would have said I loved it, but I didn't hate it. She looked like an oversized Mom as she swept into my room holding it in front of her. Junior arrived early, Aunt Mabe is here and I talked to my bestest friend. Life is very good at times.

I'm sorry about that phone call, hon. I knew I was hysterical and I tried to stop it, and I just couldn't. I'll explain properly now. You've already forgiven me but I need you to understand, too. Just the facts. Here they are.

You know this already. Junior is what we call at home a mongol child. It's known here as Down's syndrome. They want to keep him in hospital for a while, until he learns to suck from a bottle, then he goes to another hospital where he will stay. We can visit or not, as we please. In other words, he is being 'put away'.

I told Aunt Mabe to bring the car round to the back gates, where all the trash is loaded up and goes somewhere. I had my clothes on under my nightdress – I was as hot as hell, Rache. I bundled him up – George – I'm calling him George after your father – and met her at the gates. She had Vicky with her, and we were so happy going back home. She understood completely, and she said not to worry, Rex would sort it all out and we'd manage fine with Georgie. She didn't once refer to the label they've given him, Rache. He's Georgie to her, and that's that. But Rex can't use his name. He said things like, 'We can't manage with a mental baby.' 'What do you think it will do to Vicky?' 'What will people think on the complex?' And finally, 'You just *left*? What do you mean, you just left? There's a procedure for being discharged, Meriel. Are you going crazy again?' And that's when I told him to go and do something awful to Dawn – I used that word, Rache. I told him her secret that she can't have children, so he would be quite safe with her. And that's when he started to come towards me, and I screamed and Aunt Mabe appeared and said that that was quite enough, and we hadn't broken the law. And he could go and apologize to the hospital tomorrow, while she took me back with her to Orion to give us time to calm down.

And that's where I am now, Rache. I've put 'home' at the top of this letter because it feels more like home than the complex ever has. Darling, I don't feel like calming down, because it would mean I was about to compromise, and I can't do that. Rex stopped wanting Georgie the minute he saw him; I realize that now. All that frowning and shaking his head. When they explained about the Down's syndrome I was sad for Georgie, of course I was, but I actually loved him more than ever, because that's what he'll need. And Vicky loves him, too. And so does Aunt Mabe. I'm not sure about Pop, though. If it weren't for Aunt Mabe, I'd come home and use emotional blackmail on Dad to set me up in a home of my own. I'm not upset in a weepy way, Rache, I'm angry.

June 1948, home-for-now, Orion

Dearest Rache, your letters have been such a comfort, arriving every other day like they have, and then the presents. I know how tough it is back home still, darling, austerity and all that stuff, but the little bootees – yes, I saw where you had dropped a stitch and that made them so precious. And the sun hat! Oh my God, Georgie looks so cute in that damned hat. Thank you for sending an identical one for Vicky, she adores it. I am sending snaps of the two of them in their hats. What do you think?

I am so sorry that my letters are few and far between, Rache. It's not that Georgie is hard work, quite the opposite, as he is the most placid and contented baby ever, but having two is double the work of having one. It's so obvious. Rex can't understand it – if you're tied down with one kid then you might as well be tied down with two. That's what he said before Georgie arrived. So now he blames Georgie's condition for the extra work. I thought when he came down for two whole weeks around Easter he would see how gorgeous Georgie is – Aunt Mabe calls him Gorgeous Georgie – and he might start to love him. After all, Georgie is his son. But nothing happened. The strange thing is, he is quite happy to go on as we are. He's having a high old time with Dawn. I think the others on the complex look on her as a kind of nurse to him! Yes, even her husband! Have you ever heard anything so comic? Just read that sentence, Rache, and realize what it says about me. I've kind of fallen out of love with Rex, haven't I? How strange to discover that by writing to you. And I always thought that if you fell out of love you fell into hate. It's not a bit like that. I just don't mind him having this torrid affair with Dawn. I simply . . . do . . . not . . . care.

Probably I would care if we weren't so contented here in Orion. The township itself is quite small – most of Pop's pupils are bussed in from farms and big houses all over. The people who live here could be bigoted, maybe they are in some ways, I don't know. But they are not bigoted about Georgie. To them he is Vicky's brother, Pop's grandson, another Robinson. They love kids and Georgie is another kid to love. Funnily enough, he is progressing at the same rate as Vicky did. He's four months now, and I can prop him up on his pillows so that he can look over the edge of the pram – they call it the baby carriage here – and he looks. He definitely looks around, and makes note of things. Vicky was like that. You knew she was identifying things: the leaves on the trees, the birds . . . faces around her. He's exactly the same, and the face he likes to see most is hers. She adores him, Rache. And I worried about relationships!

But I do worry about Pop. I know Aunt Mabe has to have a talk with him now and then, I can't hear what she says – she makes sure of that – but I recognize her reassuring voice. It's the same voice she uses to me when she tells me to 'let things ride as they are', or when she says that big decisions often happen by themselves and we should never force them. Things like that sound like platitudes, and I take them as such. The same as when poor old Mum used to say, 'There, there, it'll be all right in the morning.' But Aunt Mabe actually always means what she says. I think she is telling me to enjoy what we have now; and then she adds that decisions will have to be made, but there's a lot to happen before that time. At least, I think that's what she means! I wonder what she is saying to Pop.

Rex is coming for the weekend. He flies to New York, did I tell you? He got promotion and is working on some programme or other. He tells me bits, but I don't really listen. He asks me questions and catches me out. Last time he was here he said Dawn always listened 'intelligently' – that got my goat. I won't tell you what I said. But it shut him up. Anyway, guess what? Aunt Mabe has made an appointment for me to have my hair cut – she's paid in advance, too. Does she think there's a chance Rex and I will get back together? Ha-bloody-ha. Give Tom a very affectionate hug, please, Rache. Tell him about how I feel so close to Mom and yet I don't believe in God or an after-life or anything. But she is with me, and his father is with him.

Gosh, Rache, just realized I've got three mothers. My poor old besotted mum, who looked after me and told me everything would be all right tomorrow. My real mother, who is now known as DM. And my soul mother, Mom Robinson, who is in my head and my heart. I'll never regret marrying Rex because he gave me Vicky and Georgie and his mother.

PS How is your mum?

Nine

August 1948, Orion

Rache, I'm going to deal with your letter here and now, and deprive you of all the news about Georgie, and Vicky, and Aunt Mabe, and Nora-Marie from next door who makes the drop scones, and Pop being awarded Headmaster of the Year by the county and Joan Greenwood who teaches at the school, and has a crush on Pop. I'm doing this quite deliberately, so that you will see that by worrying about Mrs Fritz like a dog with a bone you are missing out in a big way!

Right. Here goes. Mr and Mrs Fritz lived on the outskirts of the city in a council house. In 1944 – August thereof – Mr Fritz is in a temporary internment camp awaiting the next batch to be sent to the Isle of Man for the 'duration'. We don't know anything about his background, whether they've always lived in England or whether they just arrived before the war. She's English, he's a German Jew. He came into Gloucester on that Friday afternoon. He had borrowed or stolen a bike, and presumably got through the gates of the holding camp in odds and ends of clothing which included one of the Swallow ties. We wondered whether it was one of Hermione's old ties, but no proof. He visited his wife – we wondered whether he might have dropped in to see Mr Silverman en route, but no proof. Then he went on down to see his fancy-nancy (no proof) who lived by the pump rooms and worked in the canteen for foreign personnel. We think her name was Eva. OK so far?

On the Saturday evening he repeated the whole thing (no proof) and we picked him up as he came from the direction of Silverman's and swung alongside the war memorial on the edge of the park. He threw us off the scent, but we picked him up right outside the house, where he faced up to us and accused us of hounding him. Then he went into the house.

The air raid happened in the small hours of Monday morning. I went back to the house in Spa Road later that morning, managed to get past the police, and was convinced Fritz was in the rubble under the staircase. The warden found a tie, and later two bodies were dug out, Fritz's and Eva's. You joined me and we went to Hermione Smith's house, where we discovered that Mrs Smith was missing and had lied to Hermione about her dental appointment. Also you told me that Hermione appeared to be missing a school tie (no proof). Mrs Smith turned up.

Tuesday, you and Tom got on the trail again and investigated the scene. You discovered the exact place where Fritz and Eva had been killed. You also found some scraps of rope, which suggested that they had died before the raid and there was a possibility they had committed suicide by hanging. You then went to the temporary morgue in the infirmary and were told that they were both fully dressed, which could have been a confirmation of your suicide theory, but again – no proof. Tom then 'dragged' you round to Silverman's where you discovered his body hanging from a ceiling beam in the shop.

The result of all these disconnected incidents – well, Rache, they are only circumstantially linked, please note all the times I have had to add 'no proof' – was:

1) you and I felt responsible in some way for the deaths of Fritz and Eva. How we managed that, I can't remember after so long. I came to my senses pretty quickly, and I thought you had too.

2) Tom feels responsible for the death of Silverman because he had some kind of premonition about it and did not follow it up quickly enough.

Now, Rachel Throstle, will you kindly read through the above and accept that just because we happened to be around on that Friday and Saturday, and you and Tom were the first to find Silverman's body, does not make us in any way responsible? None of us. Tom was obviously looking for a way to beat himself up over the loss of his dad . . . I can't see why, but just know I am right. And you and me . . . well, we were just a couple of drama queens.

Yours regally, Meriel

August 1948, Orion

Dearest Rache, Got your letter and thanks. Now, no more about that. Turn the page or even close the book. I am very glad I was able to help and don't thank me. I agree with Tom that the whole business of Mrs Fritz – who, apparently, is really called Sylvia Strassen – is really funny and it serves you right for being so gullible! I just hope she doesn't try it on again – not that she's likely to after pinching your typewriter like that, but you never know. If she does you'll just have to get in touch with the police. I'm really glad you think it's now a closed book.

The trip to Huddersfield sounds rather grim to me. It's really hard to imagine you all still scrimping and saving on food and clothes and everything. America really is the land of plenty as far as I'm concerned. Rex mails me huge checks, and the ice box here is always stuffed with food.

So good to talk to you on the telephone. Yes, I love having my hair short again, all Ingrid Bergman like you did it. It saves a lot of pain too; when it's long enough Georgie loves to grab a handful and when Vicky sees him laughing about it she does it, too!

I wondered how we should get on when Pop was home for the summer but he has planned the nicest thing. He's taking Aunt Mabe for two weeks' vacation on the Maine coast, and has told Rex to 'get himself down here' to keep me company and help with the kids! I approved of the first thing – the holiday – but not really the second. Pop is hoping we'll get together again, of course. I'm pretty certain it can't happen, Rache. I know you will be sad about this, and in a way I am too. Perhaps there is some way round it all. It will have to come from Rex. Perhaps if he applied for a job somewhere else I might be willing to go back. He'll have finished his doctorate now, and that may well open up new horizons for him. Even then it would be difficult. He's not interested in the children, Rache, that's what is so awful to me. I can see that he's still shocked about Georgie. But damn it all, Vicky is still around, and she is not only lovely in every sense of the word, she is such fun, too. I didn't say anything to Pop, but I gather Rex has agreed to come for a few days. We'll see.

Meanwhile . . . Joan. She's never heard of our Joan Greenwood, the actress, but when I told her about the sexy voice she dropped hers a tone, and now speaks slowly and significantly, even when she is only asking how we all are. Aunt Mabe and I can't help giggling about it – not unkindly because she's so sweet. We thought at first she didn't have a chance after Mom – his dear Ellie – but now I'm not so certain. He's sixty and Joan is forty-five and very attractive, so he's probably flattered to bits. And I'm an expert on extra-marital relationships, as you well know. OK, he's a widower, but so recently it would be the same as extra-marital. And funnily enough, I don't think Mom would mind. She was never daft and adoring like poor old Mum was about Dad, and she would want him to be happy. Joan is bound to call and see me when Pop and Mabe are away – she is very good with Vicky and Georgie – and she just might confide in me. We'll see.

Am I getting a bit too much like Daphne doo-dah – fat girl, permed hair, loved to gossip? I'm telling myself it's because I am interested in people. I really am, Rache. Aunt Mabe said to me ever so seriously last week, 'Honey, when the kids are grown-up I think you should go to college. You should read psychology. You are good at it.' I made a face and she knew what I was thinking and she actually grabbed my arm. 'Meriel—' she always calls me Merry or honey, my full name means trouble. 'Meriel, Georgie will lead a proper life. He will probably get married.' I stared at her, amazed. 'Aunt Mabe . . . I don't think it would be allowed . . .' I stammered on those words, because it hurts to have to face up to the fact that Georgie will never be independent in this world.

She gripped my arm so hard it hurt. 'Then you make sure you know enough about psychology that you can make it allowed!' And she marched off angrily – angry with me for not having thought it through, angry with . . . everyone all of a sudden.

She apologized later. 'Things that matter, Merry . . . I either end up in tears or lose my temper. And you don't do that. You never judge people, do you, honey?' I must have started blabbering something, but she ignored me. 'I'll never forget you coming out of that hospital clutching your baby. You never blamed Rex or the hospital people or anybody. It had happened, and that was that, and you would deal with it as you saw fit. You could really *help* people.' She just walked away then, before I could say anything, probably because she was 'ending up in tears'. I know I was.

August 1948, Orion

Dearest Rache, I'm doing a Daphne doo-dah now. Joan came over to say cheerio to Pop. She's got her parents with her for the whole summer. Whether it was the feeling of being a bit restricted, I don't know. But she got Pop on the verandah, the dark end, and kissed him! And that's not all. He let it happen but didn't do much reciprocation, hands lightly on her waist, head slightly inclined towards her, but not much passion visible. Then – the hussy – she stopped hanging on to his shoulders and one hand slid over his and she moved it – his hand – from her waist to her breast! She was wearing a navy and white gingham dress buttoned to the neck with a Peter Pan collar almost up to her chin so he couldn't get past that, but he didn't move his hand, and I'm almost certain he inclined his head another two or three inches towards her. What do you think of that? Sorry to sound a bit too Daphne for words, but I slid out of sight into the kitchen, and Aunt Mabe was there washing up after dinner, and I didn't tell her. So you've got to have it, my bestest friend, whether you like it or not! Maybe this is one of my letters you'd better burn!

Wednesday

Rex is here. Came late last night. Vicky went berserk with delight and all he could say to her was, calm down. She went to bed in tears, and he asked whether she was always like this! Then I began to feed Georgie, and he said why on earth wasn't I using a formula like any other mother? I told him Georgie is six months old, and I breastfed Vicky for nine months. And he said, 'Sorry. Just thought you wouldn't want to breastfeed . . . him.'

And even after that, Rache, I let him sleep with me. I am my father's daughter, am I not?

Sunday

Rex left today. He got a taxi and picked up the Amtrak at Vermont, then he will fly 'home'. Five days. He was with us for five days. I knew that almost all that time he was itching to get away. Back to Dawn, I guess.

It's really hot and the children both sleep after lunch and he could have rented a car and taken us to the lake.

Darling, stopped abruptly there because Joan came over. Turns out she saw him leave in the cab. Rex. She's kept away these past few days to give us a bit of time alone, I guess. She must have told her parents about Rex, and her father said immediately, 'Let's take that little family to the shore for a couple of hours. Kids always enjoy water. What d'you say, girls?' So here was Joan checking that I wasn't in floods of tears and hoping it was a good idea.

Needless to say . . .

I know I'm always going on about this neck of the woods, Rache, but it is so beautiful here. I guess I appreciate it so much because I know the whole stay is just that, a stay rather than a permanency. I do hope this 'stay' will last through the winter, when the snow lays itself over everything and the trees are decorated with ice pendants. Anyway, sweetie, yesterday afternoon was grand. The lake is a sort of basin in Harrison river. It's fed from Harrison Falls so the water is constantly renewed, and is as clear as crystal. The river sort of takes time to calm down in the lake, then meanders on into the county and out the other side, and eventually empties itself into the sea – must ask Pop about it, get him to draw a map for Vicky. He's still so good with her, they draw together at the weekends. Mostly animals. I think he might like to change to maps.

It took us almost two hours to drive there because Mr Greenwood does not go above thirty. Georgie got a bit fretful, actually, which is most unusual. Joan took him on her lap and tickled his tummy, which he loves, then said a little rhyme to him which I remember my old mum chanting to the twins. 'Leg over leg, as the dog went to Dover, when he got to a stile, up he went over – up he went over.' Do you know it, Rache? I thought it was amazing, an English nursery rhyme in America.

And Mrs Greenwood turned round – very gingerly – in the front seat and said over her shoulder, 'My great-grandmother always sang that one to me when I was little. She came from Kent in England way back in 1844. Answered an adver*tise*ment in the local paper for a Kentish maid who could make drop scones. She didn't know what drop scones were, and she thought the post was for a cook housemaid! Great-Grampy's mother taught her how to make drop scones and be a good independent American wife. And she taught them all her rhymes – dozens of them, there were – some you skipped rope to, others you played ball with. She was a great grandmother and a great lady. She'd been an orphan in England, and she reckoned there'd been a mistake at the heavenly turnstiles and her family were all waiting for her in America!'

We laughed like drains, of course, but that's how I feel, in a way. I looked sideways at Joan, and knew that from now on her drop scones would always be my favourite tea-time food. And then I knew . . . she was right for Pop. It came to me there in the car, with Georgie starting to grizzle again, and Vicky repeating 'Is we there?' at every bend in the road. And at the same time, or maybe a split second after it . . . and because of Great-Grandma Greenwood . . . I also knew I would have to give my marriage another go. It's so tempting to say to you here and now, Rache, I will come home. I think about it all the time. I could live with dear old Mum – she'd help with Vicky and Georgie, I know that. I could take up Dad's offer of working at Nightingale's and I could have real fun making life for him and DM absolute hell! But . . . but . . . I'm not sure any more, Rache. And in that moment, in the Greenwoods' old car, I knew that I should give Rex another chance to love his kids. I could run away . . . it is possible. Gran Greenwood couldn't. She'd burned her boats. And now, I think I'm going to burn mine. I think you will understand.

This is a kind of farewell letter, sweetie. I'll always write, and hope you will too, and there will be visits, I'm sure of that. But I'm going to set sail for America properly, now. I'm going to work at it, Rache. I don't know about Rex, but my children are American, and my mother-in-law said we were similar, and she was American. Pop, too. And darling Aunt Mabe, who will have to leave the school house and be alone again. And now Joan and Mr and Mrs Greenwood. They've got another daughter and a son, both married with families, so I'll be meeting them and gaining lots of cousins. Oh my God, Rache. I'm sitting here on the verandah, kids asleep upstairs, so hot, no covers, fireflies and big drunken moths around the lights, and the sky just huge above the trees, and I feel I'm going to explode . . . is this my road to Damascus? I haven't told you a thing about the afternoon, and the picnic, and Vicky sitting waist-deep in the crystal water, patting it with her hands so flat they're bending backwards – like she does in the bath. And Georgie being gently, gently dunked by Mr Greenwood, going rigid for a moment with shock and then screaming with joy and waving his fists . . . and Vicky laughing her head off at him.

I must lock up and go to bed, Rache. I haven't been drinking though I know it must sound like I have. Pop will be phoning through in a minute telling me my Aunt Mabe is worrying him to phone every night. I know he's right but I'd bet quite a lot that he would phone anyway. They *are* my family, Rache. If she is *my* Aunt Mabe, then he is *my* Pop. I have to stay.

PS Darling, do you think Tom is worried about not remembering his mother? Don't answer that, of course he is. Cheer him up. Offer him one of mine. I'd offer him my dad, but in the circs that wouldn't be funny.

Another thought. I know that Mr Silverman is – was – good. And I think we both know that Fritz . . . sorry, Wilhelm Strassen . . . was evil. I don't know why I said that. Perhaps because I feel its truth so certainly, I had to see it in my own handwriting.

All my love, Rache. Merry

Ten

And then Sylvia Strassen was murdered.

I had seen her several times from the corner of my vision. When I looked at the wedding photographs I was certain she was standing on the edge of the little crowd who had assembled outside the church to see my dress and throw confetti. Meriel said the picture was too blurred, but Sylvia was smiling and the rabbit teeth were there.

She had turned up in June, just over two months ago. Tom and I were renting a flat in Brunswick Square, just across from the new technical college. We were on the first floor, so if anyone rang the bell we could inspect them from the window.

The bell rang, and there she was.

I knew her instantly: still skinny, her face all eyes and nose and teeth, hair tucked into a headband, sort of gingery. I'd . . . seen her around now and then . . . as Meriel said, we were bound to cross paths occasionally. It did not mean that she remembered me.

Tom was down in the Forest of Dean interviewing a man who had worked on the Burma railway, and I had hoped it might be him wanting me to throw down the key because he'd forgotten his. She looked up and saw me peering down at her, and her expression became a mixture of anger and fear and stubborn defiance. Just as it had back in 1944, the weekend of Holidays at Home. She held my gaze for the instant before I stepped back into the room.

The bell jangled again, imperiously. I opened the door on to the landing and waited for Mrs Price on the ground floor to answer it. She paid a lower rent because her husband did the garden and she answered the door – and sorted the post and 'ran a mop' over the hall floor now and then. There wasn't a sound from below; the whole house appeared to be empty except for me.

The bell jumped and jangled again and again. It was on a spring just inside the front door. I went on to the landing and looked over the banisters. The spring was still shuddering. Then the letterbox was lifted from outside and a shrill voice said, 'I know you're there – I saw you!'

I ran downstairs; if anyone was in the flat above and the attic above that, I certainly didn't want to call attention to myself in quite this way.

She pushed herself through the door before it was half-open and immediately started up the stairs. It put me – somehow – at a disadvantage; I hurried after her as if I were the visitor and she the house-holder. Luckily she did pause at the half-open door on the landing and I pushed past her, turned and blocked her entry.

She stood there, breathing heavily, her watery eyes enormous. She looked . . . hunted. I felt the same way. We faced each other, no more than twelve inches between us, in similar shabby outfits of blouses and cotton skirts. My sandals were the same ones I had worn the day I'd encountered her first: schoolgirl sandals, with good quality leather uppers that would long outlive the crêpe soles and hand-stitching. Her sandals had probably been bought the previous week at one of the many church bazaars where clothing coupons were not needed. I felt a terrible pang of shame for what Meriel and I had done that day. All right, as Mum was always saying, it was nothing criminal. But we had meddled and our meddling had had . . . outcomes. I stood aside suddenly.

'Come in. Sorry. Come and sit down. It's so hot.'

It took the wind out of her sails, and she came into our large living room uncertainly and made straight for the long open windows.

She glanced at the view of the square and the college beyond, and almost flung herself into one of the fireside chairs I'd drawn up to catch any breeze that might pass by. I hesitated, wondering whether to offer lemon barley, then sat down carefully and pulled my skirt almost to my ankles. There was a strange smell coming from her; it reminded me of school.

I said, 'I don't know your name.'

'I didn't know yours, either. Found it by keeping an eye out.'

Strangely enough, I felt an enormous relief. Meriel had thought I was imagining things, or that it was just coincidence. I had known it wasn't. She had been around . . . in the cinema or the Co-op or just walking in the park.

I waited and she said, 'Sylvia. Sylvia Strassen. That bloke you chased all round the city back in the war . . . he were my husband.'

I swallowed, but denied nothing. Eventually I said, 'We were schoolgirls. We didn't mean . . . anything.'

'It 'appened though, dinnit? He went off to see bloody Eva Schmidt that night and stayed there. If 'e'd come home proper, he'd still be alive now.'

It was so close to our pretend-stories: Meriel's, Tom's, mine. I kept swallowing, and she knew.

She said viciously, 'It were your fault.'

I said again, 'We were . . . children. We thought he was a spy.'

She looked surprised. 'Your dad tell you that?'

'No.' I had no saliva left to swallow; my mouth was bone-dry. 'We . . . we made it up.'

The surprise turned to astonishment, then she laughed. She looked different; much nicer. Still a rabbit, but a rabbit you might like to stroke.

She stopped laughing and said wryly, 'Well, you could have been right, you could have been wrong. One way or another I reckon you owe him something.' She looked around the room, then out of the windows. 'Nice place.' She nodded at our silver-framed wedding photograph. 'Same one as was in the *Clarion*. I saw you coming out of the church. Is he – your husband – the one who found old Silverman?'

I had to adjust my thinking to Tom and our wedding and then back to our first meeting. 'Yes.'

'Is he here?'

'No. He's working.'

'I've seen his name in the paper. Yours, too.'

'I'm the tea girl at the office. But they let me do a piece now and then.'

'That recipe the other week. It was all right.'

'It came from my mother.'

'Ah.' Her eyes narrowed. Then she said, 'Is your parents on the phone?'

She only had to look in the local directory to know they were. So I said, 'Yes.'

There was another pause, longer. I had the impression she was tensing herself to tell me something. Her hands suddenly clenched on the wooden arms of the chair.

'All right for some. Isn't it? Good jobs, nice homes, telephones . . . plenty to eat too, I bet. Plenty of folks as 'd want to do you a favour.'

I swallowed hard. 'We are very lucky.' Mr Myercroft still kept us well supplied with stuff from his greenhouse, and Mum and Dad shared their garden produce with us. We were lucky.

'Yeh. Thought so. Thought you might like to repay some of them favours, too. If you got the chance, that is. In memory of my 'usband.' And she added almost proudly, 'Wilhelm Strassen.'

I did not know what to say; was this a kind of emotional blackmail? I kept silent. Tom was good at silence; it worked wonders for him. People who had not wanted to be cooperative found themselves filling the silence with things they had not meant to say. I hadn't got the same gift, and I sat there finding it very difficult indeed to wait for her to say more. She found it difficult too; I sensed her gathering herself together.

She blurted suddenly, 'What your dad gave me din't last five minutes – oh, it seemed a lot at the time, but there was all sorts to do with it.

I 'ad to see to the remains after . . . there was a funeral. That din't come cheap. Then after the war, I 'ad to get in touch with 'is fam'ly. They din't want to know. I married Willi so that he could keep out of internment camp – they were going to pay me a lot for that. But then he was going in anyway, and then he was killed – none of it my fault, was it? But the buggers wouldn't pay up. There's the rent. I 'ad a job but there was Arnie last year and no one wants to give a pregnant woman a decent job. And now 'e's dead and gone, poor little sod, and I'm back to square one.'

It came out so fast, and there was so much information in-between each breath that I suddenly had no difficulty keeping silent. I needed to. Dad had been to see this woman? Dad had helped her out? It was so typical of Dad I could have cried.

'D'you get what I'm getting at?' she said, her voice a notch higher. 'I need some cash, else I'll lose the house. D'you get it?'

I nodded quickly. She sounded on the verge of hysteria. I seized on the other things she had said . . . she had been paid to marry Willi? Not our silly make-believe Fritz, but Wilhelm Strassen, a real man, a paid-for husband. And a lover. Eva. Eva Schmidt. Had they been so in love, so desperately in love, that they had made a suicide pact? Impossible to know that. But Arnie, who was Arnie? The penny dropped.

'You had a baby? Last year?' It couldn't have been Wilhelm's baby, then. 'Not your husband's?'

She said shortly, 'Willi's been dead four ruddy years. Arnie was born too early. He died. Had colic, fits – convulsions or whatever they call it.' She shrugged. 'I en't bin strong since.'

'No.'

I was so stupid; I just stared at her.

She leaned forward and spoke slowly. 'I got to 'ave last month's rent and next month's rent, else I'm done for. And I reckon you could afford some . . . what do they call it . . . conscience money?'

'Oh! Money. I'm sorry.' Dad was out of the picture now; Dad had helped her out of sheer generosity. But might she apply to Dad again? Mum was not up to it. Not up to it at all. I said quickly, 'How much do you need?'

'I just told you! For Christ's sake! Last month's and—'

'I don't know what your rent is.'

'Ten and six a week. Work it out for yourself. You could add something for food if you felt like it. Though I expect you'd like me to die of starvation!' she gave a hoarse laugh.

'Of course not.' But it sounded so much money. Four guineas altogether. Would four guineas buy me an easy conscience? Tom had wanted me to keep my money separate from the housekeeping. 'Let's use yours for nice things like birthdays and treats,' he'd said. There were twelve pounds in my nice new cheque book account. I felt mean, but I made out the cheque for six pounds – half and half, as it were. I flapped it in the air to dry the ink and then gave it to her. She stared at it for some moments, before giving a shout of complete disgust and trying to fling it in my face; it fluttered to the floor.

''Ow the hell am I supposed to get 'old of that?' she asked, her aggression suddenly escalating into fury.

I was angry, too. Buying an easy conscience was the same as blackmail, by the sound of things. Either way, I knew already there was no way out. And of course I should have known she wouldn't have a bank account; I hadn't had one until a few weeks ago. I stared down her incipient hysteria. 'I haven't got much here.' I went for my bag and took out the old school pencil case Mum had made for me in the middle of the war; it was now my purse. I shook it out on to the table. She got up and followed me and stared down at the ten-shilling note, the two half-crowns, a sixpence and a threepenny bit, a halfpenny and a couple of farthings. It added up to fifteen shillings and tenpence.

She said, 'That won't get me far. I wanted to walk round to the Guildhall an' get them off my back.' There was a kind of despair in her angry voice. It was so hot and the thought of walking right into town and then all the way back to the estate was . . . tough. There had been no bike parked outside; and she was so thin.

I said tersely, 'Look. Give me the rent book. I'll go and cash a cheque and pay it for you. I've got my bike under the stairs. Sit by the window and try to relax. I'll be half an hour, no longer.'

She looked at me in sheer astonishment, then she laughed. I thought at the time it was a grateful, relieved laugh, and I smiled back at her. She rummaged in her bag and produced the rent book, one of those linen- and cardboard-covered note books with cut-outs on the edge for each month of the year. I glanced at it quickly, and saw that she was telling the truth: the month of May was not signed by the clerk . . . or by her.

I said, 'You have to sign this.'

'It's all right. Other people often have to sign. Tell 'em I'm ill.' She laughed again, this time bitterly. 'Not far wrong, is it?'

I said nothing, tacitly agreeing, wondering whether she had TB or something even worse. I pressed her back into the chair and fetched the jug of lemon barley from the kitchen slab, poured her a glass and set it on the floor by the chair.

'Close your eyes, if you like.'

'What if anyone comes?'

'They won't. Ignore the bell.'

'The windows are open, they'll know someone's 'ere.'

'I always leave them open in this weather. Try to relax.'

She watched me leave. As I closed the door I turned and looked at her and smiled. She smiled back.

That was the last time I saw Sylvia Strassen, because when I got home forty minutes later she had left. So had our old three-bank Oliver typewriter. After running around the living room, bedroom and kitchen, then down the landing to the shared bathroom – as if it would be there – I had to accept what had happened. She had gone through my dressing-table drawers too; I had never had any jewellery except the silver bracelet Mum and Dad had given me when I matriculated, and that was never off my wrist. But the typewriter was important, especially to Tom. After standing for ages by the window with clenched fists, waiting for the tears to dry on my face, I had a bit of a brainwave. The Oliver was heavy and she was not strong, so she could not have carried it far. I went back into the square and down to Eastgate where Mrs Crutcheon ran her second-hand shop.

It was there. She told me she had given the young lady a fiver for it. And yes, she would accept a cheque from me, so long as I wrote my address on the back of it. It left me with less than three pounds in my lovely new account. It was a long, hot and heavy walk back to the flat; I wondered how she had found the strength to do it in reverse.

Tom's first words, after our thank-God-for-each-other kiss, were, 'Where's Ollie? I want to get started, Rache. It's been the most amazing day. Mr Harrison – I have to call him Fred – is so clear-eyed about it all, I'm not saying there's no bitterness, but he can see why a lot of the atrocities happened. He says the Japanese weren't much better to their own men.'

He was lumping the typewriter on to the table as he spoke, fetching quarto-sized paper from the bureau and winding in that first wonderful, virgin-white sheet. I just smiled at him, so happy to see him, so happy at his enthusiasm . . . it was what had made me love him in the first place, when we were following up the suspicion that Fritz – sorry, Willi – and Eva had made some kind of suicide pact.

There was a flip side to the enthusiasm, of course: he was almost obsessional about finding his father. The previous week we had had two days off and had spent them on the new British Railways, going to Liverpool to see a repatriated prisoner from the Far East who had been in the same regiment as Tom's father.

He had spent some time in a makeshift field hospital run by a Scottish doctor who distilled his own drugs from local plants and roots. The ex-prisoner, whose name was Stanley Clarke – 'Call me Nobby' – was wryly humorous. 'Luckily he still had hydrogen peroxide when I was there, otherwise I'd be dead from blood poisoning. Sometimes the concoctions worked, sometimes they didn't. He could bring down a fever, and when the quinine ran out he had something he said got to grips with malaria. But when he started boiling up grass, we knew he was on his beam-ends.' His grin was full of admiration. 'He distilled hope . . . that was what kept us going.'

Tom had said, 'When I heard that you'd been in a field hospital I felt hopeful, too.' He had tried to return the grin, but it was so important to him . . . I had been holding his hand. I had squeezed it hard.

Nobby Clarke had said, 'Wish I could be more help, son. Fact is, I was delirious most of the time. And you've got to remember, none of the orderlies were permanently in the hospital. They'd come and do a stint when they were marched back at the end of the day. When there was an operation, the Japs would let a couple of them help out. You never got to know them.' He had looked at Tom's face, and said very seriously, 'Listen, my son. If your dad is still alive, there will be news. But you will have to make up your mind to wait for it. The mess and muddle out there is pretty bad. The Japs burned every damned piece of paper they could. But you've told me a lot about your dad today and he sounds an unusual sort of a bloke – someone who will stand out in a crowd, be remembered. Drawing things all the time . . . I'd remember someone like that. Other people will, too.' He had glanced at my face, and added, 'You 'aven't wasted your time today because I'll be on the look-out now. If I 'ear of anyone who would rather do a sketch of someone than talk to 'im—' he laughed. 'Well, I'll be in touch.' He had tapped the letter on the arm of his wheelchair. 'I'll keep your letter close. Never fear.'

No, it hadn't been a waste of time, we had gone there together, and come home together. But when we were delayed at Crewe Tom had lowered the window in the crowded compartment and hung out, looking at the faces that thronged the platforms. He had forced a smile at me as he sat down again, excusing himself by saying, 'People don't just disappear.' I had smiled back. He knew, as well as I did, that people disappeared all the time. And it nearly always meant they had died.

Much later that night in June, when I had read Tom's article and we had eaten a salad and new potatoes and corned beef, I told him about

Sylvia Strassen. He stared at me in disbelief and I spread my hands helplessly.

'Sorry, love. I know I'm a complete idiot, but she was so thin. And anyway, this time I've paid for it – literally!'

Tom suddenly burst out laughing. I stared at him, astonished and a bit annoyed.

He spluttered, 'It sounds so like that farce we saw in Cheltenham a couple of weeks ago. Jangling door bells and you and this woman coming and going like blue-assed flies!' He leapt out of his chair and gathered me to him. 'Oh Rache, don't you see? You've always worried about that weekend in the war – the only one we spent together because I was posted the following week – now . . . you need not give it another thought. When that woman talked of conscience money she was right. That's what it was. You've paid your dues, imaginary though they were. They're gone.' He kissed me. He has a special way of kissing me; each time is the first time. He looked straight at me, his blue eyes so full of love it made mine water. He said very quietly, 'Maybe if it hadn't been for her and Wilhelm Strassen and Eva Schmidt and—' He hesitated a moment and forced himself on, 'and poor old Silverman, we wouldn't have squashed about three years of getting to know each other into eight hours.'

I cupped his cheek in my palm. 'There would have been another way. We could not have simply missed each other for the sake of eight hours.'

That night Tom and I lugged the mattress from the bed to the open windows in the living room. The bedroom was a cubby hole partitioned from the living room; it was airless and very hot. This way we slept practically under the stars. I thought of Meriel and her two babies in Orion, where it was possibly hotter than it was here. I thought that probably they were on their own in the house. Unless Rex was with them. I prayed that he was. I prayed that she could know just a little of the happiness I had in such abundance. I fell asleep composing the letter I would write to her tomorrow, telling her about how Sylvia Strassen pinched the typewriter. I loved the thought of her with her hair in short curls again, laughing as she read about it.

July and August were almost molten. I submitted my 'Saturday Supper' recipes and two diamond-wedding-party pieces. Katherine and Stanley Holdaway had been born in the city and married in 1888. She had been eighteen and he a year younger. It was a lovely interview; they were both warm and full of fun; he called her Mother and she called him Dad. They had no children; not one. She chuckled without bitterness as she told me 'It's all part of the wishful thinking!'

The other two had come to live just outside the city at the beginning of the war. They called themselves elderly evacuees. They still ran their smallholding, and I came home with two summer cabbages and a newspaper parcel of runner beans.

Uncle Gilbert chuckled at both the articles.

'My God, Rachel, you know all about pulling heart strings. Everyone will have a soppy smile on their faces when they read this, and there will be a few hankies in use!'

'I know it's sentimental, Gaffer, but it's absolutely true! They are still – both couples – in love! Neither of them were involved in either of the wars, though I haven't said that. But I *do* think it's something to do with peace . . . and growing food!'

He threw his head back and laughed. After a second, I joined him.

It was only a week later, the first week in September, that Sylvia Strassen was murdered. That was when I stopped thinking everyone was lovely and life was mainly hearts and roses. I had posted back her rent book. My signature was repeated eight times inside it.

Eleven

The man who killed Sylvia Strassen was arrested the next day. He had struck her from behind with her old-fashioned flat iron and then made a run for it. When they picked him up he was underneath the up platform at the old Great Western railway station. It was where all the rats were. It was ghastly; horrific. Uncle Gilbert told me this in his brusque, don't-you-dare-cry sort of voice.

He looked at me, and added just as brusquely, 'No story there for you, young Rachel. Tom can cover the arrest and trial. It will have to be carefully done.' What that meant I didn't much care, then, I was so thankful I was not to be involved any more. Not that I could ever become uninvolved. Not now. Surely even Meriel would see that?

He said, 'You'd better go home. You look as if the hot weather is getting you down.'

I went home. Tom was back from 'the scene of the crime', and just put his arms round me and said, 'It's all right, darling.' He rocked me gently while I cried. Then he sat me in the window, in the chair where Sylvia Strassen had asked for conscience money, and went to make coffee. He put it on the floor, then knelt by me and stroked my hands until I stopped twisting them. I told him what Uncle Gilbert had told me.

'What made him do it, Tom? She was such a poor thing. It sounds as if they'd had a row and he did it on impulse – oh God, the thought of that iron. And he must have hated himself so much to hide where he did. I've sat in waiting trains and watched those rats run in and out . . . oh Tom—' I shook with a spasm of revulsion, and he gripped my hands hard.

'Listen, my love. Try to concentrate on the fact that the whole thing won't be made public now. If your father did give her money for her husband's funeral, that might have come out. And then, of course, there's that blessed rent book . . .' I nodded, eyes tightly closed. Indeed, when Gilbert had told me about the arrest I had felt enormous relief. The details had overlaid that. The iron, so heavy, so lethal, actually entering her skull . . . and the desperate man hiding with the rats . . .

Tom drew up the other chair and sat close to me, then reached into his pocket and produced the rent book. 'I found this in Sylvia Strassen's kitchen. I suggest we burn it,' he said.

I couldn't stop shaking. He put the rent book away again and held one of the coffee cups to my mouth. I took a sip obediently. It did help. He spoke quietly.

'Rachel. You and I have heard some terrible stories in the time we have worked for the *Clarion.* The war still dominates lives. The search for my father has underscored all that. But when we're together we're . . . OK. It's as simple as that. We must hold on to that, darling.'

I thought about it. My eyes were still shut, but I felt my mouth lift in a smile, and I nodded. I whispered, 'I love you, Tom.'

'I love you too, Rache. And that is what I meant, of course.' He spoke very slowly. 'Here, right here, is love.'

I opened my eyes, smiling properly, and took another sip of coffee. It was a marvellous moment. The ordinary business of sharing coffee was part of it. It gave it . . . gravitas. Nothing airy-fairy about our love. It was grounded in the ordinary things of everyday life. It was . . . OK.

He sat back with his cup, and we went on sipping and smiling at each other for some time. It was a Saturday, the day for the vegetable cart. Through the windows came the unmistakable scent of horse from below.

'I've left a list with Mrs Price,' I murmured. 'Thought I might still be at the office.'

Sounds came from below: the clank of metal scales, Mrs Price's voice dictating my list. The vegetable man praising the quality of his summer cabbage and lettuce. We listened to all of it with the appreciative smiles usually reserved for a special concert at the Cheltenham Town Hall from the Birmingham Symphony . . . we never missed one of those. The cart moved off, the front door closed, there was a thump from my string bag as Mrs Price deposited it at the bottom of the stairs. Then her door closed. The world had settled comfortably around us. We went into married conversation.

I said, 'I enjoyed that.'

Tom did not ask whether I meant the coffee or the vegetable cart, he simply said, 'So did I.'

I said, 'What shall we have for lunch?'

Tom said, 'I'm really tired of salad.'

I said, 'So am I. And I've got that beef dripping. Shall I make chips?'

And so it went on. Foolish, easy. It wasn't until we'd finished eating the chips that I brought up the murder again. I fiddled with the cutlery, then said, 'Why?' And Tom knew exactly what I meant.

'I've got a very plausible theory. D'you want to hear it?' He sprinkled some salt on his bread and nibbled at it. He often did that when he was being Pierre in *War and Peace*. It took some of the awfulness out of a lot of things. I smiled, acknowledging all that, plus my willingness to listen to his theory.

'Well. I reckon Sylvia Strassen knew a thing or two about her Willi's operations. And when that didn't work as blackmail she talked about losing her baby and not being able to pay the rent. Then she might have mentioned conscience money.' He nibbled again. 'I think you weren't the only mug, Rachel. It started with your father – I'd love to know how much he donated to the Strassen fund.'

'He wasn't very well off when it happened.' I removed the salt cellar. 'I hope it wasn't too much.'

'He'd finished paying your school fees. Maybe they went into Sylvia's kitty.'

'Maybe.' I did not want to remember that time; the thought of Dad being dragged into it was awful. 'So you think there were others besides Dad and me?'

'Yes. I think there was probably the Strassen family back in Germany. And I think it more than likely that they had a lot to hide and she knew it. So it became real blackmail, nothing to do with conscience money. They could see her draining them dry. They found someone who would . . . maybe threaten her at first. Maybe hurt her a little, frighten her. Maybe he went too far.'

I looked at him. His theory hung together so well it sounded almost reasonable.

'This is the sort of game Merry and I played. Are you trying to make this whole thing more plausible?'

'No. But I am trying to answer your question. Motive. It's what the police will want to know.'

'Yes.' I cleared the plates and brought in an apple tart and custard from yesterday. 'D'you mind if we don't go to the pictures tonight, Tom? I'd quite like to cycle out to the rough road and visit Mum and Dad.'

'It's a Raymond Chandler film,' he reminded me, not really minding much.

'I've had enough murder mysteries for one day.'

'All right, that's fine. But the real-life one is over for us, Rache – you do accept that?'

I made a wry face. 'Not quite, is it? If the police go on investigating, they will pick up on the missing rent book and check at the Guildhall. I initialled the ledger thing there, too.'

I could tell he had already thought of that, and hoped I hadn't. He cut himself a wedge of pie and spooned cold custard over it. 'Please don't worry about it, darling. Please. They've got the murderer. His prints will be on the iron. They'll want it all out of the way as quickly as possible.'

He smiled at me and I smiled back. I wanted everything to be normal, I wanted that quite desperately.

* * *

We had such a good evening with Mum and Dad. Mum looked better than she'd looked for ages. They both knew the latest about Sylvia Strassen's murder; Uncle Gilbert had telephoned them immediately the murderer had been arrested. Like me, Mum had the shivers every time she thought about it. She said soberly, 'I'm just so thankful the murderer wasn't someone local.'

We were in the dining room putting out pickles and liver sausage for supper. I said, 'How on earth do you know it wasn't someone local?'

'Well . . . he'd have gone back home, wouldn't he? I mean hiding where he did . . . there are rats under that platform, you know, darling.'

'Yes.' I almost told her about Sylvia Strassen's demand for conscience money. Instead I said, 'Tom thinks it might be someone connected to Wilhelm Strassen's family.'

'What? Back in Germany?'

'I suppose so. It was just a theory he had.'

Mum was doubtful. 'The war is over, darling. And Wilhelm is dead, anyway. How could she put any pressure on them?'

'Conscience money?'

'I wouldn't have thought so. Anyway, it doesn't matter now. You'll have a lot to write to Meriel about, won't you?'

Again, I almost told her that Meriel knew

about Sylvia's visit already. Again, I stopped myself in time. We'd got into the way of trying to save Mum a lot of worry. Instead I said, 'Are these Mr Myercroft's tomatoes?'

'Certainly not. I grew them with my own fair hands!'

We laughed. I began to cut the tomatoes into zigzag shapes, Mum arranged slices of liver sausage around them. Then she upended the carving knife and fork and drummed on the table, and announced in sonorous tones the call-sign of Lord Haw-Haw's war-time broadcasts.

'Germany calling. Germany calling,' I picked up nasally, snuffling with laughter already.

She replied with the percussion on the table, 'La-la-la-Laah. La-la-la-Laah. La-la-la-Laah. La . . . Laah!' We took deep breaths and crashed into Beethoven's Fifth. I speared a tomato and held it high. She lifted her knife and fork and did likewise. We faced each other, two conductors, one brilliant symphony. We went for it. Time scrolled back. Dad and Tom appeared at the open window and became our audience. We finished our performance together, let our batons come to rest on the table, bowed to the tomatoes and liver sausage and turned to the cheering audience in the window.

Dad yelled 'Bravo!' and Tom begged an encore. It was all so silly and so marvellous.

* * *

Strangely enough, Sylvia Strassen's murder was dealt with very quietly. The man confessed and was sent to prison in Birmingham to await trial. Police investigations stopped there. Gilbert's did, too, which was a surprise. The story could have run for some time if he had given it to his chief reporter. But he insisted that it should be brought to a decent conclusion. 'We've had enough gory glory to last the old *Clarion* a long time,' he told Tom almost wearily. 'People want to hear about lighter things: weddings, fashion. Get Rachel to use her influence and do a series on Nightingale's. Dennis will cooperate all the way, such good publicity.'

We had a feeling that someone had killed Sylvia's story. Tom was thankful in many ways, but in others he had welcomed the opportunity to look into the 1944 thing. Three deaths then: Willi, Eva and Mr Silverman. Now a fourth: Sylvia Strassen. He wanted to link all of them. I pointed out that we couldn't possibly link Sylvia's murder with the three suicides, and he frowned and said, 'Maybe they weren't all suicides. Maybe Sylvia could have told us a thing or two.' But it was four years ago and now Sylvia was dead, too. We burned the rent book with mock ceremony, and told each other that was that. I went to interview Dennis Nightingale and found him far more interested in Meriel than I would have believed possible – if only he'd been like that when she was around. In the end I got more from Maria Nightingale, the dressmaker – she had changed her name to Nightingale by deed poll until the divorce was through. I wrote to Meriel to ask her whether she minded all this stuff, and she replied to say she didn't. I knew she did. But I told myself it was a job and went ahead.

October came in like a lion that year. The leaves were torn from the trees much too soon. The subway by California crossing was knee-deep in them. I made a point of walking through each day, recalling how I'd done it as a very small girl with my grandparents. The clocks went back, and suddenly it was winter.

I got in late one evening, after having tea with Dennis and Maria in the stock room at Nightingale's. I was beginning to understand Meriel's father at last. He was the usual mixture of strength and weakness. A man who couldn't say no, and needed someone like Maria to sort out his self-made muddles and messes. She was strong; powerful. Very like Meriel in a lot of ways. Meriel was coping with an erring husband and a disabled son; not just coping either, making something very good from it all. Maria had done the same. I could imagine that Dennis still strayed, and she had

had to learn to accept that. She knew she was good for him, that was the thing. He needed her. I couldn't make up my mind whether she loved him or not, but I thought she probably would never let him go again.

Anyway, it was dark and dismal, still blowing fiercely, and it was good to get inside the hall and smell that Mrs Price had run her mop over it that very day. The lights were on in our flat so I knew Tom was home; probably tapping away on the Oliver. He was. And he'd got something cooking; the smell was wonderful. And he'd put a match to the fire, and everything looked cheerful. We hadn't started regular fires, though of course there had been the incineration of the rent book.

He packed up work immediately and leapt up to grab me and waltz me round the room.

'I called on Flo and George, and Flo had made us a stew in a casserole which exactly fitted into my bike basket!'

'Oh darling . . . How were Mum and Dad?'

He stopped dancing, held me away from him. His eyes were blue. Just blue to anyone else but I could see silvery specks in them; azure.

'They've been asked, both of them, to visit the Lufthaus factory in Düsseldorf!'

I was completely astonished. The war had been over for three years. You had to be a politician or a field marshal or – or a spy – to go to Germany. Or, I suppose, a respected inventor. But if Dad hadn't developed his modification to the Spitfire fin, he would still be another draftsman; actually, within Smith's he still was. He'd got a rise and a bonus from the fin, but mostly he saw it as his special war effort; a tiny mathematical adjustment that he had come upon accidentally.

I laid the free half of the table – giving the Oliver a wide berth in case of spillages – and brought in Mum's cast-iron casserole. She had tied on the lid with string, which Tom hadn't removed when he'd put it in the oven, so I dusted the charred remains from that into the sink first of all. We sat down and discussed the Düsseldorf thing exhaustively.

At first I didn't think Mum should go; she usually went to bed for a couple of hours after lunch, and how could she do that in digs?

Tom said, 'I've misled you. The MD is going with his wife, plus two of the directors with theirs. It was the Lufthaus people who asked for George, and of course your mum was included. The MD's wife has always liked her, apparently, and has told your dad that she will make sure she rests.' He was so happy for them, his face alight. 'It's such an honour, Rache. And George . . . well, he deserves some kind of recognition. They actually asked for him.' He usually called Dad by his first name, though sometimes 'Flo' became 'Mum'. I knew why it was: he wouldn't usurp his own father's place in any way whatsoever. I did not comment. Instead I asked a load of questions about when and how . . . it was staggering to hear that they would be flying from Staverton airport. 'Private plane,' Tom put in with relish. 'Posh hotel, too. George has found out all about it. My God, the Germans might have lost the war, but they live all right.'

'People who have money generally do,' I reminded him. 'There will be others who have no money.'

We finished the stew with plenty of bread, and washed-up, and Tom got on with his piece, and I darned some socks and made notes about Nightingale's winter coats, which were all featuring hoods. Maria had plans for a mannequin parade, which I had found interesting. I frowned as I went back to darning; I had to write to Meriel and try to explain why I was getting on so well with her birth-mother. And then, or perhaps before then, I ought to call on Myrtle Nightingale in the old house and ask after the boys. She would want all the latest news about Meriel. I bit my lip, wondering whether she knew about Georgie.

'All right, love? Why the frown?' Tom was stacking pages into a neat bundle, smiling at me from beneath the desk lamp which Uncle

Gilbert had given us for a wedding present.

'I'm fine.' I turned the frown into a grin. 'Relishing the fire . . . the safety . . . every last little thing.'

He came over and sat opposite me, and nodded. 'I see what you mean.'

'Don't mock. Soak it up.'

I finished my sock. We drank cocoa and talked more about the Düsseldorf trip and wondered what sort of reception they would get from the Germans generally.

'George won't come into contact with anyone outside the factory, I wouldn't think,' Tom said judiciously. 'It might be different for the wives.'

He picked up my empty cocoa cup and made for the kitchen. 'By the way,' he said over his shoulder. 'One of the directors is the Wingco. Did you know?'

He was referring to Mr Smith, Hermione's father, husband to the very mysterious Mrs Smith. 'How could I not know? Same name, of course, though there are so many Smiths around. Mrs Smith informed Mum that her husband's father had founded the engineering firm at the beginning of the century, and as Dad worked there she expected I would befriend Hermione at school.'

'But you and Meriel—'

'Exactly. I was at least sorry for Hermione. Merry despised her. Well, until the time she gave us some ice-cold milk out of their ultra-modern fridge!' I chuckled at the thought, and added, 'Poor Hermione. She was frantic about her mother that day.'

He brought in two russets and we scrunched into them. 'Did you ever discover where she had actually been that day?' he mumbled through his apple.

'Not really. Hermione had some story about her mother meeting a friend. But she arrived home along the rough road.' I threw my core into the fire. 'Dad said she'd seen us and done a swift detour to avoid us.' I shrugged. 'Hermione looked good at our wedding, I thought.'

'Doctor Smith. Yes.' He stared at me. 'D'you regret leaving school and working at the *Clarion*?'

'And meeting you and then getting married to you?' I pulled a long face. 'How can I answer that?'

He growled, and came towards me, and swept me up into his arms.

I delivered my piece to Uncle Gilbert and told him about Dad and he asked if Mum was up to it, and I said I didn't know. We had a cup of tea together. Maxine came in and gave me a very perfumed hug. She wanted to sweep him off to get ready for a charity dinner.

She said, 'Remember Silverman's? The old

bespoke tailor in the Barton? Hung himself . . . didn't you find him, Rachel?'

'Sort of.' I recalled the sight with a shudder. It was still my private waking nightmare.

'They're taking down all the shuttering on his shop. I reckon it's been bought at last.'

'Good Lord, it'll be full of rats by now!' Uncle Gilbert commented; another nightmare. 'Anyway, I'm off, Rachel. Tell your mother to take it easy on this trip. If she gets much thinner she's going to disappear altogether.'

I gathered up the cups and made for the cloakroom, and they trooped off down the stairs. I knew Uncle Gilbert would be composing his report before any of it happened. '*The mayor's parlour was graced by several members of the county's oldest families this afternoon in an effort to raise money for . . .*' I couldn't remember which of Maxine's charities was on show this time. Gilbert had told me proudly not long ago that his wife was responsible for raising half a million pounds for one of her many projects. I hadn't believed him but as Tom said, Maxine would not take no for answer. So it was possible.

I picked up some stuff with my name on it, stuffed it in my bag, and went into the lane, where my bike waited dutifully, locked to the lamp post. I usually walked to the office, but that afternoon I intended cycling out to see Mum to talk over the Düsseldorf trip. I swung into Northgate, and then on an impulse crossed over into Kings Square and from there into Eastgate. As I pedalled towards the railway crossing I wondered what on earth I was doing, and at first told myself I would turn off at Derby Road and go to my parents' that way, maybe past Meriel's old house. But I knew what I was doing, really. And when I relocked my bike by the ash lane at the end of Mr Silverman's block, it was quite clear to me that if I could get into that house I might get rid of two nightmares: the memory of Mr Silverman hanging brokenly from his ceiling, and the terror of marauding rats. It was the sort of thing Meriel would do. 'Come on, face up to it . . .' I could almost hear her voice. 'Stop being such a ninny . . .'

Actually, it worked. The door in the garden wall was off its hinges and propped in the yard, so I walked past it and down the area steps. The door there was open; the hallway which ran past the kitchen was swept clean and painted in Walpamur's apple green and the little living room, which was directly beneath the shop, was empty of overturned chair and suspended body, painted in rosebud-pink with lino in an imitation wood-block pattern. It looked fresh, clean, and, with the wind gusting outside, offered a cheerful little sanctuary. Needless to say it was rat-free.

There were sounds from above – hammering and sawing – but I had seen all I needed. I stood for a moment and deliberately conjured up the memory of poor Mr Silverman. It was another time, and therefore another place. I turned and retraced my steps, unlocked my bike, and cycled out to the rough road and Mum.

That night Tom told me he had met someone from the *Midshires Post* who was covering the Strassen murder. Apparently the killer claimed to be the great-nephew of Alfred Silverman.

Tom was agog. 'You know how I told you the first day we met that Silverman was a marvellous man who offered asylum to Jewish refugees before the war, en route from Germany to the United States? Guess who worked with him? Eva Schmidt! You remember – Wilhelm Strassen's girlfriend. She fed the refugees as they arrived. The old man had two other houses by the pump rooms – Eva lived in one of them, and was like a housekeeper. More than a housekeeper: she translated for the refugees, helped them to organize their finances. They stayed until they could get patrons in the States to vouch for them. It was well organized. Silverman had contacts all over the place.' Tom was flushed and excited. All I could manage was a forced, 'Golly.' Tom was caught up in it again; he was rounding the bits we had into a proper picture. It would make it more and more difficult to forget the whole thing.

'Of course—' Tom swept on, 'I mentioned Dad to this reporter – like I always do. When I said Fairbrother he almost gawped at me. "*Jack* Fairbrother?" he said. "The cartoonist?" I said yes, and he went on and on about Dad's work and how he had started a trend which was being carried on by Giles . . .' Tom's face was alight, as it always was when he spoke of his father's work. He loved meeting people who remembered the old days of the *Birmingham News*. It was as if he could keep his father alive by talking about him. 'He suggested I go to the new offices in Birmingham and see if any of his stuff is still around. We could go on Sunday if you felt up to it, Rache.'

My heart sank. The past would not let go; one way or another we were still held by it. I smiled. 'Of course, darling.'

'And by the way, Rache—' Tom appeared at the bathroom door; he was scrubbing his teeth so it was difficult to decipher what he said. 'Jim reckons it wasn't suicide at all.'

I frowned. 'Who is Jim?'

He went back and I heard him spit vigorously. Then he called, 'Sorry. Jim is the chap from the *Midshires Post*. Mainly agricultural stuff, so they're loving the Strassen murder, makes a bit of a change.'

'Oh. Ghoulish.'

'Not really. Jim reckons he was such a good chap – Silverman. Had no reason to top himself. Must have been murdered.'

My heart sank further still.

I had a feeling we were never going to free ourselves from the past.

Twelve

March 1953, Florida

Dearest, dearest Rache, we are coming! At last, at long last, Vicky and Georgie are going to see the twins – and where it all began. And Rex and I can walk in the park and revisit the scene of the crime – well, the first one, anyway. Almost eight years since I saw you, Rache. And if it weren't that our poor old king has died and Elizabeth is being crowned, I wouldn't be seeing you now, sweetie. As you probably have gleaned from my previous correspondence (ho-hum) my darling husband is a snob. He wants to be able to say – and he wants his kids to be able to say – We Was There! One sad thing is, Aunt Mabe has decided not to come with us. I did so want her to see everything – not the new Queen and Buckingham Palace and the Tower and everything like that – the ordinary things, the places you and me lived in, the air we breathed, the scents we learned to appreciate or hate, the shops, the streets that were made by the Romans, Southgate where you can almost hear the tumbril rumbling up from Berkeley bringing poor old Edward's body to the cathedral. Do you know, Rache, when we used to stare at his effigy lying there I used to think it was really him turned to stone and that was how you and me would end up! Oh Rache, can we go up into the whispering gallery again? Have you got a spare bike I could borrow so that just you and me can go down to Rodley and swim in the river . . . shall we build a dam in Twyver's Brook with a special hole for the sticklebacks to ride through? But listen up, best friend, if you so much as breathe a word about Mr Silverman or Wilhelm Strassen or any of that business back in '44, you can build the damn by yourself. OK? Tom's dad . . . fine. Tom has got a good reason for being obsessed. You haven't.

Darling, Rex has come in, and says don't worry about hiring a television as we're *all* going to London, and the television at the hotel is enormous. He is insisting on doing this, Rache. It's no good your father going all hoity-toity about it. It's only a couple of nights, after all. We get the whole thing on the picture box (that's what Vicky calls it) and can step out on to the balcony to get a two-minute glimpse of the real live thing.

Now, darling, to more serious things – though what could be more serious than this wonderful trip I have no idea. Try harder with your dad. I just can't imagine him without his Flo, but it is obvious he needs to get out more. Is there anything I can do while we're over? I want to help, Rache. I thought when the twins were born that he would begin to live again: he's a natural father and I thought he'd be a natural grandfather. But it sounds – reading between the lines in your last letter – as if the girls somehow make it worse. That means he is missing out on seeing you as well, doesn't it? Oh, I know Tom has them when he's home, but it's not quite the same – for one thing, you go out to the rough road all the time. Why won't he meet you and go to the pictures? Or come with you to one of the symphony concerts you're so keen on? He can't face going out any more, that's why. There's a proper medical name for that. I can't remember it and must ask Gus next time I see him. And that's what your dad has got. And remember I always wanted him for a dad myself 'cos my dad is hopeless. So I've got a stake in all this. I'm going to crash into your old house – where angels fear to tread, apparently – and I'm going to act on him like a dose of salts. It's going to be cards on the table, and I shall tell him that if he hasn't come out of his shell by the time I come back here, then I want my money back. That's it, Rache. I'll plonk a thousand dollars on the dining table. We've got money coming out of our ears, hon. But don't tell him that. It's my stake. OK?

Enough. Let me bring you up to date on the Center for Learning. Yes, we had the visit from Eleanor herself. It was our third anniversary party and as you know, Georgie's fifth birthday. Thank you so much for the present, hon. I love it when you knit and sew things. Don't ever apologize for the mistakes, Rache, they're like pearls to me. Anyway, Mrs R. What a woman; built like a battleship, moves like one too, talks about 'my dear Franklin' as if he's sitting in that bloody wheelchair right beside her. He probably is, too, only the rest of us can't see him. Georgie held Rebekkah's hand – I told you he's in love with this little girl, didn't I? She's got cerebral palsy, and her hands fly about all over the place, but Georgie just holds on to them with a kind of grim determination. He took the flowers off her lap, put them between her two hands, and held the hands close, pushing them forwards towards Mrs R. Oh, Rache. I looked at Vicky and she was jerking her head at her father. Can you believe it – he was wiping his eyes.

I reckon he might be getting there, Rache. Difficult to say, of course, when he's still seeing Dawn most weekends. But then, I've got Gus, so neither of us cares. But I want him to care about Georgie and the other kids at the center. I want everyone in the whole world to care.

Rache, I can tell that you don't like the idea of Gus and me, so I'm not going to mention it again: either in my letters or when we're talking properly, face to face. It doesn't mean much, which is hard for you to understand. This is the Dennis Nightingale in me. The tough cookie you describe as my birth-mother . . . DM . . . she's there, too. She's saying – you're not hurting anyone, and it stops you going mad about Rex and Dawn. But I realize that you and Aunt Mabe . . . and probably your dad . . . just don't understand. So no more. Though I'm not sure that list would have included your mum. I often used to think she was tougher than you and your dad thought, right down deep inside. Anyway, no more. Don't worry, it's all well under control.

Honey, don't worry either about where we'll all stay for that precious month. Rex has it all organized. He's taken a house in Cheltenham. It overlooks the college cricket field, would you believe. But he actually took it because it's almost next door to the hospital. It's for his sake, not Georgie's. We know exactly what to do when Georgie fits, but it still almost kills Rex to see it happen. He wants to be able to get a specialist on the dot!

He was slightly fazed when Aunt Mabe decided not to come. Who was going to look after 'things'? His wife is a well-known hopeless cleaner, cook, et cetera, et cetera. But he's fixed that now. The US air force base at Fairford found him the house – lots of their officers have brought their wives across the pond and have houses in Cheltenham – and they will arrange the hired help. Rex is dealing directly with some colonel chap who is actually going to let us use his car while we're over there. Rex has always wanted to drive one of those big Jaguars with the leaping mascot on the hood and guess what – it is a Jag. Enough said. Next year, Rache, it will be eight years since he shoved me over in the park. I've changed, darling, I hope you'll recognize me. But Rex has stayed the same, so no difficulties there.

My love as always. That blob there is Georgie's fingerprint. Meriel

PS What I said before about not talking 1944 stuff . . . forget it. Talk to me about it and let me take it away with me. All this stuff about the past clawing at us – I don't like it, Rache. You sound like I felt after Vicky.

By the way, I've written to Hermione. Yes, I know we never got on and probably that will be exactly the same. But apparently she has specialized in genetic malfunctions. You never know, we might be able to help each other. I'd like her to visit the center some time, give her some ideas.

I stared at that last paragraph, caught beneath the glue of the air letter. Daisy and Rose were taking their mid-morning nap, and I had saved the letter until now, when I could read it with a cup of coffee. Tom was coming home in a couple of hours so that I could talk to Maria Nightingale about the new Coronation ball-gowns she had designed for the county Coronation dinner at the Shire Hall. Each one was exclusive; they had already sold on the design sketches alone. Nightingale's was doing better than the big shops in Cheltenham's Promenade; that had never happened before. And I was finding them a constant source for my 'Notes on a Coronation' published every Saturday in the *Clarion*. The only big snag was – I had to work from midnight to three a.m. every Wednesday night and it took me four days and nights to get over it. In fact I don't think I did get over it.

I fingered Meriel's air letter, and imagined her neat fingers holding it still while she scribbled her thoughts, and reported events, and kept an eye on Georgie – all at the same time. It sounded as though Rex had fallen into the way of trying to undermine his wife's confidence – maybe because she was so capable. I read that bit again, and decided he was not succeeding: Meriel chose what she would do with her life, and did it exceedingly well. Then I read the whole letter again, because there was a lot there. I had got used to the idea of Meriel coping with so much. I realized her life had changed completely in the last four or five years. She had accepted living back in Florida, the 'compromise' being that they moved out of the compound and bought their own house with its own pool. But when she had started running the centre, the change had been measurable from letter to letter. She had become an aggressive fund-raiser, first of all. With only three children attending for two hours a day, and a four-day week, she had demanded a Steiner-trained teacher for two of those days; and as numbers practically exploded she had found someone from the Montessori school to come on the other days. She had sent me photographs of what she grandly called 'the campus'. The toys were designed by the original Montessori chool, with plenty of input from Meriel. It was first time I had ever seen a ball pool . . . plained it to me in a later letter. The visit s Roosevelt was one of many peaks in the life of the centre. I imagined Georgie making it possible for Rebekkah to present the famous visitor with her obligatory flowers, and tears came into my eyes. They weren't simply sentimental tears, either, they came from the realization that when Meriel had said goodbye to me back in 1948 – when she had determined to 'set sail for America' and be a good American wife – she had meant it. And it had happened. Meriel was coming home; but would she still be my friend?

The other thing was her ban – and then withdrawal of it – of all discussion on the Strassen business. Surely I had put the whole Strassen thing from me by now? I might be talking about it in my letters to Meriel. Yet I was far more concerned about Daisy and Rose; about Dad; about Mum not being here to conduct Beethoven's Fifth; about Tom quite suddenly not being obsessed with looking for his dad. I wondered, not for the first time, whether he had received any official confirmation of Jack Fairbrother's death. Surely he would have told me? But the truth was, we had so little time for talking. It was getting better – Tom kept telling me that – but when we had first moved to this tall old house in Chichester Street, I had been under the impression, until we actually arrived, that we would be moving into number twenty-two not number twenty-one. Which meant the opposite side of the street, an entirely different view from the back windows, the sun with us in the mornings instead of the afternoons . . . Neither of us could understand how it had happened. I hadn't been able to view it before the auction, and we'd moved in the moment the contract was signed, so that the babies had separate rooms. We had thought that would solve our problems. It hadn't. But I preferred number twenty-one, anyway. Morning sun started the day off rather nicely. Tom had agreed with me, but said, 'We have got to start communicating properly again, Rache. We haven't had time to ourselves since the twins were born – we hurl instructions and comments between us like bullets—'

'It started before the twins. It started when Mum died,' I had said in a low voice.

I don't think he heard that. He had said, 'Everything will be better now.' He'd bought two enamelled plaques, with 'Daisy's room' on one and 'Rose's room' on the other. They wouldn't wake each other up, they could have separate naps . . . new house, new beginnings . . . That had been a year ago and life had got steadily harder. Last night there had been more snow – it was March and the daffodils were all out – which meant I couldn't take the girls to their Rhyme and Rhythm class this morning, which meant they were fed up by ten thirty. I put a record on the turntable and tried to get them to clap their hands in time to the music of Henry Hall. It was exactly the same sort of thing Daphne Beard did at her wonderful innovative music and movement class, but they weren't interested. Daphne had married straight from school and had two boys, one seven years old and the other five. She had started her class last summer, and had suggested I take the twins 'just to watch'. They had taken to it like ducks to water, mainly because of Roland and Colin. But of course the charismatic Roland and Colin weren't at twenty-one Chichester Street that Tuesday morning. After reading to the twins for ten minutes, giving them their orange juice – another five minutes – sitting them on their potties in front of the fire for all of two minutes, I had advanced the time of their naps by an hour. I sat there in front of the fire, coffee on the floor, Meriel's flimsy letter on my knee, and allowed the usual hopelessness to start creeping up from ankles to waist – and just stopped it before it reached my heart. I stopped it in the usual way. Counting my blessings.

I liked this house. It reminded me of my grandparents' cottage at the end of the Barton; it was big, and the hall floor was tiled, and the front door had coloured glass in it, so that the tiles were different colours depending on the time of the day and the quality of the light. I liked the thought that it was all ours.

But I missed Mrs Price, who had been a real brick when I had come home from hospital with the girls. I had thought Dad would be there for me – like Meriel, I had imagined the girls might take the edge off Mum's death. But Meriel was right, it had seemed to make it worse. Mum would have been so good with them, so wonderfully good. He couldn't bear the thought of what they were missing. He couldn't bear it, either, that she would never know them.

I leaned forward and warmed my hands. Nor could I bear it. I wished so much that Mum had had a sister. I wished there was an Aunt Mabe for me.

But – back to that paragraph again – I couldn't possibly have resurrected the Strassens and Mr Silverman whatever Meriel said, for the simple reason that I had no time to worry about them any longer. It took every ounce of energy – and more – for me to get through each day. I had welcomed Uncle Gilbert's suggestion that I might like to do some kind of a column to show how the Coronation of our young Queen affected the city and the people in it. I thought it would do me good to get away from babies for a while. I had not envisaged the interviews, the notes and the midnight oil once a week.

I finished my coffee and got up to make soup for our lunch, then stood there with my back to the fire, re-reading the whole letter. Then I stared through the window at the snow falling on the little canyon that was Chichester Street. It was a narrow road, the houses parapeted, so that they looked like a solid wall pierced uniformly by identical windows and doors. Covered already by the snow blanket were coal holes and boot scrapers outside each house. Meriel and I had cut through this way sometimes on the way home from school; to get away from Hermione. The road looped around then ran parallel with Northgate. I wondered what Meriel would make of the road, now I lived in it. If June proved to be a hot and sunny month, it might take on that drab, tired look so much of the city had had since the war. And when she discovered how hopeless I was at being a mother, perhaps our friendship would die a death. Would her letters become infrequent and more reserved? And then stop?

From above came the first of the wake-up calls; I took my coffee cup into the kitchen and stuck Meriel's letter behind the clock on the mantelpiece. I was willing to bet that first call came from Rose; she had entered the world first and in a dreadful hurry. I was right; as I started upstairs her familiar 'Mumumum' escalated into a screeched 'Mummee!', followed by Daisy's cry of protest from the next bedroom. I lifted them out and shepherded them into our bedroom for a really good view of the snow. It was bitterly cold upstairs, no heating of course. We sat three abreast on the top stair and eased ourselves gently down on our bottoms, pretending we were sliding downhill on toboggans. I didn't mind things taking a long time; there were still two hours to go before Tom arrived home and took over. By the time I had inserted four legs into two pairs of dungarees, fitted slippers on to four feet and topped everything off with cardigans, it was time for lunch. We sat around for as long as they would, dunking bread in our soup, trying – not always successfully – to keep the ends of our hair out of the bowls, and not to wipe soupy fingers on our cardigans. There was the usual struggle to flannel their faces and hands afterwards, then they sat on the identical wooden engines Uncle Gilbert had given them at Christmas, and shunted from kitchen to living room, while I washed up, made sandwiches, and peeled some potatoes for the evening meal.

It was heaven to see Tom. I kissed him as if he'd been away for a fortnight instead of just seven hours. He misjudged things as usual and said, 'I wish you didn't have to go out in this, darling. It's really treacherous underfoot.'

And I said, 'Cake in tin. Sandwiches. Rosehip syrup. Back for bath time.'

He groaned. 'Oh God . . .'

I said, 'Well, I'm communicating important things.'

'I know.' He gathered Rose and Daisy to him, one on each arm; it looked easy. He said, 'Shall we watch Mummy slide down the road?'

They were really keen on seeing that. Tom played with them so well . . . so well.

I had a nice time with Maria Nightingale. I wondered what Meriel would make of that. When I got home the sky was full of stars, and the snow like cake icing. I wondered whether Tom and I could stand outside for a while after the twins were asleep, but knew I would be too tired, too cold, too everything.

I let myself in and children poured over me. 'Mummee, Mummee . . .' Daisy had a new word, it sounded like 'Bandee Bandee'. She called Dad 'Grandee'; was he there, in our living room? I hurried through, Tom was in the kitchen on his own. Pots and pans were on the table.

'We've got something to show you, haven't we, girls?' They nodded, full of importance. 'Up you get, then.' They scrambled on to their chairs and knelt so that they were hip-high to the table. Rose picked up a spoon and banged a saucepan.

'Not yet . . . wait for it—'

Tom lifted a wooden spoon high, and

suddenly I knew what game they had been playing; what it was they had to show me.

Tom boomed sonorously, 'Bom, bom, bom-de-bom—'; then a semitone lower, 'Bom bom-de-bom—'. And they were off. Saucepans, frying pans, Tom's voice roaring Beethoven's famous notes.

It was the Fifth. He had taught them the opening bars of the Fifth Symphony.

Thirteen

I said, 'You haven't changed. Not a bit. You are still you.'

Tears poured down her face. 'You have changed. You're skinnier than ever and – damn it all, Rache – there's a grey streak from there to there.' She touched my hair above the left eye. 'No need for that!'

I smiled. 'You've got a rotten memory. I had it at school. When Daphne clonked me with her hockey stick – I lost the pigment or something. She reminded me just the other day.'

Meriel drew back. The tears were making runnels in her makeup. She said, 'You're beautiful, Rache. You're so like Flo Throstle. So much.'

That did it, of course. I knew I had Mum's cloud of dark hair, and her pointed chin and curly mouth and brown eyes, but to me they had never added up to Mum's beauty. I certainly did not have her luminosity. I was grey, just like the streak in my hair. I grabbed Meriel and knocked her hat sideways as I bent down and hid my own tears in her curls; yes, she still had her Shirley Temple curls. She also had a ballerina skirt layered with a great many petticoats, from the feel of her. She protested as I squashed all of them; Tom and Rex stopped shaking hands and stood by us; and the young black woman called Sheba who had come to Southampton with us from Cheltenham picked up Georgie and led Vicky towards our two girls. She knelt down, right there on the dock, and started the introductions. I could see she was going to be a gem because Daisy came forward ahead of Rose and kissed Georgie. Rose was suddenly, and not typically, shy.

Rex said, 'Listen . . . girls . . . let's get somewhere a little more private, shall we? Honey, no need to cry quite so hard . . . Tom, is Rachel OK?'

Tom had a hand in the small of my back. I glanced at him; he was smiling widely. 'I think she's more than OK. OK has nothing to do with anything much at the moment.'

I was so proud of him saying that. We might not be too good at communicating lately, but he still understood. He knew. For me, seeing Meriel again was like going back to the time when Mum was alive. I suddenly realized why Tom had chased the memory of his father so hard.

He said, 'I've got that Jaguar in the car park – not far. Shall we drive out of the town and find somewhere for tea?'

Rex's face lit up. Meriel snuffled, 'Oh Tom. That would be lovely. But how shall we all get into it? Four of us, four of you and this – this – angel of mercy.' She held out a free hand without disengaging me. 'Sheba. The Queen of Sheba, no less. Thank you so much.' Then turned back to Tom. 'Nine people?'

Tom said, 'Four of them very small. One driver and four laps.'

Rex went to sort out luggage. There were four trunks somewhere, all labelled with the Cheltenham address. There were two overnight bags. They went in the boot – trunk – then came out again so that Merry could find Georgie's stuffed rabbit, and then at last we wedged ourselves into the car, and Rex sat behind the wheel looking like an excited schoolboy. 'Gee. A stick. Look at this, honey – everything on the left . . . wow, see the clock? This car will do a hundred! See this, Vicky?'

'Sure, Daddy. Can I sit on Uncle Tom's lap? And Daisy here and Rose on Mommy's lap—'

But Georgie wanted Mommy's lap and wanted to be very close to Rose, too. I realized suddenly she was frightened of him, and that was why she was hanging back. I pulled her on to my knee, and then leaned down and put my face against Georgie's. 'Welcome to England, darling,' I said. 'We're so pleased to see you at last.'

His strangely tilted eyes studied me for a moment very solemnly, then he grinned and said, 'Me too.' He pushed out his tongue. I felt Rose tense.

Meriel looked at her. 'He does that all the time, honey. You get used to it.' Rose didn't understand, of course, she was only two. She put her head on my shoulder and kept very still.

It was a long drive and some of Rex's enthusiasm for English classic cars had abated by the end of it. The children had most definitely had enough. Sheba proved her worth over and over again, but we changed our plans at Oxford and decided Rex would drop Tom and me and the girls first and then go to Cheltenham and settle his own family without our help.

Meriel was disappointed. She wanted me to see the Cheltenham house and then have dinner and chat the night away. I wondered how that could happen. What about bed time and Rex and Tom, and wasn't she just a bit tired? I was absolutely exhausted. I managed to wave them off while Meriel screamed with delight at our boot scraper, then Tom and I gave up. The girls went into their cots without a murmur and without a bath. Tom and I had a cup of tea and some toast and staggered upstairs at eight thirty. I wondered how on earth we were going to cope with a month of this.

Vicky and Georgie were instantly at home in the Cheltenham house, the Chichester Street house, Daphne Beard's big through-room in Barnwood where they took the Rhyme and Rhythm sessions in their stride – and where Roland and Colin, Daphne's amazingly polite boys, both fell in love with Vicky – and my old home down the rough road, where Dad watched with a stunned expression as they ran around like creatures from the Amazon jungle.

Meriel said, 'Do you mind awfully, George?' Her American accent had disappeared like snow in summer. 'They're just showing off in front of Daisy and Rose. They'll calm down in a minute. Vicky knows when. If Georgie tanks about too much he can have a fit, and she hates that.'

Dad looked worried; he had never looked worried before . . . Mum. He had always been in control of whatever was happening. I tried to take Mum's place and glinted a smile at him. 'She called you George!' I said.

And, amazingly, Dad smiled back. 'It's my name. I think.' He looked at Meriel. 'May I call you Merry?'

It wasn't much of a riposte but it started

Meriel off again. It didn't take much. The sight of Twyver's Brook; my old satchel hanging in number twenty-one; the little plot where Mum was buried. She said to me, 'I had to leave it for eight years to realize how precious it all was.'

But Dad was still all right; he draped an arm around her shoulders. 'The trouble with you two girls is that you've kept such stiff upper lips all this time.'

And Meriel, acting on him like a dose of salts, as she had forecast, said, 'You're a fine one to talk!'

But all this wonderful stuff happened after the trip to London to watch the Coronation.

Rex had wanted to book us all in at the Ritz, but London in June 1953 was full to bursting point, and in the end he had got two 'family suites' in a very comfortable hotel just off the Edgware Road, where we got a glimpse of Marble Arch from one of the balconies. Heaven knows what it cost. One of the other scientists at the Space Center had a brother who knew the MD of the hotel chain . . . it got complicated, but it was an excellent hotel. Neither Tom nor I had stayed in a hotel before. Dad had been to Germany, of course, but otherwise he was as raw as we were. We delighted in our two nights of luxury, and the full English breakfast, and the dinner which commenced with Windsor soup. Rose wanted nothing else; she had four plates of Winzie soup and asked for more at breakfast time. It was the kind of hotel that agreed, smilingly, to dish up soup for breakfast, and for a long time afterwards that was what Rose enjoyed every morning.

On the morning of 2 June, we were woken by a strange murmuring sound. I glanced at the grey light filtering through the curtains and decided it was rain, but when the little chamber maid brought tea – silver tray and pot – and opened the curtains, she reported the overnight crowds just waking up. 'Poor things,' she said, peering out. 'It's a sharp breeze out there, they must be that cold.' Tom and I carried the girls to the window to join her. The narrow side road was full of people, and when we leaned out and looked towards Marble Arch we saw where they had slept all night long. 'It's a carpet of people,' Tom told Daisy. 'Look . . . can you see them wrapped in blankets? They're running about in the park to keep warm.'

Rose ran next door to call Grandee, and Dad came in wearing his threadbare pyjamas. I realized how shabby we all were. When two minutes later the Robinsons joined us, this was even more evident. Meriel's matching nightdress and negligee were pure silk, and Rex sported an alpaca dressing gown – 'I had to wear it in bed – gee, is it cold for midsummer!' But he hadn't grumbled about the food last night, unlike the Americans on the next table. He remembered the drastic economies during the war, and had guessed that we weren't far away from all that. I decided that I rather liked Rex, especially when I managed to cut out Dawn from the equation. He and Tom got on really well. And he was polite to Meriel, and loving to Vicky – and sometimes to Georgie, too.

As planned, we spent our time between the television room and the balcony. All the children preferred the television; it was cold and wet on the balcony and there was nothing to see until that glimpse of the royal coach. But when that glimpse came, Vicky surprised us all by bursting into tears. It worried Georgie; he clasped her around the waist and buried his face in her flimsy summer dress.

'What is it, honey?' Merry asked, stooping down. No chance of Rex comforting her, he was craning over the balcony rail clicking his camera wildly. But Vicky did not really need comfort, she needed empathy, which she was getting from the other children. She looked at them and wailed, 'I love her. I'm half-English so she is mine as well as yours, and I love her.' So of course Rose cried properly, Daisy forced a few tears and Tom lifted up as many of them as he could, starting with Vicky, and perched them on his shoulders so that they had the best view of all.

It was over in minutes. We had all seen the Queen on the day she dedicated herself to us, and looking around I thought that maybe the same sort of thing had happened between Meriel's family and mine. As Tom said later, 'Poor lass. She's got to take us on, warts and all.' And that's how we had to be with each other. Warts and all.

So, for the rest of that month, we did just that. Daphne Beard turned up trumps and entertained all the children once a week, while Meriel dragged me into the old house to chat with her mother. I found it difficult. Myrtle Nightingale had to be well aware that I visited Maria once a week; I had tried to make it sound as if it was all in the cause of the 'Notes on a Coronation' but she was canny enough to realize that such regular visits weren't strictly necessary. Probably Dennis, with his usual tact, had told her how well we got on together. It was just as difficult for Meriel, when we went in to the shop to see her father and birth-mother. I knew that Maria would have liked to have given her one of the Coronation 'specials', but after the fiasco of the green dress she did not dare. When we came away, Meriel actually said, 'God. I'd love one of her outfits! You can see how she nobbled Dad, can't you? Dressed up like Lady Muck, clothes rationing or no clothes rationing.'

I said, 'Be fair, Merry. Surely it was your

adopted mother who did the nobbling? You were actually born when your dad got engaged to her. Maria was left right out in the cold.'

'I'm not sure. I rather think Mum and Dad were in the middle of a long engagement when I came along. Poor old Mum was so besotted she took me on as well as him. Dad didn't want to lose her – she had money. God, he's such a rotter.'

'She still loves him, Merry. And Maria does, too. He must have something.'

She gave a rueful smile. 'Don't I know it. Guess that's why I behaved so badly when I was at home. I hated him for making me love him – hated myself more!'

'You were a crazy mixed-up kid,' I said fondly.

'And you were a spoiled only child. What a mixture.'

'Yes.' I thought back. It had been wonderful. Just wonderful.

Meriel punched my arm. 'Come on. Snap out of it. Your mum was an angel who had lost her wings. She's found them again.'

That did it. Dad came in and told us once more it was a good thing to loosen up now and then. And Meriel put her arms round him and held him close. She was doing that quite often. He held himself still at first; now he put his face against her curls and closed his eyes for a minute.

* * *

One Saturday Meriel told me she had invited Hermione to tea. 'I'll take the kids. Don't worry, Sheba is a natural with them. You write your column and get sorted. I want Doc Hermione to have a good look at Georgie in a child-oriented environment. That's medical speech for watching his normal behaviour patterns. He's due for a fit. It would be excellent if he had it while she was around.'

Sometimes Meriel amazed me. I stared at her, speechless, and she shrugged. 'I know. But what's the point in not accepting it?'

'I – I thought . . . Hermione might know of some special treatment . . .' I faltered.

It was her turn to be amazed. 'You must know that nothing can make Georgie better? I just need to hear another opinion of what his potential might be.' She checked herself and then said, 'I don't mean "better". Georgie is a complete Georgie. I need to know what I can do – how I can change myself – to make human behaviour more acceptable for him.' She shook her head, smiling at me. 'Sorry, Rache. This is something I've thought about so much. Georgie is in a minority and minorities are always supposed to conform to the majorities. Why is that? Why shouldn't the majorities change to accommodate the minorities?'

I was amazed. 'You sound very . . . political.'

'Perhaps I am.' She hugged me suddenly. 'Georgie can't argue his case, Rache. I can. If that's political, then that's what I am!'

We were on our way to the cathedral and the whispering gallery. I took Georgie and Vicky, she took the twins, and we stationed ourselves as far from each other as possible. The gallery surrounded the nave far below, and we waved across the vast space, and then Meriel's voice was in our ears. 'Hi there, Yankees. What do you think those old builders were up to?'

Vicky started to laugh and we heard Rose gasp with surprise. I said, 'I guess they ran out of wire for the first telephone?' Vicky was convulsed and Georgie whispered, 'Where's Mommee?' And jumped when her voice came loud and clear, 'Give me a wave, honey. And I'll wave back.'

We had a whale of a morning. It was mid-week and the cleaners were in. We stayed for two hours learning to appreciate those old builders. Then we had lunch at the Tudor tea rooms, where, to Rose's absolute delight, they served Winzie soup.

Rex accompanied Tom on a trip to Upton-upon-Severn where Nobby Clarke now lived. Tom had kept in touch with this veteran of the Burma railway and was delighted when Rex offered to drive him to Upton and take Nobby out to lunch. 'Give me a break from family life!' he joked. I looked at Tom but he hadn't noticed; he was as excited as a schoolboy at the prospect of introducing Rex to Nobby, and having another, roomier drive in the Jaguar.

'It will take you all of half an hour to drive there,' I said. I wasn't wet blanketing the expedition, it was going to be wonderful to have the house to myself and finish my weekly column without losing a night's sleep. Anyway, Tom was undeterred.

'Maybe we can take Nobby out for a bit of a run.' He glanced at me. 'After all, I did drive the car down to Southampton. I don't see why I can't have another go.' I grinned. Dear Tom wanted to drive the car again.

When Rex arrived he loaded the girls into the back with much arranging and re-arranging; they would return to Cheltenham and drop the twins off there to play with Vicky and Georgie while Hermione 'observed' them all. Tom and Rex would head off to Worcestershire. It was such a wonderful thing to have a car, apart from the obvious excitement of being able to go exactly where you wanted to. Trains and buses were all very well but they didn't allow for armfuls of soft toys, bottles of orange Corona, swimming costumes and so on. I wondered whether Tom and I would ever have a car. Dad steadfastly refused to get one; he used his old bike, and when that was stolen from outside the *Clarion* office he used Mum's.

I enjoyed that day. There was still almost a week before Rex and Meriel went back and already they were talking of coming again . . . of us going out there. I felt relaxed about the whole thing; that pall of exhaustion was lifting at last. I worked easily and well. It was good to think of Tom talking to Nobby Clarke, being with Rex; it was wonderful to think of Rose and Daisy playing with Vicky and Georgie, watched over by the angelic Sheba . . . and I suppose the strange doctor who was actually Hermione Smith.

It was almost time for their reappearance when Dad turned up, as he sometimes did on a Friday on his way home from paying bills and shopping. I was delighted. Usually the girls were at their most grizzly when he popped in at that time. Tonight I put the kettle on and we sat in the back garden with tea and scones and watched the willow in next door's garden moving gently in the breeze. Nothing could have been more peaceful.

Dad said suddenly, 'How would you feel if I went back with the Robinsons for a little holiday?'

I laughed. 'A contradiction in terms, if ever there was one. Holiday? Robinsons?' I glanced at him and said, surprised. 'Are you serious? You know I would be really pleased.'

He grinned and nodded, and looked like Dad used to look. 'I am serious. Meriel and

Rex have both been on to me about it. At first, of course, I simply discounted the idea – didn't consider it for a moment. But then . . . I'm not sure, Rache. I need something. It might actually be a holiday with Meriel.'

'Well . . . I can't imagine you over there. But then I don't know what over there is like. Would you go with them – by sea?'

'I haven't got that far but I don't think so. Give them time to settle back in and then maybe fly over.'

'That sounds sensible.' There was a silence. I didn't hold on to it deliberately to make Dad say anything. I simply couldn't think of anything to say. He must have made up his mind . . . he must have talked it over with Merry and Rex. He hadn't said anything till now. And neither had they.

He took a huge breath, let it go and said very quietly, 'I have to tell you something, Rache. About the trip to Düsseldorf.'

It was getting more and more surprising. The trip to Düsseldorf had been at the beginning of Mum's final illness, and we never spoke of it. Mum had said she enjoyed it, and everyone was very kind. Dad had said nothing at all. For some reason I gripped the arms of my garden chair.

Dad's voice became quieter still. 'It was the Wingco who got me in on that trip, you know.'

'Hermione's father? No, I didn't know.'

'He wanted to show me something. He wanted to show Mum as well. She did a little shopping with the other wives, but the main thing was her visit to the factory.'

'Of course.'

'Yes. Well. It was the actual production line for the Dornier props. Their main factory is in Friedrichshafen. This was where they specialized in . . . adaptations, I suppose you would call it.' He put his cup on to the grass. 'She didn't want to come. She was adamant. But the whole purpose of the trip – the real purpose – was for her to see that what I had done was . . . meaningless.'

I said nothing. Was he blaming himself somehow for Mum's death? How could he be? She had had TB, hidden it from everyone for a year.

'Smith suggested I should take the retirement package being offered to employees of sixty and over. Look after Mum.' He was looking at the grass and the cup as if he expected something. I knew he was upset. Of course. But I did not know what to do.

'It was the Dornier production line. They were making the fins.'

I just stared at him, not understanding.

'The fins, Rache. *My* fins.'

'Like yours?'

He stared back at me, obviously wondering if anyone could be that thick.

'They were mine. Exactly the same.'

'You mean . . . what do you mean?'

'I gave them to Maude Smith and she passed them to Willi Strassen.'

I barely reacted. I heard what he was saying but it meant nothing.

He glanced at me and tightened his mouth then went on. 'Strassen had arrived in this country rather late in the war and wanted to make a name for himself back home in the Fatherland. Maude Smith was under his thumb. I suppose she was in love with him, I have no idea. She knew Mum had access to the official records. She badgered her until Mum's morale was at rock bottom – you know what she was like. And you know what Maude Smith was like, probably still is. So I did my little deal. And it got her off Mum's back.' He actually shrugged. 'It was meaningless, of course. They'd already developed their fins along the same lines as us. But she didn't know that and presumably neither did Strassen.'

He took a deep breath and let it go. 'We were lucky. I don't doubt it would all have started up again except for the raid and Strassen's death.' He glanced at me again and must have registered my total confusion. He said, as if it made everything crystal clear, 'That was why I left Smith's, of course. Maude had told her husband, the dear old Wingco, that I had contravened the Official Secrets Act and he suggested I should take early retirement.'

My face ached, every muscle and nerve taut. He waited but I could not speak; I could not comfort him. I felt sick and ill.

He swallowed audibly. 'It's been difficult, Rache. The only one to stand by me was Gilbert and he did it for Mum's sake. And for yours.' He tried to smile. 'When I told Meriel about it, she immediately said I must go back with them and get into harness again. Whether she means I am to go to work with Rex . . .' he tried to laugh. 'She's a crazy girl, Rache, I'd forgotten just how crazy. But she keeps saying there's a place for me out there – that I've lost my way here and I must give it a go. And I'm beginning to believe her. I need a shake-up, my dearest girl. Can you understand that?'

The word 'understand' meant nothing. I tried to nod. But Willi Strassen, or Fritz as Meriel still called him, was in my life again with an intensity he hadn't had before. And now, linked with Willi Strassen was my Dad. Dad could not have sold anything to Willi Strassen. Could he?

He said, 'Be a bit more convincing, Rachel, there's a dear.'

I glanced at him, then away. Someone had sold those designs, and there was only one person it could have been. We were still close enough to the war for the word 'traitor' to mean something.

I said, 'It's an excellent idea. Really good. Exciting. And Meriel will look after you.'

He forced a laugh. Had he expected me to beg him to stay? He got out of the chair with some difficulty. 'I'm thankful you understand, Rachel. The war has been over for eight years but somehow it lingers. I've been trying to put it all away from me for the past three years – since Mum died. And if this trip to America will help, then I'm all for it, too.'

'Will you be able to afford it?' As I spoke the words I heard their terrible irony. Of course he would be able to afford it. Strassen must have paid through the nose for the fin designs.

'Yes. Of course. It costs so little for one person to live, Rachel. And the mortgage has been paid off.'

I leaned down, gathering our plates and cups; out of sight, I squeezed my eyes shut very tightly. How could this be happening? He had been quietly celebrated for his invention, proud of it, Mum had been proud of it . . . and he sold it. Obviously there was no crippling mortgage on the house any more. As I walked back into the house the crockery shook and clattered in my hands.

Dad noticed. Of course he noticed, he was still my father.

'Darling girl. I know how you feel. I've lived with it for so long now. We talked about it, you know . . . before she died.'

I wanted to shout at him that treason had probably been the last thing she wished to discuss. I nodded dumbly.

'Oh yes. We talked about everything. If this trip to America works, Rachel, I'll tell you what she said to me.' His voice was choking up, and the last thing I wanted was a complete breakdown. Things happen during that sort of breakdown that cannot be clawed back afterwards, and I would not want my father to know that at that moment I was bitterly ashamed of him.

'All right. That's all right with me.' My voice sounded completely normal; it was astonishing. 'Listen, Rex will be dropping off Tom and the girls in the next hour. Why don't you have a lift with them?' I'd said the first thing that came into my head and was immediately aghast. How could I bear another hour with this man who was my father, and did not seem to fully understand what he had done?

He snuffled a little laugh; the moment of near breakdown was gone. 'I've got Mum's bike outside, love. And it's a lovely evening for a ride through the lanes.'

I stood on the doorstep while he unlocked the bike from the boot scraper, then I waved him goodbye as I always did. We were so close, Dad and me. We were . . . friends.

Fourteen

Meriel was ecstatic about Hermione's visit.

'It wasn't only that she got on so well with Georgie – he doesn't like everyone, you know, Rache. It was the way she got him to do things. She brought a picture, just one. I think it was a Rembrandt, and it showed the prodigal son's return – in fact, I'm sure it was the one old Hattie used in art classes at school, d'you remember? Anyway, Hermione mentioned the colours, the clothes, the sandals. And he just nodded and said they were broken . . . the sandals. And then he was off finding those wax crayons and his scrap pad and having a go himself. He works in rectangles – I hadn't sorted that out before, but she noticed it and it's true. An oblong is a person, a square is something else – he depicted that broken sandal as two halves of a sort of rhombus. He gets the colours right, spends ages on that. Then she mounted his picture on to a card right next to the Rembrandt, and put it on the wall, and they just sat and looked at it for ages. You could feel them doing it – it was fantastic! And then after tea – we had it in the garden and Georgie really looked after her – they listened to music. She had a record with her in her briefcase. It was a Souza march. We all had to clap in time to it. Your girls just loved that, honey, it was like one of Daphne's rhythm sessions. Of course Georgie knew exactly what to do. He marched round the sitting room – the radiogram is in there, we couldn't go out, unfortunately. He lifted his legs up high and banged an imaginary drum . . .' Meriel's eyes were full of tears. She paused and grinned at me. 'I'm getting carried away, Rache. It was just so amazing to see Hermione Smith with my son. She is going to write it all up as a report for me to take back home and extract what is needed. She wants to come over and visit!'

'You're going to have quite a house full,' I said.

We were in the garden of the Cheltenham house. The paddling pool was full and the children were climbing in and out and splashing each other indiscriminately. The sort of scene I would remember through next winter . . . for ever, I suppose. I wished my comment hadn't sounded so bitter.

Meriel was still. 'He told you, then?'

'Yes. He's excited about it.'

'Yes. But he . . . *told* you about it?'

I looked at her, my heart suddenly hammering. Surely Dad hadn't confided everything to Meriel before he told me? I swallowed. Of course he had, and he had made a special call when he knew I would be alone . . . it had all been planned with Meriel.

'Yes,' I replied flatly.

She started gabbling again; she had always talked quickly: in rushes and torrents of sentences. I had never thought of it as gabbling before.

She said, 'I guess you're shattered. But . . . it's not as black and white as you think – as I thought, too.' She stood up and smoothed off her cotton skirt. 'Maybe he did do . . . what he says. Maybe money passed hands.' I stood up, too – leapt up. I wanted to tell her to shut up; I wanted to gather up the twins and run out of that lovely garden and pretend I hadn't heard her or Dad or anything. I didn't bother with brushing my skirt, but I leaned down to buckle a loose sandal and squeeze my eyes shut tightly. I was doing that a lot.

'But . . . Hermione and I talked, Rache. We never have, as you know. She was scared of me, and I despised her for being under the thumb of her mother, who was under the thumb of her husband . . . We had this conversation about when you and me tracked old Fritz that time—' She laughed and I managed to join in, but we both knew nothing was funny. 'That's what started *her* talking. She found out where her mother was that morning after the air raid. She was trying to find her sister-in-law. She had been going to see her at half past ten that morning. She did not tell Hermione – made up a dental appointment, as we know. And then, in the early hours those bombs were dropped and she was very worried about the Wingco's sister and left early on her bike, went straight to her house and got in, just as I did later on. And realized that she must have been killed. She lived there, you see – the sister. They kept it very quiet because of course the Wingco was so bloody gung-ho he would have died if anyone had guessed that he came from Austrian stock. His father had anglicized the name before the first war – the Great War – when he brought the family over. Started making stoves . . . kitchen ranges, that sort of thing. It changed during the Great War. Made guns instead. Guns that went into those funny little aeroplanes they flew then. Guns specially synchronized to fire between propeller blades. And because old man Schmidt was so patriotic and so damned clever, no one knew he was Austrian – people were worse about aliens then than in the last war. And by the time his son took over Smith's, the Wingco was in the Royal Air Force and knew everything there was to know about planes and flying. But the Wingco had a sister who felt quite differently.

She was proud of being Austrian. She did not want to embarrass her family so she broke away from them after university and worked for the Ministry of Defence as a translator. She kept her Austrian name, and because she was valuable there was no question of her being interned.'

Meriel stopped and took a deep breath before rushing on again.

'Mrs Smith did not mention any of this to Hermione until Hermione started work in the psychiatric hospital. Then she had to fill in a lot of forms and . . . well, it came up. Hermione reckoned her aunt must have been a pretty amazing person to be able to acknowledge her background the way she did during the war. Eva actually liked to be known as Schmidt. It helped when she was working in that club for the Free French and Poles and Czechs, and later when she was helping a few of the men from the holding camp for internees— You remember that was where she met Fritz. Are you with me, Rache?'

'Yes.' I felt sick. We were never to be free of the war. Not ever.

'So why was Mrs Smith meeting with Eva that morning, Rache? Was it something to do with the Wingco? Was she feeding her sister-in-law information? Was the sister-in-law giving it to Fritz? How does it all fit in with that bloody, bloody tail fin?'

It was then I realized that Meriel was as distressed as I was. Still, it offered no comfort. I almost resented it – what right had she to be so concerned for my father?

She said, 'One thing to be said for her, Mrs Smith, she was very worried about Eva's death, though in fact she never came forward to identify the body. But that morning, if you remember, she didn't arrive home until we were leaving Hermione. And then she came from the rough road. I reckon she cycled out to the holding camp and tried to find out whether Fritz was still on the loose. She knew about Fritz – Eva must have told her – maybe she had even met him and given him that blessed Swallow tie! There was more to it than just having a cup of coffee with Eva. She'd made an appointment . . . to see her sister-in-law?' Meriel shook her head. 'No. She'd made an appointment to see Fritz. She had something for him.'

I made a sound in my throat. She saw that I was at the end of my tether, and tried to put an arm around my shoulders. I straightened quickly so that my shoulders were out of her reach.

She said, 'We've got to let it ride, Rache. It's over and done with. Just let your father come to us for a while. It will work out, honey. I promise.'

I had to stop her talking about Dad. I said, 'So . . . Eva Schmidt was the Wingco's sister.

Hermione's aunt. Eva was in love with Willi Strassen. Quite a . . . a tangle.'

I looked at her just for a moment, and she nodded. She was so small and compact and delicate-looking. And she was as strong as steel. And, I realized, suddenly, I was not.

Tom and Rex had had a wonderful time at Upton-upon-Severn. In spite of losing his leg, Nobby Clarke had a boat, a big, cumbersome rowing boat: 'built like a tank', according to Rex. He had come on a charabanc trip to Upton soon after Tom and I visited him in Liverpool and had fallen in love with that stretch of the Severn. Part of the organized trip had been on the river, but only Nobby and his corporal friend had taken it up. Nobby had had to accept a fireman's lift to get into the prow of the boat and had panted, 'Never again – never a-bloody-gain.' But he had ceased to care about getting in and out very quickly. The magic of this entirely new world, of seeing things he would never have seen from the bank, had enchanted him almost immediately. The curious silence of the heavy river, the dipping of the oars and the way they had creaked in the rowlocks, had made him part of another dimension. They had come to the end of the reach and there, in a small bay of shallow water and pebbles, had lain the bloated body of a dead sheep. 'I like that kind of ending,' he told

Tom soberly. 'I never wanted to die out there, in Burma. Too far away.'

So he had moved to Upton with his family and bought the boat. ''Tisn't beautiful but I got to have something that won't tip over when I get in – I sort of fall in, see.' But there was nothing wrong with his arms, and they developed alarmingly under the regime he set himself.

Tom couldn't stop talking about it. 'Rex took him out in the Jaguar, and of course he enjoyed that. But then he wanted to show Rex what real travel was about and we went down to this little jetty and there was the tank – Rex called it that and Nobby says he'll do the same – and he sat on the edge and just let himself go straight into the stern. Getting out is more difficult.' Tom was so happy, I couldn't tell him – not then – about Dad. He already knew Dad was going to fly out to stay with the Robinsons in the autumn, and he thought I was worried about that. Plus he thought I was still dreading the end of June and the end of Meriel's precious visit. Actually . . . I think I wanted her to leave.

Before that happened, Meriel and I took Hermione to Malvern. In the Jag. There was a cricket match in the college grounds and Rex and a couple of other Americans ensconced themselves quite early in the solitary stand. Sheba was taking the children to the open-air pool in the morning where they were offering swimming lessons to the under-fives. Both Georgie and Vicky were expert swimmers and looking forward to helping the instructor. Meriel bought Daisy and Rose new costumes for the occasion. I had given up protesting about her generosity; actually, I had given up. Full stop.

Meriel and I took it in turns to drive the Jag; Hermione wasn't interested. Neither was I, but I had to keep up a constant pretence now, for Meriel. I am not sure why this was; it had just happened.

That day it wasn't too bad because of Hermione. I had always known that she was very clever, but I had forgotten that Dad had once told Miss Hardwicke that it was curiosity that drove learning. Hermione was curious; she wanted to know . . . things.

I thanked her for giving the children such a good time at Meriel's and asked her how she was herself. I expected the old Hermione-type reply, over-polite, giving nothing away.

She said, 'You mean with the job?' She was sitting next to Meriel, and turned right round to talk to me in the back. 'It's like being a detective, really. You're given clues but they're not always the right ones, and they can be totally misleading. So you sort out what you think are the real ones, then you grill the patient and hope something will kind of fly out at you!' She laughed and she was laughing at herself. She had changed.

'Was it like that with Georgie?'

She rested her cheek against the leather and her strange colourless eyes softened. 'Oh . . . Georgie. He is so special, isn't he? Mind you, most of the kids with that syndrome are the same, they're happy, they're lovable and they're different. They mustn't be lumped together as regards achievement.' She shifted her smile to Meriel, then back to me. 'Georgie could be a standard bearer. That became obvious when he helped his friend Rebekkah to hold out her flowers for Mrs Roosevelt. He is not self-centred. As well as being supported, he is himself a supporter.' She sighed. 'In Georgie's case it is a question of environment. Surrounded by loving stimuli, life will be good for him. His problems were created by us, by society in general, so we know exactly how to solve them. It's not that difficult. And though you have to name various disorders, it's a mistake to go by the labels you give out so readily. Each person is unique and it's difficult to remember that – if you've stuck a big label on them saying Down's syndrome or schizophrenic. So though you've got solutions, they have to be very carefully chosen.'

She sighed. 'It's a bit different for the patients in the psychiatric hospital. They have been wounded. No one can see their wounds but they are there. So they have to be found, and then there has to be a way to help them to heal themselves.' She shook her head helplessly. 'My prof says we're in the business of finding solutions, which means we have to identify the problems first. Sounds pretty hopeless, doesn't it? But if you can learn to be a good detective . . . well, it's possible!' She laughed again, ruefully. I found myself admiring her very much.

We climbed to the beacon and looked over all those English counties with their cathedrals and their rivers and their people. I looked sideways at the two women who had been schoolgirls just yesterday. Hermione held her skirt down against the summer breeze; Meriel let hers fly around her face. I had managed to sit on mine, so that it didn't fly and I did not have to hold it down. I wondered whether Hermione had noted our differences. Probably without realizing it, she was observing, assessing, diagnosing.

At that moment I felt pretty bad; I was in the company of two women who had accomplished a great deal already. I felt I was still at the starting line, and I was nobody's favourite. Suddenly, Meriel pushed her skirt between her knees and gripped it there, then put one arm around Hermione and the other around me.

'I wish you could meet my Aunt Mabe,' she said out of the blue. 'Here we are, still under thirty, still not really knowing anything, looking here and there and everywhere for something meaningful, something that will solve our problems, not really knowing what the hell we've been put on this earth for!' She laughed. 'Aunt Mabe never rushes. She is always just *there.* People come to her with their troubles and find solutions without her saying much – except to tell them they are marvellous people.' She sobered suddenly. 'Do you remember how, when I discharged myself from the maternity unit with Georgie, I asked her to meet me at the back gates in the car? I went out in my robe so that no one would guess I was actually leaving the hospital. She was there, with Vicky. Quite calm. Told me that everything would be fine, and of course I could keep Georgie and bring him up like a proper brother to Vicky. She told Rex to collect my stuff and make it all right with the hospital and he did it. He wouldn't have done it for me.' She squeezed us to her. 'She gave me strength. And that's what we can do for each other. The three of us. Like the bloody musketeers! We can give each other strength.'

'Oh Meriel . . .' Hermione's voice was quavery. 'That's wonderful. I've always wanted to be like my Aunt Eva who was so strong. But this would be better still. Three of us. Like an isosceles triangle!'

I heard Meriel gasp and then shriek with

laughter. She spluttered, 'You can do the math. Rache can do the English. And I'll sweep up the mess – how does that sound?'

Hermione laughed, too and after a second I joined them. It wasn't the moment to be asking what mess Meriel would be sweeping up . . . and why should it be her with the broom?

They left two days later and I cried off going to Southampton this time. The owner of the Jag, who was one of the officers at the US camp at Fairford, drove them there, and Sheba went with them to help. We said our farewells the night before; it was less of a strain for the children. Rex said that, and for once Meriel agreed with him. We hugged and she said, 'We'll take good care of him, you know, Rache.' Of course she meant Dad. And I said, 'I know that.' It seemed to satisfy her.

I didn't know what to do with myself. I think it was a Wednesday, which was the day for Daphne's Rhyme and Rhythm class, but the girls did not want to go without Vicky and Georgie. I suggested visiting Mrs Nightingale, who was living alone in the old family house and had been fervent with her invitations when we had called in with Meriel. I wasn't sorry when they turned that down. We had had a life before the Robinsons came for the Coronation, but it was hard to remember it.

It was wonderful to see Tom after lunch. The

girls no longer 'went down' for an hour's nap, and the afternoon stretched ahead endlessly. They went mad when they heard his key in the door: ran into the hall and swarmed up his body yelling 'Daddy Daddy!' I wasn't far behind them. I leaned against the living-room door, and smiled as he dropped his case and clutched his daughters instead. 'You won't be able to do that much longer,' I said. They were almost three years old, and with Tom and me as parents they were not small.

They slithered back down, and he stooped with them. 'Can't do it now,' he said breathlessly. We staggered into the kitchen while he explained that the Gaffer had declared the planning session ended when Maxine had arrived with a dog. 'It's a poodle.' He accepted a cup of tea, grinning at Daisy as she vociferously demanded a 'doodle' of her own. 'Not likely,' he said immediately. 'I'm scared of dogs.' He looked up at me. 'Can you understand why the Gaffer stands up to anyone – mayor, councillors, police, politicians . . . but not Maxine? And Maxine with a poodle, too!' He slurped his tea. 'I'm not criticizing. It means we can put you two on the bike seats and go down to the brook for a paddle!' He smiled at me. 'On the way home, we'll pop in to see George, shall we? He'll be missing them, too, and maybe getting cold feet about his trip.'

I smiled back and said, 'I don't think so.'

He raised his brows, but said nothing, and we got ready and loaded the girls on the backs of our bikes and cycled the two miles to Twyver's Brook, where the remains of the dam Georgie had built last week was still hanging on to the bank.

When the girls were in bed that night I tried to explain to Tom why I found things 'a bit flat', as he put it.

'It's something to do with losing my memories.' I spread my hands. 'Meriel revived them at first. And now they've gone.'

He tried to comfort me. In the end I had to tell him about Dad. I hated doing it; I didn't want anyone else to know that my dad was a traitor, not even Tom. But I simply couldn't keep up the pretence that everything was OK; not any more.

We were in the garden. It was that sort of summer's night. Mum used to call it balmy. Meriel would be on deck looking at these stars. Dad might be outside too, wondering what on earth he was getting himself into . . . but then he must have done all that kind of wondering before. Tom was silent; he seemed completely shocked. But then I knew he was trying to work it out. I wanted to reach for his hand, but thought it was better that he should reach for mine.

He did not.

After what seemed like for ever – he was so

damned good at these silences – he said, 'He told you this himself?'

'Yes. How else would I know?'

'You and Meriel', you enjoy cooking things up . . .'

'You think I would cook up something like this?'

'No. But sorry, I still don't believe it.'

'You said that as if I ought not to have believed it – d'you think I wanted to believe it?'

He let that one hang for another age. Tears were pouring down my face. I needed more than his hand, I needed his shoulder. I had lost Meriel, I had lost Dad and I really had lost Mum. I couldn't afford to lose Tom.

Then he said slowly, 'D'you think he believed it?'

I tried to do his trick and not speak. He must have heard . . . known . . . that if I had I would simply have exploded into sobs.

He said, 'If the Gaffer hadn't leaned on the Chief Constable and hushed up the business of Sylvia Strassen's murder . . . if the actual murderer hadn't been found hiding under the platform at the railway station . . . you might have been implicated, Rachel. D'you think something as random – accidental – as that might have happened to your dad?'

I looked at him through that summer dusk.

'The Gaffer? Uncle Gilbert? How could he

have known that Sylvia Strassen had come to see me?'

'Because I told him. Reminded him that you were his goddaughter, too.'

'Oh . . . Tom.'

'It could have happened to George, Rache. Don't ask me how. I haven't had long enough to think. And there seem to be so many people implicated. Hermione's dad as well as yours. Eva . . . Strassen himself. Even poor old Silverman.'

At last that hand came out for mine and I collapsed into his shoulder.

He whispered into my ear. 'If he'd given them the Crown jewels, Rache, he wouldn't have been a traitor. You know that.'

Of course I knew. I laughed as I sobbed. Laughed at myself for being such a fool. Then I held on to Tom. And kept holding on.

Fifteen

I thought it would be harder than it actually was. I mean Dad going to stay with Meriel. But my feelings about Dad were so ambivalent I was almost glad of his absence. I thought I'd get it all straight in a few months, and everything would somehow become all right. In fact, better. Dad would be a proper 'grandee' to Rose and Daisy, and my special friend again. I worked on this from all angles; the best one seemed to be an acceptance that the past was not real. The past was a series of dreams, cherished and polished beyond any kind of reality. I got out the folder where I kept my bits and bobs of writing, and I re-read all the stuff I'd got down about the summer of 1944, when Meriel and I had had our 'awfully big adventure'. And I saw it for what it was: a series of events that I'd threaded together to make coincidental. Nothing had come of them; the people in them were victims of the war. We – Meriel and I – were victims of the war. Sylvia Strassen's murder came under that heading, too. And nothing had come of that, either. I had thought I would be implicated, that I would drag Mum and Dad with me. Nothing had happened. The young man who had hit her with her old-fashioned flat iron had been returned to a German psychiatric hospital after a long drawn-out legal battle. He had never explained why he'd done it. No one would probably ever know, either, why Mr Silverman had hung himself. And after so many years, it was old news. It could all be filed away in the cellar beneath the *Clarion*'s offices in St John's Lane with all the other world-shattering events that had never actually shattered the world.

I told myself that Dad's horrific disclosure could go with them. It had happened, he had sold his precious invention to the enemy, and they had still lost the war. It had not made any difference. It could be filed, too. Eventually. What had emerged from all that was Meriel meeting Rex and me meeting Tom. Those meetings were what joined the past and the present. Not my father's treason.

I took out the clothes pegs which had separated my bits and bobs into what I had originally thought of as chapters, and replaced them with the shiny paper clips we used at the *Clarion*, and tucked them back into the folder. I made a note that Willi Strassen had paid Sylvia to marry him, and then had fallen in love with Eva Schmidt, who was Hermione's aunt. I wondered what Hermione made of it all. I thought I could never ask her.

Then I got out Meriel's letters.

I hadn't kept them all; the awful diatribes that had followed Vicky's birth – she had asked me to burn them and I had. I recalled the first terrible argument she had reported, then. She had wanted to call the baby Ruth; it was a running joke she and Rex had kept up during the pregnancy, but it had pleased Meriel. She hadn't been interested in the famous Babe Ruth; she had re-read the bible story and had been struck by the love between Ruth and her husband's mother, Naomi. But Rex had flatly refused to 'honour the bargain' – I remember those words of hers. He liked Victoria; she didn't. I think it was Rex's mother who had eventually come up with a compromise, and Vicky's full name was Victory; though of course it was seldom used.

But I had kept enough of Meriel's correspondence to be able to track her development: from the schoolgirl I had known, to the determined woman who had come home for the Coronation of the Queen, and orchestrated a whole new life for her family and for mine. Just for a month.

It continued to hurt terribly that Dad had confided in Merry before me, but I tried to be objective. He had wanted help and I couldn't give it to him. He had known that she could. He had recognized the power that I was seeing in her letters. Maybe it had come to the fore with Georgie's birth, but it had always been there. Meriel had been the leader and I had followed.

Eventually, after re-reading them, I found another paper clip and fastened them together; then, suddenly hating the whole idea of keeping a record of our failing friendship, I bundled them into the middle of the file. I had thought at one time that I would interleaf them into some kind of continuous narrative. But they were recording the past and . . . the past had gone.

And my father had gone.

During the next two years he came home twice; neither visit coincided with Mum's birthday or the anniversary of her death, or in fact with anything. The first time he put the house in the hands of letting agents. He wanted us to live there, but it was too far away from work and school. I had got used to being able to step out of the front door and find the city at the end of the street. Our bikes stayed down in the cellar with the coal. Occasionally we toiled up the cellar steps with them at weekends and strapped the girls into their seats for a ride down to the river. We had a favourite spot: a horseshoe bend where the current slowed right down and a sunken barge provided a safe swimming area. When their legs grew long and strong we discussed getting them their own bicycles but we never did. Terraced houses do not offer easy access for bikes. When they needed bikes they borrowed ours.

I told Dad to sell the old house. I felt as if I was issuing a kind of challenge to him to cut his ties with England completely. If I expected a shocked rebuttal I was disappointed; he frowned consideringly then said, 'You might want it one day. And house prices will never come down, not now. We'll hang on to it as an investment.'

The agents let it to a highly respectable couple; they came from London and he was something to do with the Ministry of Works. Henry and Henrietta Sims – Henrietta always did the introductions and made a big thing of their names. They'd come to oversee the sale of the old Manor House that had housed POWs, internees, Free French soldiers and many others over the six years of war. The burgeoning Ministry of Health was buying it for a psychiatric respite home. Mr Sims was in charge of the repairs and alterations. Hermione was the assistant resident psychiatrist. She stayed with her parents and spent her days poring over catalogues of the latest equipment, plans, designs . . . even landscape drawings.

Henry Sims had been in residence just over

a month, bouncing his car down the road four times a day, when the council's road workers moved in with an archaic steam roller and a boiling pot of tarmac. The rough road was smoothed and surfaced its whole length, past Twyver's Brook and down the curling track that led to the Tewkesbury Road and the manor itself. Mr Sims was a man of influence.

It took a year before he was satisfied that the manor had been suitably renovated for convalescing traumatized patients. Then he went back to London, and Hermione phoned me and asked whether she could have Dad's address so that she could either rent or buy the house. I told her to apply to the agents, but she said she couldn't do that without asking him first. The next thing was, Dad paid his second visit home in two years.

They spent some time together in our old home, talking about decorations and central heating. Hermione said that any inside alterations were down to the tenant and with his permission she would modernize the house to her liking.

'I hope I can stay for ages, Mr Throstle.' She had always loved Dad – all my friends had loved him – and she was a bit breathy and misty-eyed as she mentioned some of the wonderful ideas she had for the house where Mum and I had conducted our symphonies, and we had all hidden under the Morrison shelter like foxes in a den. 'But of course it will always be yours. If you need it at a moment's notice just send off a cable—'

'Not very likely, Hermione.'

I was an unwilling third at this meeting, and was standing by the window trying not to listen to Hermione's plans. Dad's words didn't help. I pretended very hard that I hadn't heard any of it.

Hermione said, 'The manor is a bit of a flagship for the National Health. Small. We have to refer patients to bigger places with more resources in some cases. But for others the manor is excellent. Environment is a therapy in itself, of course.' She laughed. 'Oh dear, I'm on my hobby horse again! It's just that . . . well, to be offered such a position is wonderful. And then to be able to make my own home in a place that I have always loved.' She turned pink. 'It's a happy house, Mr Throstle. Thank you for letting me have it.'

'My dear girl. You're paying a good rent. And the law protects you totally – I can't give you the order of the boot even if I wanted to.' He added hastily, 'Not that I would ever want to, Hermione. You are practically family.'

Was she? Had she ever been?

I said quickly, 'You'll need help with the garden.'

She joined me at the window, hands clasped beneath her chin. She was almost ecstatic.

'I plan to use the garden in my work. Enlist help from patients who could benefit. And put them in the position of being experts, too.'

I nodded but felt bound to add, 'You'll have to be careful, Hermione. You'll get accusations of exploitation!' I laughed but she took me seriously and nodded.

And she was happy there – and at the manor. I saw quite a lot of her as the years went on. She went out to Florida for Georgie's tenth birthday. He had been accepted at a special school west of Boston, and though Meriel had fought tooth and nail for his place, she suddenly lost her impetus and was terrified she had done the wrong thing. She wrote to Hermione, who took her first holiday and went out to go with Meriel and Georgie to the school. They stayed with Jack and Joan Robinson and visited every day. Hermione was ecstatic when she told me about it.

'They're using the best bits of Steiner, Morgenfrau, Montessori . . . all of them! Every child an individual, every child with their own personal mentor, but they can chop and change whenever they want to. Music, movement. And the environment – you know what importance I give to that, Rache. New England is just beautiful. I saw it in the fall, of course, but Meriel has been there for all the seasons.'

'What did Meriel think about the school?'

'She got back her confidence. She only needed one thing to make it whole. And that was Georgie's happiness. To see that he was happy. And he is happy. His Pop and Joan are two hours' drive away. He can go there at weekends.'

'What about my father? Is he happy, too?'

'I think so. He loves visiting the Robinsons, but the climate in Florida agrees with him. I didn't realize he had so much arthritic pain, Rache. He never talks about it, does he?'

'No. He doesn't.'

Sometimes I thought I had never really known my father.

I kept in touch with the first Mrs Nightingale and very occasionally I saw 'the boys': Barry and John. They were both married with young children, both living in married quarters at Plymouth, both carbon copies of their father. Myrtle Nightingale spent her time between them, acting as baby sitter and general dogsbody, as far as I could make out. But she was happy, too. At some point during the last ten years she had stopped being unhappy. I had mentioned this to John once, and he had grinned at me knowingly.

'Come on. You know as well as I do why she is quite content with life at the moment.' I had opened my eyes, spread my hands helplessly. He had laughed.

'Dad came round a couple of years ago when we were both here. He wanted to patch things up. For Mum's sake, he said. Barry got it right away. It was for Dad's sake. So that he could come and go as he pleased even if we were around.'

I had felt my jaw sag. John had guffawed. 'Come on, Rache! Dad's got it made. Maria tells him what to do at work, and everywhere else. Mum never tells him anything, except that she adores him. So he has his cake and he eats it! Typical of Dad, isn't it? In other words, nothing has changed.'

I had been aghast. 'But what if Maria finds out?'

John had made a face. 'I think she probably knows. She must be pretty tough. She gave Merry to Mum to look after . . . Mum always knew about her. Now she knows about Mum. Sounds fair enough to me.'

I suppose it was fair. Almost. The odd thing was I liked the second Mrs Nightingale. I recognized Meriel in her; the old Meriel.

Something else rather odd happened during this loop of time when Daisy and Rose were growing up and up; and – over in Florida – Victory Robinson had her first 'date'; and nearer home Dennis Nightingale kept two women happy; and Hermione Smith named our old home 'Rough Road Cottage' and kept notes that would one day become a bible for anyone dealing with traumatized patients; and Tom became editor-in-chief of the *Clarion*, though the Gaffer was still very much a presence in the office. The 'something else' was that we had our usual Christmas card from Nobby Clarke with a message inside it.

> Tom and Rachel, It will be 1963 in two weeks time, twenty years since I worked on the BBR (Bloody Burma Railway to you) . . . Some of my stuff turned up last month. Sent on by my old RSM who got it from a monk, who got it from Buddha knows where! Letters and so forth. Gave me a bit of a turn, you can imagine. Twenty years is a long time. Anyway, tucked inside one of the envelopes was this sketch. That's me at the end of the railway sleeper. Took ten of us to carry it down the track. We were as weak as kittens. Does it ring any bells for you? Hope your kids are doing fine, and you too. Try to pop up next summer and we'll go fishing. Happy Christmas.
>
> Your friend, Nobby

I had recognized his hand writing, so had saved it for Tom to open. He read the note aloud and we looked at the sketch together. It was done on part of a cigarette packet: a pencil sketch, a line of men in long khaki shorts and hats, home-made sandals on their feet, their skeletons showing clearly beneath weathered skin. They were carrying a railway sleeper.

I said, 'Oh, dear God. You know it happened but to see it . . . recorded by someone who was there—'

'Recorded by my dad.' Tom spoke flatly, without emphasis.

I jerked my head round to look at him. His arm was loosely around my shoulders so that we could both look at the sketch. He felt my gaze and turned to meet it. Very slowly his eyes filled with tears. I said, shocked, 'Tom!' And he laid his forehead on my shoulder and cried; properly cried.

I gathered him to me and held him tightly against enormous sobs. He wept for some time: maybe three or four minutes, but it seemed so long. I made noises but did not speak words. I had learned from him when to be wordless.

As he gradually quietened we moved to the sofa and sat down. The fire in the grate was full of caverns and we watched them change colour and collapse on themselves. Tom took my free hand, kissed it and held it to his face. Then he spoke. 'For the first time, I feel the absence of my dad. Isn't that strange, Rache? I know he did that sketch, that he was there, that it was 1943. Evidence of life. Yet . . . there would have been others, wouldn't there? And this is the only one.' He kissed my hand again and turned to look at me. 'He's gone. You and everyone else have always known it. And I wouldn't accept it. What does Hermione call it – a state of denial?'

'You simply held on to your hope, Tom. And why not? Nothing has changed, really. Except that you have the most extraordinarily special Christmas present anyone could possibly have.'

He gave me a watery smile. Then he said, 'You show the girls, Rache. I'd cry again and that would upset them. But make them understand how important it is, won't you?' And then of course I cried.

That spring Uncle Gilbert began coming back to work on a regular basis. I think Aunt Maxine made him work twice as hard at home. He had never given up his big office which overlooked St John's Lane; Tom was accommodated in a very small room on the other side of the landing, and used the big room for interviews only. Gilbert – the Gaffer – telephoned me on a nasty day at the end of April, and asked me to slip in and have a cup of tea with him before the girls got home from school. I took my file containing notes on forthcoming articles; the Gaffer was still a force to be reckoned with, and I thought he was going to use words like 'parochial', 'claustrophobic' and – quite probably—'incestuous'. Indeed, he started off that way.

'It occurred to me the other day—' he

nodded at the armchair, which meant I wasn't actually in trouble, and I sat down gratefully. 'That you have rarely left our historic and illustrious city, Rachel.'

I smiled and said nothing. My best friend and my father might well live in America but not many Gloucestrians strayed far from the shadow of the cathedral tower in those days. Gilbert knew this as well as I did.

He asked a direct question so that I would have to speak. 'Let's see . . . where did you go last summer? Dorset, was it?'

'Devon.'

'That's right.' It sounded as if he might be congratulating me on getting the answer right. 'I remember those two articles well. I'm sure the hotels and landladies of Hope Cove and Slapton Sands must have doubled their profits in the last part of the summer. You made the whole place come alive.'

Compliments from the Gaffer were rare, and I almost goggled at him. He went to the window and looked down into the lane. The April rain fell inexorably. He said, 'Your Aunt Maxine was saying the other evening that the *Clarion* is missing out on something rather special. A letter from America.'

I felt a little spurt of enthusiasm. 'You always said Meriel would have made a good reporter. Yes – Maxine is right – it would run for quite a few weeks—'

He cut me short with a backward flip of his hand, then turned and came back to the desk. 'No one remembers Meriel Nightingale now, let alone Meriel Robinson. But they know you. You are one of them. If you went over and wrote a series of articles on various aspects of ordinary domestic life – maybe interspersed with a few of your homely political comments digestible with Saturday morning's breakfast toast – the weekend sales would increase still more. And if you were visiting your father – who *is* still remembered, and your friend, who happens to be the daughter of Dennis Nightingale . . . the sales would hit the roof. We would be connecting Florida and Gloucestershire. Can you see it, Rachel – can you visualize it?'

I could, of course. But I visualized something else, too.

'Are you worried about Dad?'

'Not worried. I'd like some properly subjective news of him. And I don't think he's coming home again, so you are my best bet. And you're never going to go out there just for a holiday. But you'll have to go out on this assignment, because I'm telling you to!' He tried hard to look belligerent.

I wasn't keen, of course. Meriel was looking after Dad now, and I didn't have to think about any of it. I said, 'You could do it. It would have far more impact if your name was underneath.'

He leaned on the desk. 'I don't want that sort of impact, Rachel. I want the gentle under-the-skin, day-to-day stuff. Your readership will be comfortable with that. When you make any broader comments they will be acceptable and comprehensible. Not something to be skipped over. You can do it, girl!'

'I'm not sure about Tom and the girls – time off school and work—'

'Christ, I'm not talking about the whole bloody family going with you! D'you think the *Clarion* makes that sort of profit? We're still independent, Rachel, not many of us left. We work on a bloody shoestring and this isn't an all-expenses-paid holiday, this is a proper assignment.'

'You said a subjective view of Dad—'

'Exactly. Not a blurred unnatural view because he's got his granddaughters jumping up and down in front of him. A quiet, ordinary view built up over fourteen days. Time when you can talk together and find out what he is really thinking.'

'All right, all right, I get it. So it would be before or after the summer holidays?'

'Before. June. June would be a good time. Things to do, preparations to be made. You would fly, of course. Everyone does now.'

I bleated, 'June is just over four weeks off!'

'Exactly. You'll have to get cracking. Maxine will help you. She can talk to Tom. And she'll keep an eye on the girls, of course. And your friend Daphne can help out. Piece of cake, really. You'll be home in good time for the school hols and another break in Dorset.'

'Devon.'

'OK, Devon.' He beamed at me. 'You'll do a good job, Rachel, I'm certain of that. And it will do you good as well. Maxine is always telling me you're much too thin. But your mother was the same.' His smile died. 'You are the spitting image of your mother, Rachel.'

I put my hand to my hair self-consciously. It really was the only thing I had inherited from Mum. Uncle Gilbert was wearing the wrong glasses.

That was how I came to go to see Dad and Meriel in Florida that June of 1963.

Sixteen

The Visitation – that was what Meriel called it – was much too short, of course. Besides taking endless photographs with a physical camera, I did lots of filming the way I'd done as a child, focusing intensely on a 'frame' and almost burning it into my mind. It means that I saw Meriel's kitchen in two-dimensional blocks and have to concentrate hard on moving around it, and mentally joining it all together.

I loved working in it; it was so light, so airy and so big. The gadgets were never put away because we actually used them on a daily basis. The juicer was a delight; the electric blender, the cake mixer, the vegetable chopper . . . even the toaster was quite different from mine, with six slots if you needed them. I became an expert cake maker and copied out all Aunt Mabe's wonderful recipes for use in my *Clarion* column.

Aunt Mabe was a delight; she was the same age as Dad, but seemed more like a grandmother than a mother. Rex was there for breakfast, and very occasionally for dinner. He took us out to restaurants and talked to Dad about his work. 'Classified information', he called it. 'But it's safe with you,' he said, clapping Dad on the shoulder. Little did he know. Meriel did not even meet my swift glance, and I had a feeling she had completely forgotten about the betrayal. I did mention it at one point, and she looked surprised. 'You mean that misdemeanour of his – obviously, honey, he knew what he was doing. It was too late in the war for his invention to be any good to the Germans and he needed the money for your mother. No National Health then, was there?' She smiled wryly, she too had missed out on the National Health; subject closed.

After the middle weekend we paid a visit to Joan and 'Pop' Robinson. Georgie's school was closing for the summer, and we were to collect him and bring him back to the Florida house.

Jack Robinson had been retired for some time, and he and Joan had become almost caricatures of good solid citizens. In many ways life in Orion was Dickensian. Joan headed a team of ladies who had made 'caring' into an art form. Soup in the winter, angel cake and blancmanges in the summer. Pop put chains on his car in the winter and drove people from place to place every Wednesday and Thursday. They both belonged to a reading group and a chess club. They kept weekends for Georgie

– though this term he had joined a choir who were much in demand for church services on Sundays. They told us very seriously that with the extra time on their hands they had thought of taking badminton lessons.

Meriel was different with them; she could relax properly, say what she thought. The second of our nights there, they talked about Ellie. It could have been tricky for Joan, but she too had known Jack's first wife and had loved her. There seemed to be very much more love around in the States. Perhaps we had been fed on hatred for too long; we had to learn to be open and loving again. Or perhaps it was a national failing. Caution, protectiveness . . . I wasn't sure. I decided I would float the idea in my articles, and see what sort of response I got back home.

Joan said to me, 'You know, Rachel, Ellie thought that she and Merry were very similar. She told Mabe she wanted Merry to do the things she might have had a shot at. That was why we have all encouraged Merry to enquire about the psychology course at Bristol University.'

Meriel flashed a grin at me. 'I haven't told Rachel about that, Joan. I suppose I'll have to, now!'

Joan wasn't a bit fazed. 'I should think so,' she said. 'Do it now, while Jack and I get some supper. Once you take Georgie out of school, there won't be much opportunity to talk it over.'

We did not exactly talk it over; we strolled down the 'yard' to the stream at the bottom and watched a pair of blackbirds on the opposite bank, and Meriel talked while I listened.

'It's Aunt Mabe who keeps on about it,' she said half-laughing but very serious, too. 'She says it's the ideal time because Georgie has got another three years at this wonderful school, and she's still around for the vacations, and Joan and Jack are always there, and Vicky will be in college . . . and she's right. There's no provision for Georgie once he's nineteen. Well, that's not quite true, but what's on offer would not interest him. Carpentry, gardening. You know the sort of thing. He loves music. He'll never be a musician, but he loves music.' She took my arm suddenly. 'Oh Rache. He loves music.' She was weeping. I remembered him ten years ago at Daphne's Rhyme and Rhythm sessions, banging a drum. I put my other hand over hers.

'He'll always have people who love him, Merry. That is what counts.'

'Vicky . . . yes. Oh yes. But what if he wants to marry someone? What if he wants an ordinary home and children?'

I swallowed, not knowing. We protected disabled children even when they grew up . . . didn't we? Could we let them take the enormous adult jump of marriage and family life?

Meriel said, 'Aunt Mabe wants me to have qualifications.' Her voice became stronger, steadier. 'So that when I voice an opinion it has . . . weight. This course at Bristol offers teaching qualifications and a degree in psychology. Armed with that I could do a doctorate back here at home. And then I would have some . . . what did we used to call it? Clout. I would have some clout.'

'What for? I mean how would you use this clout?'

'Getting . . . stuff . . . for Georgie.' She waved her hands. 'I could write a textbook – Hermione would help me.'

'My God. What you're saying . . . you're being political again!'

'I don't know what that means, really. But like I said before, if it turns out to be political, then that's OK.'

I suddenly remembered how she had coped with Mrs Roosevelt's visit to her tiny Center for Learning . . . Georgie at five years old, cupping his friend's hands around some flowers and presenting them to their illustrious visitor.

I said slowly, 'You could do it, Merry. And if it's the ideal time . . . why don't you start next September?' I was startled at my own words. 'What about Rex?' I asked.

'Grandee has talked to him about it. He

would be delighted.' She made a face at me. 'Clear field with Dawn from Devon!'

I was startled all over again. 'Not still?' I asked incredulously.

She nodded self-mockingly. 'He would be so much better off with her, Rache. And he's stuck with me. And he's stuck because of Georgie. If I moved into the front line he would feel free to ask for a divorce.' She shrugged. 'Sounds crazy, I know, but he's a good man basically. He would never leave me out on a limb, as it were. It would be different if I was completely independent of him – he would still see Georgie, but it would be different.'

'I think I know what you mean. And Vicky would always be a bridge between all of you.'

It was as if we had made an agreement. She brought up the subject in front of the whole family back in Florida, Dad as well.

'Aunt Mabe and Joan and Pop and now Rache . . . they're all keen on me doing a course in Bristol. Psychology with a Certificate of Education thrown in.' She looked at Rex. 'What do you say, honey?'

He flitted a grin at her. 'You know what I would say.'

It was the Nightingale situation all over again. Complicit. Horribly, unnaturally civilized.

'I'd rather you said it, and in front of witnesses.'

'I think it's a good idea. We all know that

you need to go to the limit with your crusade. That's what it will become, Merry. You know that.'

She nodded. 'It's what I want,' she said simply.

Meriel had also talked to Georgie about going to Bristol. She was constantly consulting Georgie, he was never left out.

He said bleakly, 'I won't see you.'

'I'll be home every time you are.' She looked into his strange eyes. 'I promise. I'll telephone you at Grandee's house. I'll write to you every week. Just as I do now.'

I knew those letters, because she had insisted I put my piece into them while I was staying with Dad. They were simple diaries: they recorded the weather, the latest flowers in the yard, the pool man's annoyance with the drifting leaves, Vicky's opinion on the Polaris agreement and the riots in Alabama. Vicky was determined that her brother should be aware of the world beyond school and family. I heard her say angrily, 'If you want him to have the same opportunities as everyone else, then you must let him feel responsible for – for – everything!' Meriel told me later that she had provoked Vicky by her 'condescension'.

'We were looking at a newspaper photograph of Jackie Kennedy, and I said she should send it to Georgie because he loved beautiful people. I didn't mean they were the only people he could appreciate – my God, he appreciated Mrs Roosevelt all right!' Meriel looked at me and issued a challenge. 'Dammit, Rache, you're in the business of communication. You write to him. See how you do!'

That was when I started to write to Georgie. My letters weren't a bit like hers. The first was one of my recipes for drop scones. The next day I copied out Blake's 'Jerusalem' and sent it to him. I showed them to Dad when he got in from the day's golf. He grinned, just as he had before Mum died. 'If you go on doing this, Rache, tell him about the time we were all foxes in a den.' Then he stopped smiling, and said, 'Get Tom to do some sketches. To go with your letters. He'll say he can't do it. That's because his father was so good. But he could do it after a fashion, and he should.' He saw my astonishment and all the questions I was going to fire at him, and he said dismissively, 'Just a thought. I must have a shower. Mabe is cooking supper tonight.' And he was gone.

The plane landed at Stansted and there was Tom and the car I thought we'd never have; before I even asked he said, 'Daisy and Rose are staying overnight with Daphne. As they are both in love with her boys I'm afraid you lost the contest, love.'

I butted my head into his arm. 'At least you turned up.'

He kissed me, then said, 'And at least we've got the house to ourselves till about four o'clock tomorrow afternoon.'

We held on to each other, drew apart, looked and looked. I steadied my voice to say, 'And Daphne was also a Swallow girl, so she will know what their uniforms should look like.'

He nodded, half-smiling, running his hand over my hair.

'They've made a list of questions so that you can prepare your answers.' His voice did not shake so much as wobble. I'd only been away a fortnight, but we hadn't been apart that long since we were married. 'It's a long list but a lot of them are duplicated and involve the sort of makeup Vicky is wearing and whether Georgie and Rebekkah will get married. And whether Grandee has met anyone else.'

'D'you think they're sex mad?'

'No. But they are going through a silly stage. They catch each other's eye, and for no reason at all they fall about laughing.'

'They're laughing at us. They realize that life is absurd. They think they are the only people in the world to know that.' I kissed him again, laid my head against his arm and closed my eyes blissfully. 'And of course, they are twelve years old.'

By the time we got to Oxford I was asleep.

It was good to be home. The two weeks in America had been amazing. I had tried to 'do a Hermione' and observe it all as dispassionately as possible. Uncle Gilbert was paying for this trip and I had to bring back 'letters from America' that were both everyday and chatty, yet conscious all the time of the different cultures, the poverty gap, the frantic efforts to gather all those disparate peoples and make them into a nation. I had found it incredible that even at Georgie's 'special' school the day began with the national anthem, the flag, the reminder that first and foremost came the United States of America. Learn that and everything else would follow. And by everything else, most people meant wealth. At the same time I noted the generosity and kindness. There seemed almost too much of everything, especially food. I had not realized that almost twenty years after the end of the war we were still so careful of food and belongings; we had not yet entered the throw-away world.

Personally, the most important thing I observed was Dad's apparent happiness. It didn't go deep and it certainly wasn't the sort of happiness he had had with Mum, but he looked very fit and well. Retired men in Florida played golf, and he joined them and liked them well enough. He seemed to have no wish to come back to this country. He was absolutely delighted to see me at first, and then there was almost a caution about him; as if he dared not let himself go. As if he had fenced himself away from all his old life. I couldn't believe it. It was as if the whole Strassen thing had gone; in fact as if the whole of England and his life at Smith's had gone.

When I reminded him that he had not seen the girls since they were five years old – which was when he had let Hermione have Rough Road Cottage – he looked vague. 'Guess I should come and look at the house.'

I was nettled by the fact that Daisy and Rose came after the house.

I said, 'Hermione is taking great care of it. She loves it. Reckons she had the happiest times of her childhood there. I think she came round about half a dozen times, didn't she?'

'Golly, Rache. I don't remember.'

That was how he did it, of course, by not remembering. When I was rattling on about the girls and Tom I often felt him shut down. He rarely mentioned Mum. He was only seventy-two and he was deliberately losing his memory. He didn't ask about Hermione again. I wonder whether he even remembered her.

I found it terribly difficult to tell Tom all this. When he asked about Rex and Meriel and Vicky and Georgie, I couldn't stop talking. But when it came to Dad it was different. 'You'll have to wait for me to do my letters for the *Clarion*,' I told him. 'I've got heaps of notes. There's just too much to remember and regurgitate.'

Long before I got the very ancient Oliver on to the kitchen table, Meriel's first letter had arrived. It was very short.

> Darling Rache, I am missing you so much. Maybe more than I would have done had we had the kind of holiday together I planned. I knew you were coming out to see your father, of course I knew that, but I still thought that in-between – not even in-between but all the time, there would be that bond between us. I'm not saying it's gone, Rache. It can never just disappear. But what we had in Coronation year, that wonderful month when it seemed as though nothing happened and everything happened, we didn't have that, did we?
>
> Perhaps I'm sounding neurotic. It's just that . . . well, you know me, Rache . . . I have to have everything out in the open. So if there is anything, just tell me. Please, please, Rache, just tell me.

That was all there was, and she must have written before I actually left, because airmails took five days to get across the Atlantic and this one arrived on my first 'normal' day – when in fact I planned to start on the 'letter from America'. I stared at her sprawling signature almost vexedly; I did not want anything to come before *my* letter. Gilbert had commissioned it so that I could go over and check on Dad . . . we both knew it. So the letter – the excuse for going – had to be . . . good. And as for Meriel wanting to have stuff in the open – it was ridiculous.

I put her letter on the kitchen mantelpiece and got cracking. I didn't even hear Rose's key in the door at four thirty. Not until she slammed her satchel on to the table with such force the Oliver lifted half an inch.

I stopped work and tried to hug her; she was stiff. 'What's up?' I asked.

'Daisy's got a date.'

Her voice was almost sullen. She shrugged out of her blazer, put it on the back of one of the kitchen chairs, and made a sound of annoyance as it slid to the floor. She made no attempt to pick it up. I demanded to know who Daisy was with, and how she could just walk off without letting me know. They both knew the rules: they came home from school immediately and directly.

Rose looked grimmer than ever; after all, why should she have to put up with my anger at first-hand when it was nothing to do with her? I shook my head in a sort of apology and kissed her.

She said, 'The date's not today. You've forgotten she's got tennis practice down at the park. You forget everything lately.'

'Oh . . . of course. And I'll be OK once this article is done. So what's all this about a date?' I gave up on the Oliver, lugged it over to the dresser, then grabbed the kettle and filled it. I hadn't eaten since seven thirty and had not even peeled a potato for our evening meal.

'Colin Beard.'

'Colin? Aunt Daphne's Colin? But he must be . . . fifteen?'

'Nearly sixteen,' Rose said with a touch of satisfaction at my reaction. Obviously, she thought 'the date' was my fault because Daphne was my friend and Colin was her son; and just as obviously she enjoyed making the age difference even wider and more horrific.

I spooned tea into the pot and glanced over my shoulder. 'Pick up your blazer, it's not meant to be a door mat. Then go and change your clothes. We'll have tea outside, and you can tell me all about it.'

I had been home three days and was sounding like Meriel. But Rose instantly picked up her blazer and disappeared, so it worked. And I made the tea and went for the phone. Daphne had long given up on Rhyme and Rhythm and now ran a cleaning agency. She also lived back home with her widowed mother; home was an enormous house with its own tennis court and swimming pool. She cheerfully confessed that her husband had dumped her for his secretary. The boys, just as cheerfully, said Dad couldn't stand the noise when they took up drumming. He visited them all once a week and said he hadn't known when he was on to a good thing. But he always went back to his blonde, slim and very pretty secretary. Daphne was still overpowering.

Her voice on the other end of the line was warm and welcoming.

'Welcome home, darling. Have I already said that? The girls were marvellous – and I have definitely already said that! Are you working hard? We must get together and have a good chin wag.'

'Yes.' I sounded perfunctory. 'I just wanted to know . . . Rose tells me that Colin is taking Daisy . . . somewhere?'

'Colin? Daisy?' She sounded genuinely bewildered. 'Oh, you mean the coaching? Colin offered to meet her out of school tomorrow and bring her up to tea, then have an hour on the court. He says she's got potential.'

She didn't laugh so there was no horrible pun intended. It was, as usual, Daphne and her boys being nice. My feathers were smoothed instantly, and I felt a bit ridiculous and overprotective. My God, Vicky had been 'dating' since she was thirteen. But my girls weren't thirteen yet.

I swallowed and told Daphne how marvellous Colin was, and yes, that would be fine, and thank you so much.

'Why don't you come, too, Rachel?'

'I need to finish this article for the *Clarion* – the reason I went to the States, after all. But it was great to see Dad and Meriel and the children.'

'I tried to fill in for you. I adore your girls, as you know. And Hermione was like a lost soul on her day off, so we went to the cinema.'

'It was so good of you. Thank you a thousand times, Daphne.' I had already thanked her but Daphne needed more than that. There had been so much catching up to do. I reminded myself I must buy her flowers and chocolates. I had got American sports shirts for the boys.

'Darling, it was a pleasure. I mean that. Come on over as soon as you can.'

I replaced the receiver and thought how marvellous Daphne was. Then felt cross with Rose. Then told myself I did not understand what it must be like to be a twin. Was Rose feeling left out in some way? She had been the front runner of the two since birth – she had arrived first. But things were changing. I had noticed for some time that there were the subtlest of differences developing in their faces and Daisy's combination of dark hair and blue eyes made for an attractiveness that Rose's just missed. It was giving Daisy a confidence she hadn't had, bringing her into the adult world faster than her sister.

We sat under next door's tree-overhang and she reluctantly admitted that Daisy was going to be coached by Colin.

'So. No need for me to come the heavy mother?' I smiled at her, trying to convey that there was nothing here to worry about.

'I suppose not.' She took a slice of cake, one of the many I had left for them before I went to Florida, all still in their tins. 'I'm better at tennis than Daisy but no one offers me any coaching.'

'If you're better than Daisy, there's the answer. You don't need coaching.'

She nodded, but we both knew that was not the point. The twins had adored Daphne's two boys since they were two-year-olds. I apologized mentally to Uncle Gilbert as I consigned the letter from America to an imaginary pending tray.

'Listen. Daphne invited us all to tea tomorrow. I said no but if you'd like to go, we could have the car and drive out together. The three of us.'

'No.' She looked at me. 'I know it's only coaching, Mum, but it's Daisy's . . . thing. Colin is cycling in at half past three to meet her and he'll bike back with her, too. It wouldn't be the same if we all went.'

I looked at her, then reached over the cake tin to take her hand and sort of shake it. 'You're right.' I wanted to congratulate her but knew I mustn't. 'Have another piece of cake,' I said instead. And she did.

Everyone seemed to like the American piece. Gilbert ran it over four Saturdays and suggested I expand it for a book. I was astonished; it was so ordinary, a lot of it quite personal. I insisted on keeping anonymity. I used the pseudonym Mary Silver: Mary was the name of Tom's mother, who had died just after he was born. I often felt that in his anxiety about his father's fate she had been almost overlooked, and this was my way of reminding us both that he had a mother and I had a mother-in-law. Silver I used in memory of Mr Silverman the tailor, who had saved so many lives before losing his own. Tom still believed he had been murdered by Willi Strassen, and I told him he should write a book himself. He shook his head gently. 'You know that one day I am going to write a book about my father. I've got all that material from the *Birmingham News* group, and loads of background from Nobby Clarke.'

I felt the usual pang. I could have written a memoir – maybe – of my father: who had spoiled his wife and daughter, who had been a wonderful mathematician and invented a special tail fin for fighter planes that had perhaps saved lives. And then had sold it to the enemy. Instead I said, 'I've promised Merry I will write to Georgie – I did a couple of letters while I was over there. Dad thinks you should illustrate them.'

'Does he, indeed?' He looked at me knowingly. 'In other words you think I should try to emulate my dad? You know I can't draw, Rache.'

'Dad *said* you would make that excuse.' I hugged his arm. 'Georgie would love it, Tom. Next week it's the school summer concert. Do a couple of stick figures – Daisy and Rose – playing their violins. He still loves music.'

He gave me the silent treatment, but kissed me to show there were no hard feelings. I had had Nobby Clarke's tiny cartoon framed for him, and he often stood in front of it: looking at the few lines which made up a picture of unendurable poignancy.

The following week he handed me a square of card, the perfect size to accommodate a sketch of our daughters playing their violins. I could practically hear the ghastly scraping sounds that so often came from their rooms. They were never going to be musicians. I enclosed it with my letter to Meriel. I had never left a reply so long, especially when she was asking for reassurance. I gave it to her and signed my letter 'your equally neurotic friend'. I knew that whatever happened nothing could really – not really – come between us. We were two sides of a coin.

The summer holidays began, and in July

we went to Devon and lived in a tent for two weeks. It was wonderful. We came home and Colin called for Daisy, and Rose refused to languish and started on a letter to Vicky. She carefully folded those maddening little edges and stuck it down; I never knew what she said in it. But I never doubted that she lit the fuse that eventually blew up the events of that winter. Two weeks later, Meriel telephoned me to say that Dad planned to come home this autumn – perhaps they might travel together, but probably not, as Meriel wanted to come earlier to get a flat in Bristol and settle in properly before the term began. Anyway, what did I think about Dad staying with Hermione? Apparently he was absolutely certain he must be in his old home again. Did I think Hermione would mind?

I had no idea whether Hermione would mind at all; in fact she telephoned that evening to say she had just had a chat with Dad and was delighted that he was going to be staying 'for a bit' at Rough Road Cottage.

I minded. I minded quite a lot.

Seventeen

Dad arrived home on the day President Kennedy was assassinated. He had not heard the news before he left, and knew nothing about it. We did not mention it during the drive home. He looked so different from the man I had left on the golf course last June. His tan wasn't quite right in England's November, it made him look as if he were running a high temperature, when actually he was shivering in the English chill.

Two weeks ago, just when I had thought he had shelved the whole idea of coming home, he had telephoned Hermione and announced his arrival time, before ringing us and asking if we could meet him. He had not sounded excited or even mildly happy about the visit. I had said tartly, 'I can tell you don't want to come, Dad. Why not simply cancel the flight?'

Amazingly he had replied, 'Don't be silly, Rache. I've got to come now!'

I had not wanted to enter into a discussion

transatlantically, as it were, so had made a non-committal sound.

And here he was, shivering and not looking very well. All right, I had been really upset about his unexplained wish to stay with Hermione, but now I was suddenly thankful. Hermione had had central heating installed when she first took on Rough Road Cottage. It was much warmer than number twenty-one Chichester Street. It felt freezing as we drove down the Pitch and crossed the city boundary on the road to Tewkesbury. The flat river lands stretched bleakly around us and there was no getting away from the wind.

We told Dad about President Kennedy just before we reached the rough road, but he was by no means devastated. 'People who need power take that risk, I guess,' he said slowly. 'He's got kids, too.' And that was that. He looked at the line of willows that marked Twyver's Brook. 'This new tarmacked road is much better for the car suspensions, but it takes some of the character away.' I recalled that was how he had been last June; a suitable response to any kind of news and then back to the minutiae of the moment. And then Tom was turning the car into the driveway and Hermione was at the front door waving a tea towel. As far as I know Dad did not mention the assassination again.

At first Hermione had insisted she would

move out, back to her parents further up the road. As they were both practically reclusive now, and disapproved strongly of Hermione's work, choice of home, clothing and food, I said that wasn't a good idea. Then I told her that Dad wanted her to be there: he had said he needed to have a good talk with her.

'What about?' she had asked nervously.

'I don't know.' I had shrugged. 'You could both have come to us each evening and picked up where you left off, I would have thought.'

Actually, though Dad had been cryptic, he had said he wanted to talk to her about her parents. I hadn't taken that very seriously. Neither had Meriel when she came over at the start of September to fix her stay in Bristol. She had been as confused as me. 'Never mind the bloody Smiths – I'm coming over, and I'll spend every weekend with you!' She was determinedly happy, though I knew her heart was breaking because she would be leaving Vicky and Georgie. I loved her again, then. She was . . . gallant.

She had said three must be our special number. 'Nineteen forty-three, '53, and now '63!'

I had reminded her that the air raid that started it all had been in 1944.

'I still maintain that '63 will be a very special year.'

'You're going to be here. And Dad is going to be here, unless he changes his mind. And I came over to Florida . . . that will make it special.' I had looked at her. 'Why has Dad made this sudden decision – do you know anything I don't?'

She had frowned. 'Well, it must be something to do with Rose's letter to Vicky. Vicky is so impulsive in some ways. She went storming over to George's apartment waving the letter like a banner and telling him what he should do. And don't ask me what that was, because I don't know, and she wouldn't tell me, and George wouldn't tell me. But she said he should go back home and sort things out. That was last month some time, and he's not said too much about it lately. Bet he'll come. No one can stand out against her bullying tactics.'

'I wonder where she gets those from?' I had answered. She laughed.

'We OK now, honey?'

'We were never anything else,' I had come back quite sharply. That was the attitude I had taken after her letter. Of course I had known what she meant, but I didn't see how we could hope to maintain the sort of thoughtless relationship we had once had. Obviously we were getting older and our friendship had to be conducted at arms' length most of the time.

* * *

She went back home to spend time with Vicky and Georgie, and returned at the end of September to start the three-year course at Bristol. She found a flat in Clifton and Hermione and I helped her to furnish it and thoroughly enjoyed ourselves. Just for that day in September we were all girls again. The dynamics had slightly changed: Meriel and Hermione had a lot of shared interests and I felt just a little outside. Probably I felt the way Hermione had felt twenty years ago.

Meriel's new life absorbed her totally. She loved it. 'It's good doing all the practical stuff first and then discovering that the theory fits so well! And when it doesn't you have to adjust the theory, not the practice! David Harmsworth – he lectured last week – suggested I ought to teach some of the classes!' I could imagine. When I met Professor Harmsworth eventually it was obvious to me he was in love with Meriel. That didn't surprise me, either. She was still a tiny firecracker, her energy ferocious.

Once Dad had moved into our old place I learned that Meriel telephoned Hermione at least twice a week to discuss a lecture or a textbook. She telephoned me, too; we talked about student fashions and how crazy they all were . . . and how young and wonderfully thoughtless.

When she came home at weekends she always stayed at Chichester Street. The girls loved seeing her, and she loved being with us. She had a very low sports car that could eat up the A38 between Bristol and Gloucester, and she calculated she could be sitting at my kitchen table in under an hour from leaving the university. I waited for her to suggest that she should stay with us and commute on the days she had lectures. She never did. Neither did I.

So Meriel was living in Clifton practically next door to the main university building, and after the awful Kennedy murder Dad was living in our old house along the no-longer-rough road and with Hermione Smith. It seemed to me the oddest set-up I could have imagined. Even Tom was sufficiently intrigued to have a word with Rose.

'Now you're a teenager—'

'Only just,' she said defensively.

'Only just a teenager, I think it's all right to tell us what you put in your letter to Vicky that has brought your grandad back home.'

'Nothing.' She looked innocent enough. 'He's been home before. I expect he wants to see Daisy and me before we get married.'

Tom ignored the red herring. 'So he stays with Hermione.'

'Yes. Well. It's probably better that way. We go to school every day. And you two go to the office.'

'And Hermione goes to the manor.' He turned suddenly and caught Daisy making a face. 'So you're the one at the bottom of the plot,' he said in a friendly voice. I was washing up at the sink and couldn't see any of them, but I knew the way things were going. Tom could use silence and friendliness in most unusual ways. The girls both knew that, too.

Daisy stammered, 'There isn't a plot. It's just that when Vicky was here for the Coronation, Roland Beard fell in love with her – they were both seven – and they've always written to each other since then, and now they're seventeen . . . well, he wants her to come over—'

Tom nodded, still friendly. 'I see.' He waited.

The girls stuck it out for as long as they could, then Rose blurted, 'They want to get married.'

'So Vicky has sent your grandad over to make the wedding arrangements?'

Both girls laughed, obviously relieved, then realized Tom was waiting for something else. Daisy frowned and chewed her bottom lip consideringly.

'I rather think,' she began portentously, 'that Grandee is supposed to speak to Roland. You know, like fathers do. To make sure his intentions are above board and all that sort of thing.'

'I see,' Tom said again, but this time he

stood up and picked up the tea towel. 'Actually Grandee is not Vicky's father.'

'No. But he's English and he knows Daphne a bit. Besides, he's worried about the Smiths.' She fielded a warning glance from her sister, and added, 'I think.'

Tom dried two plates and put them in the dresser.

'If there's nothing much on the television this evening, d'you want to have a go at the Souza march again? I got two new kazoos today. Good ones. Mum could have the wooden spoons and the kettle and I could manage both tambourines. What d'you say?'

The girls thought they were off the hook, and were full of enthusiasm. Meriel had brought snapshots and tapes of Georgie, and they were practising the march ready to tape it for him at Christmas. They had become teenagers in August and it was good to see them revert to being little girls again. They broke into raucous song immediately, and when Tom produced the kazoos – plastic with fretted ventilation – the noise was ear-splitting. I covered my ears and begged for 'Yankee Doodle Dandy', which was another from the repertoire. And in the laughing respite, Tom said, 'Actually, I rather gathered that Vicky was getting bored with Roland's letters, and he was trying to pep them up a bit by mentioning that Mr Smith's sister lived with a German collaborator during the war.'

The silence was deafening for all of two seconds. Then Daisy said in a bewildered voice, 'How would that get him back in her good books?'

Tom said nothing, this time because he was baffled.

Rose said, 'Oh, tell him, Daisy. He knows Vicky wants to be a writer like him.' She turned to her father. 'It's a load of rubbish, Dad. Roland would say anything to get Vicky interested. He probably hasn't mentioned getting married. He just wants to make the – the situation here – exciting. So he made up this story that Maude Smith was a murderer.'

Daisy was aghast. 'You promised me . . . I promised Colin I wouldn't say anything to any of the grown-ups!'

Tom and I looked at each other blankly. It was my voice that asked the question.

'Who did she murder?'

'Someone called Silver Man. I mean . . . pretty stupid, eh?'

Rose giggled. 'We thought Grandee was coming over to have a go at us! We felt terrible.'

Daisy said, 'Well, it was you who wrote to Vicky!' She dried her kazoo carefully and added, 'Anyway, you wrote ages ago and he's only just come so it's probably nothing to do with your letter at all.'

There was a little silence. Rose said uncertainly,

'Who was Mr Smith's sister, then, Dad? And who was the German collaborator she slept with?'

Tom said, 'Sorry, girls. I just threw that in to try to shock you into telling us what was really in that damned letter you wrote.'

Rose half-laughed. 'Well, that's all it was.' She looked at her father. 'Honestly,' she added.

So we got the kettle, the kazoos, the wooden spoons and the tambourines and began practising the Souza march again.

Tom said, 'All that old stuff coming up again. We know it's not true – we discovered the body, for goodness' sake!'

It was cold in the front bedroom and my dressing gown was at the cleaner's. I huddled into one of our old army blankets and stood by the window, looking out.

I said, 'Killing people . . . it doesn't stop even when war is over. Imagine someone planning Kennedy's murder.'

Tom said, 'Unless there was something we didn't know. It was hushed up so suddenly, wasn't it?'

I knew he wasn't talking about Kennedy; I watched someone cycling from the Northgate. A sudden gust of wind made him veer into the kerb, and he almost fell off. I said, 'Does it matter now? It's so long ago.'

'It matters. Even when we don't know, and

might never know, what happened, it matters. Like my dad.'

I dropped the curtain and went to the bed and put my arms around him. My blanket dropped away, and I shivered, and he tucked me under the covers, and we held each other. He whispered, 'I know what you mean. What matters is you and me here, now, right now.'

I whispered back, 'Are we going to grow old together, Tom?'

'I pray about that, Rache. I pray that we will.'

'So do I.'

Eventually we slept.

The next day Tom took the car. He was driving Uncle Gilbert to a lovely old inn at Broadway in the Cotswolds, where he was lunching 'intimately' with the lord lieutenant and a select few of about a dozen people who actually ran the county. That evening there was going to be a reception at the Shire Hall where Uncle Gilbert would be given the freedom of the city, but the lunch was what he called the 'real McCoy'. He had always been able to pull strings and now that was being officially recognized. I was invited to the evening's reception, but certainly not the lunch. I think Uncle Gilbert had had to pull lots of strings to accommodate Tom.

As soon as he had left and the girls had

plodded off to school I fetched my bike from the coal cellar, flipped a duster over it, went upstairs, put on some extra clothing and different shoes, and set out for the no-longer-rough road, which had been 'adopted' by the County Council and named Winterditch Lane. It would always be the rough road to me.

It was a typical December morning; the combined river mist and city smog made it intensely cold, but there was no ice about; it was what my grandmother had called 'roar' meaning raw. There was no wind either, so I made good time once I was out of the city. I zoomed past the Nightingales' house and cut left where the old-fashioned finger sign said Cheltenham and Tewkesbury. Then I was between low hedgerows and felt the flat lands all around me, though I couldn't see them. It was incredible – impossible – that Mr Silverman had been murdered, but I had to talk to Dad about it. He'd been home almost three weeks and I'd seen him every day and never known why he had come to this country at this time and why he was staying with Hermione. All right, it was his home still, but . . . Hermione?

I sped down Winterditch Lane; no more pot holes, no more skidding. Rough Road Cottage was looking good; Hermione had had it painted for Dad's return. The outside of the house was of course his responsibility, but I doubted whether she would mention the painting, and he probably hadn't noticed it. I realized that Hermione had been in a tizz about Dad coming back ever since I told her about it, which was ages ago now, back in the summer some time. It was a strange situation for her; she was put into the position of being a cuckoo in the nest – or was that Dad?

I propped my bike against the side of the house and fiddled for a handkerchief to wipe the moisture from my eyes and nose. During the war the rough road had been graced with several enormous oil cans which were lit by the air raid wardens when an alert sounded, in order to screen the ack-ack guns in a pall of oily smoke. Afterwards we used to be blowing soot into our handkerchiefs for ages. It felt like that again as I mopped at the smog on my face and fumbled round to the kitchen door. It was a bit of an anti-climax to find it locked. If Dad had been in it would have been open; Hermione fed Mr Myercroft's cat and he had access to the porch, where there was always a saucer of fresh milk.

Even so I peered through the dining-room window, then went to the front of the house and cupped my hand against the glass to see into the sitting room. No one was there. I should have phoned, of course, but somehow I had wanted to surprise him.

I was at a completely loose end, my sense of

anti-climax rolling in with the fog. I wheeled my bike to the road and cycled slowly back the way I had come. Conditions, as they say on the wireless, were worsening, but still I saw something I hadn't noticed earlier. Hermione's bike was parked outside the Smiths' house. Hermione used her car for getting to and from the manor; Dad must have borrowed her bike.

I propped mine next to it and went up to the well-remembered front door. It had been maroon, and was now sunbleached and almost free of paint. The Smiths were very comfortably off, it didn't make sense. I knocked and then crouched to open the letter box. 'It's only me!' I called. Silence.

I lowered my head until I could see through the narrow space. The stairs were on the left, the banister on which Hermione's school uniform had hung minus the tie was just visible. Behind the stairs the hall led down to the kitchen. To the right it led to the dining room and then the sitting room. The telephone had been there. If I pressed my face hard to the letter box I could just see it. It was still the old fashioned two-part arrangement, a separate mouth and earpiece. The earpiece was dangling on its cable, slightly swinging.

I bawled, 'Dad! Where are you? It's me – Rachel!'

His voice came back immediately; the usual, unruffled tone.

'Just a minute, honey. Hang on.'

I straightened, holding my back in sheer relief. I don't quite know what I had imagined; perhaps Mrs Smith knocking Dad unconscious with the frying pan? Voices came through the letter box now, Dad's soothing, Mrs Smith's even higher-pitched than normal. Grumbling about something, grumbling more than normal, in fact hectoring, in fact escalating to hysterics. Then Dad saying something quite loudly and Mrs Smith shutting up, cut off instantly.

The kitchen door opened and Dad's voice spoke clearly, 'No need to see me out, my dear.'

Mrs Smith said, 'The phone—'

Dad said, 'I'll see to it. You'd better sit down again.'

There was a pause. Perhaps he was shrugging into his top coat. Then there was a clatter and he said, 'I told you to sit down. Now put your legs up like a good girl.' It was sickening. Mrs Smith had never ever been a girl, let alone a good one.

He moved around in the hall quite a lot, probably replacing the phone and finding his cycle clips and gloves . . . he opened the door, gave me a reassuring grin, glanced back down the hall, then closed the door with a very sharp click.

'Damned thing needs oil.'

He took my arm and manoeuvred both of us down the path to our bikes. For some reason I hung back.

'Dad, what's happening? Is she all right?'

'She is now. She got upset. Hermione doesn't have much to do with her, so she rang up last night and said some awful things. I told Hermione I would warn her off. And I have.' He swung his leg over the saddle. 'There was a bit of a scuffle when she tried to ring the police.'

I looked at him, expecting him to grin at me; he didn't.

We got on our bikes and went back home. I made some coffee. Dad knew his way around the kitchen and produced a biscuit tin full of home-made biscuits. I raised my brows; he shrugged. 'Hermione should have a husband and a family; she is a beautiful, intelligent woman. The Smiths put the kibosh on that, of course. Things were much better when she moved here, but her mother is going to wear her down eventually. She should go and live in America the way I did.'

'You were running away – is that what you mean?'

'I was running towards warmth. She would be running towards excellent funding for her work. Maybe that husband I mentioned. She's not forty yet.'

'Dad . . . she won't let them rule her life again. She's strong.'

'None of us are that strong, Rache. You would have done lots of things for Mum and me.'

'I *loved* you both!'

'That's the most powerful weapon of all. Funnily enough, Hermione loves that vampire too.' He jerked his head in the direction of the rough road. Then he shrugged. 'Kids love their parents even when they're beaten and starved. Hermione knows that. She is doing some research into it at the moment.'

I drank some coffee, coughed on it, spluttered a bit and managed, 'Dad, what is happening? I don't understand. Have you come home to – to sort out – something? Roland Beard made up some story and told his brother Colin, who's got a crush on Daisy. So of course he told her, and she told Rose, who wrote to Vicky. The story was that Mrs Smith had murdered Mr Silverman.'

Dad looked into his coffee cup as if he might find an answer there. Then he looked up, frowning slightly.

'Yes. That's it in a nutshell. Vicky said I'd got to come back and find out the truth. Because if Mrs Maude Smith had killed Mr Silverman, then Hermione would know about it and would be in danger.' He sighed. 'I prevaricated like hell, Rache. Because you and Tom had found him hanging.'

'We did. If he'd been murdered . . . there would have been . . . signs. Surely?'

'Yes. That's what I thought. I didn't want to open it up all over again, Rache. Mum was at peace and Florida . . . nobody cares out there what happened in little old England nineteen years ago. Meriel is my link with home. And her family treat me like one of themselves. Why turn the clock back?' I waited. He took a breath. 'Vicky questioned Roland like mad, and he fed her more stuff. Roland's father drinks with the Wingco. Who is scared of Maude. Scared of his own wife. Scared for himself. And scared for Hermione. And the Wingco was taken into hospital with food poisoning four weeks ago.'

'Oh my God.'

'Yes. Maude didn't mention it to Hermione until last Monday. And Hermione went to see her father in the evening. She was in a bit of a state when she got back. Obviously she wouldn't tell me why, but she did say that her father does not want to go back home. So on Tuesday I went to see Gilbert Carfax. He'd done the cover-up when the bodies of Strassen and Eva Schmidt were dug out. He did another when Sylvia Strassen was murdered. Had he done a third when poor old Silverman died?'

'Uncle Gilbert?' This was fast taking on the proportions of a nightmare; I tried to wake up and nothing happened.

Dad nodded. 'He would have done anything for your mother. You know that.'

'*Mum*? What has *Mum* got to do with any of this? My God, Dad, Mum is *dead*!' The fog was pressing against the window, and it was almost dark in the dining room.

He looked surprised. 'I thought you realized, Rache. It has all been for Mum. All of it.'

I stared at him, thinking he was talking about his own actions in selling the designs for the tail fin. I said – not without sarcasm – 'And what are you going to do this time . . . for Mum?'

'Darling . . . you're not listening. This time it is for Hermione. And I am going to murder Mrs Smith before she can murder her daughter.'

I kept staring at him, then felt for the edge of the table, found a chair, pulled it out and sat down with a crash.

Eighteen

I told myself this was actually happening, and was not a nightmare at all. Dad had said he intended to murder someone. This was no joke. Even so, I said, 'Dad, stop messing about.'

He gave a little smile, pulled out another chair and sat down. Our knees were touching; I knew mine were shaking but his were steady.

He leaned forward and took my hand. 'Darling girl. I couldn't talk about it when it happened back in '44. I almost said something when you and Merry got involved with Strassen . . . I was terrified, actually. But then he was killed in that raid and . . . well, it was best forgotten. Then almost ten years later, when Merry suggested I go for a holiday to Florida, I told you then. Just in case there was a plane crash or something.' He tried to laugh at himself, but I just kept staring.

He squeezed my hand. 'Rache, it was nothing. Not really. Mum was such an innocent, she handed over a name to her posh neighbour, Mrs Smith, whose husband was a wing commander and on the board of Smith's Aircraft Company. She was so respectable she frightened Mum to death. Almost literally. Mum's job entailed keeping records of men who were working for the Allies in France. She found the name Mrs Smith had asked for; he was based in Lyons, a railway engineer. He had died in a sabotage operation that had gone wrong. Of course it was still covered by the Official Secrets Act, but when Mum saw that the man was dead, she saw no reason to hold back – Mrs Smith said she wanted to help his family. Mrs Smith actually gave Mum her very own ration book as a reward. You know how Mum loved to feed us, however difficult it was. It wasn't like taking money – she couldn't have done that. But, well, you have guessed it, Mrs Smith didn't stop there. She wanted other names. She had other ration books.'

I was gripping his hand tightly. Mum . . . so sweet, so kind, such a low opinion of herself. I said hoarsely, 'How many ration books?'

Dad shook his head. 'Mum was innocent, but not stupid, Rache. No more ration books. She hadn't used the one she had, and she gave it back the moment she realized what was happening. Mrs Smith tried to paper over the cracks – used to sit by you in church, didn't she? Mum found out that the man's family had been evacuated to America soon after the outbreak of hostilities and she felt better about it. But of course her morale had hit rock bottom. It was Gilbert who suggested to me that I let Mrs Smith have the designs for the fin. He said it would shut her up, and be good for Mum.' He shook his head wearily. 'Sounds crazy now, doesn't it? But the war was almost over, and when I looked at bits from some of the German crashed planes it seemed as if they were already developing their designs parallel with mine.' He lifted his shoulders. 'It so often happens, Rache. Mum gave out that name in all innocence, because the owner of it was dead. And I did the same. My invention was dead.'

I discovered I was weeping. I said, 'I don't get it. Why did Uncle Gilbert think it would help?'

'He *knew* it would help. And it did. Mrs Smith left Flo alone. She thought she had landed a much bigger fish. Anything to impress Willi Strassen, of course. She even killed Silverman when he threatened to expose Strassen . . .' He paused morosely, recalling that time, and then grinned unexpectedly. 'Mind you, how long Mum would have been free of her is a moot point. But the Nazis sorted that one out!' His grin became rueful. 'Mum didn't believe I'd actually given away my precious tail fin. Not at first. Then I dragged her to Düsseldorf with me after the war was over and she believed me then.' He nodded. 'Actually, it did make her feel better about the whole nasty business. We were in it together, you see, Rache. Even treason!' He tried to laugh, then added, 'Like you and Tom. Mum was so thankful for Tom.'

I broke down completely. If only he'd talked like this years ago.

Dad took me on his shoulder and patted my back and said that he had thought I would put two and two together and see exactly what had happened. He described the 1944 events as 'a storm in a teacup', Sylvia's death four years later as 'a tragedy'. I managed to tell him about our Oliver typewriter and the rent book so blatantly signed by me.

'Ah. I don't think Gilbert realized that. He just saw the name Strassen and thought that the whole horrible business might rear its head again and Mum would be back to square one. By that time she was really ill.'

I controlled myself gradually. It was past midday and we were both hungry. Dad made some more coffee and I cut cheese sandwiches.

I said, 'There's no way Uncle Gilbert could cover up Mrs Smith's death. And anyway, Dad, you couldn't kill her.'

'You should have seen me earlier this morning. I nearly broke her arm when she tried to phone the police.' Again, I could not laugh, and he said seriously, 'What a waste, Rache, if at the end of it all Hermione is poisoned. Or her car brakes don't work. Or her dear mum visits her and pushes her down the stairs.'

'Uncle Gilbert would not even try to cover that up.'

'No. But Hermione might still be very dead or injured. And the Smith woman isn't fit to live, anyway.'

'Dad. You cannot do it. That's that.'

He put more coal on the fire and settled back down with his lunch.

'I've thought about it so much, Rache. I confronted her this morning about her husband. She said she had also been sick four weeks ago and it must have been the fish they had eaten. I asked her whether she had used the same poison she'd used on poor old Silverman. She said the post-mortem had not shown any poison so far as she knew, and anyway how would she have hoisted a man, even a little man like Silverman, up to a noose on the ceiling beam? I told her she had done it with Strassen's help while we were at the park celebrating Holidays at Home. I told her she'd killed Silverman because he'd threatened to tell the authorities what she was up to. She denied it all, of course.' He looked morosely at his plate. 'Nothing rattled her, Rache. She is without conscience.'

'The jury will see it as without guilt.'

He looked up at me. 'We can't take her to court, Rache. She would drag Mum's name into it.'

I met his eyes. They were no longer vague; Dad was focused for the first time since Mum died.

I said, 'You mean we're going to forget Strassen and Eva and Sylvia and Mr Silverman?'

'Of course not. But revenge is never sweet, my love. I'm not going to kill anyone for vengeance. But to prevent another death . . . yes. If that is the only way, and I cannot think of another one, can you?'

'Not at the moment. It's all been rather . . . bloody awful.' I don't think I'd ever sworn in front of Dad before, and he widened his eyes.

'It's a shock. I thought you were au fait with a lot of things. I've had a long time to get used to it, and my one thought was to protect Mum.'

I glanced at the clock. 'Dad, I must go. The girls will be home at four.' I stood up. 'Look, please don't do anything . . . precipitate. Give me a day or two. You've shown your hand to Hermione's mum – you might even have frightened her off.'

'Not very likely.'

'Meriel will be home tonight. She's driving back straight after her last lecture so that she can be with the twins while Tom and I are at the reception at the Shire Hall. Let me talk it over with her. Please, Dad.'

He held my coat for me. I think it was his hesitation that convinced me of his intentions. My heart hammered.

'Dad . . . I couldn't care less about Mrs Smith. But you . . . Uncle Gilbert will never be able to cover this up. And it will finish you, Dad.'

'Let me work that one out, Rache. It will be all right.'

He cycled back with me as far as the Pitch. The fog was dense. I promised to ring him when I got in. It was so good to see the street lamps each with their foggy aureole, to turn into Chichester Street, lug my bike up the two steps and go into the hall. Mrs Smith a murderer? All I cared about was getting a cup of tea and stirring up the fire. But there was something . . . not right . . . about Dad's story. I couldn't think what it was, then. But it sounded so much like something Meriel and I might have cooked up when we cycled to school each morning. Up to a point we were spot-on with our pretend games; but then there was something wrong. They became phoney.

The Shire Hall was ablaze with lights; there was a red carpet following the treads of the steps. On the opposite side of the Westgate, the cathedral, shadowy in spite of the floodlighting, rose above the houses and illuminated the river mist into a separate entity: a silvery cloak. Meriel had arrived just as we were dressing and was now somewhere in the small crowd on the pavement with Rose and Daisy and a camera. She had been fiddling with it as I told her briefly what had happened since her last visit. She had just nodded and peered through the view-finder. The photography crew from the *Clarion* were there in force but she wanted personal family snaps to send back home for Georgie.

Tom gave up the keys of the car to someone called Stan and took my arm for the walk up to the resplendent figures just inside the doors. Besides the lord lieutenant there were the mayor, the sheriff and a horde of councillors, all accompanied by bejewelled wives, mothers and daughters. Two Jamaican couples hovered uncertainly next to the mayor, looking uncomfortable in English evening clothes. Our ancient schools were represented, and as we shook the row of hands I spotted Miss Hardwicke, marvellously severe in silver-grey satin. I did so hope Meriel had got a snap of her as she swept up the steps. Somehow, be it second- or third-hand, Vicky and Georgie had to get a glimpse of Miss Hardwicke. Tom and I took a glass of something from a silver tray that appeared before us and moved to join her.

Tom looked suddenly middle-aged in the evening suit we had hired from Nightingale's. I realized I usually saw the Tom I had first met in the lower office of the *Clarion*; I hadn't noticed that he had changed. The nervous business of covering his slightly prominent teeth with his upper lip had long gone, and he smiled often and without embarrassment. People took to him instantly because of what he called his rabbit smile. Miss Hardwicke had met him at parents' evenings, and held out a hand, smiling herself.

'How lovely to see you both. Mr Fairbrother, you look very handsome.' She sounded surprised, and then even more surprised as she turned to me. 'And Rachel, at last you're not ashamed of your height! As you came into the room you were moving so freely! Remember to keep those shoulders well back at all times.'

I nearly spluttered into my wine glass and Tom said, 'Both kitted out at Nightingale's, of course. I rather think you did the same. Am I right?'

I was amazed by his sheer cheek, but Miss Hardwicke dimpled – yes, she actually dimpled, something I had never seen before.

'The families of my girls are – it naturally follows – my own family. And we have to support our families, don't we?'

I could imagine how Dennis would love this. Actually Maria had chosen my dress, and told me how to walk in it so that I wouldn't tread on the fishtail train at the back. It was a strange blue, which shaded into black as I moved, darkened my eyes and made my cloud of dark hair nearly exotic. Tom had already told me what he thought; Miss Hardwicke's comment increased my self-confidence.

Uncle Gilbert was announced, then, and everybody put down their glasses and clapped. He was a popular figure, and cultivated his resemblance to Winston Churchill. Maxine was nothing like Clementine. She clung to his arm as if she expected to be torn from it at any moment. The white feather boa which wound itself around her bare shoulders appeared to be tickling her nose, and she screwed up her face occasionally and responded to the applause with little snuffling laughs. She had not aged at all as far as I could see, though Uncle Gilbert had mentioned trouble with her weight now and then. They moved from group to group easily, expertly. People still chatted, but very quietly, and it was plain that they were waiting their turn. When he reached the three of us, Gilbert gently detached himself from Maxine and held out his hands to me.

'My goddaughter,' he explained to Miss Hardwicke over my shoulder, and planted a kiss on my cheek, then added into my ear, 'You are so like Flo, it hurts.' And then he put Maxine's hand back on his arm, and spoke to Tom and Miss Hardwicke together. I hardly heard what he said, and whether they responded. My cheek burned. I remembered Dad saying that Gilbert Carfax would do anything for Mum. Would he approve . . . even help with . . . the murder of Maude Smith? I shook myself. It couldn't happen.

We followed Gilbert and Maxine Carfax into the banqueting hall and took our places with much fuss and reading of place cards. The soup arrived and turned out to be brown Winzie, which made Tom and me smile and touch hands beneath the knife edge of the starched table cloth. Tom turned to share the joke with Miss Hardwicke, who appreciated it.

'Knowing Rose, I think you were very lucky she took to any of the hotel food,' she commented. 'She professes to be disgusted by everything Cook makes for school dinners!' Tom made an apologetic face, and Miss Hardwicke added, 'She eats as much as the others, in spite of that.' I smiled, and felt some kind of normality washing around me. Rose being awkward, Daisy being sunny, Tom always being there . . . trying to find time for my weekly contribution to the *Clarion* . . . promising myself that one day I would write a book . . . this was my life – these were the links in the chain of my life. Not old conspiracies and present-day planned murders.

As usual, Meriel had tried to take the whole thing on to her own shoulders. 'Don't worry, I'll think of something. Just enjoy your evening.' Then she had looked past me and said, 'She wouldn't harm her own daughter.'

The evening began to take shape around me, someone whispered to me, 'Isn't that the old headmistress of the Swallow School? My

God, she must be nearly a hundred!' And I laughed, because of course Miss Hardwicke looked exactly the same as she had done back in 1944. There was an entree, fish, I think, then very unexpectedly a small sorbet to freshen the taste buds – my knowledgeable neighbour told me that – then beef cut from an enormous joint lying on a gigantic trencher at the side table. It wasn't even a joint, it was a section of the actual animal. Tom said it was a bit too Henry the Eighth for him but, like his daughter, he ate as much as those who had no criticisms whatsoever. The puddings came on tiered trolleys, one for each side of the table. I had something that tasted a bit like sherry trifle; Tom had lemon meringue pie, which was all the thing at that time.

After the cheese and port came the speeches. Some very nice things were said about Uncle Gilbert; I found myself believing them until I caught Miss Hardwicke's eye. She didn't exactly wink, but the impression was similar. As Tom said later, 'He's an old rogue, but that's all right when he's on your side.'

(I repeated Tom's words to Dad when I saw him next and added, 'We've got a lot to thank Mum for.' I spoke without thinking, but Dad gave a rueful smile and shook his head with a kind of resignation.)

There was a lot of talk about the independence of Jamaica. We had quite a few West

Indian Gloucestrians now and Uncle Gilbert had floated a scheme for cultural exchange: he and Maxine were taking the mayor and his wife to Jamaica to promote English local government; the medical officer had recently joined the group. Tom had suggested to Gilbert that some representatives of the West Indian community should join the 'Benevolent Society bash'. Tom could get away with saying things like that; he added with a grin, 'Make it less of a benevolent society, if you get my meaning.'

Anyway, the mayor explained it all in his speech and made it sound amazingly innovative and democratic; more smiles were directed at Gilbert and Maxine, then, as an afterthought, towards the Jamaican group, who smiled back with generous flashings of beautiful teeth.

We did not stay long. Maxine kept chatting for ages in the cloakroom, asking me whether I would have Frou-frou while she and Gilbert did their Jamaican 'exchange'. 'I cannot bear to be separated from her, Rachel darling. But Gilbert can't live without me, and of course she would never survive the quarantine.'

Only then did I remember Frou-frou was her poodle. I accepted willingly; this was the sort of thing we did, this was 'normal life'. When she told me it would mean she had to visit me every afternoon so that Frou-frou could get used to my 'premises', I wasn't quite so willing, but by then the die had been cast.

Stan was magically waiting for us on the steps; he had just delivered Miss Hardwicke's car and held the door for her with suitable reverence. We waved and wished her a happy Christmas, and then Stan disappeared to fetch our car, and we drove to the old stables at the end of Chichester Street and walked down to number twenty-one almost on tiptoe. It might be the swinging sixties elsewhere but at midnight in Gloucester everyone had been in bed for some time. Except Meriel, of course.

She was waiting in the kitchen, the oven lit and the door open. It was bitterly cold and the insulation we had acquired from food and drink had gone during the short walk from car to house. We huddled around the cooker and gave her an outline of our evening, and she was the usual wonderful audience, clueing in to the funny side of it, rejoicing at the thought of Miss Hardwicke in her silver-grey satin. She opened her eyes wide when Tom told her about Gilbert and Maxine going to the West Indies.

'All expenses paid?' she asked.

I saw a furious political diatribe opening up and was thankful when Tom said, 'When we were waiting outside the cloakroom the Gaffer mentioned he might have to help the Jamaican nurses with their fares, but otherwise the trip would be self-funded.'

Meriel couldn't quite let Uncle Gilbert get off scot-free and put her head on the table giggling helplessly. 'Self-funded? There's a new one! I predict we're going to hear high usage of self-funding!' She poured the last few words down her nose exactly like poor Mr Kennedy might have done, and I have to admit Tom and I laughed too.

Tom put an end to the long, long day by switching off the cooker. We all stood up. Meriel kissed us both and walked to the living-room door where she turned and smiled at us lovingly.

'I know we don't want to mention that woman, but I've had all evening since the girls went to bed to think about it. And the answer is right under our noses, and so perfect it's almost unbelievable.' I felt Tom's hand between my shoulder blades so knew I had visibly tensed. Meriel smiled slightly then said, 'Dear George and Hermione should get married. She can't kill off the two of them but just in case, George deposits a letter with his solicitor to be opened . . . if necessary.' She flipped through the door, then opened it again and looked through. 'It would be so *good* for George to have someone to look after again. You and me, Rache, we've always been so bloody self-sufficient. You're lucky, you're in a partnership. And George knows that.'

She was gone again and Tom and I looked at each other blankly.

'I don't get it,' I said. 'It doubles the problem, if anything.'

'It does and it doesn't,' Tom said helpfully. He held the door open for me and I ducked under his arm which, somehow snake-like, then encircled me and held us together. He whispered, 'Could your father love her, d'you think? They're both scientists, they're living together very comfortably, as far as we know—'

'Dad is *lodging* there . . . in his old home—'

'But they both seem so at ease with the situation.'

'Hermione feels safe. She always did with Dad. Dad is – must be – on tenterhooks the whole time, living so close to the woman he is convinced murdered that poor man—'

'Darling, your dad is facing up to life again. Which he hasn't done for fourteen years.'

'How can you be so – so precise?'

'Because your mother died just before the girls were born and they are now thirteen years old.'

I was silent, digesting this, although I knew immediately that he was right.

He whispered, 'You are so beautiful, Rache. I wanted to shout it out tonight: This is my wife, and on the day we met we found a dead body, and we've been investigating it ever since!'

'No, we haven't.' I kissed him. 'We've been living ever since. That is what we've been doing, Tom Fairbrother. We were shown the importance of living and we've done it. And will go on doing it. In spite of – or perhaps because of – your father and mine!'

He clamped me to him; my chin on his shoulder, his on mine. Both of us filled with sheer gratitude. But then he said right into my ear, 'I wonder what that harridan of a woman had got on your mother.'

I whispered, 'What do you mean?'

'How did she make Flo Throstle smuggle secret information from the records office? It must have been blackmail, Rache. It wasn't money. Flo would never have been bribed. She was blackmailed.'

I held on to him tightly. That was what had been phoney about Dad's story. There had been no reason for Mum's actions; none for his, either.

'What do you think it was?' I asked obscurely.

Tom knew what I meant and sighed into my neck. 'Well . . . if it is still bad enough to make your father consider murder, it's not very likely we will find out. Is it?'

We looked at each other in the darkness. And then we went to bed.

Nineteen

None of the events of that Friday stopped me sleeping like a log that night. Tom and I were still curled together like an upper-case S when Daisy knocked very circumspectly and then entered at Tom's drowsy 'C'min'. She had two enormous pint mugs of tea inside a washing-up bowl. We had devised this adaptation of the usual tray and cups when she had first started the tea-in-bed thing aged seven. It saved a lot of frantic mopping-up.

I opened one eye but could not move. 'How absolutely lovely,' I said, eyeing the steaming tankards and wondering whether I could ask for a straw.

Daisy said, surprised but very interested, 'Have you got a hangover?'

Rose came close behind, clutching a packet of digestive biscuits. 'Of course they haven't,' she said scathingly. 'It's Mum and Dad!'

Tom started to giggle first, but I wasn't far behind. We couldn't stop. We couldn't move.

Tears streamed down our faces. The girls stood there looking disgusted. Eventually, after they had told us how pathetic we were, they placed the washing-up bowl and biscuits on the floor, my side of the bed, and left. 'Hope Aunt Merry will be more sensible!' was Rose's parting shot.

Once they'd gone we simmered down, and Tom shouted his thanks, and we struggled up in bed, and I placed the washing-up bowl on the bedspread. We sipped and grinned and almost giggled again with sheer pleasure. It was eight thirty. Tom worked out that we had had seven hours' sleep, which was sufficient for people of our age, and we should be up and sweeping the snow from the doorstep.

'Snow?' I asked, seriously alarmed.

'Metaphorically speaking, of course.'

That started us off again. We couldn't understand it. There was still the awfulness of discovering that crabby old Mrs Smith had probably murdered someone, plus the fact that my father was proposing to follow in her footsteps. Oh – and also the fact that Meriel thought he should marry Hermione Smith. Hermione Smith, daughter of the horrible Mrs Smith! And there was something else, too . . . what was it . . . it was the extent of Uncle Gilbert's wheeling and dealing. Perhaps we were hysterical. It was enough to cause hysteria.

Meriel yelled from the landing, 'I'm hogging the bathroom for half an hour!'

And that seemed funny, too.

Eventually we staggered downstairs and joined Rose and Daisy at the kitchen table with the cereal. Rose made toast and demanded details of last night's dinner.

'Miss Hardwicke there? You didn't tell us that! Oh, sewers and drains – what did she wear?'

We told them. Daisy said, 'Silver satin? So romantic. D'you think—'

'We're talking about Miss Hardwicke,' Rose said repressively.

'By the way, we're going to be looking after Frou-frou for Aunt Maxine when she goes to Jamaica,' I mentioned. The response was overwhelming. Daisy clasped her hands ecstatically. 'How lovely! How simply lovely! She can sleep with me. Oh, darling Aunt Maxine! I just love her!'

Rose said, 'Jamaica? Why? When? But mainly, why?'

Tom took over and was half-way through when Meriel appeared and confessed to having shaved her legs and blocked the bath outlet. 'It's OK now, I'm rather good at plumbing. You didn't mention about Jamaica last night. When are you going?'

Both girls screamed at her. Everything was sorted out. I went upstairs to wash and dress and tidy the bedrooms. I felt happy. I really felt happy. Like Dad said, all that had happened back in the 1940s was no more than a storm in a teacup, and I was almost certain that what was happening in the 1960s would be written off the same way.

We had an early lunch because the girls were going to the Plaza cinema with Daphne, Roland and Colin to see *Summer Holiday.* Meriel had work to do. Tom suggested we get the car and drive to Huntley to see the Gaffer.

'We might be able to sort it all out. Between us.'

I was doubtful at first. But then I remembered Frou-frou. 'That can be our excuse. Maybe we can take her home with us, get her used to the car. The girls would love to see her.'

He looked at me. 'Why can't we go straight for the jugular—' he imitated a German accent. 'Did old man Silverman hang himself or was he murdered?'

'You can do that. I'll talk to Maxine about Frou-frou's likes and dislikes.'

'Hang on, Rache. The Gaffer and I have a purely working relationship. It's you he's close to. Last night . . . I thought he was going to cry when he set eyes on you.'

I sobered somewhat. 'It caught him unaware. My likeness to Mum.' I sighed. 'I grew up knowing he was an old boy friend. Over the years I've realized he put her on a pedestal.' I recalled last night and his emotional greeting. I had been . . . embarrassed. I said quickly, 'Thank goodness for Maxine.'

He looked at me in the mirror, then said, 'She certainly keeps him on the straight and narrow.'

We drove slowly along the drive of Clarion House. A row of beech trees, last year's leaves rattling in the December wind, defined the boundary on the right and swept around the house, carelessly magnificent. On the left the land dropped away in a series of lawns joined by ha-has. A few sheep were grazing on the furthest lawn; Uncle Gilbert had never seen the point of mowing machines when sheep could do the job silently and constantly. We drew up on a gravel sweep in front of the house. Uncle Gilbert's Riley was on one side of the pillared porch, Maxine's Wolsley the other, so they were both at home. Tom said, 'Once more unto the breach . . .' and opened his door, and at the same time, the wide front door under the portico opened and there was Maxine, arms outstretched in welcome.

'You *never* call unannounced, darlings!' She got her arms around us both, and I realized her sleeves were rolled up and her hands, held above our shoulders, definitely floury. Maxine cooking? 'Has something happened?'

Tom kissed her on the cheek with enthusiasm. 'I've always thought you looked wonderful, Maxie, but in an apron, with your hair in your eyes and flour everywhere . . . you look more like Betty Grable than ever, with a touch of the Doris Days, too!'

She pecked him back, but still looked anxious. I was about to reassure her when he chipped in again. 'It's a bit too fraught at our house. We've come here to escape. Is it inconvenient?'

'No, no, no! Certainly not.' She stepped away, hands still held high. 'In fact, you can come and sample some of my Victoria sponge.' She smiled at me. 'Your mother taught me how to make sponges. In the days when it was powdered eggs and any old fat you could get hold of!'

She did not often refer to Mum, and it always came as a shock to remember that they had been friends. In fact, had Mum actually introduced Maxine to Uncle Gilbert? Surely not?

We followed her across the hall and beneath the arching staircase into the kitchen, which Dad had always called the ballroom. It extended the width of the house; and the windows looked out on the sweep of beech trees, and followed them down the hill to where we knew the home farm, which dealt with everything muddy, smelly or noisy, sat by the road.

Maxine said, 'Gillie is sorting out the sheep. They need to be moved up to the pasture for the winter. He won't be long. He likes to chat to Arnold and be a farmer for five minutes.'

'No longer?' Tom asked, all innocence.

Maxine laughed. 'You know him better than we do, Tom.' She dusted her hands and then put them under the tap. 'It's good to see you. You haven't been out for ages.' She dried her hands and filled the kettle. 'Sit down, both of you. We'll have to stay out here otherwise I'll forget the sponge and it will burn.' She switched on the kettle and sat down at the table with us. 'What did you think of last night?'

Tom said, 'Jamaica? We were amazed. And impressed. The Gaffer has still got it. And those nurses – a touch of genius.'

'They're lovely girls. And so excited at the thought of seeing their families again. What about the food? I wasn't sure about the sorbet, but we were in London last summer, and they served it between courses at Grey's, so I thought it must be all right. And I read up about the syllabub. When Cromwell lodged here, there was reference to syllabub and a 'baron of beef'. So it seemed sort of right.'

I said, 'Did you take on the catering, Maxine? My God, it was superb! I didn't realize it was syllabub – of course it was – how absolutely marvellous! You must have been sweating blood all evening – no one gave you credit or anything.'

She laughed and flushed with pleasure. 'I thought you would know, of course. I usually arrange the catering for these sorts of things, I should be used to it. But this was so important. I'm really glad you liked it.' Of course, that was how Mum had known her; they had been waitresses together.

'Oh Maxine—' I was overcome. 'And there was me thinking all you cared about was Frou-frou!'

'Well, of course. And Frou-frou is always top of the list but . . . well, you know—'

I thought back through all the years, how I had pigeon-holed Maxine as just a symbol of Uncle Gilbert's . . . what . . . virility? I said, 'I'm so sorry, Maxine. I've never realized you were—'

Tom took over. 'You're part of a team, Maxine. We took you for granted.' He sniffed. 'Is the sponge OK?'

She leapt to her feet and grabbed a fancy oven mitt. The sponges – two of them – were perfect. She waited until we had finished our tea, then turned them out and spread them with jam.

'I know you should wait until they are cold, but hot cake is so special.' She cut three large slices, and we started on them ecstatically. We smiled at each other. We had never been so close to Maxine.

Tom finished first, took his plate to the sink and swilled it. He looked at her over his shoulder.

'Maxine . . . can I ask you something rather personal? Just between the three of us?'

She opened her eyes wide and swallowed. 'Is it something awful?'

'Yes,' Tom said unequivocally.

'Oh God. Well, you have to now, don't you? Go on.'

'Mr Silverman. You remember? The bespoke tailoring business?' She nodded with a kind of resignation. Tom said, 'Rache and I found him, you know. Back in '44. Hanging from his living-room ceiling.'

'Do you think I could have forgotten that?' Her voice was low. 'I told Gillie you would guess some day. I told him. But he said he knew you were both bright but not that bright.'

There was a silence; the sort that Tom liked because it gave him time to work things out.

He said, 'What did he tell you about it?'

I held my breath. Was she going to say that Uncle Gilbert was a murderer? She clasped her hands around her plate, and kept her eyes on it as she took a deep breath. 'He didn't have to tell me anything. I was there. I helped him.'

Tom flashed me a look of pure horror and blurted, 'You didn't kill him, did you?'

She was just as horrified. 'Tom! Of course not! Your Uncle Gilbert is absolutely incapable of violence.' She lifted her head to look at him, then at me. 'You know that, Rache! He dotes on you. He always thought you were his. But of course you weren't. Any more than Hermione Smith is George Throstle's daughter.' She smiled. 'Isn't it odd that men are shocked to bits if they think they've got someone pregnant? But when the child grows up they want a piece of it – have you noticed that?' I must have looked terrible, because she said quickly, 'Oh Christ! You didn't know? I thought that was one of the reasons why you were here . . . Rachel, Gillie is not your father. Flo was so sorry for him she might have . . . slept with him. But he cannot father a child. George knew that, but when he found out about Flo sleeping with Gillie, he – he – well, turned to someone else – just for a moment.'

My mind leapt back to what she had said at first and I choked. 'Mrs Smith? He wouldn't – he hates her – he wouldn't—'

Tom was behind me holding my shoulders.

Maxine said on a note of pure astonishment, 'My God – Hermione isn't Maude Smith's child! She belongs to Eva Schmidt. Surely, surely you knew that?'

Tom said quietly, 'As you see, Maxine, we did not. It explains a great deal.'

He slid his hands down to my waist and crouched, holding me against the chair back. I stopped sliding off on to the floor. Maxine got up and fetched a glass of water. She too, crouched by me and offered the glass.

'Listen, darling. I've always known about it, so it does not seem shocking to me. Gillie was sort of pining away, rather. I did the best I could, but he was like a lovesick boy. Eventually dear Flo . . . your mother . . . she must have been trying to comfort him, she was so soft hearted. It . . . escalated – is that the word? into something else, and Gillie must have boasted to your dad. It went no further. We're talking about the mid-twenties, Rachel. Nobody spoke about things like that, then. It was so easy to keep it all hushed up.' She shrugged. 'I can't tell you what went on between your mum and dad. Presumably there was a row. He's not a vindictive man – you know that – but he had always admired Eva Schmidt. When your mum was pregnant and Eva was pregnant too . . . Gillie put his particular two and two together and made four. They sorted it out between themselves, of course. Maude Smith took on Hermione without a murmur. And George . . . well, George probably knew all about my Gillie so he never doubted that you were his. Gillie knew, too, but sometimes he likes to – to pretend. Now and then.' Her eyes were full of tears. 'I've let him do that, Rachel. It doesn't seem much to do for him, does it? It would be cruel to spoil his dream.'

There was a silence. I wanted desperately to

cry with Maxine but I couldn't. There was still the question of Hermione. It seemed to make complete sense that Maude Smith was not her mother – any more than dear Mrs Nightingale was Meriel's mother – but who was her father? How could Maxine be so certain that Eva had not comforted Dad as Mum had comforted Uncle Gilbert? Were Hermione and I half-sisters? So much began to make sense. Dad's protectiveness towards Hermione, and his loathing of Mrs Smith. The fact that when they moved into the rough road at the start of the war I was expected to befriend Hermione, take her to school, 'keep an eye' on her. Snippets of memories blew around inside my head. What had Mum thought about all this? How had Mum borne it? Why hadn't she told me . . . anything? Something?

The three of us sat and crouched there, digesting all of it. I wondered whether Hermione knew anything about her parentage, anything at all. I suddenly knew how Meriel had felt, discovering who her real mother was when she was living on another continent. I had to talk to Meriel. I had always known, but now suddenly fully comprehended, the way that every single action we take as individuals affects so many others. I shivered, and Tom gripped me tightly.

Eventually Maxine straightened painfully, and looked through the window. She said in a low voice, 'Gillie and Frou-frou are on the lower lawn. Please don't tell him what I have said. You were children . . . we wanted to protect you.' She looked round at us. 'If it seems right, I will tell him. I promise.'

He came bursting in. He'd seen the car. Why hadn't we phoned? He'd only been sorting out the bloody sheep, had Maxine looked after us? Hot cake sounded wonderful, and where was his? He kissed the top of my head, clapped Tom on the back, and gave Maxine a bear hug. His grin literally spread from ear to ear.

'What brought you here, for God's sake? We should do this more often. Rache, you look like death warmed up!'

Maxine laughed as she refilled the kettle. 'Probably the hot cake, darling. I think you're not supposed to have it straight from the oven and soggy with jam!'

'That's the best way.' He sat opposite me and frowned. 'Overdoing it, Rache. Too many late-night dinners with beef and syllabub! What did you think of it – wasn't the food in keeping?'

I pulled myself together. Tom was sitting by me now, and I took his hand and squeezed it reassuringly. 'It was wonderful. All of it. We were so proud of you both. And all we can do in return is to look after Frou-frou. Where is she, by the way?'

'Left her in the porch. It was a bit muddy in the farmyard.'

'Gillie! You should have carried her!'

'Well, I didn't. She needs the exercise. Where's my cake and ale?'

Maxine presented his tea in a pint mug, just as the girls had that morning. He took the rest of the cake and set to.

Tom said, 'We came to see whether we should take her home for the night. What do you think?'

'I think most definitely.' Gilbert spoke through his cake. 'Then I can chase Maxine around the house without the bloody dog yapping disapproval at every scream!'

Maxine simpered, then drew out a chair and sat down. 'Actually, darling, these two came to ask about Mr Silverman.'

Tom and I stared at her, and she looked at us with a tiny smile. 'I realize I talked about last night's dinner and making sponge cakes, but that *was* why you came, wasn't it?'

Uncle Gilbert stopped eating quite suddenly, and became wary. No one said a word. Maxine's smile seemed fixed on her face.

I thought that so far Maxine had opened flood gates one after another, and deserved a bit of help. Or perhaps I just wanted to shock this man who had tried to mess up my parents' marriage so long ago. I said, 'Did you kill him, Uncle Gilbert?'

He exploded cake crumbs. 'Did I *what*?' He turned on Maxine. 'What the *hell* have you been saying, woman?'

Her smile did not change. 'Sponge cake and syllabub.'

Tom was clutching my hand like a drowning man. I said, 'Tom and I found him hanging. Now we hear from Vicky Robinson that he was murdered. We are asking you whether you did it.'

'Who the *hell* is Vicky Robinson?'

'Don't pretend to be an idiot, Uncle Gilbert. She is Meriel's daughter. In correspondence with Roland Beard, who met his father last summer and heard, or invented, a story about Mrs Smith killing old Mr Silverman. We thought you might know something.'

'Why on earth would I know anything about a teenage boy making up stories to impress a girl who lives on the other side of the Atlantic?'

Tom squeezed my hand, then said, 'You're a fixer, Gaffer. People tell you things so that you can fix them. That day in August 1944, Rachel and I gave you jolly good evidence that Wilhelm Strassen and Eva Schmidt had committed suicide but you did not follow it up. In effect, you covered up that story. And you reported the Silverman business on page four in . . . six lines, I believe it was.'

Uncle Gilbert stopped looking wary and shrugged. 'The war was still going strong. There were other more important things needing space. Remember the paper shortage? We were allowed a double spread and that was it!' He was gaining confidence. 'Anyway, Tom had dragged you into that house, Rachel – literally, if I remember correctly. Whether you liked it or not you were involved. I wanted to keep your name out of it.'

'Just as you did after Sylvia Strassen's murder? Anyway, you had no idea I was involved with Strassen when poor old Silverman hung himself.'

Uncle Gilbert began to look angry. 'There was no need to protect you after the Sylvia Strassen murder. The man was discovered the very next day beneath the platform at the railway station.' He huffed audibly. 'I don't have to sit here and take this from you two. Let's just cut to the chase. I did not murder Mr Silverman, and actually I did a good obit for him. You can look it up, if you want to.'

He went on huffing and puffing. Maxine put a comforting arm around his shoulders. He was about to tuck his head into her neck, when she said very gently, 'I've told them we were the ones who found the body, sweetie. I didn't mention that it was obvious he had been clubbed, and that we assumed it was Wilhelm Strassen who had done it just before the raid, so we hoisted the poor old man up on to the beam.' She looked up at us. 'By this time Strassen and Schmidt were lovers. I think Eva must have been sorry for him. Or perhaps she hoped to keep him quiet about the Smith connection. The Wingco was her brother, after all. She had given her child away to her sister-in-law – she must have known by then what sort of woman Maude was. We know her state of mind was . . . desperate. Suicide seemed the only solution to her.' She paused and we all sat and considered the dilemma Eva Schmidt had faced.

Then she added thoughtfully, 'I sometimes wonder whether Strassen intended to go through with the suicide. Whether he thought he might still get away with it. Maude would have helped him. What ironic justice if he was killed by one of his own bombs.' She sighed sharply. 'Getting back to Gillie and me finding Mr Silverman's body . . . our one thought was to keep everyone we knew and loved out of it. If the two bodies found in Spa Road were the result of suicide, why not another one? All that silly treason business could be forgotten. None of it mattered. The information was already obsolete. But the authorities might not have seen it that way. So anything that might link Strassen with your family was dangerous. So we faked Silverman's suicide. He was already dead. The mark on his head was nothing much – if it was murder, then he was knocked out and finished off some other way. Maybe poisoned. We didn't hang about making guesses. We managed to . . . well, you know what we managed to do. We figured out that if Strassen had had anything to do with it, he paid the price. His own people killed him, in a way. And poor Eva Schmidt who had to spend her life in the shadows for fear of embarrassing her brother . . .' She smiled. 'Was it so terrible to hide what lay behind their deaths?'

Neither Tom nor I said anything for ages. Uncle Gilbert bumbled on about it being 'long ago and far away', and that he had had to do something for his family. When he told us that he had stolen and burned the register of corporation houses – which contained my signatures against Sylvia Strassen's rent – I realized that 'family' included me.

Eventually they pretended that they took our silence for total agreement. More tea was offered. We told them that the girls had gone to see the latest Cliff Richard film and even if they had tea at the Tudor tea rooms they would be home soon. I didn't mention that Meriel was there to welcome them back and listen to their chatter. It was almost dark, anyway. We needed to go.

Maxine cleaned Frou-frou's paws and packed her 'weekend case'. A typed list of instructions was tucked into the outside pocket. The past was tucked away, too. Maxine said nothing about Dad's precipitate return to this country or Mrs Smith's implication in . . . well, everything. I wondered whether she knew – had we mentioned it? – that Mr Smith was in hospital with food poisoning.

We stood under the portico to say our farewells, and Uncle Gilbert clasped me to his shoulder as usual, then said very solemnly, 'I'll make some enquiries, Rachel. I'll sort it out – I'll sort it all out. Don't worry any more.'

They waved us goodbye and Tom tooted the horn cheerfully, as if everything was hunky-dory. And I wound down my window and flapped my glove at them, then wound it up quickly so that Frou-frou would not catch cold. I had no idea what Uncle Gilbert was going to enquire about, or what he was going to sort out. Strangely enough his final words made sense, because I wasn't worried any more.

Tom said grimly, 'This is how it has to be, isn't it? Our box of secrets. We might well open the lid now and then and look inside the box, but mostly we will have to keep it locked.'

I put my face down, so that Frou-frou could snuffle her kisses just under my chin. I said deliberately, 'The girls are going to adore having this little dog in the house.'

For a moment he was astonished, then he laughed. 'OK. You're so thankful that your father is still your father. What else?'

'Gilbert and Maxine come out of it rather well, I thought. Especially Maxine.'

'Yes.' He concentrated on turning into the main road. Then said, 'Your dad almost got it right, except that it wasn't the ghastly Maude and Strassen who hoisted Silverman up to the ceiling, thank God.' He steered the car carefully past one of the enormous coal wagons and I was reminded of the Shire horse whose hoof I had narrowly missed all those years ago. 'Poor George. He's been haunted by the Gaffer, in a way. He can't see straight now, and he couldn't see straight then. When Maude Smith blackmailed Flo into breaking the official secrets thing, your Dad must have seen it as proof that Flo slept with Gilbert, who quite possibly fathered you. I guess if it hadn't been for protecting Flo and you, he might have murdered Maude then and there. And now, when the threat rears its head again, he thinks he can get away with it. I'm afraid he probably wants to kill her, Rache. He might even be looking forward to it.'

I was quiet, simply because I did not know any more who ought to know what. So many people appeared to have the keys to our box of secrets that they were no longer a tool for blackmail. And the secrets themselves proliferated almost daily. I had to hang on to the two most important ones – and surely they weren't even secrets? But Dad was Dad and Mum was Mum and that was all that mattered. Except . . . except that it was possible I had not been an only child and that Hermione was my half-sister. Why else would Dad be trying to protect her? And if Dad wasn't Hermione's father, who was? It looked as if Willi Strassen had only appeared just before the war. He was most likely one of Mr Silverman's protégés. So if he wasn't Hermione's father, who was?

Twenty

It is strange how the mind works. On Friday afternoon, cycling back into the city from my old home, I had been full of an unreasoning terror in case my father was, even then – at that moment – donning the dark cloak of a murderer. All right, I know that sounds beyond melodrama, but the whole day – wrapped in mist and mystery – had been like that. And then, quite suddenly it seemed, we were dressing for our evening out, dramatic enough, of course, but full of quirks shared with Tom. For instance: Uncle Gilbert, oozing good works but managing to feather his own nest very nicely at the same time, and Maxine, worried about Frou-frou, hanging around Uncle Gilbert's neck like an overblown trophy. Dramatic or not, it seemed ridiculous to think of Dad donning that blasted black cloak. And then Saturday, which began with giggles, ending with more enormous secrets. But also with Uncle Gilbert's promise that everything was going to be all right.

Meanwhile there was the business of Frou-frou. Meriel hated her, the girls adored her and Tom knew it was politic to give her a trial run for the weekend; but it was me who took her into the garden for her bed-time toileting. The girls then gave her some supper, so it was they who gained her gratitude. We went to bed fairly early and left her in her basket near the banked-up fire in the living room. Meriel needed to work, and kept a suspicious eye on her from the kitchen table.

I said to Tom, when we got to the safety of our bedroom, 'We should have her with us – she always sleeps with Gilbert and Maxine.' Tom treated me to one of his silences and I changed the subject quickly. 'And I don't quite know how Gilbert will ever sort everything out as he promised. Maxine is letting him believe he is my father, and how on earth he thinks he will discover Hermione's real father, heaven only knows!'

Tom came up behind me and wrapped me in his long arms, then put his cheek against my nape. 'Have you noticed how problems seem to . . . I don't know . . . sort themselves out?'

'Oh, Tom.' I lifted one of his hands from my waist and kissed it. My mind had leapt again. 'Poor Mr Silverman. Even if we'd gone straight to Eastgate that day, we couldn't have saved him. It must have happened the previous Saturday.'

He turned me and looked into my eyes. 'How do you do that?'

'Do what?'

'Tune in to my thoughts like that?'

'I didn't know I was. But I've always known it worried you that we might have saved Mr Silverman. I wondered whether, in a way, it might be a tiny bit of relief to know we couldn't.'

We had switched off the bedroom light because the street lamp was only two doors away. We looked at each other in the strange artificial gloaming and experienced one of those amazing moments when it seemed as if our minds touched and overlapped; and in that moment I thought I knew something else about Tom. Nineteen years ago he felt he had failed Mr Silverman, who was a good man, an unsung hero. And over the next decade he had linked that failure with another. The failure to find his own father. He knew it was a superstitious, touching-wood kind of thing, but buried deep in his mind was a conviction that if he had saved Mr Silverman that day in August, he would also have saved his father.

I whispered, 'All that blood . . . when you fell against the wall—'

He whispered back, 'And when you fainted,

right there in that little room . . . and I thought you had died, too.'

It was as if we were reminding each other that we had done what we could. I said, 'What can we do now? Nobody could stop her then – surely now—'

The moment was over, though we still stared into each other's eyes. And then he heard Meriel coming upstairs, and on impulse I went to the bedroom door and beckoned her to join us. She was carrying two hot-water bottles, a book and a thermos flask. She crept laboriously along the landing past the girls' bedrooms.

'What's up?' she asked going to the window where Tom was standing, apparently looking out. 'Don't tell me Mr Dawson has lost his cat again?'

Tom said, 'No. It just crossed my mind that in a way it's a pity George cannot marry Hermione now. He needs someone to look after.' He looked round and beamed at Meriel. The lamplight reflected on his teeth. 'You would have been absolutely spot-on for the job except you're so bossy, and of course already have a husband!' He laughed and added, 'You're not so lumbered as usual – where are the sandwiches?'

'Never mind the bloody sandwiches. Why can't George marry Hermione? You can see with half an eye how close they have become!' Tom tried to stifle his escalating laughter and she made a sound like a kettle coming to the boil. 'And I am not bossy, Tom! I simply know my mind and speak it. I would never try to force anyone to do anything they did not want to do.'

'Sorry . . . sorry. As for your query about Hermione, after what we were told at Clarion House it doesn't seem a good idea any more.'

'Who cares about Gilbert the Great?'

'Well actually we do, and that includes you. Because he is going to sort it all out for us.'

'But not for Hermione, by the sound of it.'

Tom glanced at me and I made up my mind on the spot and told Meriel that there was a remote possibility Hermione was my sister.

'I don't believe it,' she said flatly. 'Your father and Mrs Smith? Are you mad?'

'Try – my father and Eva Schmidt,' I suggested.

It stopped her in her tracks. I saw her considering the idea, gnawing her bottom lip. She didn't like it, but she tried to be fair.

'I'll have to sleep on that one,' she said. 'Uncle Gilbert again, I take it?'

'No,' I shook my head. ' Maxine.'

She raised her brows, turned down her mouth, nodded thoughtfully.

'Well, well. I respect that woman. As you know, she turned my dad down.' She turned, hugging both hot-water bottles to her. 'If I don't sleep a wink it's all your fault.' Then, just before the door closed behind her, she added, 'Anyway, nobody will murder anyone tomorrow. It's a Sunday.' The door clicked shut and we fell into each others arms, laughing helplessly.

Our tea duly arrived in the washing-up bowl the next morning. Rose's face was long and mournful, even Daisy looked solemn. We sat up in bed, and said how lovely, and waited to hear what they had to say. The silence was deafening, in spite of the creaking of the bed as we settled ourselves among the pillows and wedged the bowl between us.

Tom, who could bear only his own silences, said, 'The light seems odd. Has it been snowing?'

Daisy leapt to the window. Rose said repressively, 'Don't be silly, Daisy. If we didn't see snow from the front door when we waved goodbye to Aunt Meriel, we're not likely to see it from the upstairs windows, are we?'

She could be insufferable at times. Daisy did not care. 'The sky is yellow. Grandee always says something about that.'

Rose joined her. 'Yes. He says red sky at night is shepherd's delight.'

Daisy improvised quickly. 'And when sky is yellow, snow is mellow.'

I was glad when Rose laughed and gave her a friendly shove. I said, 'Don't tell me Meriel has gone to church?' I lay back in bed and sipped my tea. I could see that it was another murky day.

Rose's face lengthened again. Daisy said, 'More impossible than that, even! She's gone back to Bristol early because she's got lots to do, and it's always left to her to sort everything out, because the two of you are ungarageable.'

Rose said, 'Incorrigible. Mum and Dad aren't cars!'

'OK. What does it mean?'

'I think it means they're hopeless.'

I wailed, 'She's gone back already? Hermione and Grandee are coming to lunch. We've got pork and apple sauce.'

Rose mentioned she did not like pork because it tasted like a pig. Tom said, 'She didn't say anything last night about leaving. She must have thought it up in the night.' He finished his tea and frowned. 'She's going home for Christmas soon, isn't she?'

I looked at him, eyes wide. 'Oh Lord. Her flight is next Thursday. And she hasn't even said goodbye or taken the presents for Vicky and Georgie or – or – anything!'

'It's only a month, Mum. She'll be back in the middle of January.' Rose patted my hand and Daisy scooped up the bowl and mugs.

'But I'd got jam for the Greenwoods, and an old war-time recipe book for Joan and Jack with a foreword by Lord Woolton.'

'We'll go to Bristol on Wednesday to say goodbye and take the stuff.' Tom relieved Daisy of the washing-up bowl, put it on the floor, and gathered us all into his long arms. 'We'll give her a great send-off and just show your Aunt Meriel that we're not that hopeless after all!'

Dad was late for lunch, and by himself. He left his bike by the boot scraper and scrubbed his feet assiduously on the door mat. 'I wish it would actually snow,' he said, sounding unusually grumpy. 'This blasted fog makes you wet. You can shake the snow off.' He made a fuss about spreading his coat over the newel post, and suggested that for our Christmas present he should get central heating installed in the house. I stayed by the front door waiting for Hermione to appear. The girls ushered him into the front room where the tree was already up, ready for decorating, and the fire glowed.

'You can shut that door, Rachel,' he called, mollified by their welcome. 'Your bestest friend in all the world has taken Hermione with her to Bristol, and intends to take her further still, to Florida.' He waited till I came in then added, 'She browbeat Hermione. The poor girl had to pack a case, leave her cards and presents on the hall table for me to deliver, sort herself out at work— They gave her four weeks' leave, can you believe it? Times have changed. My God, they've changed.'

'Hermione works hard, Dad. She deserves a proper holiday.'

He nodded contrition. 'I know, I know. I'm not up to these sudden decisions.' The girls were jigging around him wanting to know why and when, and telling him of our plans to drive to Bristol on Wednesday with the presents. Tom joined us, pushing the girls' old dolls' pram full of bottles and glasses. It was the usual melee. Dad accepted a glass of ginger wine. We all clinked glasses. Dad said, regretfully, 'She could have stayed and joined in with us.' He sighed deeply. 'Except that she couldn't.' The girls laughed at that, but Tom and I knew what he meant. And when we were washing up and the girls were watching *A Tale of Two Cities* on the television, he admitted that Meriel had done the right thing.

'Poor old Derek Smith died late last night. Luckily the sister rang Hermione as well as Maude Smith. When Meriel rang Hermione very early this morning to ask her over to Florida for Christmas, Hermione told her, and Meriel's invitation became urgent. Very urgent. She arrived soon after in that blessed sports car, and we thrashed it all out. Hermione wrote a letter to her father's doctor requesting a post-mortem. I rang Gilbert – I wanted to cut him out a bit. He's getting rather too big for his boots. Plus he's such an old woman. But I told him he'd got clout and if he wanted to use it in the right way he would make sure the Wingco had a post-mortem examination.' He grinned. 'He said he'd do anything I asked. I nearly made a list. Then I told him Hermione was going to the States for Christmas and I wanted it all sorted out before she came home.' He cleared his throat as he reached up to a high shelf to put away a milk jug. 'I think I actually said that Maude Smith must be behind bars by then. Can't quite remember.'

I pulled the plug and watched the water swirl away. Tom was in the larder finding room for the leftovers. I said quietly, 'Dad . . . tell me straight out. Is Hermione your daughter?'

He was so shocked he dropped the tea towel. I said quickly, 'Don't panic. No one else knows. Just Tom and me. We went to see Uncle Gilbert and Maxine yesterday.' I whipped up the towel and tried to grin. 'Sorry . . . sorry. Shouldn't have mentioned it.'

'You didn't *believe* him? My God, you did! Rache, you lived with Mum and me. You knew us. How can you imagine for one minute that I would have cheated on my beautiful Flo?'

'Dad. I'm sorry. Uncle Gilbert was full of a kind of awful nostalgia. We went to ask him about Mr Silverman. He thought Strassen had killed the old man. I should have known then that everything he said was suspect.'

'Not quite. He told you about . . . other things, I expect. They were true.' He didn't wait for my answer and his voice toughened. 'It made me angry. I called on Eva, intending . . . I'm not sure now. It's nearly forty years ago. I'd always admired her for admitting she was an Austrian Jew. Always. We knew her quite well in those days. The war was still a long way off. But already Silverman was getting Jewish people out of Germany and settled in this country, and she helped him. It wasn't easy for her. Her brother had married Maude, who was a social climber of the worst kind and wanted to forget the whole foreign side of her new husband. Eva ignored her and kept going. Yes, I admired her a lot.' He sighed. 'She listened to me going on and on about Gilbert Carfax seducing my wife with his pleas for sympathy. She even let me hold her hands . . . drink her whisky . . . dammit, I think I cried at one point. And then I tried to kiss her. I was probably drunk by then.' He sighed again. 'It's all right, Rache, don't be embarrassed. It stopped right there. I knew she was going to talk me out of it. But she didn't even do that. She just laughed. And she kept on laughing and told me to go home and stop acting like an idiot.' He looked up. 'Rache, I couldn't have done it anyway. Flo . . . your mother . . . was everything to me.'

I thought for a terrible moment he was going to cry again. I felt his loneliness like an enormous void. I went up to him and put my forehead against his.

'Dad, it's all right. It wouldn't have made any difference. I promise you that. I'm glad for your sake, not for mine. And I'm glad that Hermione had a mother like Eva.'

'Hermione is glad, too,' he said in a low voice.

Behind Dad, Tom came out of the larder and made signs at me. I straightened so that I could look Dad in the eye. I gave the smallest smile.

'Uncle Gilbert was out when we got to Clarion House and Maxine did quite a bit of talking before he came in.' Dad smiled, too, and nodded. I said, 'You do know that Uncle Gilbert cannot have children, don't you?' He stopped smiling. 'She wanted me to know that. In case I got any strange ideas that Uncle Gilbert might be my father.'

He stared at me not speaking, barely breathing. Then he said, 'I knew that. Yes. But Gillie is so . . . possessive at times.'

'He . . . pretends. Like Meriel and me. And – I suppose – sometimes, he believes his own delusions. Maxine goes along with it.'

'But, Rache . . . you were our wonderful reconciliation. It was so awful – we both thought we'd scuppered ourselves. And then . . . well, we hadn't. He can't not know – he's got no right—'

'Dad. Stop. The important thing is that we three – you and Mum and me – we still belong to each other in every possible way. Uncle Gilbert . . . is . . . well, he's Uncle Gilbert!' I tried to laugh. 'You said – not long ago – that all that terrible business at the end of the war was no more than a storm in a teacup. And so was this.'

I saw him swallow. He seemed afraid to take his eyes from my face. He said, 'You see, Rache, Mum always felt terrible about ditching Gilbert the way she had. I suppose it was awful. They were at this dance together and I was there – a complete stranger – and I asked her to dance and that was that. So she introduced him to Maxine – she worked with Maxine, as you know – and they got on well and they got married. Then he was ill and everyone thought he was dying and Maxine sent a note for Mum and she went and just . . . stayed. I didn't think she was coming back, Rache. I hated Gilbert. I almost hated Flo. And I went to see Eva . . .'

'Dad, I know. You just told me. But then, afterwards, you and Mum were so happy, so together.' I wanted him to tell me it had been all right; everything had been all right. Just as I remembered it.

'We were. We really were. We never spoke about it. We were probably both suppressing it – that's the sort of thing Hermione says about her patients. They suppress things and think they've forgotten them for ever. But then . . . they haven't.'

He swayed slightly and Tom bounded forward and pushed a chair against the back of his knees. He sat down abruptly. He said, 'Rache, d'you think Mum ever believed that Hermione was mine?'

I said swiftly, 'Of course not.'

He said, like Rose needing reassurance, 'Did I wonder whether you were Gilbert's?'

'Of course not. And you certainly weren't idiotic enough to let it spoil anything. Remember Beethoven's Fifth?'

He looked puzzled for a moment, and then, quite suddenly, he was himself again. 'Beethoven's—? Oh yes. Of course.' He smiled and leaned back and felt Tom's hands on his shoulders and directed the smile upwards to include him. 'She was an amazing woman, Tom. No real confidence in herself, yet somehow she radiated warmth and light. That's why I needed Florida. I couldn't see properly any more, and I was always cold.'

'Oh Dad.' I crouched before him and took his hands; they were warm.

We stayed like that for what seemed like ages, though it was probably only a minute. Then the phone rang in the hall and the sitting-room door opened, letting out a blast of sound from the television, and the next instant Rose was yelling down the hall that it was Hermione. Tom went, giving Dad and I time to collect ourselves, stand up and hug, half-laughing, half-crying.

'I wish we'd done this years ago,' he said, pushing his chair beneath the kitchen table again.

'That's the thing about suppression. It works!' I looked at him and just for a moment I saw an old man; he was, after all thirty-five when I was born, and I was edging up to forty.

'Yes.' He grinned and slid back into being just my dad. He and I, we'd always been such friends, and I had felt terribly deserted for the ten years he had stayed away. His grin broadened, as if he knew my thoughts, and he said, 'Prepare yourself, Rache. I might have to disappear again quite suddenly if I do manage to finish off that crazy woman.'

I shook my head at him. 'There will be a proper post-mortem on the poor old Wingco. She's cooked her own goose!'

We both went into the hall to speak to Hermione. I expected her to sound scared to death by Meriel's sudden intervention, but she was nothing of the sort. Perhaps she had been scared for years, and now that Meriel had taken over she felt only a glorious relief. What had surprised her – and me, too – was that Meriel had her old boy friend in residence. The doctor who had looked after her when she was pregnant with Georgie sixteen years ago had taken the flat next door to hers in Clifton. As I said to Tom later that Sunday, 'I suppose we should be honoured that she spends every weekend with us! What the hell do he and Professor Harmsworth do when she disappears?'

Tom shrugged, then joked, 'They have a darned good rest, I would think!' He smiled almost sadly. 'Strange to think that we take Meriel's freedom for granted now. But in the mid-twenties it would have been such wonderful blackmail material. Poor George. Poor Flo.'

Dad stayed with us that night, sleeping in Meriel's bed until the girls had gone to school and Tom to work. He said he had a lot of catching-up to do. I telephoned Meriel's flat thinking Hermione would be feeling deserted. I was wrong again. She couldn't stop for a chat then, because Gus Michaelson had popped in for coffee.

I replaced the receiver and stood looking down the hall at the layers of coloured light coming from the stained glass on the front door. I seemed fairly good at judging events and people wrongly. Absolutely and totally wrongly.

I made tea and took it up to Dad, and when he smiled at me I knew that, misjudgement or not, things were all right between us. We could pick up where we left off when Mum was alive.

Then the phone rang again and I got to it as quickly as I could, because I thought it would be Hermione again. It was Tom.

'Thank God Dad spent last night with us—' There was no preamble at all. 'Rough Road Cottage was burned out in the night. It was quite deliberate, neither Hermione nor Dad would have stood a chance.'

Twenty-one

The really awful outcome of that blatant arson attack was that Mr Myercroft died. Dad maintained that he would have had his heart attack fire or no fire. But the fact remained that, when Dad and I failed to get a response to our knocks and shouts, and eventually used his spare key, the familiar bungalow – which Mum had tried to keep clean and tidy after Mrs Myercroft died – was full of the acrid smell of smoke; as indeed was the whole area. And Mr Myercroft was not even in bed. He was sort of neatly folded-up in the kitchen, where he had had a slit of a view through the laurels to our house.

Dad comforted me, and the two policemen who had come with us suggested that perhaps the old gent would not mind if I made some tea, as I probably knew where to find it. The ambulance men took Mr Myercroft away; Tom arrived; the policemen were talking to Dad in the sitting room where a portrait of Mrs

Myercroft smiled at them benignly from above the tiled fireplace. I began the dreary business of making tea. I had known twenty years ago where the Myercrofts kept their caddy, sugar, crockery; they were still there and probably had not been moved since Mum died. The cutlery drawer was full of newspaper cuttings and notes about repairing the greenhouse and buying Jeyes Fluid. I boiled a kettle of water and used it to scald spoons and mugs, filled it again and watched Tom clearing a space on one of the cabinets, where it looked as if Mr Myercroft had done his repotting. Some of the old pots were growing various moulds.

I said, 'Mum used to come round and see to things now and then after Mrs Myercroft died.'

Tom nodded. 'Even without her he was better off here than in a home. His garden . . . he still loved it. Look at this.' It was a grubby list of next year's planting with a plan of the enormous garden. I gazed at it desolately. Mr Myercroft had always been . . . there.

And he had always been old. He had to have been well into his nineties. Tom said, 'How is Dad taking the loss of his home?'

'It's not his home any more, not really. It's Hermione's. She had the heating put in and all her things were about.' I started to cry weak tears. 'She won't go off with Meriel now. And she's got nowhere to live. And she could – so easily – have been my sister.'

I put my hands to my face, and Tom gathered me up and said humorously, 'I don't think so, my love. And probably the police won't object to Hermione going to the States. Why should they? She wasn't even here at the time of the fire.' He dried my eyes and held his handkerchief for me to blow my nose, as if I were Rose or Daisy. 'In fact,' he went on, 'in case they don't catch up with Maude Smith, who is obviously completely crazy, I think Hermione should be right out of the country. Once Maude knows she wasn't in the house after all, she will be after her like a rabid dog.'

We took tea into the sitting room, where Dad was frowning prodigiously over the outrageousness of what he was saying to the police. Mrs Smith, probably insane with grief at the death of her husband, was trying to kill her own daughter? It didn't make sense. We all knew we had stepped out of the realm of sense, but even in that no-man's-land how could we – let alone anyone else – accept such an illogical scenario?

We saw the Wolsley draw up outside. Never were Uncle Gilbert and Aunt Maxine so welcome. The thunderous knock on the front door, Maxine's voluminous fur coat which enveloped the two of us, her fluting enquiries about Frou-frou . . . we gladly let them take over, and I am fairly certain the two policemen were just as glad. The Carfaxes appeared to know exactly what had happened, and what should be done about it.

Strangely enough, the only thing to survive in our old home was Hermione's car, mainly because the garage was right away from the house and was made from panels of asbestos. She had let Dad have the keys before she left, and we phoned the local garage, who sent round a mechanic to check that the car was in its usual pristine condition. We left Gilbert telling the police that he had insisted on a full post-mortem to be carried out on Mrs Smith's husband, and we drove slowly back into town. We were all nervous; even Dad kept glancing out of the rear window as if he expected that sit-up-and-beg bicycle to be following behind. I was terrified Mrs Smith had booby-trapped the car, which was just as ridiculous: Hermione had had to change fuses since she was seven years old because Mrs Smith couldn't do it – and besides, Mrs Smith would not have been able to lift the car's bonnet.

Tom said, 'I'll ring Miss Hardwicke when we get in. It might be as well to keep the girls home until the police pick Mrs Smith up.'

Dad said, 'Why don't you go down to Bristol tomorrow – take the girls?'

We were making Maude Smith into some kind of evil-genius, ready to pop up at any moment and finish off the whole family!

Tom lit the fire in the sitting room, Dad made tea; I took Frou-frou into the garden, and almost laughed at the look of relief on her small woolly face as she squatted among the chrysanthemums. Then I sat by the fire and cuddled her until Gilbert and Maxine arrived. There was another flurry, somehow typical of Gilbert and Maxine. Gilbert said he had told the police 'everything'. We didn't question him; we desperately wanted him to take it all on and tell us what to do. They left an hour later after he had telephoned the insurance people.

'I'll leave you to get in touch with Hermione,' he said, accepting a cup of coffee and sipping it appreciatively as he stood in the hall. 'I don't know the girl all that well but she must be in as much danger as you are, George. Why don't you get yourself down to Bristol for a couple of days? You could probably live in Meriel's flat, couldn't you?'

Dad said, 'If Maude Smith can't find me or Hermione, she'll doubtless go for Rachel and her family. She's tipped over the edge, Gillie. I think we should all go somewhere – anywhere, really – until they catch her. It can't take long. Where will *she* go? She's not in her house. Her bike's not there either. She's going to be fairly conspicuous cycling anywhere in the county.'

Hovering in the sitting room, I said to Tom, 'It's absolutely ridiculous. All of us terrified of one elderly lady on a bike with nowhere to go!'

Tom frowned. 'She's got the advantage of not caring any more about anyone at all. She must have stopped enjoying her role as wife to a wing commander. Perhaps he found out about some of her dealings during the war and threatened to expose her . . . who knows? Whatever happened it has made her into the equivalent of a Japanese kamikaze fighter. She just wants to take as many people with her as possible.'

I shivered.

Tom met the girls from school while I cooked an enormous stew, then telephoned Meriel's flat. She was at the final seminar of the term and Hermione sounded very awkward. I was in the mood to panic.

'Are you on your own – is someone with you?'

She said, 'No to the first question. Yes to the second.'

My heart was leaping around already. 'Just say yes or no . . . is it your mother?'

She did not answer immediately; my heart stopped leaping and threatened to stop. At last she said slowly, 'You must know that my real mother has been dead for nineteen years, Rachel. The person who is with me is Meriel's doctor. Gus. From what you have said, I gather that my foster mother has . . . disappeared?'

I heard my own breath leave my lungs in sheer relief. I simply said, 'Yes.'

'Ah. Then it seems Meriel was right to practically drag me here.' I could hear the smile in her voice and she seemed to be including Gus in her next comment. 'I am constantly surprised by Meriel's intuitive perspicacity—' there came a gurgle at her own pretentiousness. 'All that frantic packing as if the Hound of the Baskervilles were after us!' She laughed; her flippancy was annoying, to say the least.

'She's burned down the house, Hermione—' I meant to sound angrily strong, but my voice was a bleat. 'And Mr Myercroft is dead!'

There was a shocked silence, and I regretted my words and started to add that we had no proof as yet, and though the 'fire people' knew it was arson they could not know who was responsible.

She said – almost calmly – 'I had better come home immediately.' She must have slightly tipped the receiver as she added, 'Will you take me, Gus? She's after me. My friends must not be involved like this. Rachel and Tom, Rose and Daisy and dear George – nothing must happen to them – you do see, don't you? Nothing must happen to them.'

I didn't hear what Gus said, of course, but even if I had it would not have impinged on that moment of . . . what to call it? Comprehension is not sufficient. It was a moment of sheer enlightenment. It was a moment when the events of 1944, 1953, and 1963 came together and made sense. So much love . . . so much pain and hatred, too . . . but we had all overlooked the love.

I blurted, 'No – you mustn't, Hermione. You mustn't.'

She had very gently replaced her receiver. And anyway, I knew that she must.

The three of them arrived in Gus's hire car two hours later. Tom had fetched the girls from school, and we had laid a sort of buffet in the kitchen, and Dad had stoked up the sitting-room fire. And though it was still much too early we had fetched the tree decorations from the attic and were all taking turns at hanging on the baubles. Gus hung about in the hall, shaking Tom's hand again and again. The girls stayed by their creations on the tree and peered at the pantomime of Hermione, Meriel and me hanging on to each other desperately. It wasn't for long; we broke off and talked to them in very obviously normal voices, which did not fool them for a second. But they were good girls, well-trained by Miss Hardwicke, and they played along with us and explained to Gus that there was a story behind nearly all the baubles, then proceeded to tell him the best one of all: the glass swan that Daddy's daddy had bought for him when he was five years old and that had been made for Queen Victoria. Gus, totally out of his depth, registered astonishment. 'Say! Is that something! Queen Victoria herself, huh?' And Daisy gazed at him adoringly and said, 'You speak proper American, Mr Gus!'

She brought the house down.

Strangely, everyone was hungry and we ate some stew and then opened four tins of apricots and a tin of condensed milk – Daisy's favourite, and just for tonight she was belle of the ball. Then I shepherded her and Rose upstairs and superintended the washing and the hair-brushing; I hung up their clothes and tucked them both into Daisy's bed.

'Is *everyone* staying here, Mum?' Rose asked rather anxiously. 'There's only one packet of cereal left for breakfast.'

'I don't know, really.' Actually, I had envisaged us sitting up through the night . . . just in case. I didn't want the girls to know that, of course.

Daisy said, 'Why are they all here? I thought we were going to see them off on Wednesday!'

'Well . . .' I bit my lip. 'I didn't want to tell you but, actually, Grandee's house – Hermione's Rough Road Cottage – has been almost totally destroyed. There was a fire in the early hours of this morning. We didn't hear about it until after you'd gone to school.' I cupped their faces. 'Don't look like that, my lambs. It can probably be rebuilt, and the insurance will see to it, and Grandee and Hermione weren't there . . . but probably Hermione won't go to the States just yet. There will be things to sort out. So Meriel brought her home. And Gus – he was her doctor when she had Georgie – was visiting, and came too.'

I made it sound quite normal, and of course they hadn't had the experience of actually seeing the smoking ruins. I kept quiet about Mr Myercroft. They held my gaze, shocked but not horrified, then Rose leaned forward and pecked my cheek comfortingly.

'It's where you grew up, Mum. Where you and Aunt Merry . . . were.'

'Yes. But this is where I am now. With you and Dad. And, thank goodness, with Grandee!'

Daisy said very practically, 'I think they should go and stay with Aunt Daphne. She'd love it and she's got a big freezer full of food, so she won't have to worry about shopping and everything.'

I hadn't thought of Daphne. She probably knew all about Maude Smith anyway after Roland's drunken get-together with his father, and the ensuing correspondence of last summer with Vicky. It struck me suddenly that if Roland had confided in his mother, it was more than likely that a lot of people knew about Maude Smith.

'That's a good idea, Daisy. I'll put it to the committee!'

Rose said, 'By the way, Mum, Aunt Merry has finished with Gus, hasn't she? Only I think he's got a thing about Hermione.'

I laughed, once more astonished by their sheer empathy, kissed them both and tucked them in tighter, making the three-foot bed look like a giant papoose. I wondered whether they would talk about this into the wee small hours, but when I checked on them less than an hour later they were both asleep, arms and hair everywhere.

Meanwhile we finished clearing away supper and went back into the sitting room to 'make a few decisions', as Meriel put it. Tom stoked the fire again, Dad fiddled with the tree lights and got them going, Meriel sat on the rug, Gus took the space next to Hermione on the sofa, and Dad, Tom and I eventually collapsed into the remaining chairs. I found myself eyeing Hermione and Gus, and then wondering how on earth I could do such a thing in the middle of this horrible crisis. But, somehow, it helped.

I said, 'Daisy suggested that Daphne Beard could help out with sleeping arrangements. Shall I telephone her?'

We thought about it. Gus said, 'This is crazy. What are the police doing?'

Dad said, 'They're keeping an eye on her house. And on the shell of our house—' he glanced at Hermione, who seemed her usual calm and collected self. 'They think she might go back to look through the rubble. For bodies.'

Gus drew in a breath and said again, 'This is crazy – just crazy.'

Meriel said, 'Back home there would probably be an armed posse looking for her. Well, they would have found her by now during the daylight hours. Such a small area—'

Hermione said, 'They would also probably have shot and killed her, too. She needs treatment. At a hospital. She must be in hell. All that deception and betrayal and death.'

Gus repeated, 'It's crazy. Totally crazy. And she's your mother?'

'No. Actually she is not. She did not tell me until after my mother was dead. By which time *she* was almost my mother. I'm proud that Aunt Eva was really my mother but I can't love her like I loved . . . this other mother.'

Dad said quietly, 'She wants to kill you, Hermione.'

'She wants to be rid of me, certainly. It would have been some kind of solution for her if I'd been in that house. But when – if – she discovers that I wasn't, I am absolutely certain she will feel relief.' She turned her head to look at Gus. 'She needs help.'

He said, 'It's crazy, honey. She is insane. It's just not possible—'

Meriel said, 'It's the same situation as I was in, don't forget. Poor old Mum might lose her mind – I think she is slightly senile, actually – but she would never want to kill me.'

Dad shifted in his armchair. 'She killed her husband, however. She loved him – she was proud of being the wife of a wing commander. But when he found out about Mr Silverman—'

Hermione said, 'She did not love my father. He had slept with his sister and produced me. She hated him for that.'

She paused. The last piece of the jigsaw fell into place. It made such . . . sense.

Hermione lifted her shoulders slightly, acknowledging our shock. 'Yes. I am the off-spring of incest.' She smiled, a proper smile. I thought of her childhood and shivered. She went on in her calm, objective way, 'Then Strassen arrived. Mr Silverman had bought him a bride . . . but he fell for my mother. Eva. My other mother, Maude Smith, was in love with Willi Strassen. She worked for him. She was devastated when he died.' She looked at Gus again. 'And we have no proof that she killed my father.'

He was almost pop-eyed by this time. 'It's crazy,' he protested yet again.

Tom said, 'You're right, Gus. It is crazy. And we have to think how far that craziness will extend. And that is why we are so anxious for Hermione.'

'Hermione—' Gus said, then stopped. I made a vow never to call him in a medical emergency. Then he seemed to get a grasp of the situation. 'I'll take her back with me. On Thursday, as arranged. She can have your ticket, Meriel. We'll stay at the hotel overnight. She's a sitting duck here. She can't stay here.'

'I have to stay here. I'm the only one who can talk to Mother.'

Gus said warningly, 'Hang on. You might be able to talk to her, but will she listen?'

'Of course. She's looking for a rescuer – you know that, Gus.' He tightened his lips and she took it as agreement. 'I'm the obvious person. She needs my forgiveness and my total understanding.' She turned her face to Dad. 'She'd like it to be you, George. But she knows it can't be. Because of your Flo. I've got no one like that. Only her. I have to convince her that I still love her.'

Meriel said, 'You're going to let her find you? There won't be time for chit-chat then, honey. You'll probably be struck down from behind – isn't that how they put it?'

'No. I'll go to her.' She looked up, surprised by our protests. 'I know where she will be. Where he was living most of the time. Strassen.

Willi Strassen.' She rolled the name around her tongue with distaste. It was the nearest I'd known her come to showing dislike. But then she smiled. 'Thank God my father was my real father. Its dreadful to think I might have been fathered by Willi! Its very lucky he didn't appear in this country until many years after I was born.'

Gus opened his mouth – probably to mention the craziness again. But then, thankfully, shut it.

Tom sighed. 'Of course. She will go to the manor, the old internment camp. And you know that area so much better than she does.'

Hermione nodded. 'Not all the huts have been removed, by any means. We use some of them as wards but there are others, almost derelict. She will be in one of those. They are linked to the tannoy system. I can talk to her from my office.'

'My God!' Gus smiled at last. 'You are brilliant. You are completely brilliant!'

Dad reached across from his chair to mine and took my hand. 'There's been so much coming and going. Bogey men – or women – in every turn of the road. Now I think we will be able to sleep.'

I smiled back at him. And Hermione said, 'George, I'm so sorry, but there won't be much sleep for any of us tonight. I would like you to come with me, and I suggest we go now.' She smiled apologetically at me. 'You do understand, Rachel? Your father knows everything about her. And she knows that. It makes her want to kill him but it also makes him a hated friend.' She turned to Gus. 'Perhaps you would drive us there, Gus? As your car is outside and you are such an unbiased observer of all this. But no one else. It will frighten her into doing something out of character. It is important that we know who we are dealing with.'

No one argued. I could see why Hermione was so good at her job. She laid down facts so calmly they became laws.

But in the end they did not use Gus's car. Someone had knocked out the headlights. Someone had left a hammer in the road as proof of responsibility. Dad recognized the hammer immediately. It came from his old tool shed.

Tom fetched our car and Gus slid behind the wheel of that. And then they were gone. It was ten thirty.

Twenty-two

Tom did not even suggest that we should go to bed. He filled two hot-water bottles and handed one to Meriel, the other to me. It was only then that we realized we were both shivering in spite of the fire. It was so dreadful to think that while we were discussing what we should do – six of us separated from Gus's hired car by a wall and a boot scraper – Maude Smith had actually been out there with a hammer. Why hadn't we heard her? Those were not the days of double glazing; why hadn't we heard Dad's hammer crashing through the headlights? Meriel and I clutched our hot-water bottles and crouched by the fire. Tom went upstairs to check on the girls, and then came down and said that probably Dad would spot Mrs Smith in his headlights long before they reached the old manor.

Meriel said, 'Is that what she wants, d'you think? I mean she is taking such risks, does she want to be caught?'

I was past trying to fathom Mrs Smith's motives, but Tom said, 'It could be. Yes, it could be, couldn't it?' He crouched between the two of us and put his hands on our shoulders to keep his balance. 'Strange, this need to hide . . . hide our secrets and then hide ourselves. There must come a point when it seems pointless and we throw it all to the winds.'

Meriel nodded at the glowing caverns of the fire. 'We had a psychology lecture on that sort of thing. It showed up during the First World War, apparently. The men came back and couldn't talk about what they had experienced because they couldn't bear to think about it.' There was a silence while we all stared into the caverns. Then Meriel added, 'That could have happened to your dad, Tom. It's called voluntary amnesia.'

Tom nodded. 'Imagine the opposite. Hermione derided every day for being . . . illegal?' He stood up, and Meriel and I shuffled to the sofa and flopped on to it.

She said, 'It's amazing that she got away from her foster mother, trained, has such a good reputation already. In fact Maude Smith's constant insults were counter-productive, weren't they? Hermione is thankful and proud of being Eva Schmidt's daughter.'

'As well as the daughter of Eva's brother,' I said in a low voice.

Tom caught my eye; we exchanged looks. He said, 'Yes.'

Meriel took a deep breath. 'She's a doctor. She understands all the . . . genetic things. Implications. She still loved him, and is proud to be his daughter as well as Eva's.'

We were all silent for some time. The fire fell in again and Tom said, 'Yours is the best way, Merry. Protest as loudly as possible about all injustices. Tear up the dress made by the mother you didn't want. Tell the world that you had Vicky so that you could shake the dust of all of it off your tiny feet!'

We all laughed. She shook her fist at Tom. That interval of terrible grief for Hermione was somehow absorbed. And then the door bell rang.

I leapt up, finger on lips, and whipped out of the sitting room and up the stairs, along the landing and into our dark bedroom. The curtains were still tied back, and I peered down into the street. Mr Dawson was standing there. He was an elderly man who lived on the other side of the road and had built a life around his ancient cat. I ran to the top of the stairs and nodded at Tom who was on the alert in the hall. He opened the door.

Mr Dawson said, 'There must've been an accident, Mr Fairbrother. The front of this car is badly damaged.'

'Yes. We do know, Mr Dawson. We have no

idea how it happened. We heard nothing.'

'Reported it to the police, have you?'

Tom looked back at me. We hadn't. 'I was just about to do so,' he said.

'Only there's a bit of woolly stuff under the bumper there. Could be an important clue.' Mr Dawson was speaking over his shoulder while he clambered down the kerb as if it was Everest, and gathered up the 'woolly stuff' and came back with it. I had seen Maude Smith in that cardigan. And it solved another little mystery. We had not heard her smashing the headlights because she had wrapped her cardigan around each one while she carefully knocked it out. It had not been an act of pure rage; it had been carefully thought out and executed. We did not ring the police about the car because no sooner had Mr Dawson disappeared over the road than the telephone rang and it was Dad.

'We're in Hermione's office and she has just put out her first message on the tannoy.' He spoke so quietly I could barely hear him and he seemed to realize that and gave a small laugh. 'Sorry, love—' his voice came over clearly and amazingly normally. 'The temptation to whisper is ridiculous. We found we were doing it in the car! We came across country fairly slowly – this damned mist all the time – and went down Tewkesbury Road, parked in the courtyard. Dashed over to the two occupied wards, alerted the staff there, searched, locked them. Came back here, looked in the three consulting rooms, big sitting room, dining room . . . everywhere. No sign of her. We reckoned it would take her at least an hour to cycle from town, so Hermione is just putting out the first message. Can you hear?'

He must have held the receiver in her general direction. I heard her voice, a kind of double echo, gentle and calm inside the office, nasal as it bounced back against the windows.

'Mother. It's Hermione. Your little Hermione. I know you want to see me and tell me how you feel about Dad and Aunt Eva and George Throstle and everyone who has hurt you . . . betrayed you. You want to tell me so that I will know the truth. And because, in a way, when all those people betrayed you, they betrayed me, too.' There was a long pause while she waited for her words to stop echoing outside and penetrate Maude Smith's illogical mind. If indeed Maude Smith was within hearing distance.

Then that strange double-edged voice filtered into my ear again.

'We were there, mostly just the two of us, alone in that house day after day while everyone else went on living. When you met Willi at Eva's house, that was when you took hold of our lives, Mother. Tried to change things. You got that name for him from the records office, d'you remember? And then – best of all – got those drawings from George Throstle. Everything would have been all right if Willi hadn't died, wouldn't it? You even got rid of that old fool Silverman for him. Nobody had anything on him. You had taken it all on yourself. And he would have realized that. He would have left Eva for you. After the war we could have gone to Germany. Together. Could we still do that, Mother? Let's talk about that. Just come over to the front door and ring the bell. I'll make some tea, shall I?'

She went on about cooking a late supper but Dad was back on the line again saying, 'She is going to repeat that sort of thing until midnight when, if Maude intended to come here, she will have heard it. Then we are going to eat something and she will start again.'

'Can't be too good for the other patients,' was all I could say.

'They had already been sedated for the night when we arrived. And remember, they are used to Hermione's voice.' A pause, then he said quietly, 'She's pretty marvellous, isn't she?'

I was choked. Not only because Hermione really was marvellous, but because I had not been able to see any of this from Maude's point of view. Hermione had opened a door for me.

He did not wait for a reply. 'By the way,

Rache, unless you've already done so, don't bother to report the car thing to the police. We did it when we got here and told them what we were doing. Gilbert must have convinced them that she started the fire, anyway. They will be here as soon as we need them.'

I cleared my throat and said, 'We've been talking about it. We think she wants to be caught.'

'Yes, Hermione thinks that, too. I am still worried that she might want to take . . . others . . . with her. Just in case we are completely off-track, my love, keep an eye on the twins, OK?'

I felt sick but said, 'OK.' Then I put down the phone and took the stairs two at a time. Needless to say, both girls were still fast asleep. I went to the window and lifted a corner of the curtain. The garden was in complete blackness, a slight movement from next door's silver birch proving that there was still a breeze. I stood there for some time, then turned with a gasp as Tom crept in.

'Why have you been up here for so long?' he whispered.

'Dad said something . . . I wondered whether we were on the wrong track and she had stayed around here. She could shelter in one of the garages.'

'What would be the point, love?'

'How could she hurt us most – all of us?' I turned my head and stared at the bed.

He shuddered, but murmured calmly, 'The gate to the ash lane is bolted. She might climb over it, but then the kitchen door is also bolted top and bottom.'

'I've managed to get in when I've forgotten my key.'

'How?'

'The dining-room window. Slipped the old gardening knife up between the top and bottom, pushed the fastener to one side, and lifted the sash.'

I heard him swallow but his voice was still calm when he replied. 'You are agile, Rache. Come on, can you see Mrs Smith climbing through the bottom sash of our dining-room window?'

Of course I couldn't, but Mrs Smith had done some other things I couldn't imagine. Anyway, we went downstairs – Meriel was waiting in the hall, completely on edge at our sudden disappearance, and we stood around the fire again while I told them what was happening out at the manor and how marvellous Hermione was. Then Tom went into the dining room to try to secure the window, and Meriel and I made cocoa and put some food on a tray, and we gathered in the sitting room again. It was going to be a long night. Tom had screwed down the window, and in any case we were still certain that Hermione was right and Mrs Smith would make for the manor; but we were frightened on so many levels that there was no hope of us relaxing in the chairs. Meriel said it was like the war again, and in many ways it was, but then the enemy had been unknown, impersonal. Now the enemy was a woman we all knew and had simply thought was a shrewish, curmudgeonly snob.

Yes. It was going to be a long night.

Dad phoned at four thirty and told us it was all over. I had picked up the receiver and the other two crowded into the hall watching my every reaction. I just nodded reassurance at them. I could tell Dad was at the end of his tether; I started to ask a question and he seemed not to hear me. He spoke slowly as if reciting a script. He said, 'Maude Smith is dead, Rache. Hermione tried to stop her and was injured. Gus dealt with it, and she is all right, but not fit to be moved. They've got everything here, no need to move her. Gus is glued to her side. The police are dealing with Maude's body.'

I must have made a sound that got through to him because he paused, and then added quickly, 'She stopped being mad, Rache. Just for a moment she saw the whole thing properly. It sort of . . . made sense. At last.' He paused again, and then said, 'There's stuff to do here, Rache. With the police and everything. But I will be with you as soon as I can. It's all right. I promise.'

I replaced the receiver very carefully and turned to the others and passed on Dad's words. 'He'll tell us everything soon—'

And Tom said, 'Is he all right?' And I nodded gratefully.

A December light began to filter down Chichester Street just before eight o'clock; the girls still slept, and we drooped in our chairs looking rather like three very tired horses. 'Ready for the knacker's yard.' Tom murmured. We hadn't been able to face our cold bedrooms and had thought we might sleep by the fire, but it had not happened.

Dad arrived just as the street lights went out. I whipped to the door in time to see him park well clear of the glass from the shattered headlights and emerge very stiffly indeed. I ran out and flung my arms around him, and we almost fell over.

'Hey, hey . . . I'm OK, honey. OK.'

He sounded like an American; he often did. I began to cry. He shepherded me back into the house. It was bitterly cold. Tom was stoking the fire yet again, and Meriel came from the kitchen wheeling the tea trolley, which was absolutely loaded with tea things, toast, marmalade, boiled eggs. When had she done that? Had I fallen asleep and not known it? The sheer ordinariness of the room, the tree, the trolley . . . seemed wrong. It was all . . . skewed. Incongruous. The tired horses had leapt into action, and though we were prepared after Dad's last phone call, still the meal and the welcoming fire and the much-too-early Christmas tree seemed like a conjuring trick in the good old Victorian melodramatic tradition, and it was made more so when Dad took off his coat, held me again and whispered in my ear, 'Now we can go back to normal.'

I looked at him wildly, hoping for a few words about normality. He smiled at me and lifted his left eyebrow just like he used to do years ago. And I knew he was going to be all right. Then he ushered me ahead of him, and I followed Meriel and the tea trolley into the tired familiarity of our sitting room, where Tom was now pushing back the curtains and revealing our safe and secure city street with its lamps and its boot scrapers and the damaged hire car . . .

Dad smiled round at all of us with – with – love. More than affection. This love included himself; it started there and flowed out to us. It warmed us. We sat down, smiling too, our backs straight again. Tom said, 'Are you all right?' And when Dad nodded emphatically – and we could all see he was very much all right – Tom finished, 'In your own time, then,' and grinned widely.

He didn't launch into things immediately; it came in bits and pieces, gestures with the toast in one hand and a cup of tea in the other.

We had to fit it all together slowly. We were tired, our minds were still numb. It was simple enough, really.

Like so much that had happened . . . nothing happened. Not for ages. But as Dad said, through a spoonful of boiled egg, 'That's not true. I have been building a relationship with Hermione over the past four weeks but I've realized I still hadn't grasped the essential . . . being! I thought that when she learned about her real mother and father she would have . . . gone into herself. Not a bit of it. She is so proud of being the child of a brother and sister . . . she says it is a – a unique love, this incestuous beginning. It starts in the womb, and only ends in death, whatever the two partners do with their lives. She—' He spluttered a little laugh into his toast soldiers. 'She is writing a book about it. Of course!' He spluttered again and took a gulp of tea. 'She has this ability to take something intrinsically shocking – to the rest of the world – and make it into something wonderful!' He looked at Meriel. 'You're doing it, Merry. We have to learn to do it, Rache.' I nodded, I knew exactly what he meant. It was so much more than making the best of things. It was knowing that what was happening *was* the best.

And, after a pause to finish his egg, he went on with his story. It was simple enough. As we suspected, at some point during yesterday's early darkness, Maude had wrapped her cardigan around the headlamps of Gus's hire car and smashed them. Dad called it her message in a bottle. She had then pedalled like mad through the lanes, and got to the manor ahead of Dad and the others. And she had ignored the cold empty huts and the ones full of sick people and hidden in the attics of the house. Twenty years before, she and Willi had explored the manor inch by inch to find escape routes for him, and one of them was a flat roof above the toilet block with access to the storage tanks inside the attics. She got there easily through a system of fire escapes discovered by Willi during air-raid practices. The locks had never been changed, and she had keys. The attics were rabbit warrens full of old furniture, books, stacks of files, obsolete kitchen equipment; the police had found a camp bed and blankets, a packet of digestive biscuits. There were several trap doors, most bolted from the inside. Two were unbolted, one of them directly above Hermione's office, so Maude could probably hear and see everything below her. The other was inside a linen cupboard in the corridor outside. The piles of sheets and blankets muffled her exit, and had proved good cover for the half a dozen petrol cans she had been bringing in one by one. She was the same age as Dad, and had been clambering up and down ladders carrying heavy weights every night for almost a week. Dad wondered how she had felt when she had peered through a crack in the office trap door and seen three people. She must have thought Dad and Hermione were already dead, incinerated in Dad's old home. That must have set her back. She might have been planning to lead Meriel and Tom and me to this place. She had always loathed Meriel, and I had inadvertently been a thorn in her flesh for a long time. How had she felt when she had identified Dad and Hermione, and another man she had never seen before?

Dad reckoned she could have gone over the top then and there; raved and screamed and crashed in on them brandishing her knife – she had a knife, a ridiculous thing in a leather scabbard around her waist. That was part of the horror of the whole thing: Maude Smith, an elderly woman, with a scout knife.

Anyway, she did not go over the top then. She hatched a new plan on the spot. Dad knew this because she told them. She wanted to split them up. Deal with them one by one. Prolong her reign of terror. Show them who was boss.

She started by tapping on the radiator in the cupboard. The internees had done that during the war, using Morse code. Mrs Smith did not know Morse code except for the three longs, three shorts and three longs again of the international call for help, SOS. She thought it would bring one of the three out into the corridor to investigate.

Strangely enough, it was Gus who heard the tapping first, and he assumed that the old heating system was playing up. Hermione was talking to Maude, her words never quite the same, her voice always very calm. He waited for a pause then said, 'Honey, something is wrong with the heating.' She clicked off the tannoy and the three of them heard it immediately. Dad knew what it was and therefore who it was.

He said tersely, 'It's Morse. SOS.' He told us that Hermione's face 'melted'.

She clicked on the tannoy system again and said, 'Mum, I can hear you. It's all right. Come to us. Please come to us.'

As Dad said, 'She never uses the word Mum. It's always been Mother.'

We all thought that it was that word – Mum – that brought Maude into the office at a run. And three policemen, called by Dad from the enormous foyer when they had first arrived, must then have started to close in.

Dad said Hermione and Maude had perhaps three or four seconds before the police arrived. Maude burst in and came to a halt about three yards from Hermione, who had stood up and turned to face her. Hermione was weeping, controlling her breathing against sobbing so that the tears simply ran unchecked down her face like rain on a window pane. Maude was dry-eyed, but her face was twisted as if in terrible pain, and she appeared to be fighting for every shallow breath. Dad and Gus could not move; in fact, nobody moved. When I first heard the term freeze-frame many years afterwards, I knew that, just for those seconds, life had frozen so that Hermione and Maude could make contact and say goodbye.

And then the door, still open, was filled with the three policemen. They came in and made a triangle which enclosed Maude. She saw them and roared. Like a lion, Dad said, throaty, furious. Hermione said, 'Mum, it's all right.' She actually held out her arms, though she must have seen the knife. And Maude launched herself.

The policemen grabbed her, but not before that knife had missed Hermione's jugular by an inch and blood was everywhere. Dad and Gus piled in, Dad snatching the clean tea towel neatly placed by the tea things as if for just such an eventuality as this, Gus expertly applying pressure with his fingers. But there was still blood, spurting and pouring, and it was not until Hermione reached with her right hand for Maude's pinioned body that we realized it was Maude's blood as well.

As Dad said, 'She was always one for being pernickety. She knew that there was nothing left for her and it would be a neat and tidy ending to the long-drawn-out vendetta.' He shrugged, there was no relief in such neatness. He added, 'Hermione does not remember us putting that tea towel there. She wondered whether that might have been her mother's doing as well.'

It must have been quite a mess in the end. But perhaps Maude would have liked that, too. Hermione pronounced her mother dead. She used her doctor's voice. Then said shakily, 'It's what you wanted. Goodbye, Mum.' Then she asked Gus very politely if he could help her over to the self-harm ward where there were 'oodles of sterile dressings'. Gus picked her up bodily and carried her down the corridor – she directed him. He was still with her. Dad thought Hermione would like it if Tom, Merry and I went to see her later. After the morning rounds.

Dad went to bed. The twins got up. Merry got their breakfast and told them briefly what had happened, and they were stunned and frightened and just a little bit intrigued. Daisy said, 'Roland will say I told you so.'

Rose sighed, 'Well, he did.' They wanted to know how we were, and Merry told them we were in the sitting room, and probably asleep on the sofa.

We weren't asleep. We sat side by side and shared our thoughts silently as we so often did. Then I said, 'Where will they take Maude?'

'You know where they will take her, Rache.'

'Will it be in the same place now?'

'No. That would have been the final irony, wouldn't it? Maude ending up where Willi and Eva did.'

We thought of that day when we had found the temporary morgue in the hospital. The heavy sheets soaked in disinfectant, the anger of the pathologist.

Tom said – exactly mirroring my own train of memory, 'Maybe the Gaffer shouldn't have sent a couple of kids like us on a job like that.'

I said, 'He didn't know how good we were!' and we snickered an imitation laugh. I added, 'He's not going to be able to do a cover-up job about this.'

'Not fully, no. The *Clarion* will report that Doctor Hermione Smith failed to prevent her mother's suicide attempt, and as a result sustained injury to her shoulder. Her mother took her own life while the balance of her mind was disturbed after the death of her husband, a director of Smith's Aircraft Company . . . you know the sort of thing.'

I nodded. 'It's raining,' I said.

Tom glanced out of the window and groaned. 'And here comes Mr Dawson, wanting to know what the police made of the damaged car.'

I followed him to the front door, I could not

bear to let him out of my sight. I could hear Merry and the girls behind us.

Mr Dawson stood there, the few hairs over his bare head miserably bedraggled.

'Thought you might be wondering about my cat. He was run over last night, you know.' He turned to look at Gus's car. 'No luck with the police? They're not interested in the likes of us.' He hunched his shoulders into his coat and shook his head. 'Better get back. The vet's coming for the body. He'll want me to have another one. I can't. Not yet, anyway. That old moggie, he was a faithful friend.'

I realized belatedly what he was saying and made a sound of distress. Tom said, 'Come in and have a cup of tea, Mr Dawson. We ought to tell you what has been happening here. You've always been such a good neighbour . . .'

It's strange, but after weeping with Mr Dawson, normality . . . happened. Our unhappiness was permissible. And our recent terror simply showed how much we cared about each other. I tried to tell Meriel this, as a kind of apology for ever imagining that she had taken Dad from me – yes, I could admit it at last.

She looked at me in astonishment. 'You need to face up to the fact that he felt rejected by you, Rache!' She gave me a quick hug. 'I'm fed up with tea, hon. Let me make you a proper cup of coffee. Then we can clean up. I reckon there will be a full house here for Christmas. We've got to get cracking.'

And we did.

Twenty-three

In the end we went to Clarion House for Christmas lunch and it was wonderful. Maxine did 'the works' and wore her waitress's outfit with aplomb. The girls pestered to be her assistants and she got out her old uniforms, which had been beautifully pressed and layered with tissue paper, and they looked like 'a million dollars', to quote Gus. Poor old Gilbert got misty-eyed because he said they reminded him of Flo when he first knew her. I caught Dad's eye and winked, and after a second he waggled his eyebrow at me.

Hermione was with us. Her left arm was in a sling, and she was even paler than usual but she insisted the whole dreadful experience had been good. 'It helps me to know the other side of the coin,' she maintained.

I still felt we were related in some way, and I said like an anxious aunt, 'You were already rather good at that, Hermione.'

She thought about it. 'I could *see* the other

side, yes. But now I know it.' She touched her shoulder briefly and smiled right at me. 'I know it, Rache. With my muscle and bone!'

I think if it hadn't been for Gus, the two of us would have embraced then, but he got in first and she did not protest. In fact after a quick glance at Meriel she darted a kiss at his cheek that landed on the tip of his nose.

Meriel chuckled. 'No need to check up on me, Hermione. Gus and I finished ages ago.' She looked at him. 'He's been a good friend. Saved my life – certainly my reason – once or twice.'

Gus was unembarrassed. 'You're welcome, Ma'am,' he said cheerfully. 'I told Eve here that you wouldn't mind. Been telling me for ages to lay off.'

We almost missed the last few words because we were saying in unison, 'Eve?' Rose and Daisy came in carrying vegetable dishes swathed in towels, and they said, 'What?'

Hermione was bright red. Gus said, 'Hermione has never liked her name, apparently. And she thought she would like to take two-thirds of her real mother's name. So she is now Eve Smith; soon, I hope, to be Eve Michaelson.'

Hermione gasped like a schoolgirl. 'You never said – this is the first time—'

'Well, do you like it?' he persisted.

She swallowed, and then coughed, and then said, 'Yes.'

Meriel said, 'It sounds like a famous psychiatrist's name to me.'

Daisy put down her dish and looked at her sister. 'Was that a marriage proposal?'

Rose said, 'I think it was.'

Daisy turned swiftly towards Hermione and said, 'Eve . . . sounds OK . . . do you want to have two bridesmaids?' I was suddenly so proud of her. Actually, neither of the girls had ever voiced a wish to be a bridesmaid. I knew that Daisy's plea amounted to a confirmation – of Hermione's new name and Gus's marvellously opportunistic proposal. I glanced at Tom. He waggled his eyebrow. Of course he did.

We sat around the enormous fireplace until it was dark. All of us still looked desperately tired; but at least we were now warriors talking about our battles, not poor old horses waiting for the knacker's yard. Daisy and Rose sat at Hermione's feet – it was going to take a long time for me to think of her as Eve – and talked weddings. Tom, Gus and Dad went to sleep in their chairs and Gilbert became maudlin. Meriel smiled and nodded at him. Maxine and I made tea and warmed mince pies.

We left at five, six of us in our car, leaving Gus and Hermione to drive to Gloucester in Hermione's car – they wanted the rest of the day to themselves. We drove a little way down the road, then turned off to visit Daphne. She was laying up a tea for a regiment of soldiers; it seemed it was for us. Roland came in rather sheepishly and apologized for 'starting this whole thing off'.

'Not entirely his fault, my dears,' Daphne said briskly. 'If his dad knows about something the whole of Gloucester soon does, too. Tom, I hope your boss can make a comprehensible story of it. Sounds ridiculously complicated to me. After all, at the end of the day, Hermione Smith's mother committed suicide. No need to drag up old sins, surely? Justice has been done, and has been seen to be done.' She looked confused and amended her words. 'Or is it "and has to been seen to have been done?"' She shook her head. 'Who knows? Is Hermione all right?'

We told her about Hermione's change of name, and Tom said something about Gilbert Carfax being used to inventing the news, and Meriel held my arm and said, 'Just like we used to do, Rache, huh?'

Daphne took off her apron. 'Oh, come on. He couldn't have invented the war – he couldn't have invented any of what has happened, not really. He just sort of . . . tidied it up a bit. And you two—' she glanced at Meriel and me dismissively. 'You were just a couple of bored schoolgirls who should have joined the drama club.' She flapped her apron at the boys. 'Take Rose and Daisy into the playroom, Roland.' She turned to Tom. 'We've set up a ping-pong table. Good practice for next summer's tennis tournaments. You and I'll have a go later on, Tom. Do you good.'

Actually, it did. Daphne beat him every time, but he went back for more after tea, and she told him graciously he was coming along nicely. On the way home Meriel said from the back seat, 'You've got to beat her, Tom. Is there somewhere you could practise in your lunch hour? Miss Hardwicke used to have that table up in the old attics, Rache. I'll give her a ring and explain the situation.'

'What situation?' Tom asked.

'Daphne's situation. She needs to lose at *something*.'

'Merry! She lost at marriage, for goodness' sake.'

'She did not. She is the only woman I know who has made a huge success of divorce!'

Rose said sleepily from within Merry's arm, 'And actually, she threw Reggie out . . . he didn't actually leave her.'

'No.' Daisy sounded equally sleepy. 'But he's got someone else.'

Rose said, 'She won't marry him, though, will she?'

'Well . . . he's pretty boring.'

Tom was shaking with laughter by my side. Meriel said in a soothing drone, 'Go to sleep, both of you. I'll wake you when we turn into Chichester Street.'

And Dad, supporting Daisy, said, 'My God, Merry. You sound just like Flo!'

'That's the best compliment I've ever had, George. Thank you.'

Thank God, I felt not a pang of jealousy. My Mum and my bestest friend in all the world.

Meriel went back home two days later, but Gus stayed. She telephoned to say she was safely home, and Rex had decorated everywhere with fake holly, and Vicky and Georgie had worn Santa Claus hats when they met her at the airport. It was all so different over there, I found it hard to imagine. Merry would be back before the end of January; she seemed capable of straddling continents. When I mentioned this to Tom he looked surprised. 'You did it so easily last June, my love. And you brought back a sort of essence of America . . . you'll have to do it again. You and Merry between you . . . you're good at it.' I suppose he was right – because we have gone on doing it ever since.

When Meriel came back it was 1964 and another winter had set in with a vengeance. It meant that during that spring term we saw very little of Merry. I went to Bristol on the train twice but the 'icy conditions' went on for ages and we had a snowstorm the day she flew back home for Easter. It wasn't until Whitsun that we resumed our regular weekends together.

It was almost five months since Maude Smith had 'committed suicide' and in that time we had sorted out adjustments to our usual pattern. Eve Smith and Gus Michaelson were living at the manor and planning a July wedding, and Gus was practising unofficially, running an unpaid consultancy for some of Eve's patients. Dad was living in Maude Smith's old house on the no-longer-rough road, and, besides the wedding, was overseeing the rebuilding of 'Hermione's Cottage', as we all called it now. For the rest of us, life seemed to return to what it had been; but there were subtle changes in relationships, which we were all well aware of. Gilbert moved from his honorary avuncular status to something more official, though it was hard to identify. He filled a niche somewhere between a grandfather and an uncle. And Maxine's light shone as she chattered on about the things she and Mum had done together. 'She was my best friend,' she said to me one day. 'Like you and Merry. We were silly together. But after she met George, she asked me to look after Gilbert. And I did.' She put her face into Frou-frou's topknot and said in a stifled voice, 'That was why I didn't stop . . . what happened. I was still looking after Gillie. Can you forgive me, Rachel?' It had never occurred to me that she bore responsibility for any of the events before my birth. It never would. I realized again that no two marriages were the same, and there must have been an element of passion in my parents' marriage, recognized by Meriel but not by me.

The twins showed the greatest change; we had, of course, protected them as best we could from the nightmarish elements of Maude Smith's madness, but they knew that she had burned down Rough Road Cottage and had tried to stab Eve before she killed herself. They also knew that she was not Eve's real mother, but we told ourselves this was made more acceptable for them by the fact that Meriel was so free with what she called 'maternal arrangements'. For the moment that brought them close again, close to us, too. They needed to know each other's plans and exactly where Dad and Mum were, so each morning we exchanged timetables. If we were going to be out when they got home from school they often went to the cathedral and spent an hour drawing and sketching and making peculiar maps of the building. Tom said gloomily, 'You know what comes next, don't you?' I nodded and he finished, 'They will tell us they intend to become nuns.' And I nodded again.

The only people who stayed the same were Tom and me; I was certain of that. We knew each other as we knew ourselves, our thoughts would mingle effortlessly. We were growing old together. Tom was forty in May. And then it was Whitsun, and Meriel arrived with the usual car boot of books, and a case on the seat next to her, full of clothes for Maria to alter. She had got into the way of doing that 'as a punishment for DM'. But we both knew it was her way of acknowledging her real mother, and perhaps forgiving her.

I knew something was wrong almost immediately; she had lost her 'edge'. The sharp, lemony zest that was the essence of Meriel was not there any more.

The first Saturday night – it was just June – I asked Tom whether he had noticed anything. He hadn't.

'She's wrapped up again in her course, love. And she's always missing the children. That's one of the reasons she wants to be with our two.'

'That's another thing. Maria Nightingale put on a spring fashion show this afternoon – proper catwalk and everything. They wanted her to go with them. Got her a ticket. She said she was too tired.'

'You were going, so it made no difference to them.'

'I had to go – promised Maria the publicity, for what it's worth. I couldn't even stay back with Merry, get her some tea.'

'Presumably that was what she wanted. Peace

and quiet. And though she gets on all right now with Maria and Dennis, it can't be easy for her. I mean, the whole situation is simply ridiculous now.'

I suppose it was; Dennis visited Myrtle every other weekend, quite openly. It seemed to suit everyone. Even Meriel.

'It's not . . . Merry. She was so polite about it all. Would we mind if she had a nap? That is not Merry. She should have told us to clear off and give her some peace.' We were in bed and I stared at him in the darkness. I said, 'D'you think she is ill?'

He started to laugh quietly, then checked himself and thought about it, then said, 'No.' He cradled me comfortingly. 'Give her some elbow room, Rache. We're all still reeling from last winter. If there is anything wrong, she'll confide in you soon. You know that.'

But the next morning I got up early, thinking I would go to church. I tapped on her door before eight o'clock with a mug of tea.

'I know you're awake,' I opened the door a crack. 'Heard you in the bathroom while I was making tea.'

It was a wonderful June morning, light was streaming in and revealing strewn clothes everywhere. That didn't worry me unduly, though actually Merry lived out of her suitcase very neatly each weekend and it was unusual. What was worrying was that she was sitting up in bed, obviously trying to work, her face streaked with tears. She looked up, and forced a smile.

'A brew that is not twin-made?'

'Exactly.' I put the mug on an empty chair and carried it carefully to the bedside. I said quietly, 'Can I do anything?'

She did not prevaricate. She simply said, 'No.' She picked up the mug gratefully and held it in both hands as if she was cold. 'I must sort this lot out and go to see Hermione today. I mean Eve, of course. Is she still living at the manor? How on earth does she stand it after what happened there?'

'She's got Gus with her. It's a beautiful place, especially in the summer.'

She glanced up at me. 'You'll miss her.'

'Yes. But . . . well, it's so great. What is happening to her – to them both. You're all right with it, are you, Merry?'

'Of course. He was there when I needed him. I know he's a good man. It couldn't be better.' She put down her mug, gathered up a sheaf of papers, and tapped them into shape. 'You're going to church. Say one for me.'

I hovered a moment more, then left. I was not reassured. I had not been there for her when she arrived yesterday, and today she was going to the manor.

*   *   *

I wasn't a bit keen on Dad living in the Smiths' old house. After all the fuss and bother had abated after Christmas, Hermione – Eve – had declared she would sell the house as it stood; she could not bear to live there. Dad had immediately made an offer which she had refused. 'It will suit you to live there for a while, I can see that,' she said. 'But it's not a happy house. I can't let you buy it, George. You're having such fun designing Hermione's Cottage. Live in my house while you do that, and then move down the road and I will sell mine.' And Dad, being Dad, began to clean and paint Mrs Smith's domain so that it no longer looked dark and frightening.

He still came to us for Sunday lunch, and he was disappointed that Meriel was not there.

'The thing about last winter was – all that danger pushed us together. It was the war-time feeling all over again.'

'Oh Grandee,' Rose protested. 'All this talk about the war-time feeling. You sound like Miss Hardwicke!'

Daisy warbled, 'There'll be blue birds over . . . the white cliffs of Dover . . .'

'No respect,' Dad mourned pitifully.

Tom handed him the carving knife. 'You're the only one who can carve decently,' he said reverently. And through the laughter I remembered how the war and its aftermath had split us so badly that Dad had left us for ten whole years.

Daisy said unexpectedly, 'Aunt Merry was sick in the night. I think she's got an upset tummy.'

But even as I voiced my concern, I knew the sickness was a symptom of something much more serious. Meriel would have said frankly that she was 'up-chucking' and asked for a day in bed. Instead she had already left the house when I got back from church. And I was convinced she had gone to see Gus, not Eve. She had wanted to see the doctor who had helped her in the early years of her marriage.

The following week Daisy was chosen to represent the Swallow School in the Gloucestershire junior tennis championships. Mrs Rolfe – still the school secretary – was busy, and Miss Hardwicke telephoned to ask whether I could drive her and Daisy to Stroud. It was grey and overcast as we set out, but Miss Hardwicke immediately pointed out that it would stop the players overheating. She had nothing to say when a light drizzle blurred the windscreen.

We parked and hurried to the pavilion, where there were changing rooms and the absolute luxury of hot showers. The six courts in front of the pavilion were still being dragged as we paused beneath the verandah and took it all in. The school groundsmen were loosening the nets slightly, and girls milled around outside the high wire netting, some with umbrellas but others almost relishing the rain. The umpire platforms were wheeled in, the ball girls took up positions, a loud speaker crackled, Daisy left us hastily, and we settled ourselves beneath the verandah as the first announcements were made. Nothing at all was said about the rain, and as if suddenly ashamed, it gave up and a watery sun appeared.

Play began at ten thirty and stopped for lunch at twelve thirty. Daisy was still in there. We met her in the school hall where a marvellous buffet was laid out along the edge of the platform. She ate sparingly. She was sparkling. 'It's so exciting, Mum. I never thought it would be like this. I thought I'd lose my nerve. Colin keeps telling me I'm good and I thought it was just because . . . you know . . . *because.* But then Rose watched me in the heats and she said I was really good. Seriously good. And I knew she wouldn't say it just to get in my good books like Colin so . . . I started to believe it. It was when I beat that girl in the second round. You know, the one in the tiny shorts. Denise Elmhurst. I'd watched her and I knew she was bloody good. And I beat her! So I must be bloody good myself!'

I glanced at Miss Hardwicke. Apparently she hadn't heard. She was dealing with some crab vol-au-vents.

Anyway, Daisy became Junior Girls' County

Champion at the end of that afternoon, and we returned home flushed with victory and so pleased for her. She was pleased, too. She thought Rose and Dad and Grandee would be pleased. And Colin. Colin Beard, she explained carefully to Miss Hardwicke. The one who had given her so much coaching. Miss Hardwicke said she remembered his mother, who was an old girl of the Swallow School. I thought perhaps all this optimism was a good omen and Meriel might not be terminally ill after all.

On 21 June there came a telegram from Worcester General Hospital. It announced starkly that Stanley Clarke was a patient and would like to see us. It was over a year since Tom had visited him at Upton-upon-Severn and much longer than that since they had had a 'float-in-a-boat', as Nobby put it. I telephoned Tom in the office, where he was putting the weekly to bed. He said, 'Bring the car round to the house, love. Get some Players from the corner shop. And some fruit, if you like. No flowers. Nobby wouldn't want flowers. Be with you in under an hour.'

He was sooner than that; the Carfaxes were on another of their cultural visits and life was much easier without Gilbert's help. Tom dashed in, swilled his face at the sink, changed his jacket and we were off. We did not take in the mid-summer scenery – the A38 was still a country road and the weather was glorious – we used the windscreen wiper to get rid of pollen from the cow parsley . . . none of it mattered. Nobby had become a life-line for Tom, his link with his father. We knew this was the end.

He was in a side ward and on his own, a sure sign that he was almost there. A nurse told us he was sleeping, and if we could not wake him we could still talk to him. 'At some level he will almost certainly know you are here,' she said. Then she closed the door gently, and we stood and looked at the unnaturally supine figure in the bed, vaguely outlined by a blue counterpane, the head of wispy hair barely denting the starched pillows. His hands, incredibly gnarled, ropes of veins weaving across their backs, lay across the turned-down sheet. Tom took them both in his and crouched by the bed.

'We're here, Nobby.' He spoke loudly. 'Rachel and Tom. We came as soon as we heard. How's it going?'

There was no answer, but as I fetched a chair and manoeuvred it into the back of Tom's crooked knees, I thought I saw the shadow of a smile float across Nobby's face. It was what I wanted to see, of course.

Tom said, 'Well, we're all in this together, old man. Just like in the boat. The same boat. We're all in the same boat, Nobby. Me and Rache in the bows, you rowing. Your wooden leg stuck straight out, ready to tip us in the river at the slightest provocation—' He went on like this, then leaned closer and said, 'Where are we going, Nobby? You're taking us somewhere new. Where is it?'

We both saw the smile, then. And we heard the sigh which emerged as a long drawn-out, 'A-a-ah—' I reached over and held his elbow, and felt his muscles contract as he pulled on Tom's hands. Then the door opened again and a green-overalled woman entered. She looked about sixty. She gave us a delighted smile, turned and towed in a trolley containing a large brown enamel teapot, flanked by cups, saucers, a large milk jug and sugar.

'I know Mr Clarke won't be bothered but I thought you would like a cup of tea. He might manage a beaker, actually.' As she spoke she was pouring tea and adding milk. She said, 'You must be Tom and Rachel. He spoke about you so often. Only . . . let me see . . . yesterday? No, it must have been the day before. Because he wanted you to have something that arrived in Monday's post. He was quite agitated about it. I said to him that Sister would let you know, but then he said she wouldn't, not till the end.' She beamed at him, as if he was sitting up and taking notice. 'He didn't want you hanging about too much, you see. Did you, Mr Clarke? They're busy people, aren't they, Mr Clarke?' She pulled forward a bed table and put the three cups on it, then leaned across Tom to the locker and reached inside it. Tom was forced to release Nobby's hands and lean back. I went to the other side of the bed and leaned down until my mouth was next to his ear. 'Not yet,' I whispered. 'Don't leave the boat yet.'

She heard and laughed. 'He's always on about his boat.' She looked down at him. 'I've done what you asked, Mr Clarke. Your friend has got that letter right and tight now. I'd better get on.' She pushed her trolley to the door. 'He's a good sort. He wanted to hang on till you got that letter in your own hands. Didn't want it bundled up with his effects and maybe burned.'

Tom was holding the letter and looking bewildered. He thanked her, but said it was addressed to Nobby himself. She said, 'It's yours now.' And the door swung shut. And still Tom just held the envelope by a corner.

I said as steadily as I could, 'I think he's gone, darling. Should I ring the bell?'

Tom was stricken. 'He can't have! He was trying to pull himself up just a second ago.' He dropped the letter and felt frantically for a pulse. It was so obvious that Nobby had simply vacated his body. I rang the bell. Sister must have been right outside the door, and almost burst in. She put three fingers against his neck. We waited. She said, 'I'm sorry.' Just for an instant she moved her hand to his face, then straightened. 'He would not let me send that telegram until this morning. I think he knew exactly when the time was right. Immediately he saw you . . . that was the time.' I could feel myself filling with tears, and I swallowed fiercely.

Sister said, 'I am so pleased. He wanted to be here when you got that blessed envelope!' There was a smile in her voice. 'And Mrs Draycott – the tea lady who is in the Women's Institute at Upton – had promised him she would make sure you got it. Things don't usually work out so well.'

Neither of us replied. Tom was now holding Nobby's hand, and I had his elbow cupped in my palm again. She said, 'Would you like ten minutes alone with him before my nurses tidy up?'

Tom nodded. She left us and we leaned across the bed, joined by Nobby, and closed our eyes. Tears oozed out of mine, probably Tom's too.

We read the contents of the envelope when we got back in the car. There in the car park, with the hurly-burly of that busy city going on around us, we jammed together behind the steering wheel and looked at the envelope. It was addressed to Sergeant Stanley Clarke, written in a childish hand, enormous block letters. After that came his home address at

Upton-upon-Severn written in open, generous italics. Then yet another hand had scribbled, 'Please forward to Worcester General Hospital'. It was stamped with an English first-class stamp and on the back was a small, silvery address label that read 'Mr & Mrs Carter' and gave an Upton address.

We stared at it silently, then Tom upended it and shook out the contents. There was a letter, typewritten. Folded inside the letter were half a dozen sketches very similar to the one Nobby had sent us before. I could hear Tom breathing, almost gasping for air, flipping through them frantically. I took them from him, smoothed them out, and, using the typewritten sheet as a base, laid them out against the steering wheel. They were all tiny portraits of bearded men standing around a table. One of them was of the table itself and a lone man lying on it. His face was turned full on. We stared at it in disbelief for a long time.

Tom whispered, 'Is it?' And almost at the same time, I said, 'It's Nobby. A young Nobby.'

We peered closer. All the sketches were in pen and ink. The closer you looked, the less you could see. I took the typewritten sheet away from the steering wheel and held it against the windscreen. Tom said, 'This is what Nobby wanted us to see. He was ill when he got this. He must have felt so – so—'

'Excited,' I supplied. 'How wonderful. To

travel those last few days in a state of excitement. How wonderful.'

We dried our eyes and turned to the other sketches. We recognized no one else. Tom said, 'One of these men is my father. And my father from over twenty years ago. I *must* know him!'

'It was drawn . . . since then, darling.' My voice was hoarse. 'My God . . . this is done in biro. There were no biro pens in Burma in 1943.'

Tom extracted some recently acquired spectacles from the glove compartment and put them on. He studied the biro sketch, holding it close, then away, then approaching it from different angles.

He whispered, 'Do you think . . . what do you think? When did they start flooding the market with biros? And I still can't see him – surely he would be there?' His voice became querulous, then frustrated. I glanced at him. I had thought I knew everything about him.

I said uncertainly, 'Maybe he's not there. He's the observer. The artist. He did not include himself in his drawings.' I went on, 'Read the letter, Tom. Is it official?' I gathered the sketches and put them back into the envelope, while he glanced at the type, turned the page over and back again.

He said, 'Not a bit. It's signed by someone called Frank. Look.' He put his arm around my shoulders and drew me close. And then we were silent, poring over the letter. Almost immediately Tom made a sound of distress and began to tremble, and I tried to hold him still. We both had trouble with our breathing. At one point we were both weeping, dashing tears away so that we could finish reading that letter. It said:

> To Sergeant Stanley Clarke.
>
> Dear Sir. I get flashes. You are in them. And now I've got your name. Nobby, they called you. You were very brave. I had to hold you down when they sawed off your leg. I don't know if you are alive. The Burma Star man visited today and the wife said she would try to find out things when she went home. She will take this letter and try to send it to you. If you read it you might remember me. I doubt it. You were very ill and then I was ill. I woke up in a hospital bed. I was born again. No you. No anyone who wasn't in front of me. No words, no walking, no eating. No name, no hair, no nails. They called me Frank because the animals came to me and the first thing I learned was to feed them. I was so happy. I could have learned to walk and talk and read and write in a few months but I didn't. I couldn't stop my finger and toe nails from growing, nor my hair and beard sprouting, but I hung

on to everything so that I could taste it and smell it and know it was happening. I stopped time. Even now I do not understand the nurses here. I draw messages to them. That is the one thing I have always done. I draw my life. They smile at me and nod and hug me.

Then three or four years ago, after one of my flashes, something strange happened. You were there. You were in a boat. Three people. The Burma Star people leave me books and I read one called *Three Men in a Boat*. So I thought it was that. I thought perhaps you had read that book too. But then some time after, it happened again. And this time I knew that one of the people in the boat was you. And your name was Sergeant Stanley Clarke. And you were the same brave man I remembered.

I want to say two things. I am still so happy. When I laugh they call me crazy Frank. They learn words to say to me. Crazy Frank laugh, they say. How else can I share such joy? And I want to know that you are happy like this also. We are connected. Look at these sketches and remember. And I will know.

Yours faithfully,

Frank. I have read about Francis of Assisi now.

Eventually the letter slipped on to Tom's knees. He turned to me and we held each other, and as we wept the strangest thing happened. There was joy in the confined space of the car. It was June and the sun was bright. But this was something else.

Twenty-four

We noticed everything on the way home, every spray of blossom, every ripening plum in the Pershore orchards. I remembered my grandmother's amazement when at last she gave in and wore spectacles. 'Everything is so beautiful – the colours are just right and bright!' And she went around the garden every morning, rain or shine, to make sure those magical glasses were still working. It was like that. Seeing things for the first time.

'This is what he meant,' Tom said.

'It's what Hermione meant at Christmas when she recognized the difference between imagining the feelings of others and . . . knowing. What did she say – she knew it with her muscle and bone?'

'It's adding a new dimension. Colours and shapes and how to draw them.' He slowed to go through another village. Then added, 'I wonder . . . Rache, I wonder whether he is still alive.'

I had known this was coming. I felt cautious but could not say so; Tom's tiny hope was like a light shining again. For so long now he had 'accepted' his father's death; suddenly he had this hope. I said, 'The Burma Star Association. They're the ones to contact. And this couple in particular: The Carters. They brought the letter home and found Nobby's address.'

'But if he is, what then? How fragile is that happiness he feels? Have we got any right to threaten it?'

I waited until the road widened again. 'Well . . . just to know he is alive would be enough at this point, wouldn't it?'

He was silent for ages, then nodded. 'Yes. I have to know if he is alive.'

Nobby's sister-in-law, and the friends who had supported him domestically, arranged the funeral, and the church at Upton was full of people who had appreciated his courage and his eccentricities. He had been a 'character' as well as a hero. Afterwards in the local pub we heard some very amusing stories. Nobby would be missed. The Carters were there and local members of the British Legion. The girls asked whether they could come with us. It was their first funeral, and they were suddenly hit by trepidation as the coffin was brought into the church. We all held hands very firmly.

*   *   *

Then it was time for Meriel to go home for the summer. Since her trip to the manor to see Gus, she seemed slightly better and the amazing letter from 'Frank' had rushed all of us into another place; she had been as incredulous and amazed as we all were. But that last weekend with us seemed to drain her energy again, and she sat at the kitchen table and stared into the garden, opting out of the fervent discussion going on around her. Tom had spoken with the Carters at Nobby's funeral, and again by telephone. There was a feeling now of urgency; Jack Fairbrother – if it was him – was the same age as my own father and had been institutionalized for the last twenty years. Eve and Gus talked to us of the cushioning effect of amnesia. I remembered Dad living those ten years in Florida: a half-life.

It was Saturday, and Tom was at the office, so I was trying to explain to the girls and to Meriel how ambivalent Tom felt about the whole thing.

'Frank's fingertips were damaged and his teeth pulled, so there was no easy identification method.' The girls moaned softly; we had spoken of the torture aspect very matter-of-factly, not glossing over it; but I was glad it had not escaped them. 'Even so, it is almost certainly Jack Fairbrother. The sketches are sufficient evidence for us.' I looked directly at Meriel. 'I've got no doubts about it whatever. Do you agree, Merry?'

I did this every time she slipped into her special reverie, forcing an answer from her.

She must have been listening properly because she immediately responded, returning my look with a small smile. She knew exactly what I was doing.

'Of course I agree,' she said. Then, as if to convince us of her complete understanding, she went on steadily, 'The Carters heard of this hospital in Singapore because of the drawings – didn't they say there was a framed collage of them in their hotel room? One of the hospital staff must have saved them from the incinerator – maybe to show his family? Whatever. They made enquiries and paid a visit. And found one of the patients was English. A leftover. No identification, so no papers, so no slot in the system. Also no memory, except these flashes, as he calls them. And always of his captivity. And absolutely no trouble to anyone.' She glanced at the girls morosely. 'A lesson here, yes? You don't get noticed if you're too . . . amenable.'

I said quickly, 'No problem for you two, then.' They cast me exasperated looks, but then smiled. They would not be fourteen until August and were entitled to another few years of childhood. And then Rose tipped her chair and turned to me.

'Listen, Mum, why don't we tell Dad to get himself over there? Just be with this man and find out if he really is our other grandad. Then we can visit him too, and perhaps one day he will be able to visit us.'

Daisy nodded. 'Dad has to go there. I reckon our grandad might die if we take him away from the heat and the sunshine. And his world – the world he has made inside his head – would go away.' She nodded again, emphatically. 'Much better for Dad to go there.'

Meriel smiled properly at them. 'Oh, girls. You're wonderful. You prove all the time that two heads are better than one. How long do you think your father could stay over there?'

They looked at each other; they were so close I often wondered whether their minds could connect in some way, as Tom's and mine so often did. They started one of their dialogues.

Rose said, 'We could manage for a while without him. Somehow.'

'We would. Of course we would. We would make ourselves.' Daisy's hand, lying palm down on the table, clenched itself into a fist.

'It would be awful if he stayed over Christmas.'

Daisy forced a laugh. 'It's only June now, six months till Christmas.'

'Six months. That man – Frank – he's been on his own over there for twenty years!' Rose set her jaw. 'I think Dad and Frank ought to live together properly, get meals and things. It might take a year. But it has to take as long as . . . it has to take!'

Daisy nodded judiciously. Meriel said, 'Do you mean that? Your father does such a lot with you.'

'You come over here, Aunt Merry, and Vicky and Georgie manage.'

'I know. I feel awful about it, actually.'

'But it's not really for long.' Rose became very earnest, leaning forward across the table. 'And it gives you lots to talk about when you go home. And Dad will have such heaps to tell us about our new grandad.'

Daisy said in the same tone, 'It's the only way, really, isn't it? For you and your family, and for us and our family.' She turned to me. 'Tell you what – Grandee would like to go and he'd help Dad and our other grandad. When he's finished planning Hermione's Cottage he'll need something else, and it would be like one of Miss Hardwicke's projects!'

My heart sank: no Tom and no Dad. Yet Dad would look after Tom.

Meriel gave one of her old sly smiles. 'There's always Uncle Gilbert to look after you. And I could have a word with my dad.'

We all laughed. It was a good time.

Tom must have talked to Gilbert that same morning, because when he got home he seemed feverish with excitement. Gilbert and Maxine were still full of their trip to the Caribbean; they had entered into this new journey with total enthusiasm. Maps and airline timetables had appeared; the service to Australia nearly always stopped to refuel at Singapore. Tom telephoned the Carters and they confirmed that the journey was not difficult and Singapore was a beautiful city; and Frank's English, though rusty through under-use, was simple and direct and intelligible. We all went to see Meriel off, and in a sudden fright I made her promise to return in September.

She laughed. 'I've talked to David Harmsworth. You met him, Rache. A really good man. He seems to think it'll be all right. So yes, I promise I will return!' She mimicked the narrator's voice in a Victorian crime series on the new commercial television channel, and I laughed back at her obligingly. I assumed she meant that her exam results had passed muster. It was such a relief. I knew better than anyone how much work she had put in to this first year of the course.

The rest of that summer went by much too quickly. When Dad and Tom left one pearly dawn, the three of us clasped each other and wept as if we would never see them again. The house almost rang with emptiness. The slightest thing set us off; I ironed the clothes the men had been wearing and wept; Rose and

Daisy found the kazoos and dripped tears on to them, so had to dry them and wrap them in tissue ready for the next musical concert.

We thought time would hang heavily and pass very slowly, but after a few days it seemed to work the other way. We got letters or phone calls two or three times a week, and felt as if we were living half our time in dusty old Gloucester and the other half in the exotic Far East. The first time Tom visited the hospital, Dad stayed in his hotel room and wrote to us about what he could see through the window; the palms and the shops and beyond them the sea; how anxious he was about Tom going to the hospital alone, and how homesick they both felt. 'I know now, my darling girls, that I cannot live in Florida again. Please investigate the golf courses in the county!'

Back home, Myrtle Nightingale surprised everyone by learning to drive. She took us to the river to swim every day during the short, fierce heatwave of August. Barry joined us with his second wife and her three small boys. The girls came into their own as nursemaids; they found some old planks and made a raft and towed the boys up and down between the barges; Myrtle absolutely loved watching the girls regress to being ten-year-olds again.

In the midst of all this, Gus and Eve jettisoned all the plans for their wedding and 'fixed everything up' at the registry office. Gus added, 'Once George and Tom left, we didn't want anything grand, but we wanted it quickly.' I thought I knew why. They were planning to go to the States.

The girls had their fourteenth birthday without Tom. Colin and Roland Beard took them to dinner at the sixteenth-century New Inn, and Gilbert and Maxine did a jelly and bun party the next afternoon with paper hats and crackers. The girls from the Swallow School pretended it was a bit of a joke, but everyone enjoyed it so much they asked whether they could come again next year. After they had followed the treasure trail laid by Gilbert through the fields to the home farm and back again they abandoned Miss Hardwicke's rules on pestering and *begged* to be allowed back next year. The treasure was a cultured pearl necklace each.

Maria Nightingale designed two dresses for the girls and 'did them a deal'. She was planning another show in the autumn and asked them if they would model the dresses.

In fact people were so anxious to fill Tom's absence that both girls had the time of their lives. But when all the festivities had died down and the new term began, they started asking whether Dad would be home for bonfire night. It seemed he would not. He wrote to us at the end of September.

Darlings, this is going to be a long job. Frank is definitely my father and your grandfather. When I saw him first I recognized him instantly: he can still wrap his big toes around the others, he is ambidextrous (look that one up!) and he has a sort of lisp. But even without those things I would have known, just as you would know me in twenty years' time. Unfortunately it doesn't work the other way round. Not only does he definitely not recognize me, he shakes his head at the idea of ever having had a son. As for my mother, he smiles and says what would a nice girl be doing with a bloke like him? Yes, he has a go at a bit of a joke now and then. And today we had a breakthrough. He was interlacing his fingers when I arrived and I told him it reminded me of an action rhyme he used to do for me when I was small. He didn't understand the term 'action rhyme' and I showed him. You know the one, girls, you loved it too. 'Here's the church, here's the steeple, open the doors and here's the people . . .' and so on. I was half-way through when he actually picked it up and went on with it. 'Here's the parson running upstairs, and here he is saying his prayers . . .' It was marvellous. I cheered, and the little Chinese nurse came running, thinking there was trouble. But that was it. He sat there smiling like a Cheshire cat, but nothing else happened. Patience. We must have patience. Grandee is coming again tomorrow to play dominoes. My father can play dominoes. Before all the other soldiers left, they taught him dominoes and he's hot stuff. Just a word for Mum, then I must go to bed. There's a big fan over my bed and it's heavenly.

In his postscript to me he told me how sad it was. And then he said he loved me and I must take care. And other things.

Suddenly it was October and Meriel's new term had started, and there was no Meriel. I telephoned Florida, and Vicky's voice came down the line. I almost sobbed. 'Oh darling. It's so good to hear you. You are the one person who will tell me the truth. I need to know – we're such old friends – I can come over if there is anything—' At that point Vicky interrupted me brusquely.

'Hold on there, Aunt Rachel. What's going on? Put Mom on the line, will you? I haven't heard from her since she left and—' She stopped talking because I gasped a small scream, and then I did actually sob, and she said, 'My God. What's happened? Try to talk slowly. The line is not wonderful. Is my Mom ill?'

I put my hand over my mouth and tried to still my whole body. Vicky waited. I said very carefully, 'I don't know. She is not here. She has not come back for the new term. Gus has been to Bristol. No one has heard from her.'

The silence was terrible. I wanted to hold Vicky to me. I could feel her anxiety move to terror. Yet when she spoke her voice was completely level. I remembered that this girl had lived with Meriel all her life; she knew about her father and the girl from Devon . . . Dawn. She was devoted to her brother, and had been involved in all the work towards making a good life for him and for children like him. She was mature well beyond her years.

She said, 'She was flying to New York and then on to London. We saw her on to the plane. There have been no crash reports.' Her voice wobbled up a register. 'That was almost a week ago, dammit! What the hell is she playing at this time?'

I said, 'Vicky, your mother would not worry us all deliberately—'

'Oh yes, she would. Not us specifically. Especially not you and me, Aunt Rache. But she would do it to Dad. They've had a few rows this summer. I thought that kind of thing was over . . . anyway, I have to make some calls. I'll come back to you as soon as I have some news.' She cut me off straight away. I sat there on the stairs and stared at the coloured tiles of the hall floor, and tried for a moment to imagine the kind of life Meriel had in the States. I had been only too willing to accept that her efforts to become a good American wife, and to put her soul into her work with children, had brought her into some kind of stupid harbour. As if Meriel could ever accept any kind of tranquillity. And if she was ill, terminally or not, where could she be? As I reached this point the post came through the door and I recognized the airmail envelope; but before I had read the letter I knew where Meriel was. It was written from Orion.

I glanced through it and then rang Vicky to tell her, and later I sat down and read it over and over again.

> Darling Rache. I've been dickering about for ages and now have made a decision and feel . . . well, not better exactly, but sort of whole again. I'm not coming over this term, honey. I've talked to the Prof. I can do the rest of the course later – they arrange these deferment things now for people like me. Actually, I could do it now but I want the baby to be born over here whether Rex likes it or not. And I want to take time to be a mother again. I want to have another shot at being a wife, too. Because, guess what, Dawn disappeared last Easter, and it was while I was comforting poor old Rex that I fell for number three!
>
> Anyway, I know I should have told you

before I left, but I guess you know anyway – old Hawkeye Throstle! Rache, I'm kind of scared about being pregnant because I'm getting close to forty, and after Vicky and then Georgie . . . well, I'm more than scared. I was going to tell Gus and ask for some of his magic pills, but in the end I didn't. The awful thing was, when I told Rex he wanted a termination. And he still does. We've had a couple of fights, which kind of end up in bed again, but then he says things like he'll go for good if I don't get rid of this one. He can be cruel, Rache. But I understand him. I can't talk about it much because your marriage is so different. I think your parents might have bridged the gap. They were a real passionate pair, weren't they? Anyway, Rache, I think Rex and I could make a go of it if I did have a termination. But . . . isn't it strange . . . all the soul searching I've been doing through the summer, comes down to knowing – *knowing* – like Hermione knows things – that I can't do it. This is my baby. And what's more, it's Rex's baby. I can't do it to me and I can't do it to Rex and I certainly can't do it to Junior.

So I'm here, honey. Aunt Mabe is here, too. I love her. We're in a kind of cocoon where we don't think about anything or anyone except ourselves – and that includes the Florida family, Georgie, you . . . everyone.

Joan brings us drop scones and we walk out to look at the fall colours. I'm sorry, honey, but this is all I can say right now. Underneath all this selfishness I love you still. I envy you and Tom, darling, and I hope he realizes his dream for his father. You are such gentle, good people, it is wonderful you met when you did. I'm going to bed now. Pop will pick this up in the morning and take it to the post office. Rache, don't worry about me. I am happy.

From your old friend, Meriel

I wanted to tell Tom. Right then and there. And I couldn't. I phoned Eve at the manor. And then I put the letter inside my jumper and tucked it into my bra. I don't know why, I just did.

Twenty-five

Practical Rose telephoned Maxine before she went to school. She told her Meriel's wonderful news and asked her whether she could pop into town to see me. I heard Rose say, 'No, really. She's fine. A bit overcome with all of it.'

When she came into the kitchen to pour more tea, I snuffled, 'No need to send for anyone, darling. I really am fine, you know.'

And she said, 'I know, but it's a bit . . . tricky . . . for me and Daisy to leave you here in floods, and we have to go in because of this chap coming to talk to us about careers.'

I didn't realize I was 'in floods' but it was great to see Maxine and be enveloped in that comforting bosom. I sort of gave up trying to stifle my sobs and just let her murmured words soak into my consciousness . . . 'it'll be all right in the morning' . . . 'cry it all out of you'. Uncle Gilbert, who had come too, tried to do what Tom and Dad would have done. I couldn't accept his tobacco-impregnated hugs but I appreciated him saying, ‘Let’s sort it out, and it will come to no more than a tin of beans. Just like the whole sordid Strassen affair, even mad Maude Smith—’

And though I gasped at him, ‘It’s a baby, Uncle Gilbert! A *baby*! And she’s so at risk, so terribly at risk—’ I could almost hear Dad, all those years ago in the war, saying something similar to Merry and me, the original bike spies. And he’d spoken the words slowly and reasonably, just as Uncle Gilbert was doing. And then I knew that Uncle Gilbert had always tried to be Dad. He had protected Dad as much as he had protected Mum. He loved them both.

I started to cry all over again.

Hermione came over and explained the psychological reasons behind my total melt-down. Funnily enough, that dried me up instantly.

It was the girls, our lovely twin daughters, that raised my behaviour to something else. They arrived home early from school, and served tea in the washing-up bowl – they had made spillage into an art form – along with jam sandwiches cut into bite-sized pieces. When I started crying again and tried to tell them how absolutely sweet they were, Rose said in her matter-of-fact way, ‘It’s because she’s so happy, of course.’

And Daisy picked up the dialogue as usual

and nodded wisely, 'Nothing could be better, really, could it? Babies always seem to solve everything.'

'I'm glad it's Aunt Merry and not Mum.' Rose held the tea to my lips. 'If she's like this about her friend's baby, she'd never stop if it was ours.'

My sobs ceased, the tears dried. I looked at them and they looked back; we were all startled. I said, 'Does that mean that secretly you have always wanted a sister or a brother?'

Rose put the cup back on the table. 'No,' she said in that way she had. 'When we were little kids we asked Dad about having a baby and he said you weren't strong enough. He thinks you grew too quickly in the war and you did not have enough to eat.'

Daisy nodded. 'And then he told us about our grandma having TB, and being anaemic and everything, and how the doctor has to keep an eye on you.'

Rose grinned suddenly. 'Anyway, we'll have Aunt Merry's baby next year, won't we? She'll bring her over to show us. And then, when she starts back at the university, probably Eliza will come too.'

I said, 'Eliza?' I took the tea cup from Rose and warmed my hands around it.

Daisy nodded. 'We thought Eliza sounded just right. Vicky will choose her name. And she's always been dotty about having a half-share in the Queen. So it will definitely be Elizabeth. And Rose and I thought Eliza sounded special. We are going to suggest it to her.'

'And so sweet, too.' Rose sighed ecstatically. 'There's such a lot to look forward to.'

I nearly started crying again, but I knew she was right; the future suddenly did look crowded. Which meant the sooner I got started, the easier it would be.

I drained my cup. 'This tea is good. You're learning.'

Rose took a breath, ready to protest, then let it go. She said, 'Listen, Mum. If Aunt Merry won't be here this winter, and Dad and Grandee are still away, why don't we get the central heating done? I know the house will be upside down, but the three of us can cope.'

I suspected that Gilbert and Maxine had put the girls up to this, but as I swilled my almost empty cup I saw that it was a splendid idea. A proper welcome for Tom and Dad, who would surely feel the cold terribly after the tropics. The girls had a sort of innate, down-to-earth wisdom that had completely passed me by. That night I sat up in the double bed and cut off all thoughts of loneliness and longing and made a list of things that simply had to be done. Soon.

Vicky phoned from Orion.

'She says she's too embarrassed to come to

the phone. So I'm telling you that she is fine and you are not to worry.' She paused for breath and then said lovingly, 'I could kill her, sometimes.'

I said, 'Me, too. But please tell her that the relief is just enormous. I thought she had some terrible illness.'

'She has, in a way. She – she's such a disruptive influence!' Vicky paused, frustrated, then said slowly, 'It's not all Dad's fault, Aunt Rachel. He just doesn't know how to deal with her. She has to take some of the responsibility for what went wrong. Dawn was so ordinary and predictable. She gave Dad a bit of peace and quiet. That's all.'

'Oh Vicky. It must be tough for you.'

'No – not really. Because I'm both of them, aren't I? Mom is terrific – you know that. But Dad has this great brain, and he just loves his work and he can't always tune in to her . . . her . . . otherness. It seems to him like selfishness. And maybe it is.'

I could hear desperation coming at me all those miles away. I said, 'It's nothing to do with selfishness, Vicky. It's protectiveness for the people she loves. Just hang on to her. At the moment she needs protecting. And you're good at that.'

'Am I? D'you think I am, Aunt Rache?'

'You saved Hermione Smith's life by taking Rose's letter round to my father and badgering him to come to England and sort everything out.'

'Oh no. But thank you. Listen. I'll work on Mom, and make her ring you.'

'Darling, it doesn't matter. Tell her I love her, and I am so happy about Eliza I can't stop crying. Well, I have now because of the central heating. But even when the house is ripped to pieces by the plumbers I'll still be sending my love straight across the Atlantic.'

There was a bewildered pause, then Vicky said, 'I think you've caught Merielitis. Write to us. Explain.'

'Goodbye, darling. The pipes are just being delivered and the phone is in the hall so there's nowhere to stand.'

'I know. There never is, is there?' And she was gone.

The plumbers were marvellous. They had done a lot of work for Hermione at Rough Road Cottage. 'Part of the fambly, we are, Mrs Fairbrother. That young doctor, she said as how you was all one big fambly, you and your husband at the *Clarion*, your dad prac'lly running Smith's all through the war, your friend's dad being Nightingale's outfitters . . . and herself, too. Wonderful doctor, her. And now us. Peter's Plumbing. That's me and my two boys. At your service!' This was after his third cup of tea in as many hours.

The heating was fuelled by a tank of oil installed in the cellar, and fed from the street through the metal trap of the coal chute. Two hectic weeks later, I looked at the dials and the taps, and waited for the girls to come home from school and tell me how to use them all. Peter had gone through it with great care and left me a leaflet, but Daisy had promised that Colin would be with them that evening and give us all a proper lesson. We wanted a grand switch-on in time for Bonfire Night.

It was the first time we'd had no fireworks in the back garden. The nails hammered into the wall twelve years ago especially for Catherine wheels stayed empty; I'd saved no milk bottles for rocket holders. Instead we ranged around the house, peering through every window to watch other displays, glorying in the steady warmth everywhere. That night I sat up in bed; lonely, yes, cold, no. I wrote to Tom first and then to Meriel.

The next day brought a letter from Dad.

Dearest Rachel, Tom is so busy. Try not to worry about him, it's better he should be. You will have guessed immediately that I am writing to say that Jack Fairbrother has died. We were both with him; I stayed in the background, obviously, but I was there in case I was needed. I wish I could tell you that Jack recognized Tom as his son. I simply do not know. There may have been a look between them, as there was between Hermione and Maude Smith. But as far as I could tell he closed his eyes and slept his life away somewhere between three and four this afternoon. We had been playing a silly game of cards, and he was tired. I retired to the window, and watched some of the patients walking in the garden with their visitors. It's a beautiful place. Tom stayed by the bed, almost as if he knew. He stood up at four, came over to me and said, 'Dad, I think he's gone. Can you come and check?' He always calls me George. He called me Dad. We went to the bed together, and I just nodded. Tom put his cheek against Jack's cheek, and I left him and went to find the interpreter-chap and the sister. As luck would have it, I found the English chaplain first. He's a good man. One of Wingate's crazy bunch. He picked up some of the lingo during that time, and decided to come back out here and see if he could do anything useful with it. He will be worth his weight in gold to Tom just now. He agrees with Tom that Jack's body should be buried in the small English cemetery here. Jack was indescribably happy here. Ironic, isn't it?

That's all, love. You will be hearing from Tom, probably tomorrow, but I am writing this while Tom sleeps for a while. He's in one of those long steamer chairs made of bamboo, couldn't stand the mosquito nets any more, so came out here on the verandah with me. Don't be unhappy for him, darling. He has had almost four months with his father. He found him just in time. He will explain better than I can. But I have to say that this has been a very good time for me. I think I was the archetypal father, Rache. I always liked Tom, but frankly never thought he was good enough for my only child. I was wrong. It occurred to me, during all the hoo-hah with Maude Smith, that when I 'gave you away' at the wedding and had to keep looking at Mum for support, I was giving away nothing and gaining everything. Tom wanted to share with us the woman he married. I couldn't see that – so worried about Mum and everything. I see it now. I love you both. Please take care of each other so that I can go on sharing everything you have.

There was more. It was quite a letter for a woman of nearly forty to get from her father.

They got home just before Christmas. Uncle Gilbert drove us to London to meet them, and the four of us squashed into the back seat while Dad and Uncle Gilbert chatted sporadically in the front. I had known before that Tom was 'all right'. His letters had told me that. But to sit there with the twins between us, asking questions, no inhibitions, the usual feeling built up between us. We flowed together; I knew his grief and, at the same time, the enormous consolation that went with it; and he understood the strangeness of my life without him. Dad looked back at us as the car was lit sporadically by street lamps. He grinned and said, 'Like foxes in a den, Rache.' The girls demanded to know the story behind that, and Dad told them about our tiny experience of total war, but not all the consequences that had rippled into their own lives so recently. Perhaps they would never know.

Eve and Gus were anxious to leave for Florida, now that Tom and Dad were home. Eve had sold her mother's house for an enormous sum; all the houses in the rough road had sold for six hundred pounds before the war, now they were valued at three thousand pounds. She took Uncle Gilbert's advice on investing her nest egg. She bought a small cottage near Clarion House as a base. It was cheap because sitting tenants occupied it, but in any case I think we knew that she would never come back to this country permanently. As I write this, I can say very honestly that she has made a respected name for herself in America for her work with disadvantaged children. In particular, she is a trustee of the Robinson Foundation and has been directly responsible for their input into the visual arts scene. Their travelling exhibitions at the big New York galleries are extremely popular. She encouraged Georgie Robinson to set up the music department in Florida. He works throughout the year to produce the annual open-air concerts at the foundation. So far no performer, however world-famous, has said no to Georgie Robinson. He is much loved and respected in the musical world. And by everyone who knows him.

Meriel finished her course, and did in fact bring Eliza with her. This time they both stayed with us; Meriel drove to Bristol three times each week, then worked at the kitchen table on our Oliver three-bank typewriter. When it came to her thesis she bought one of the new electronic typewriters and took over the attics. She finished it on the day that Eliza Robinson took her first tottering steps along our hall. Rose stood at one end, Daisy the other, and with joyous upraised arms Eliza discovered a rolling gait that moved her towards Rose – who ran to meet her – and then to Daisy. Their screams brought Meriel and I running. It was the summer of '66. The girls were almost sixteen; they had my mother's cloud of dark hair and Tom's blue eyes and prominent teeth. They were tall and slender and incredibly beautiful.

Tom is still the boy he was when we married,

just as I am still that girl, but we have both taken our places as the older generation. Dad died very soon after taking possession of Hermione's Cottage. He had a full summer there when he harvested raspberries, rhubarb, Victoria plums and runner beans, just as he had done when Mum and he had lived together. That winter he had caught a cold which developed into pneumonia. He knew it was the end and told me he didn't mind. 'It's so lucky that I had a second go at life,' he said, one word to each outward breath. That was it, but that was enough.

So Tom and I grew up at last. And I suppose Meriel did too, though I find it hard to believe when I see her damming up Twyver's Brook with Georgie and Eliza, making a hole for the sticklebacks to go through . . . she comes home every summer. I must regress in the same way; Tom produced a snap the other day where I am almost waist deep in water on the full side of the dam as I try to shore up a break in the twiggy wall. Daisy is shouting something at me from the bank and I remember Vicky saying, 'It's more like a beaver's den than a dam!'

Stories like this usually end with a death, but though we lost our fathers and one other, life went on, obviously. It continues to be rich and eventful. But all journals have to end somewhere and Meriel probably deserves to have the last word.

Darling, I know you will be grieving for me today but please do not. You only met Aunt Mabe two or three times, but know her through me as well as I do myself, so you must know that like your dear father, she was ready to 'lay down her arms'. It was the last joke she made, and she put her gnarled hands high above her head and then let her arms collapse on to the pillows.

Strange, isn't it, that my own mother gave me away, my dear foster mother only really had eyes for my father and Rex's mother became so dear to me and died so soon? And then in surged Aunt Mabe, and did the job properly. I had four mothers, and she had no children until she found me. She made my inadequacies into strengths, she taught me so much, Rache. I think I've come to love all my mothers, but Aunt Mabe I loved best. I will miss her. Of course I will miss her. But how thankful I am that I knew her, loved her and – best of all – told her so.

During these past few weeks we have talked about everything: the children, Rex; Ellie and Jack, then Jack and Joan; you and Tom and the girls; and Tom's father finding such ecstasy in a place that had almost killed him. And she said something I found startlingly true: it was simply that people have to learn to love unconditionally. Did we do that, Rache? I think you might have done. I remember being pretty scathing about Eve. And no one could have loved her mother, surely? But the Wingco . . . loving his sister . . . how unconditional was that? Eve is so wonderfully normal; I know that Gus still grieves that she refused to have children herself. He still calls her a mother-in-waiting. But she is also a scientist, and said to me one day, 'It has to stop somewhere. And my family is now enormous.' She was talking about the kids at the foundation. She's quite right, they all love her.

Anyway, darling, I am rambling. These few days in beautiful Orion, waiting for the funeral, have encouraged an unusual nostalgia in me. I can remember so well tearing along to the subway under the railway lines, skidding around into the Barton, picking up the scent of our own – our very own – spy, and never guessing what consequences would follow. We would have done it anyway, Rache. Nothing could have stopped us then. I'm ashamed of what I did afterwards. How I encouraged Dad to complain to Rex's CO so that he got a dressing-down, making that an excuse to see him and apologize oh-so-prettily, inveigling Rex into . . . well, you know all that. I was determined to get away from Dad and all his shenanigans, only to find I am just like him. Conniving, using sex as a weapon. God, it's horrible, Rache. That's why I had to keep trying to make it work like a proper marriage; to make Rex happy, and stop him looking for another Dawn. I don't know whether I've succeeded totally. When I phoned him about Aunt Mabe he started up with the excuses – too busy to come for the funeral, that sort of thing. I told him OK, if he felt like that it was the end for us, then I slammed down the phone. He came next day. It was the first time I'd cried for her. He held out his arms, and I went into them and cried. Marriage is such a strange thing, Rache. But I believe in it. I don't regret Vicky leaving Ralph, I shall most definitely regret it if it has put her off marriage. I don't think it has. That boy of Daphne's is over here for a couple of months. We'll see. She is very keen for all of us to come home for Christmas. She wants a repeat of the Coronation year. Perhaps she and Roland plan to get married then. It's a bit soon after Ralph, but she knows what she's doing. How about it, Rache? Gilbert and Maxine and Miss Hardwicke and my mothers. Maybe I could talk Eve and Gus into joining us. Too cold to make dams, but we could show them how The Song Birds sing carols – remember The Song Birds, Rache? And we could take Eliza to the whispering gallery. And have a treasure hunt. And look at Hermione's Cottage.

Darling, I expect you know that Tom has been sending Georgie comic strips he draws of what you are all doing. They're superb. So simple and accessible. One of Gilbert and Maxine going for a walk with Frou-frou Number Four and falling into some mud. Another of you writing up a cake recipe and then mixing it in with the cake. And what Tom calls the Throstle orchestra – all of you with saucepans and kazoos playing Beethoven's Fifth . . . that is definitely Georgie's favourite.

Bless you, my child. Until Christmas 1973 . . . I wonder what will happen next?

With love and anticipation, your bestest friend in all the world, Meriel Nightingale-Robinson.

SEARCHING FOR TILLY
by Susan Sallis

A journey into the past, and hope for the future . . .

Three women come to a remote Cornish village for the summer: Jenna, only 26 and grieving for the loss of the love of her life; her mother Caro, whose husband Steve has also died; and Laura, who had been married to Caro's beloved brother Geoff. They are staying in a house called Widdowe's Cottage – a poignantly suitable name.

In that tiny Cornish community they discover many strange memories of their forebears, and especially of Tilly, Caro's mother, whose family history seem[illegible] of their own. They b[illegible] dramatic story of Tilly[illegible] which takes them on [illegible] the West Country an[illegible] amazing fa[illegible]

978055[illegible]

CORGI